The Lanimer Bride

Also by Pat McIntosh

The *Lanimer Bride*

A Gil Cunningham Murder Mystery

Pat McIntosh

CONSTABLE • LONDON

CONSTABLE

First published in Great Britain in 2016 by Constable

A CIP catalogue record for this book
is available from the British Library

ISBN: 978-1-47211-860-8 (hardback)

Typeset in Palatino by Hewer Text UK Ltd, Edinburgh
Printed and bound in Great Britain by Clays Ltd, St Ives plc

MIX
Paper from
responsible sources
FSC
www.fsc.org   FSC® C104740

Papers used by Constable are from well-managed
forests and other sustainable sources

Constable
is an imprint of
Little, Brown Book Group
Carmelite House
50 Victoria Embankment
London EC4Y 0DZ

An Hachette UK Company
www.hachette.co.uk

www.littlebrown.co.uk

For Alys's paternoster maker, Dame Christiane; and
for Timothy, who wrote to me, and his mother Thea;
and for Martin
SEMPER
et in saecula saeculorum.

Author's Note

I have taken some liberties with the geology of the Mouse Water Valley, endowing it with an extra cave where I needed one. Most of the other landscape details are at least known to history, though they may not be visible now.

The burgh of Lanark still celebrates Lanimer Day, which falls now on the Thursday between the sixth and twelfth of June each year. The boundaries are traced, and there is a Lanimer Fair with Victorian accretions such as the procession of the Lanimer Queen. Lanark expatriates try to get home for the event, which is widely reported in the Lanarkshire papers.

Ever since it became a kingdom, Scotland has had two native languages, Gaelic (which in the fifteenth century was called Ersche) and Scots, both of which you will find used in the Gil Cunningham books. I have translated the Gaelic where needful, and those who have trouble with the Scots could consult the online *Dictionary of the Scots Language*, to be found at www.dsl.ac.uk. In this book there is a smattering of the tinkers' or travellers' cant, which I have also translated where needful.

This book has had a longer gestation and a harder labour than usual, for a number of reasons. Many people have encouraged me, nagged me and helped me; they know who they are, but my sister and Gil's godmother are certainly top of the list. I am deeply grateful to all of them.

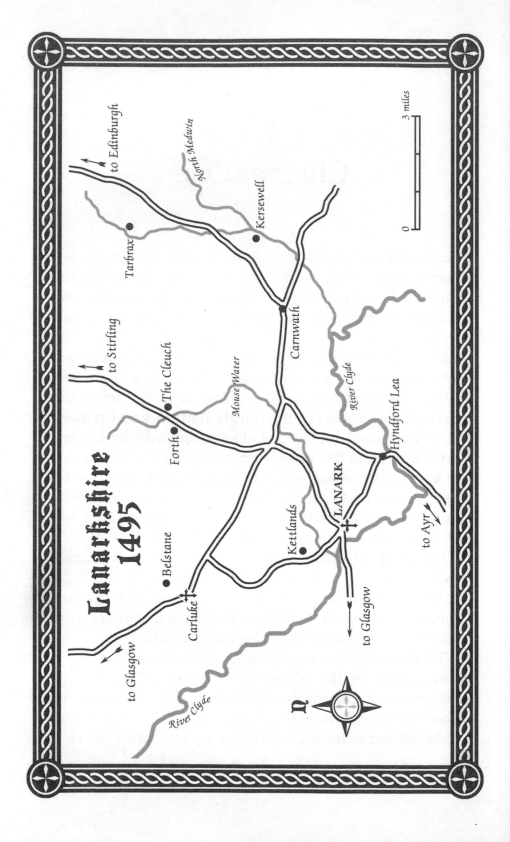

Lanarkshire
1495

to Edinburgh

North Medwin

Tarbrax

Kersewell

to Stirling

The Cleuch

Carnwath

Forth

Mouse Water

River Clyde

Hyndford Lea

Belstane

Kettlands

LANARK

to Ayr

Carluke

to Glasgow

to Glasgow

River Clyde

N

3 miles

0

Chapter One

When the news of Mistress Audrey Madur's disappearance reached Gil Cunningham, he was walking with his young wife Alys in the orchard by his mother's house of Belstane, enjoying the green shade of the high fruit trees.

The weather was unusually warm for a Scottish summer, and the airs of Glasgow had been close and muggy for days. Alys, discovering a week since that measles was abroad in the burgh, had packed up most of the household, including Gil's small ward John McIan, and removed to the fresher air of Carluke. It had taken Gil a few days to deal with the outstanding work on his desk, and he had only just been able to follow her, leaving his young assistant to mind the legal practice and Alys's aged companion to mind the house.

'It's much healthier up here,' Alys observed, gazing up into the quince tree, the sunlight edging the high bridge of her nose. 'The air is cleaner, and there are breezes. Look, there will be a good crop this year. Your mother has promised me some quince leather.'

'True,' said Gil to her first statement. 'And there have been deaths in the lower town. Your father is very concerned for Ealasaidh and the boy. You were wise to leave Glasgow. Is John behaving?'

She turned to look at him, brown eyes dancing.

'Do you think he can behave? He went after the cockerel's tail feathers yesterday, such a squawking and shrieking in the henyard you never heard. Alan wished me to beat him, but your mother only laughed. I think Alan fears John will lead his boy into trouble.'

'Very likely,' said Gil, grinning. 'I remember raiding the henyard for feathers too. They make rare plumes for a helmet.'

'Maister Gil!' a voice called under the trees. 'Mistress?'

'We're here, Alan,' Gil answered, and turned to stroll towards the orchard gate. 'What's he done now?'

Lady Cunningham's steward appeared, hot and flustered in his gown of office, shaking his head.

'It's no the wee boy, maister, it's Mistress Somerville from Kettlands, over by Lanark, wanting a word.'

'Somerville,' Gil repeated as he reached the man. 'Come under the shade and catch your breath, it's ower hot to be hurrying. Is that Yolande Somerville? James Madur's widow? What's she after?'

'Aye, that's the lady.' Alan Forrest fanned himself with his straw hat, but drew gratefully into the shade. 'Mistress.' He bent the knee briefly to Alys. 'She wedded her youngest lassie a year back, a plain quiet lass, no a great dower seeing her daddy's gone, so Mistress Somerville took the lanimer man from Lanark for her.'

'What, Brosie Vary? That's no such a bad bargain,' Gil said in surprise. 'I'd ha thought he could do better than that in the burgh. He was a couple of years ahead of me at the college in Glasgow,' he added to Alys. 'He'll be past thirty by now, and well established.'

'Well, no,' Alan said awkwardly, carefully not looking at Alys again. 'He's a younger son, after a', and buried three wives a'ready, two in childbed, one fell sick while she was carrying. They're a bit wary o him in Lanark now, or so I hear. Any road,' he said, returning to the point, 'his wife, Mistress Somerville's lassie's missing and she wants a word wi you.'

'Missing?' Alys repeated in astonishment. 'What, has she run away?'

'Mistress Somerville says no,' said Alan.

'What does Vary say?' Gil asked, opening the orchard gate for Alys to pass through. 'Is he here? What's it all about, anyway?'

'Maister Vary's no present,' said Alan in neutral tones. He turned to close and bolt the gate, and added with no more expression, 'Best if Mistress Somerville lets you have the tale hersel. She's wi the mistress the now.'

Gil looked at Alys, raising his eyebrows. Presumably his mother was taking this seriously, if she had sent Alan to fetch him in.

Egidia Muirhead, Lady Cunningham, was seated in the hall of her tower-house, very upright on the oak settle by the cavernous empty fireplace, her stout maid-servant Nan watchful by the wall. The chatelaine of Belstane was wearing an elderly but still respectable wrapped gown of fine dark red wool, suitable for the warm weather, with her second-best girdle about her waist, the one shod with silver and garnets, and an old-fashioned flowerpot headdress from which wisps of iron-grey hair escaped under her fine linen veil. The gown was clasped on the breast with the jewelled badge of her service in the late Queen's household. Gil recognised that his mother had had warning of this guest and dressed to make a statement. She could command respect wearing muddy boots and one of her dead husband's old gowns; like this she was magnificent.

Opposite her was a rather different lady. Short and plump, she was clad in fashionable black silk brocade,

3

with extravagant cuffs on her tight sleeves. A braid-trimmed French hood and black velvet veil were clamped down over a snowy cap; a finely pleated barbe probably concealed more than one extra chin, and a thick layer of dust powdered all above her waist. She was accompanied by a scrawny maid and a groom in velvet livery.

As Gil and Alys entered the hall she was almost bouncing up and down on her padded backstool, saying in agitated tones, 'But where can she be? Vary's no concerned, but I ken my lass, madam, I ken what she'd be like to do, and where would she go in her state anyway?' She gestured down her own ample front, describing a swollen belly. By the empty hearth Socrates the wolfhound, sleeping off the twenty-mile journey of the morning, did not stir at Gil's footstep.

'When's the groaning-ale to be brewed for?' Lady Egidia asked delicately. 'Has she long to go?'

'Four weeks, no more, that's why I'm—' Mistress Somerville shook her head so that the barbe swept to and fro across her bosom. 'She wouldny— and any road, what, where would, who would—'

'Gil,' said Lady Egidia in some relief, catching sight of her son. 'And Alys. Mistress Somerville, have you met my good-daughter?'

In the little flurry of presentation, bowing and curtsying, one of the servants entered with a tray. Alys sat down beside her mother-in-law, and while Gil poured well-water with fruit vinegar and handed the platter of little cakes, she said, 'What has happened, madam? It sounds very serious.'

'Oh, aye, it's serious, lassie.' Mistress Somerville dabbed at her eyes with her free hand, then took two cakes as the platter passed her again. 'My lassie's vanished away, and no knowing what's come to her, and her man's no like to seek her.'

4

Gil looked round at this, and met Alys's puzzled glance. He nodded agreement; something did not make sense.

'Tell us from the beginning,' he suggested. 'What's your daughter's name, for a start?'

'Audrey.' Mistress Somerville took a draught of her beaker, grimaced at the acid taste, and began again. 'Audrey Madur. My youngest. It's no a common name, Audrey,' she admitted. 'It's my grandam's name, that was an Englishwoman from Ely or Norwich or somewhere o the sort. My lassie's wedded on Maister Ambrose Vary, that's notary and liner in Lanark, and her first bairn's due in a month or so. She rid out to see me ten days since, wi her groom, young Adam, that's been her groom since she was twelve, and she stayed a few days, but she would ride back in for the Lanimer Fair, for that it was the first anniversary o their marriage the day after it and they were to hear Mass thegither in St Nicholas' kirk.'

'Lanimer?' said Alys. 'What saint is that?'

'Not a saint. It means a land boundary,' said Gil. 'They hold the fair at the same time as they ride the bounds of the burgh. It's a great celebration, wi races and drinking and dancing. It aye falls around Pentecost. It must ha been last week, mistress?'

Mistress Somerville nodded, and dabbed at her eyes again.

'Last Thursday,' she confirmed, 'that was June tenth. So she set off on that very day, to ride back to Lanark, thinking the fair wouldny be over when she got there. I waved her off, her on the wee jennet Vary bought her and Adam on the powny, and I thought no more o't.'

'She was riding?' Alys said.

'Aye, on a proper lady's saddle, wi her feet on a foot-board and a good stout safeguard to keep the dust fro her skirts. I know what's due to my lassie.'

5

Since both his mother and his wife habitually rode astride, Gil refrained from catching anyone's eye. Instead he said, 'And when did you learn she was missing? I take it she never reached Lanark?'

Mistress Somerville nodded again, biting her lip.

''Twas only yestreen. I rode in to visit wi Mistress Limpie Archibeck, that's a French lady residing in Lanark the now, and called in at Vary's house on my way home, seeing I was close, and I thought to see her. And the look on Vary's face when I fetched up at his door asking for her!'

'What did he say?' Alys asked.

'Oh, he denied she was there, and the servants said likewise, and then he said, *Did she no stay on wi you?* And I said, *No, she would come in to the fair.* And he said, *I bade her stay till after it, I didny wish her at the fair in her state. I took it she'd minded me for once,* he says.'

'Was that all he said?' Gil prompted, when she paused again. One part of his mind was grappling with Mistress Archibeck's name (Archibecque? Archévecque? But what could Limpie be?) while another was trying to recall Ambrose Vary from ten years since. The image conjured up by the name was of an awkward young man with few social skills and an astounding grasp of Euclid. Attempts to get him to expound the art of mathematics to his fellows had been unsuccessful, since he had stammered and stuttered, forgotten people's names, reacted badly to misbehaviour, and generally failed as a teacher, but it seemed to Gil that the ability would serve him well in determining boundaries and building lines.

'Hah!' said Mistress Somerville bitterly, and paused to take a draught of her beaker. 'No another word did he have for me, that's her mammy and beside mysel wi anxiety. Went into his closet wi his instruments o

6

surveying and shut the door. When I bade them open it till I asked him what he'd do, he was just standing by his desk polishing some brass thing and never looked round.'

Gil looked at Alys, and found her round-eyed with amazement. He was considering his own possible reaction in a like situation, and found himself wondering if Vary thought his young wife had left him.

'Do they get on well enough?' he asked. 'Are they fond? It wasny a love-match, I take it, he's a deal older than she is.'

'No, no a love-match,' said Mistress Somerville, bridling slightly, 'but they get on well enow for all that. She's an obedient lassie, I raised her to be a good wife, and to ken how to manage a house to please a husband. What are you asking that for?'

A woman is a worthy wight, she serveth a man both day and night, Gil thought, and did not glance at Alys. How did it go on? *And yet she hath but care and wo*, that was it. Perhaps some women were content with that fate; he was sure Alys would not be.

'No chance,' said Lady Egidia, breaking a long silence, 'that the groom's run off wi her? Adam, did you say his name was? If he's served her a long time, maybe he's a notion to her.'

'Nothing of the kind!' said the other lady in rising indignation. 'He's a good lad, aye been a faithful servant, and besides, his leman's saving up to their marriage. I gied her a couple of groats mysel just the other day. No, there's some ill befallen the both o them, though what it might be I darena think, and I need you to seek for her, maister, seeing her man's doing nothing about it.'

'Have you sent out a search?' Gil asked. 'Could she have gone to any of her sisters?'

'Oh, aye, as soon's I reached home yestreen I sent out all the men, beating under bushes all across the muir, hunting the river banks, till it was too dark to see, and then had them out again the day morn, and one to ride to her sisters, and her brother up at Harelaw, no to mention sending to Sir John here at the kirk in Carluke, asking his prayers for us to St Malessock, as well as my own. We've found nothing, maister, never a trace, nor her kin's never seen her.'

'It's four days,' said Gil, 'and it's been dry. There'd be little to find by way of tracks, even if you ken what road they took from your house to Lanark.'

'Never a trace,' she reiterated. 'Will you help me, maister? Your mammy here's tellt me a few tales, how you've tracked folk down, the collier fellow, that lassie at Glasgow Cross last year and the like.' The barbe swept across the wide black brocade bosom again as Mistress Somerville turned a pleading gaze on Gil. 'Will you find my lassie?'

Gil raised one eyebrow at his mother, who stared back at him without comment. He was aware of Alys rising, excusing herself, slipping from the chamber, while he turned Mistress Somerville's account over in his mind. There were several possible explanations for young Mistress Madur's disappearance, none of them particularly good. Accident, mishap, a panicky young woman running away from something (but what?), abduction.

'Was there anyone else had a notion to her, afore she wedded Vary?' he asked. 'Any that might have stolen her away? Any she might have turned to if she was alarmed or frightened?'

'What, heavy wi another man's bairn? Surely no!' Mistress Somerville paused to consider, but shook her head again. 'Her and my brother's youngest had a liking for one another when they were younger, and made plans the way young ones do, but Somerville had other intentions for Jockie. He's away at the College at St Andrews now, studying to be a priest. There's been none other I can think on.'

'Any other friends she might ha gone to?'

'Oh, she's friends round about,' conceded Mistress Somerville, 'but why would she want to do that? She was happy enough at going back to her own house, talking about the sewing she's doing for the bairn, telling me of the cradle Vary's ordered. I was right pleased,' she divulged, 'to hear he's no looking for her to accept any of the other cradles he's had in the house. I'd no want to see my grandchild in a dead bairn's cradle, knowing its mammy had dee'd and all.'

'No, indeed,' said Lady Egidia. 'That's kind in him. I think he's a good provider, mistress. It's a good match.'

'Mind you,' said Mistress Somerville, 'I hardly like to say it, but your good-brother had a notion to her at one time, maister.'

'My good-brother?' Gil repeated, startled, aware of his mother's chin going up. 'Which one? D'you mean Michael Douglas? Tib's husband?'

'Aye, Lady Tib's husband. His faither Sir James had approached me, but I thought the lad ower flighty for my lassie.'

'Oh, he's no proved flighty as Lady Isobel's husband,' said Lady Egidia tartly, emphasising the name. 'He's steady and reliable, he and my daughter are doing well thegither, and his faither's well pleased wi his management of the coalheugh.' She turned her penetrating gaze on Gil. 'I think you must lend your aid, Gil. Mistress Somerville is right anxious about her lassie. Barely a year wedded, still a bride indeed, since the bairn's yet to be born, and gone missing like this, it

9

would drive any mother to distraction. What a blessing you hadny got your boots off, you can ride out again as soon as our guest's ready to leave. And Mistress Mason with you,' she added as Alys came into the chamber from the stair, clad in her wide-skirted riding-dress. 'Nan, will you call Alan, please, and have him send out to the stables?'

Mistress Somerville rode, like her daughter, on a lady's saddle, perched sideways with her feet on a foot-board. She also wore a canvas safeguard to protect her skirts from the dust of the roads, and inserting her into this vast bag, fastening it about her waist, and hoisting the resulting sarpler on to the saddle took the best part of half an hour, thanks to her contrary instructions, complaints and objections.

Watching the process, Gil said quietly in French to Alys, 'What do you make of this? It's a strange tale.'

'I think the girl has not left her husband of her own will,' said Alys promptly, 'though he fears she has.' Gil made an agreeing sound, and she went on, 'Your mother dislikes this woman, but she has directed you to help her. She also thinks the girl has met with a mischance, I would say.'

He glanced at his mother, standing tall and cool by the mounting-block, holding the reins of Mistress Somerville's solid bay mule. The animal nudged her as he looked, and she obediently began caressing its soft chin, still watching the maid and two grooms assisting Mistress Somerville. Another groom hovered carefully beside her, and her own man Henry stood at a distance, ready to bring forward the Belstane horses. Next to him one of the two men Gil had brought out from Glasgow, the ubiquitous Euan Campbell, gazed round him at the bustle.

'James Madur, the girl's father, was injured at Sauchieburn,' Gil said. 'On the Prince's side. So he got a gift of land, a customs post, other favours, and his wife was much made up by it all and boasted about it. He died a year or two after from the wound, but my mother never forgave her.'

'I can imagine,' said Alys. She tucked her hand into his arm. 'How tactless, to boast in front of someone who had lost a husband and two sons on the late King's side. Is it worth speaking to her men, to get a clearer idea of where they have searched?'

'I was thinking that myself,' said Gil. He succeeded, finally, in catching the eye of Mistress Somerville's third groom, and summoned him with a jerk of his head. The man, accepting Lady Egidia's ability to hold the mule, came over to them, ducking his head in a brief bow. He was a broad-shouldered fellow in a leather doublet, dyed the same serviceable blue as the indoor man's velvet livery; brown hair in a neat clip showed under his woollen bonnet, and his eyes were intelligent.

'Maister?' he said.

'This is a strange thing about Mistress Audrey,' Gil said. The man simply nodded, concern in his face. 'Have you been out with the search? Where have you covered? Was there any sign at all?'

'No sign that I seen, none at all,' agreed the man. 'The roads are no that busy, but there's enough traffic, you couldny make out what was five days old and what was seven under the dust. Her jennet's got wee dainty feet, I thought once or twice I'd a glimp o its marks, but I lost them again.'

'Were those on the road she'd ha taken?'

'Oh, aye. Nothing unexpeckit.'

'What was her groom riding?'

11

'One of madam your mother's breeding,' the groom said, grinning awkwardly. 'A wee sturdy bay gelding wi a sock and a star, out that bay wi the four socks she's got.'

'Bluebell.' Gil nodded. 'I'll ken that one if I see him. Bluebell aye throws true like hersel. Did you speak to any on the road?'

'Aye, we asked all we met had they seen them, and at the houses at the roadside and all. One fellow close to home had met wi them, about where I seen the jennet's marks, but we've no more sightings this far, save for an idiot that's talking o a lady and a battle.'

'A battle?' Alys repeated.

'Aye,' said the groom sourly. 'Twelve big men, he says, hitting one another wi swords, and a lady cheering them on. Wasted an hour getting him to show me where it was. Turns out he canny count past three, and makes up these tales a' the time.'

'Was there any sign where he said the battle had been?' Gil asked.

'None that I could make out.'

'Haw, Billy!' shouted one of the grooms by the mounting-block.

'I'll need to go, maister,' said Billy uneasily.

'Aye, you will,' Gil said. 'I'll get another word wi you later.'

'A bad business this, maister,' said Euan Campbell chattily in his ear as Billy made his way across the yard. 'What d'you think will be coming to the lady? Is she lying dead on the moorland, maybe, or is she hidden away somewhere?'

'That's for us to find out,' said Gil, his tone repressive. 'Away and get yourself on a horse if you're coming with us.'

Mistress Somerville was now enthroned on her saddle, her feet on the foot-board and the safeguard

12

rising in stiff folds about her knees. Billy mounted and took her leading-rein, her maidservant was put up behind another of the grooms, and the Belstane horses were brought forward, snorting at the strange beasts, for Gil and Alys to mount. Henry and one of his minions fell in behind them, Euan joined them, Lady Egidia delivered a suitable blessing for travellers, and the cavalcade set off at a brisk walk, a speed at which Gil reckoned it would take them well over an hour to reach Kettlands.

'You could get a word wi Mistress Somerville's woman,' he suggested quietly to Alys. She nodded, and began to thread her way through the procession while he turned his attention to the third Kettlands man.

This man could add little to the tale Billy had told. He had seen no trace at all of Mistress Madur's jennet or her groom's beast, and reckoned the girl had run off with some chance-met stranger, a pedlar or the like.

'Stands to reason,' he said, with a wary glance at his mistress. 'Maister Vary's a dry stick o a fellow, and buried three wives a'ready. No lassie's going to stay wi a fellow like yon.'

'You think?' said Gil.

The present house of Kettlands, on the top of a rounded rise in the land, was quite modern, and boasted a stone ground floor with two further storeys of wood perched on top, and a tumble of outhouses within the barmekin wall. As soon as they were seen approaching several servants ran out into the road, peering anxiously under their hands; from their demeanour there was clearly no further word of Mistress Madur.

Gil, having spent the most part of the journey listening to Mistress Somerville's alternate lamentations and accounts of her daughter's excellence, refused her invitation to step in for a mouthful of ale.

13

'I'd as soon get a look at the land and get back to Belstane while the light lasts,' he said. 'Show me what road they took from here, and then I think you should try to rest.'

The maidservant, just being swung down from her pillion seat, threw him a sharp glance, but Mistress Somerville took the words at face value.

'I'll no rest till my lassie's returned to me, maister, but it's kind o you to think it. They went out that way.' She pointed south-eastward, rather than due south. The fields fell away from the barmekin wall, rolling down to a line of trees a mile or so away which Gil knew marked the valley of the Mouse Water.

'So they went by the mill-bridge,' he said, 'rather than down to the crossing at Cartland Crags.'

'Oh, a course,' said Mistress Somerville, startled. 'We aye use that road into Lanark, it's closer by far.'

'And what time was it when they left?'

'About this time, a couple of hours afore supper.'

'So maybe four or five hours after noon.'

'Aye, about that.' She rubbed tears from her eyes again. 'She'd ha been in Lanark for her supper, so I thought. Oh, maister, find her for me. Even if her man's no troubled about it, find her for me!'

'The maidservant's name is Christian,' said Alys. 'She says Audrey was just as usual when she was here, talking of her sewing, asking about family names to give the bairn and who might stand godparent and the like. She seemed very happy, apart from the backache.'

'That bears out what Mistress Somerville says.' Gil was peering down at the roadside, inspecting the drifted dust and cracked earth.

'You see what I mean, maister,' said Billy, twisting in the saddle to look back at them. 'There's no telling whether it's marks from yesterday or marks from ten days since, aside from the jennet's prents I showed you.'

'So they'd ha rid along here,' said Henry, 'and past yon ferm-toun, Brockbank is it, Billy? And down to the Mouse past the mill. Naeb'dy at Brockbank saw them pass, then?'

'Just this daftie I was telling you o,' said Billy. 'Wi his tale o a battle.'

'Where was the battle?' Alys asked, a moment before Gil could do so.

'Yonder,' Billy nodded, 'down the banks o the Mouse. Gied me a lang tale o't, but there was naught to be seen. Him and his twelve men!'

He spat into the dust. Gil straightened up, gazing about him.

'They'll be able to start the haying soon,' he observed. 'They might get two cuts if the weather keeps up. So there was nobody about, the same as now?'

'A couple o folk said they was out weeding the bere and oats,' Billy said, 'but they never looked up. I suppose if they'd their backs to the road, maybe at the foot o the field,' he waved at the infield where it sloped away from the track, 'they'd never ha heard them.'

'That's an amazing thing,' said Euan, 'that anyone might pass along the road and never be noticed, let alone be spoken to.'

Ignoring this, Gil nudged his horse forward.

'We'll get a look at this battle,' he said. 'I'm not acquaint wi this road, I take the other way down to Lanark from Belstane. How steep is the climb down to the waterside?'

'Steep enow,' admitted Billy. 'It goes sideyways down the brae. If we've goods to bring by cart fro Lanark we take it round by the other road, but this is shorter if you've no wheels to worry you.'

'Now that is wise,' approved Euan. 'But was there no battle? No fighting at all?'

'None that I could see a sign of,' said Billy glumly. 'Maybe you'll do better.'

They moved on, without haste. Gil was studying the verges, which were thick with wildflowers, clover and vetch and trefoil, campion and bellbine. Bees hummed busily in the great drifts of foliage, and a rowan tree in full blossom spread its cloying scent on the breeze. There was no disturbance, no sign that anything untoward had occurred.

'I suppose,' said Alys when he remarked on this, 'if anything had happened here they would have seen or heard it from Brockbank, so open as this country is.'

'Aye, quite,' he said. 'But I'd as soon make certain.'

'Audrey is a name I haven't heard before,' she went on.

'It's a shortening of a saint's name,' Gil said, still reading the verge. Most of these marks were older than he looked for; the road was not much frequented. 'She's a local saint in some part of England – Norwich or Ely, as Mistress Somerville said. I think the whole name is Edreda or Etheldreda or the like.'

'I see,' she said doubtfully.

'What's puzzling me,' he added, nudging his horse forward, 'is the French lady's name she mentioned. Limpie Archibeck? Archibecque or Archéveque, I suppose, but Limpie?'

'Olympe?' Aly, suggested after a moment. 'That would be, Olympias.'

'The mother of Alexander of Macedonia! Of course, I should have thought of that.'

'I wonder what a French lady is doing in Lanark? It's a long way from Edinburgh or the court.'

'I'm surprised my mother hasn't mentioned her.'

16

'Perhaps she does not know of her.'

'Is that likely? Is it even possible?' he asked without looking up. She giggled, but made no answer.

They came to the edge of the river valley without finding anything of significance. It was a steep-sided winding cut in the landscape, heavily wooded, the track curving down to their right through oak and beech and hazel. Looking out and down from the brow of the slope, Gil reckoned the river they could hear was a good forty fathom below them. A quarter-mile away on the other side of the gorge, lower than this one, were more fields, a couple of ferm-touns, and off to the left among trees the roofs and smoke of what must be Jerviswood, one of the Livingstone strongholds.

'We need to send to the Livingstones,' he said aloud, 'ask if any of theirs were on the road that evening.'

'Aye, and Woodend over yonder,' said Billy. 'I only got started this morning, and then the mistress would ride to Belstane, which took three o us off the search. I sent a couple more lads on towards Lanark to ask about it, but I took it they'd no luck, since there was no word at the house the now.'

Gil leaned over the cantle, studying the immediate footing and the young bracken fronds at the edge of the trees, then turned his horse and began to make his way down the track, saying over his shoulder, 'Follow me, but not too close.'

'A rare place to take someone by surprise,' observed Henry, as he obeyed.

'I was thinking the same,' said Euan.

'My thought and all,' agreed Billy. 'It aye makes me uneasy coming down this bit.'

Here among the trees, sheltered by the sides of the gorge, there was little or no breeze. Sunlight lay in patches on the track and on the tangled growth on the raised banks at either side; insects flickered among the trees, bees hummed, there was birdsong all about them. A cloud of butterflies rose up as Gil passed through a clearing.

The sound of the bees grew louder. Something must be attracting them. He looked about, but could see no flowering tree, no bank of wildflowers. The sound was more of a buzz than a hum, higher in pitch. Were they bees, or were they flies? A faint unpleasant scent touched his nostrils, and he tipped his head back, sniffing.

'Maister?' said Euan from ten feet behind him. 'What are you scenting?'

'I smell it and all,' said Henry in ominous tones.

'Where?' Gil said, turning from side to side. 'Can you make it out?'

'The flies are thicker that way,' said Alys, pointing ahead and left, down towards the river. 'Gil, do you think—?'

'I hope not,' he said, and swung down from the saddle, handing his reins to Henry's silent minion. 'Bide here, all of you.'

A few steps down the track he paused, looking about him. The roadway itself told him little, but one of the overhanging oak branches showed scores as if some-one's booted feet had scuffed it, and something large had come down the bank from the right in two strides, breaking the stems of vetch and ragged robin, probably a few days since. He craned to see the top of the bank, and found a trampled spot by the rugged bole of the oak tree. One or more people had waited up there, and at least one had been in the tree overhead, hidden by the leaves, where he could leap down in front of the right passer-by.

'What have I missed, maister?' asked Billy, disquiet in his tone. 'I'm no huntsman, tracking was never my gift. What have I missed?'

Where had they left their horses, Gil wondered, ignoring the man. He turned slowly, extending all his senses into the summer evening. A pair of titmice exchanged their metallic, monotonous call, a blackbird scolded somewhere. The roadway still held no signs, its dry dusty surface telling only of the lack of rain. The flies buzzed endlessly, and the familiar, sickly scent floated past him. The sound of the river blended with it all, but the buzzing seemed loudest, as Alys had said, downhill from the track.

He crossed to the other bank and set a foot on it with caution, gazing down the slope. Below him, a stand of bracken was unfurling, the scrolls so light a green they almost seemed to glow in the dappled shade. He considered it; at this time of year the stuff appeared to rise while you watched it, like bread. Five days ago the fronds might have been no higher than the rest of the green stuff around them. And beyond them, a cloud of dark flies whirled and hummed.

He stepped up on to the bank and picked his way carefully down the steep slope, moving from tree to tree, looking intently about him. When he saw the first boot he was unsurprised; when he saw the second it told him how the body which still wore them was disposed, and when he pushed the bracken aside, he knew that he had not found Mistress Madur.

'What d'ye have there, Maister Gil?' asked Henry from the track. 'Ye've found something?'

'A young man,' he answered. Somebody above him groaned. 'Leather doublet. Fair hair.' He stepped closer, holding his breath. 'His throat's been cut. Billy, come down and see if you know him.'

The body had been here for several days; it was already beginning to melt into the landscape, the limbs flattening and taking on the curve of the earth beneath

19

them. The young face was not as the lad's mother, or the sweetheart whom Mistress Somerville had mentioned, would wish to remember it; the crows had got his eyes, and something had chewed one hand. Gil crossed himself and muttered a prayer for the dead while Billy slithered down the bank towards him.

'Aye,' the man said heavily after a moment's inspection. 'That's young Adam. Poor laddie. I should ha found him yestreen. I should ha seen the sign you found. But where's Mistress Audrey got to? What's come to her, maister?' He looked wildly about, as if expecting to find the lady under another tree.

'I wish I knew,' said Gil. 'But I intend to find out.'

'Gil?' Alys was staring down at him from the road. 'Did you say his throat is cut?'

'I did,' he agreed. 'No sign of the lassie, but I suspect she's been stolen away and hidden somewhere, otherwise she'd have turned up by now, one way or another.'

'He's had more than his throat cut,' said Billy, muffled behind his hand. 'His doublet's all to ribbons.'

'Aye, they've been making certain, though he was dead already. Only the cut throat's bled, to judge by the state of his shirt. Then they pitched him down here among the trees.'

'What, you think he was killed up here and then thrown down the slope?' Henry said from the bank.

'I do.' Gil was looking about him. 'No sign of a fight down here. Whose knife is the longest? We need to make a litter for him.'

'Och, indeed, that is easy done,' said Euan. He drew his big gully-knife and addressed the nearest stand of hazel.

'Then we need to cast up and down the riverside,' Gil added. 'There's still a cuddy, a gelding of Bluebell's get and Mistress Madur herself outstanding. We need to be

20

certain none of them's under this bracken afore we take young Adam into Lanark.'

'Lanark?' said Billy sharply. 'How no back to Kettlands? What's Lanark to do wi't?'

'This is murder,' Gil said. 'He's been slain and then hidden to conceal the killing. The Provost must hold a quest on him, to determine how he died and who's to blame, though that's none so easy to discern. After that he can go home to his own.'

'Maister Gil?' called Henry from the road. 'I've found where he was slain, most like.'

'I think so, Gil,' Alys chimed in. 'They have tried to cover it up, but Henry has swept at the dust with a branch, and uncovered a great patch of dried blood.'

Gil nodded, accepting this new fact.

'The mistress willny like it,' said Billy, as Euan began trimming the first pole. 'If he goes to Lanark no Kettlands I mean. She'll no be pleased.'

'Is he still in her employ?' Gil countered. 'I thought he followed Mistress Madur to her husband's house. Strictly he's a Lanark man now.' He looked past the groom to Alys. 'Will you go home to Belstane, sweetheart? Henry can convoy you. You'd be home in time for supper.'

She shook her head.

'No,' she said firmly. 'If you're to speak to the husband, I'll come too.'

Chapter Two

'You've no need to trouble yoursel about my wife,' said Maister Ambrose Vary.

Gil stared at him.

The man was very much as he remembered him, gawky and awkward in build, with a thin face and staring blue eyes. As Gil had told Alys, however, Vary was no more than a year or two past thirty, and just now he looked fully ten years older. Dark shadows ringed the blue eyes, the fair hair had been well barbered but was growing out uncombed, his clothes were of good quality but had been dragged on all anyhow and he seemed, despite his words, to be consumed with anxiety.

'Has she left you, maister?' Alys asked gently. Vary cast her a glance like a beaten dog's.

'Aye,' he said briefly.

'Who has she gone to?' Gil asked. 'Her mother's beside herself with fear and worry, Brosie, she needs to learn where the girl is.'

'If I knew, I'd tell you,' said Vary. He seemed to speak with difficulty, dragging the words from a great distance, his lips stiff.

'Have you had no word?' Alys asked, still in that gentle tone.

'None.'

'We've just found her servant murdered,' said Gil, 'a fellow that's been with her since they were both bairns, by what the mother says. I'm not convinced she's safe. Are you not concerned for her?'

Vary turned away, looking down at his desk, and shrugged his thin shoulders. Gil considered the desk too. An abacus, a green-glazed pottery inkstand, two ledgers, a cheap set of tablets and a leather pouch with another set, a stack of paper, were arranged with meticulous neatness. In the shelves on the end of the structure, leather cases presumably contained surveying instruments.

They were in Vary's closet, where he had taken them as soon as he realised what news they had brought him. It was a spacious panelled chamber built on from the end gable of the house, with windows looking up and down the street. The dwelling as a whole was a substantial edifice, of two jettied wooden storeys over a stone-built ground floor, though its resemblance to the Kettlands building stopped there. Recent paint made the outside bright in the sunlight, but indoors the atmosphere was oppressive, as if the whole house was holding its breath. The serving-man who had admitted them, the maidservant who had brought the jug of ale, were grim and silent, treading softly around their master. Here, surrounded by the paraphernalia of his profession, Vary had the air of an animal in its refuge; Gil had a sudden recollection of a past lapdog of his sisters', hiding under a bed from a threatened bath.

At his side, Alys leaned forward from the backstool where she was seated.

'Will you show me the message?' she said coaxingly. Vary's back went rigid, his head turning in the same moment. One hand moved jerkily, as if to touch or cover something on the desk, then was thrust down at his side.

24

'What message?' he said after a moment, his voice harsh. 'No message.'

'There might be something in it which would tell us where to seek her,' Alys said.

'No!' he said, with sudden violence, and then more moderately, 'No, there was no message. You needny trouble to seek her. It's, it's some accident befallen young Adam, no need to worry yoursels.'

'The boy's throat was cut,' Gil said, 'and then he was hacked about and thrown down the hillside. A strange sort of accident.'

'I don't wish you to worry yoursels,' reiterated Vary.

'And what do I tell your good-mother?' Gil asked, exchanging a puzzled glance with Alys.

Vary turned to look at them. His cheeks were wet, his jaw working. After a couple of attempts to speak he managed to say, 'Just leave. Leave now.' He swallowed hard, made a huge effort, and added with grotesque courtesy, 'It's right good to see you, Gil. Maybe another time we can get a good crack thegither, but it's no a good moment, as you can see.'

Alys rose and went forward, putting her hand on Vary's arm.

'Will you not tell us what you know, maister?' she said. 'You must be concerned for her.'

He leaned a little back, staring down at her, drew a shaky breath. Before he could speak she put her other hand to her brow and reeled convincingly, propping herself on the desk.

'Oh! I feel so dizzy!' she said, contriving to sound helpless. 'Oh, maister – might I have a drink of water?'

'Water,' he repeated, as if he had never heard of the stuff. 'Oh – water! Here, sit down again! Gil, your wi— your wife!'

25

He thrust her down onto the backstool, and hurried past her to the closet door to shout for water. Behind him Gil moved to Alys's side as she turned the cheap set of tablets in her hand, pulling a face at the crudely painted woodcut pasted to one panel in place of the carving which ornamented better goods. He was just in time to catch Vary's arm as he turned back and lunged at them.

'No! That's private, that's my— I've no to tell!'

'You haven't told us,' Alys said reassuringly. 'We'd guessed.'

She looked down at the tablets again, unwound the string which held them shut, and opened out the two leaves. In clumsy, unaccustomed letters, gouged into the wax, they bore the legend: *SEIK NOT YIR WYF DO WIR BIDDIGN.*

'Seek not your wife, do our bidding,' Gil repeated. 'Who is "we"?'

Alys clapped the tablets shut as the same maidservant entered, broad middle-aged face drawn and shadowed with concern, a jug of water in her meaty hand.

'Was the ale soured, maister?' she asked. Vary gestured feebly at Alys, and Gil took the jug with a word of thanks.

'Mistress Mason was dizzy,' he said. 'I'll pour for her.'

The woman retreated reluctantly, and Alys opened the tablets again.

'Who is it from, maister?' she asked gently. It occurred to Gil that she was dealing with Vary as if with a nervous child or animal. 'Who was the messenger?'

Vary shook his head, gulping for air, and folded up on to another backstool.

'I don't know,' he wailed. 'I don't *know* who has her!'

'Begin at the beginning,' said Gil, and Alys nodded approval. 'When did this message reach you?'

26

'Friday,' said Vary. He wrapped his arms about his chest, rocking slightly. 'Friday. The, the morrow after the Lanimer riding. I thought— I'd bidden her no to come down to the fair, no in her condition, and when she didny return by the evening I took it,' he bit his lip, 'I took it she was still angered at me. We parted on no very friend-like terms. I hoped she'd be back in good time to hear Mass on the Friday. And then this came.'

'And who brought it?'

'I don't know,' the man said again. He stilled his rocking, and concentrated. 'Jessie said it was a laddie brought it, and one she'd not seen about the town. You get all sorts in from the farms for the fair and the riding,' he explained, as if they could have no idea about it, 'no to mention the folk that's here to buy and sell.'

'What time of day?' Alys asked. 'And if it's any comfort, Mistress Madur seems not to have told her mother she was at outs with you, maister. I think her anger has not lasted. What time did the message reach you?'

He glanced at her, and away again.

'Atween Terce and Sext. Maybe nine o the clock?' He shivered. 'I ran to the door, but I never saw a laddie like she described.'

'What did she describe?' Gil asked.

'A black-avised barefoot laddie in a tattered plaid, so she said, that handed her the tablets and ran off, and never spoke.'

'A tinker laddie, maybe?' Gil suggested.

Vary shook his head, as if trying to dislodge something, and began rocking again.

'Gil, you need to leave it. I canny have her sought.'

'Why not?' asked Alys, still using that gentle tone. 'Do you not wish for her return?'

'They said,' said Vary helplessly, nodding at the tablets still in her hand, 'they said. You see what they

27

said there. And, and,' he swallowed, 'the same day, as I was crossing the marketplace through the Fair, for the Provost wished a word, a man spoke in my ear and said, *Tell nobody. No a word to a soul.*'

'Did you see who it was?' Alys asked.

'I turned, you can believe it, and there was two-three men at my back, and a duarch, no bigger than Big Will of this burgh,' he held out his hand to show the low stature of the man, 'and some country wives, but they none o them saw who spoke to me, nor heard, for there was a piper and a dance going no ten feet away. Then they asked what he'd said,' he went on, in increasing desperation, 'and I had to leave it, say it was no matter.'

'No other word since?' Gil asked. 'No instructions, no bidding?'

'Nothing. I'm waiting! I'm waiting for— and I don't know, Gil, I canny tell what they'll ask o me, if it's something I'll be able to perform or no. What if it's no within my power to borrow what they ask? I don't even know if she's safe or no! And her mother shouting at me yestreen, and naught I could say.'

'Who could have taken her? Who is there that might wish you ill?' Gil asked carefully. 'You're not unco well to do, are you?' He gestured at the house around them. 'You're comfortable, but I'd say the Provost is a richer man and he's not the wealthiest in Lanark either. It seems to me the object may not be to get money from you.'

Vary looked at him, frowning, still rocking slightly, apparently construing this remark with difficulty. Alys looked down at the tablets again, studying the message.

After a moment, Vary said cautiously, 'I canny think that I've enemies. I do my duty to the burgh, I've displeased a few by it, but that's by the way. I've no enemies that I know of.'

28

'Is anything about to come to the Council that you would advise on?' Gil suggested. 'Is anyone planning to build in the burgh, or the like? Have you ordered anyone's foreshot taken down, any middens moved?'

'If it's yet to come to the Council, how would I ken?' said Vary, making the question sound reasonable. Gil, indweller in a burgh not much larger than Lanark, was unconvinced; in his experience the gossips on the High Street knew the business of Glasgow before the bailies did.

'You keep a register,' Alys prompted. 'An account of all the decisions you advise on. Could we see it?'

'A casebook, you mean?' said Vary, staring at her. 'Aye— aye, I do. But what would— oh. You think I might ha something writ down that would tell me who has my lass?' Alys nodded, and he turned away, looking in the shelves on the end of his desk, and then at the bookshelf, finally lifting the upper of the two ledgers lying on the desk. Checking the flyleaf, he handed it to her. 'Yon's the current one. But I canny think you're right. Who would steal away my wife, just to get my agreement to— it must be siller they're after. I'm just the one voice, I canny sway the Council.'

'You're their expert,' Gil observed. 'You're employed of the Council to deal wi boundaries and roadways, if your duties are like your fellow's in Glasgow.'

'I think we need to study this,' said Alys, looking up from the pages of tiny, neat writing. 'May we take it away, maister?'

'He what?' exclaimed Mistress Somerville, on a rising note of indignation. 'He had a message? Do you tell me he kent from Friday things was amiss, and never sent me word? Nor stirred himsel to seek my lassie? The pultron!' she uttered explosively, this time genuinely bouncing up and down on her plumply upholstered daybed, so that her cascade of chins quivered and a long grey braid escaped from her plain cap. 'The dastard! The faizart tillieloot! I'll have his liver to my pigs!'

'Indeed, madam,' said Alys soothingly, 'I can see that you must be distressed. But Maister Vary is equally distressed. I think him paralysed with indecision, and the message did direct him to tell no one, for your daughter's safety.'

'That's no the point.' Mistress Somerville pulled her tawny brocade bedgown more firmly about her massive bosom and looked determined. 'I should ha been tellt. I should ha heard. And as for Adam, poor laddie, that's ill news indeed, and how I'm to tell his sweetheart I canny think. And my poor lassie,' she burst out, 'seeing him cut down afore her een! Oh, it's ill to hear, maister. And Our Lady send,' she crossed herself swiftly, 'the bairn doesny come out scarred or marred by the sight that's met his mother's een. Oh, my poor lassie!'

They were seated in her solar, a much-furnished upper apartment crammed with curiosities and religious bijouterie, from a Crucifixion carved from an oak-gall to a writing-slope so curiously wrought it was hard to see how it could be used for writing on. The lady had received them there with apologies for not descending to greet them, the bedgown sufficient explanation for that, and listened to them in increasing distress while her tirewoman served strong ale. Now Gil nodded, took another welcome draught of the ale and glanced at the window, where the sky was light and bright. They would still get home in daylight.

'Ill news indeed,' he said, 'and I'm sorry to be the bearer. Mistress, can you think who might have stolen your daughter away?'

She stared at him in surprise.

30

'Who but the tinkers, maister, that was in the neighbourhood for the Fair. You think it's no them? What would any honest man steal a lassie for, in her state? No, no, I canny think it's any other than the tinkers! I'll have the men out first thing the morn, to speir what way they went, raise the neighbourhood to pursue them. You'll ride wi them, maister, I take it?'

'Vary has had written word from someone about her,' Gil said firmly. 'That's no tinkers' work, it's someone who can write. I think she's been taken by someone as a threat to Vary, to make him do their bidding.'

'Then how has he no done so,' she demanded, 'to get her back? Oh, my lassie! And in sic a state! She should be getting treasured and nourist for her ain safety, no harried about the country at sword's point, and her ain groom, that she's kent since they were bairns, slain afore her face!'

The maidservant murmured something, put a beaker into her mistress's hand, and began to tuck the escaped braid back into the cap. Mistress Somerville paused to take a gulp of the ale, wiping at her eyes with her free hand.

Alys said, 'Has your daughter ever mentioned any who hold her or Maister Vary at odds? Has anyone tried to persuade her to something she'd not wish to do, or to a promise she'd not wish to make?'

'No,' said Mistress Somerville flatly. 'Never. And Vary wouldny let me ken if they did,' she added. 'No, I canny see that that's how to find her. If you'll no ride out wi them, maister, I'll have the men search on their own. Somebody will have seen the tinkers, seen what way they left the neighbourhood. They'll no be hard to track down.'

'Where did they camp?' Gil asked.

'Where they aye do, I expect.' She drained her beaker and set it down. 'On the Burgh Muir, to be handy for the races and that. The men can get up there first thing, them that's no needed for this quest on young Adam, poor laddie, and then we'll can bring him home and bury him in Carluke where he belongs.' She wiped at her eyes again.

Finally escaping Mistress Somerville's lamentations, they mounted and clopped wearily onwards, up the long hill towards Carluke where the road ran as a hollow way between the tofts. To either side the dwellings were set back amidst summer growth of potherbs and salad crops, a drift of sweet peat smoke rising through the thatch of the smaller roofs, white strong-smelling coal smoke from the bigger houses.

As they drew near the church, Henry observed from behind Gil, 'They were saying in the kitchen at Kettlands, the mistress had sent over to ask Sir John's prayers to St Malessock.'

'And the gift o a pound of wax, and all,' Euan said over his shoulder. 'Is that the holy man that was coming out of the peat on Belstane's own land? I was hearing how he protects all this parish, and turned back an outbreak of the summer fever from Lanark when they bore him round the bounds last year.'

'Aye,' said Henry, very drily. Gil slid a sideways glance at Alys, and found her wearing a studiously serious expression.

He was in more than one mind about St Malessock himself. The shrivelled, leathery corpse, naked but for a fox-skin girdle, with its battered face and shock of bright red hair, which had emerged from the peat two years since a few miles away on his godfather's land, could have been anyone. It was almost certainly not St Malessock, if there had ever been anyone of that name, but the parish priest, discovering a hagiography in his vestry with the ink very nearly dry, had declared this to be the original evangelist of Kirkmalessock in the south of the parish, hastily cleared St James the Less out of a side chapel and installed the pitiful thing in a handsomely painted kist below the altar.

Small miracles had begun to happen almost immediately, warts and boils cured, a lost cow found safely, but what Gil found more convincing was a dream he had had not long after the finding of the body, in which a red-haired man, stark naked but for a fox-skin girdle, had addressed him like a fellow baron, and offered him a token which had saved Alys's life the next day. Whoever the man was, it seemed he still guarded land and people about Carluke.

'You want to step in and offer a prayer now?' he asked. 'Audrey's a Carluke lassie, it can do no harm to ask aid for her.'

'Och, yes indeed!' said Euan with enthusiasm. 'I have not been in the kirk here, and it's good to remind Our Lady who I am from time to time.'

'We could,' said Alys doubtfully. 'Aren't you hungry?'

'Very wise,' said Lady Egidia. 'Prayer is never wasted. But could Yolande Somerville be right? Could the girl have been stolen by tinkers?'

'She could,' said Gil. 'All things are possible. But it doesny seem likely to me, what wi the note.' He leaned back on the settle, stretching his legs. 'I'll sleep the night, I tell you. I've ridden further than I ever intended this day.'

They were gathered in a far less cluttered chamber, off the main hall of the tower-house, where Alan Forrest had set out a late supper for them as soon as they rode in. Cold cooked meat, bread and new butter, and a dish of raspberries and cream, made a feast for two hungry people; Gil hoped Henry and the other men were as well served.

This close to midsummer, the sun would set well north of north-west; the long golden light flooded in by the windows which looked across the wide valley of the Clyde towards the Campsie hills, lit up the little chamber, caught the bridge of Alys's nose where she bent over Maister Vary's ledger, outlined the oval of her face beneath her white indoor cap.

'But who else could have lifted her?' persisted Lady Egidia. 'And her groom dead. It looks bad, Gil, very bad.'

'I'd noticed that,' he said politely. 'The boy had been cut to pieces, I'd say by more than one attacker. Someone expected Mistress Madur to ride that way, lay in wait, and made sure to be able to take her by force.'

'And it's been kept secret,' said Alys, immersed in the ledger. 'It isn't known in Lanark.'

'Exactly,' Gil agreed. 'Whoever it is, either he can command silence or he can keep his men out of Lanark. I'd say we're looking at someone on the lands round about, rather than in Lanark itself. Does the family have enemies? I'm out of touch with local politics, but I'd have thought Lockhart, for instance, or the Livingstones, were more peaceable these days.'

'Her kin,' said his mother obliquely.

'Is any of them involved in the burgh?'

'I've not heard it, if so.' Lady Egidia nibbled a fingernail, considering. In the basket by her chair, her grey cat rolled over and dislodged a single fat kitten, which squeaked plaintively. Socrates, sprawled by Gil's feet, raised his head to look, and the cat hissed at him and began to wash the kitten. 'She has three uncles, if I recall, and two brothers. The brothers are at some distance, one at Harelaw, one in the Lothians. I don't see how

34

threatening Maister Vary would be of any use to them, but the uncles . . .' She paused again. 'There is Robert Somerville on her mother's side, and Henry Madur of Madursmains and Jocelyn Madur on her father's. Robert and Jocelyn are mostly short of money, and Jocelyn cheated me over a horse once. I suppose either could have some scheme afoot that would need the liner's consent. I ken nothing against Henry Madur,' she finished on a note of faint regret. 'He's said to be a good superior, a good landlord, but a wee thing tight-fisted.'

'And Maister Vary's kin?' asked Alys. 'Does he have brothers?'

'One is a priest, in Lanark I think,' said Gil, 'and the other holds the family lands over by Carnwath.'

'Ah.' She looked down at the ledger again. 'I have never seen such tiny writing, one could do with a flea-glass to read it. This must be the priest brother. *Ser Jerom Varrie desirus to sell ii huses in friers wynnd to wm cunnighame, pottar.* No kin of yours, I take it, Gil? No, I thought not. *Disputit on account o daunger of fyre fro the sedd wms kiln.* I suppose there is no reason for a priest to withhold from killing the manservant, if he was angry enough.'

'I suspect you're right,' Gil said. 'And Brosie thought he had made no enemies in the burgh! Are there more such, sweetheart?'

'Several.' She turned back a page. 'Someone called William Mowat, ordered to take down his foreshot. What is a foreshot, Gil?'

'A chamber built onto the gable of the house,' he said promptly, 'projecting into the street. Merchants build them to do business in. Brosie's closet is in one. It's all very well on the High Street of Lanark, which is the widest I've ever seen, but when it reduces the way so a cart canny get by it's another matter.'

'That's what has happened here. It came to the Council, who supported Maister Vary.'

'Mowat is a house carpenter,' Lady Egidia supplied. 'Easy enough for him to put up and take down sic a thing. I am amazed that Vary let you bring this ledger away.'

'It took some persuasion,' said Gil. 'It's all Council business, after all; it should never be out of the burgh.'

'And this one,' Alys continued. 'Alexander Qhippo – what a strange name! – complains that his neighbour Walter Lightbody's garderobe discharges foulness into his cellar. The said Walter ordered to rebuild or remove his garderobe.'

'Lightbody?' said Gil.

She glanced at him and nodded, and leafed further back through the ledger. 'I think this has been at dispute for four, no, five years.'

'A long time to deal with a stink in the cellar,' said Lady Egidia. 'What would provoke either party to action now, after so long?'

'Anyone can lose patience,' said Gil. 'I suppose we should speak to all these folk. Are there more?'

'Likely,' said Alys. 'But it seems to me,' she went on diffidently, 'these cases are ended. Well, not the stink in the cellar, but most of the others here are concluded. Should we not be looking at matters which are pending, or even not yet come to the Council?'

'I think we should,' Gil admitted, 'though I'm at a loss to know how we track them down.'

'Send Euan round the countryside to ask people if they're planning anything,' Alys suggested. Her quick smile came and went, and he grinned in answer.

'It would certainly keep him out of my way. He was no help at all in Lanark. Which reminds me, mother:

36

have you met this French lady that's staying in Lanark? Olympe Archibecque is the name.'

'I haven't,' she said. 'I take it you have? What like is she?'

'Striking,' he said thoughtfully, taking care not to catch Alys's eye. 'Aye, that's the word. Striking. *To hear her sing, to hear her dance! she will the best herself advance that ever I saw.'*

Leaving Maister Vary's house, after Gil had spent some time trying to reassure him and Alys questioned the servants, they had set out to walk down the High Street to the St Nicholas Inn to meet Henry and the other men. The street was not busy, but a few people were out enjoying the still, warm evening. Gil was pacing in silence, thinking at once of the problem before them and the feel of Alys's hand tucked into his arm, when the hand tightened.

'Look, Gil!' she said softly in French. 'Isn't that—? Surely it can't be!'

He looked where she indicated, and saw a tall figure approaching, clad, remarkably, in a wide-sleeved, wide-skirted gown of sky-blue and tawny brocade, topped by a short cloak of cherry-coloured taffeta rather than a plaid as most Scots women wore, and crowned by a complex green velvet hat like a man's, its trailing feathers brushing the broad shoulders. A stocky maidservant carried the long brocade train. Several small boys followed at a respectful distance, goggling.

'Sweet St Giles,' he said, 'I think you're right.'

As they drew closer he saw that the face was elaborately painted, in a way which would certainly make the boys and their parents stare, and the high-sketched eyebrows were rising in response to his scrutiny.

They both stopped. Gil bowed, Alys curtsied, they said together, 'Madame.'

'Madame, monsieur,' responded the strange figure, and curtsied deeply in response. 'I fear you have the advantage of me.'

'Forgive us, madame,' said Alys, and Gil realised they were still speaking French. 'We took you for a dear friend whom you resemble closely.'

'Oh!' A large white hand batted the statement away. 'Of a certainty there can be none like me. The good God broke the mould when he made me.'

'I believe that must be true,' Gil said. He replaced his hat, and the pale blue eyes under the painted brows flickered at the gesture. 'Forgive us – I am Gil Cunningham, and this is my wife Mistress Alys Mason.'

'And I am Olympe Archibecque.' She curtsied again, just as deeply. 'I am enchanted to meet two speakers of the beautiful language in this small place. You must call on me.'

'That would be delightful,' said Alys warily. 'Where may one find you?'

The pale eyes sparkled at them. The pudding-faced maidservant stood stolidly holding the folds of silk out of the dust, and Madame Olympe pointed at one of the gables across the street.

'I am lodged very comfortably there, in the house of Walter Lightbody,' she mangled the name extravagantly, 'who is a baker and confectioner. I have a set of chambers, quite private, looking on the street. Perhaps tomorrow? Tomorrow after noon? *Ah, madame!*' She curtsied again, less deeply, to a passing townswoman, who returned the courtesy. Alys turned her head to consult Gil, her face expressionless, and he nodded. It would fit with what he planned for the day. '*Ah, c'est merveilleux!* I shall swoon with anticipation whenever I think of it. *À demain, madame, monsieur!*'

She curtsied again and swept on. Gil, taken by surprise, just managed a nod to the maidservant as the woman hurried past at her mistress's back, and got a faint, approving narrowing of the eyes in return. Alys turned to look after the pair as Madame Olympe crossed the street to greet another couple out strolling in the evening sunshine.

'Well!' she said quietly.

'Well indeed,' he said. 'Shall we go and find the men?'

'How good is her Scots?' asked his mother now. 'Mistress Somerville seems to have taken her up, and I've no opinion of her French.'

'I expect she gets by,' said Gil offhandedly. 'We spoke in French.'

'And what is she doing in Lanark? She must stand out like a papingo in a henyard.' Lady Egidia leaned back as her grey cat, having washed the kitten into sleep, sprang on to her knee. 'Talking of henyards, John wanted to play with the kitten. Your girl made a to-do about the scratches, but as I said to her, he has to learn some time, even if your kitchen cat lets him pull her about, Silky and her kitten are another matter entirely.'

'Is the kitten harmed?' Alys asked anxiously.

'It seems unhurt.' Lady Egidia looked down at the sleeping scrap of fur. 'It will be a pretty thing, with those grey stripes.' She stroked the adult cat on her lap, trying to discourage it from working its paws in her gown. 'No, no. That's why I changed out of my court dress, Silky. So tell me what the Provost said when you handed him a corp. And one five days old, at that,' she added in distaste.

Gil shook his head.

'I sent Henry and the other men to him, with the corp on a litter, and bade them tell him where we found the laddie and why we were searching, and that I'd call on him the morn to discuss matters after I'd spoken to

Brosie. I'm troubled now,' he admitted, 'for given the manservant's been found it must be known abroad that the lady's missing. The word will spread like wildfire, no matter what their instructions were to Brosie.'

'It would have got out as soon as Mistress Somerville learned of it,' said Alys. She closed the ledger and rubbed her eyes. 'I have had enough of this writing for now. So far I have only found Maister Vary's kin mentioned, not the girl's, no Somervilles or Madurs. How far out of Lanark do they dwell?'

'No more than ten miles out, for the most part,' said Gil. 'I wonder, would Michael help? He must know them all at least as well as I do, and he made a fair fist of helping me two year ago.'

'Will he wish to leave Tib?' Alys objected.

'Tib has a few weeks to go,' said Lady Egidia. 'Mistress Lithgo is summoned to her for the middle of July—'

'Mistress Lithgo? Beatrice Lithgo?' Gil interrupted, while Alys's eyes widened. 'Is she hereabouts again? I thought they had all moved across the Clyde to Cadzow.'

'She tells me she and her good-daughter are ill assorted,' said Lady Egidia. 'I knew that son of hers had poor taste, not like you, dear, and it seems there have been disagreements and pulling of caps, and she planned to move back into this parish after Tib's time is over. I've invited her to live here,' she said airily. 'She'll have the cottage at the back of the stables, indeed, she has moved some of her goods in already, and I'll be glad to have someone so herbwise on hand.'

Gil opened his mouth, and closed it again, thinking of Mistress Lithgo. They had encountered her at the same time as St Malessock had risen from the peat; she was a sharp-brained, sharp-tongued woman with a gift for herbs and remedies, who had dealt with the ills and

40

injuries of the folk up at the coalheugh until her family left the place, and he knew she was much missed in the area.

Alys said, 'I can see she might not be easy to live with, but that's no reason for it to come to such a pass.'

'Quite so,' said her mother-in-law. 'I think she's away the now, the cottage is empty again. She's maybe gone to gather the rest of her goods.'

Gil, contemplating the effect of two such strong-minded women within the same barmekin, was unable to comment. Instead he said, 'It has been a very long day, and there's another the morn. I must bid you good night, mother. Alys?'

She rose immediately, accepting his outstretched hand, her fingers tightening briefly on his. Lady Egidia smiled enigmatically and delivered the blessing she had used since his childhood: 'Christ and His blessed Mother guard your sleep, my dears.'

Much later, curled warm and sated against him in the box bed in their chamber, Alys murmured,

'What do you suppose Ma— Madame Olympe is doing in Lanark? Such a small place, away from the court and the coast?'

'Don't let the Provost hear you describe it like that,' he said lazily. 'It's one of King David's burghs, after all. I've no idea what Madame Olympe might be doing here. I hope we'll find out tomorrow.'

'Mmm.' She was playing with the hairs on his chest. 'She was very quick to invite us to visit. I suppose she wants your help.'

'I've no doubt of it.' Gil grinned into the darkness, thinking of his previous encounter with the individual now calling himself Madame Olympe, who was in fact his kinsman Sandy Boyd and was probably spying for

41

the Crown. That occasion had nearly ended with Gil's arrest for murder, while his cousin vanished into the night.

'You'll be careful?' Alys was obviously thinking of it too. 'No more housebreaking at midnight?'

'Hardly, at this time of year, we'd be seen. I'm more concerned about Audrey Madur. I wish there had been some sign of where she was taken, which direction, who was with her.'

'Why she was taken,' Alys added.

'Did you learn anything from the servants?'

'A little. Mistress Somerville is right, she has taught her daughter well. The servants like her, think her a good mistress for all she's so young, seem attached to her and to Maister Vary. It's a well-run household.' She wriggled closer to him. 'The woman Jessie, the one we saw, acts as her tirewoman, and says she seems happy, looks forward to her baby, has no reason to run away or anyone to run to. She took her husband's side in a disagreement with his brother, which is a good sign. The servants are as concerned as their master.'

'Has she friends in the town?' he asked.

'I have one or two names. I thought I would try to speak to them tomorrow, before we call on Madame Olympe. Audrey might say more gossiping with friends than she would to her tirewoman.' She paused, still twirling the hairs on his chest round her fingers. 'You know, Gil, I keep thinking about her. A lady who rides like that, sideways on the saddle, very often knows nothing of controlling the beast. She can't use the reins, she doesn't know how to make it go faster. They were attacked, and her servant killed, and she could do nothing to escape, and even if she managed to dismount she was caught up in that great sack, she couldn't run. I hope they have her safe somewhere.'

'She could hardly run anyway, in her condition,' he pointed out.

'I suppose.'

He captured her hand and began to nibble at her fingers.

'Either you stop doing that, or we begin again,' he said round them. 'I've missed you.'

'I noticed that.' She freed the hand, which returned to its previous occupation. He chuckled, and flung his arm across her shoulders again.

'I meant what I said.'

'I know.'

Chapter Three

Following Alys down the stairs in the morning Gil was relieved, though unsurprised, to find his brother-in-law Michael Douglas standing in the hall, eating porridge and toasted bread and discussing suppliers of materia medica with Lady Egidia.

'If Andro Bothwell's shop was still there,' she was saying, 'it would be simpler by far. Good morning, my dear,' she said as Alys came to kiss her. 'Did you tell me Andro's son was set up in Glasgow, Gil?'

'And his daughter, both.' Gil bowed to his mother, acknowledged his dog's welcome, then accepted a dish of porridge from Alan Forrest, and added butter with a generous hand. 'You could send to either for what you need, or send to Alys and she'd see to it for you. Aye, Michael.'

'Aye, Gil.' Michael, compact and well-barbered, as much at ease as any man in Lady Egidia's presence, set his empty porringer on the tray at the steward's elbow. Socrates' disappointed gaze followed it, and his long nose twitched. 'What's this I hear,' Michael began, and paused because Alys was enquiring, with resolute concern, for his wife. Dealing efficiently with this, he went on, 'What's this I hear about the lassie Madur? Madam our mother sent for me,' he bowed slightly to Lady Egidia, 'but she bade me wait till you explained what it's about.'

'Indeed, it is very distressing,' said Alys.

'She's missing. It seems she's been lifted away by force.' Gil outlined the situation briefly, aware of Alan listening by the plate-cupboard. Michael heard him out and considered the tale.

'You'd think we were in the Marches,' he said at last, 'wi Armstrongs and Johnstones at war all around us. It's as if she'd been taken by one of the surnames to get back at another. Tib will be right distressed to hear it.'

'If we were in the Marches she'd ha been better attended,' said Gil, spooning porridge.

'I'd not let Tib ride out wi one man only,' said Michael firmly. 'Nor the miners wouldny permit it either,' he added.

'I'm glad to hear it,' Lady Egidia said, detaching the fat kitten from her sleeve. 'Silky, take your baby away. Go teach it to catch mice. But Audrey was only a couple of miles from Lanark town, not away up on the moorland like you. You'd ha thought she'd be safe.'

'Could it ha been some of the tinkers and the like down in Lanark for the Fair?' Michael suggested.

'That's what her mother reckons,' Gil said, 'but I canny see such folk sending her husband a ransom note, more likely to be a spoken message brought by a fleet-footed laddie. And by the sound of it she's further on than Tib. I'd not have thought they'd steal her for, well, for other than ransom, not when Lanark's full of willing lassies.' He bent to set his empty bowl down for the dog, who paced over to accept his tribute with dignity. 'No, I think we're looking at the local barons, and I hoped you might give us a hand there. Alys and I have tasks in Lanark, speaking to the Provost for one, and I'll be needed at the quest on the servant, as finder. Sending one of the servants round all her uncles to ask for her would get us little forward, it needs to be someone who can speak to the landholder rather than the steward and gauge his reaction.'

Michael eyed him warily.

'And what's my reason for seeking Mistress Madur? If Vary's been told to tell no one, how come we're seeking her?'

'Tib has had no word for a week or two,' Alys suggested. 'It makes her anxious. You would naturally want to indulge her the now.'

Michael coloured up.

'Well, I do,' he muttered. 'Aye, that would work. I'm riding round her kin seeking her, since she's not at home. And watch their eyes, I suppose, when they answer. Who d'you need to ask? Is it just her kin, or should I search wider than that? I'll need a list of names.'

'Somerville, both the Madurs,' Gil said. 'Gregory Vary.'

'Gregory's no like to be home,' Michael said. 'The most of his holdings are over in Lothian. There's only the family lands here in Lanarkshire.'

'Talk to his steward, then. And anyone else, any household that seems good. And if you can find out without asking whether there's any business interests planned in Lanark, anything Vary would have the power to deny them, it would be a good thing. Oh, and if you or whatever man's wi you could check the stables for a dainty jennet and a bay gelding wi a sock and a star, one of Belstane Bluebell's, it would be a help.'

'I'll see if they ken where King Arthur's buried and all,' offered Michael without expression.

Alys giggled. Before Gil could answer, small feet stamped on the stairs. Alan the steward stepped hurriedly aside as the door was flung open and Gil's ward John McIan hurtled through it, brown and bare-foot, tall for nearly four, his little red linen tunic already

47

decorated from the morning's activities. He was beginning to look very like his father the harper, and he had definitely grown since he had left Glasgow. Socrates padded over to lick his face, his stringy tail waving, but John pushed him away.

'Daddy Gil!' he shouted. 'Daddy Gil! I catched a hen and he bit me!'

Nancy, the quiet girl who was his nurse, followed him into the hall with chiding noises. John stopped, looked over his shoulder at her, then performed a very creditable bow to Lady Egidia, gabbled, 'Good morning madam I hope I see you well,' and flung himself at Gil without waiting for her reply. 'Come and see! I show you which one I catched. See where he bit me?' He exhibited a red mark on one lean arm. 'It hurted, but Nancy put nointment and it went away.'

'You mustn't chase the hens, John,' Gil reproved, 'or they'll give you no eggs for your dinner.'

'No, no,' John shook his head so that his mop of black curls danced, 'Jackie said he never gives eggs, cos he has a black tail. I wanted his fevvers off his tail, but he bit me.'

'If I tried to pull your curls out,' Gil suggested, 'you might try to bite me.'

John considered this, dismissed it, and tugged at Gil's hand.

'Come and I show you which hen,' he ordered. 'Come now!'

'I have to go to Lanark,' Gil temporised.

'Let him show you the henyard,' said Alys. 'It won't take long.'

Admiring the henyard, and particularly the cockerel's black tail feathers, Gil found himself subjected to a volley of questions. Why did the cockerel shout like that? Why did that hen run away from the other? Why did they not fly away like the sparrows? He parried these as best he could, while the cockerel glared balefully from the peak of the henhouse and crowed defiance.

After a while the questions died away. Gil was gazing about him, at the back of the stable buildings and the distant view of Tinto Hill, when John said, 'Daddy Gil, what's baron mean?'

'Baron?' he repeated, looking down at the boy. 'It's a man who holds land for the King.'

'Oh.' John scowled, digging with his bare toes in the dust. 'But if it's a lady?'

'A lady can hold lands,' Gil said. 'Lady Egidia holds these lands. But she canny be a baron.'

'But if it's a cow?'

'A cow?' Gil realised, with a sinking feeling, what was coming. 'It sounds the same, but it's a different word. If a cow, or a lady for that matter, is barren, it means she has no babies.'

John thought about this, scraping dust into a heap with the side of one high-arched foot.

'Lady Gidia had babies in the olden days,' he said after a while, 'cos she's your mammy, and Lady Kate's mammy and all. Even though you're a big man.'

'That's right,' Gil agreed.

'Jackie's big sister said. Mysie said my mammy's a barren.'

'Your own mammy's dead,' Gil reminded him. 'Did she mean Mammy Alys?'

'Maybe.' The bare brown foot patted the heap of dust flat. 'But Mammy Alys hasn't got no babies. She's got me.'

'She does,' Gil agreed. He hunkered down so that he was on a level with the boy. 'She's got you, but you were never her baby. You ken that.'

'I'm her wee boy,' stated John hopefully.

'That's right. And the best wee boy in Lanarkshire.'

'Jackie says he is, his mammy said it.'

'Jackie's wrong.' Gil rose, and lifted the child onto his shoulders. 'Come on, we'll go in and find Nancy.'

Making his way among the outbuildings, past the stableyard, towards the stair of the tower-house, Gil wondered whether he should tell Alys of this conversation, and how one might prevent John from playing with Alan Forrest's son, the only other child in the household close to his age. On the whole it seemed inadvisable—

'That lady that's got lost,' said the little voice above his head. 'She's got a baby.'

'No just yet,' said Gil, 'but she'll get one soon.' *Little pitchers have big ears*, he thought.

'She never had it when she got lost,' John stated in a different tone, 'but she's got it now. When you find her you'll see it.'

Now that, Gil recognised, he would certainly have to tell Alys.

'Aye, you're in an awkward position,' agreed Provost Lockhart, lifting the jug again.

A bulky, self-consequential man, he had clearly assumed his best gown to receive the Archbishop's quaestor and his lady, and was immersed in mustard-coloured velvet turned back with green silk, and perspiring heavily. His pink face gleamed in the sunshine which flooded his private closet.

'More wine, mistress? Maister?' he suggested. He poured carefully into the little glasses and set the jug down again on the tray. At Gil's feet Socrates watched him closely. 'I'll hold the quest this afternoon on the laddie your men brought me,' the Provost went on, 'gien that he'll no last much longer. You'll attend, seeing you're the finder, and I can get it brought in persons unknown, easy enough. But by rights I ought to call Brosie Vary to identify the corp, it being one o his household, and by the sound o't it would embarrass him badly. So tell me the tale again, Maister Cunningham. What was the lassie doing out and about this near her time, anyways?'

'It's all a mystery to me,' said Gil ruefully, with a brief glance at Alys. 'If my wife vanished, I'd be out scouring the countryside for her, no matter the threats I was sent, but Brosie seems like a man frozen, can neither act himself nor agree to action by others.'

'He's a high-strung fellow,' said the Provost. 'A good liner, a good lanimer-man, but high-strung. His brother's the same, Gregory. You ken they're twins? Seven-months' babes, lucky to rear them, but they were aye high-strung, easy owerset. And they never got on. Not them nor the younger one, him that's a priest. Jerome, he's cried. The faithers o the kirk. Named for the great authorities, they are, instead of for their grandsires like a'body else, but it's done them no good. Brosie's a gentle enough soul, but the other two, well!'

'Twins? No, I didn't know that,' said Gil in surprise. 'I suppose that's why the brother went to St Andrews and Brosie to Glasgow – to separate them.'

'Aye, the brother's the older, by half an hour they say, so they sent him to St Andrews. Wi it being the older college,' Lockhart explained, making matters clear. Then, returning to the matter at hand, 'Where did you say you found the laddie?'

Gil repeated his account of the discovery, and what he had deduced at the time. Lockhart nodded as he listened, and finally said, 'Aye, aye, that's about what I thought. As you say, the laddie's throat slit and his back and

51

chest cut to ribbons, they've made sure he wasny able to follow them. But who were they? That's what I'd like to ken.'

'I suspect Maister Vary would like to ken it and all,' Gil said drily. Lockhart acknowledged this with another nod. 'The lassie's mother reckons it was tinkers, but I'm no agreed. Tinkers would never send a message in writing.'

'Aye, I'd say you're right there. Forbye, the tinkers is all moved on. I set the constables on them the day after the Fair, and they'd ha noticed a Lanark lassie among them.'

Gil, having met the constables, felt this argument was not convincing, but went on, 'Who would you think might choose that spot?'

'Someone that kens the lie o the land,' said Lockhart. 'But that doesny narrow it down much, maister. That road's well used, any fighting man that travels it's going to recognise the possibilities. It's the road out o Lanark for Carluke, for Edinburgh, even Stirling.' He hitched up the mustard velvet, which immediately began to slide down his shoulders again. 'What's more, it's about the only place you could set sic a trap, atween Lanark and the lady's mother's house. So it doesny even rule out those that dwell south o Lanark.' He tapped his teeth reflectively. 'I'm agreed wi you, it's likely no money they're after. I could name you two or three men o the Council that could ransom their wives to more effect than Brosie Vary. And one or two that wouldny if they were asked,' he added, chuckling.

'Is there anything,' said Alys, speaking for the first time, 'is there anything due to come before the Council, sir, any business within the ports, that Maister Vary could support or deny?'

Lockhart studied her for a moment, and nodded again.

'Aye, I see what you're after. There might be,' he conceded. 'There might be. But it's a matter o Council business, mistress, if there is.'

'There's a lady's safety at stake,' said Gil, more firmly than he had intended, 'if not her life. We need to work out who might ha lifted her, maister.'

'I've heard o nothing definite,' said the Provost, equally firmly. 'I'll enquire.'

'What's puzzling me,' said Alys before Gil could speak, 'is where they might have taken her. It was broad day when she was captured, they could hardly gallop through the countryside without being seen, and nobody on the Carluke bank had anything to tell. Can you suggest any place they could hide until twilight, sir?'

Lockhart gave her an approving look.

'A good thought, mistress. Let me see.' He hitched up his gown again, and stared at the ceiling, considering. 'Livingstone has a barn on the Newmainshill, near the Carluke road, but that's in plain sight, hardly secret. What's down in the glen? There's the old mill, I suppose, though that's no safe, it's as like to fall round your ears and drop you in the mill-leat, or at least it was when I was a boy, it's likely fell in by now. No shelter there.' He sat up straighter. 'Aye, but I mind another thing when I was a boy. Did you ken there was caves in the bank there?'

'Caves?' repeated Gil. 'No, I never heard that.'

'It's maybe a thing Lanark laddies keeps to themsels.' Lockhart moved the tray aside and drew a snaking line on the table-carpet with a plump pink forefinger. 'See, if that's the Mouse Water, and that's the Carluke road brig, and here's the Hamilton road brig,' he placed his empty glass and the inkwell to mark these, 'the caves'd be about here, atween the two roads. On the far bank, the Carluke bank, where there's an overhang. There's no path,' he went on, still studying his plan, 'you're best going in from the Carluke road brig, cut across this bit o land here and then stay at the waterside so far's you can.'

'At this time of year, if they've used that, there should be tracks,' Gil said. 'How deep are these caves, do you mind?'

Alys drew out her tablets and began to sketch. The Provost, watching her, shook his head.

'One's little more than a hollow in the bank, enough to keep the rain off you. The other's deeper, and high enough to stand up in, but you'd no want to dwell in it, though I mind,' he grinned at the recollection, 'I ran away from home one time. Took all my worldly goods, which was my own wee bow and my bools and my bag o knucklebanes, borrowed a pie fro the kitchen, went and slept in the cave. April, it was. Never been as cold in my life. I was quite glad my faither found me the next day, for all the skelping I had for frighting my mither. Aye, mistress,' he leaned forward, peering at Alys's tablets, 'that's about right. Maybe nearer to the Carluke road.'

'Is there anyone else might have an idea,' said Gil, 'of who might be about to bring any matter to the Council that Brosie would have a say on? Would your burgh clerk ha heard anything, maybe?'

'Dodie Ballantyne, you mean?' said Lockhart. 'Aye, well, you could ask him, I suppose. Mind, he's a sticking chiel, he'll likely no tell you anything you're no paying for. Makes him a good custumar, but never play at Tarocco wi him.'

*   *   *

54

'Caves,' said Alys when they had stepped out into the street, Lockhart bowing them from his door, clearly about to shed the heavy velvet gown in decent privacy. 'But not big enough to live in or keep the girl in, I think.'

'They don't sound it,' Gil agreed. 'We can look on the way out of Lanark. Right now I want to speak to Maister Ballantyne, and I think you had calls to make?' She nodded. 'Take the dog, and Euan will attend you—'

'Och, will I not be helping you make enquiries, maister?' protested the lanky Erscheman. 'I could be helping you question this Ballantyne.'

'You'll attend your mistress,' said Gil firmly. 'Did you learn anything to the purpose in the Provost's kitchen?'

'Och, well,' said Euan, 'it seems it's all over the burgh now that Mistress Madur's missing, for they were speaking o little else. Some would have it she'd run off wi a lover, another says no, she's a decent lady. One reckons it's the Armstrongs or the like has lifted her away for a vengeance on Maister Vary, but the rest laughed at that. Could you ever see Maister Vary doing anything that would bring a vengeance down on his head, they said.'

'Useful,' said Gil. 'Now away with Mistress Mason and see what else you can learn.'

Following the directions the Provost had given him to Maister Ballantyne's house, Gil found himself in front of a tall timber-framed edifice near the West Port. Three jutting storeys rose above the iron-bound front door, and beside it a foreshot nearly as high as the first upper floor caused anyone passing towards the port to take a significant detour round it. Thinking that it was a good thing foreshots were not used in Glasgow, Gil rattled at the pin by the door.

A harassed and hatless fellow answered it, his shirt-sleeves rolled up, doublet half-unlaced, smudges of soot on his face and garments, though his bearing was that of an upper servant.

'He's in his chamber, maister,' he said before Gil could speak, and pointed towards the extension. 'In the fore-shot. The door's at the other side. Why's the whole o Lanark wanting him the day, and Steenie clerk away, and it no even Market Day? You'll ha to forgive me, maister, we've the—'

A screech, a prolonged clatter of pewter dishes, inter-rupted him. He cast a glance over his shoulder into the house, then stepped hastily aside as something black and monstrous flapped towards him down the wide hall, uttering hideous honking sounds, pursued with shouting by an equally blackened man.

'Haud her! Stop her! She'll be away!'

Gil recognised what was happening just in time, and stepped aside like the manservant as goose and man leapt down the steps, shedding clouds of soot, and plunged into the busy street.

'—sweep in,' said the manservant, watching with resignation as the pair zigzagged towards the High Street, followed by shouts of fury as passers-by found themselves blackened. When the sweep had vanished behind the foreshot, he shook his head sadly and retreated into the house, where someone was scolding shrilly while the pewter rang and clattered.

'She would have them swept,' he said as he closed the door.

Gil, grinning, made his way round to the other side of the foreshot, and rattled at this door in turn. He could hear no sounds of movement, no footsteps of anyone coming to the door, though since the sweep and his assistant were still causing a commotion beyond St Nicholas' church it was hard to be certain. He rattled the ring up and down the twisted pin again, and a voice

56

called, 'Come in, whoever that is! Come and gie's a hand here!'

A woman's voice.

Alarmed, puzzled, one hand on his whinger, he raised the latch and pushed at the door. It opened on a small waiting-room, with a bench and a locked press; beyond another door was hasty movement, a soft scuffling, someone gasping for breath.

'Who's there?' he said sharply. 'Maister Ballantyne?'

'Come away ben!' said the woman urgently. 'I need a hand here!'

Stepping round the inner door, he was confronted by a grim sight. A man lay flat on the floor, blood on his linen cuffs, his plain dark garments disarrayed. There was more blood around him on the broad planks, on the light oak of his handsome desk, and on the skirts of the woman who knelt over him. Her hands were crimson, as was the cloth she was pressing onto his chest; Gil saw the trailing ties and realised she had used her apron, just as she raised the crimson bundle to peer under it, and clamped it hastily down again.

'Call for help!' she ordered him. 'Get linen if you—'

The man under her hands choked suddenly; his eyes flew open in what seemed like surprise, a great gout of blood ran from his mouth, and the outflung hands relaxed. Gil looked at the narrow face, the bloody, grizzled beard, then bent his head and crossed himself. This man would never play at Tarocco again.

'Too late, I think,' he said. 'It's a matter of the hue and cry now. What happened?'

'Aye.' She sat back on her heels, crossing herself likewise and muttering a prayer, then grimaced down at the state of her skirts. 'I wish I'd had a right look at them.'

'It's Agnes, isn't it?' said Gil, recognising her. 'You're serving—'

'Madame Olympe, aye,' she confirmed. 'I think you're to call on us later? Wi your bonnie wee wife?'

'I am.' Gil considered the dead man again. 'I'd hoped for a word wi Maister Ballantyne first. I take it this is him?'

'I take it,' she agreed. 'I was waiting out yonder, to appoint a time for Madam to see him, and there was shouting within here, and then two great men ran out sheathing their swords as they went, and I heard him groaning. So I came to look, and here he was.'

'How long since?' Gil asked.

She shrugged. 'The quarter of an hour?'

'I can hardly ha missed them by much,' he said. 'I was at least the half of that time at the door asking for the man. You've no idea what way they took, I suppose.'

'They ran past this window,' she nodded at the aperture, 'for I saw them as I cam through the door. They'd be making for the port.'

'Ah,' he said. 'I came by the other way, down the hill, so I'd not ha seen them.' He looked about the chamber. There were papers on the desk, tumbled about as if someone had searched them hastily, and a town map. *West Port* and *Castle Gate* were marked; it might be a plan of Lanark, though most burghs had a west port. Another piece of paper lay near the door, as if dropped; casually he bent to lift it, and tucked it into his doublet along with the map. The woman Agnes was still kneeling, attempting to wipe her hands on the cleaner portions of her skirt.

'Well,' he said, 'best we get this over wi. You've no knife on you, have you?'

'None that would cause this much damage.' She lifted the blood-soaked cloth cautiously, to reveal the gaping rent in the dead man's clothing and flesh. 'That's a sword cut, and no a whinger either, it's a good hand's-breadth across.'

'You're right there,' Gil acknowledged, and went to the outer door. He thought briefly of the owner of the scolding voice, who must now be a widow and who would likely never be able to look at a chimney sweep again. Then, drawing a breath, he shouted, 'Murder! Raise the hue and cry! Bloody murder here!'

'Och, it's the speak of the town,' said Madame Olympe. 'What were they quarrelling about, Agnes? Maister Lightbody's servants told me it was something Ballantyne cheated them in, that they'd had that from you.'

'They never,' said Agnes stoutly, standing in the midst of the chamber, trying not to touch anything. 'Like I said to Maister Cunningham here, I heard shouting, and then after they ran out I heard the man groaning. I never caught what they were shouting about, save that one said, *You'll do as you promised or it's the waur for you!*'

'You're certain of that?' her mistress pressed her. She nodded. 'Agnes, away and shift those dreadful clothes. They're for the flea-market as soon as they're washed.'

'If they wash,' muttered Agnes. 'This cheap woollen, it'll turn to felt.' With great caution she lifted a bundle from a corner of the chamber and removed herself to another, inner room.

Madame Olympe turned to Gil, her former manner dropping back into place like a veil. She was garbed today in a wrapped gown of red and green brocade, its vast sleeves turned back with rose-coloured silk; her headdress was an elaborate structure of folded linen such as Gil had seen in the Low Countries.

'And such good fortune for my servant, Maister Cunningham,' she said in French, one long white hand at her throat, 'that you were there and could prevent the mob taking her up for murder.'

59

'Equally fortunate for me,' Gil responded. 'I've more to do than sit in the Tolbooth lockups until the Provost sent to free me, trying to reckon why the man was killed.'

'Indeed, a mystery!' pronounced Madame Olympe. She turned to the tray set on a stool beside her, and poured something into wooden beakers. 'You will forgive the rustic service, I know. Our lodging is comfortable, but not fashionably appointed.' She handed him a drink, then sat back and lifted her own. 'A toast, maister. To the goddess Mystery, who provides a living for some.' Gil drank obediently, some kind of fruit vinegar; she emptied her own beaker and set it down on the tray with a click. 'Now, maister, what happened when the hue and cry began?'

'The usual.' Gil grimaced. 'A crowd of onlookers, before you could blink, all eager to see how much blood there was. I had some ado to keep them out in the wait-ing-room. Then the constables arrived, and were for arresting everyone within twenty yards of the body.'

'Oh!' said Madame Olympe, and tittered. 'The Lanark lockup must be vast indeed!'

'Quite. But as you say, Agnes and I could speak for one another, and the man's whole household had been caught up in the chimney-sweeping and could vouch for all. If they could have laid hands on the sweep and his goose they'd have arrested them, I believe, but in the end they let us away and saw Ballantyne borne off to be laid out for a quest, and then set about questioning folk in the street about the armed men.'

'And what did they learn?' The pale eyes were intent. Gil grimaced again.

'Nothing. Strangely, though many had seen the men running, nobody had recognised them, and their numbers were anything from two to five.'

'I saw two,' said Agnes firmly, emerging from the inner chamber in a handsome striped kirtle which must be her Sunday best, her fouled garments held at arm's length. 'Two ran past me, both with their swords out, and then they were two that passed the window.' Her French was clumsy, ill-pronounced, but adequate.

'Description?' said her mistress. Agnes shrugged, her pudding face screwed up in thought.

'One in a dark blue worsted short gown,' she said in Scots, 'blue velvet bonnet, couple of feathers in it. About your height, madam, thin face, his hair clipped short so I never saw the colour. One in tawny worsted, a red felt hat, longer hair of a brown colour, maybe a handspan shorter than the other and heavier built.'

'Adequate,' pronounced Madame Olympe. 'It's a start.'

'Aye, well,' said Agnes. 'I'll away and get these put to soak.' She crossed the chamber and opened the door, falling back to let someone in: Alys, her gaze going immediately to Gil, her expression changing to one of relief. Socrates pushed past her and came to sniff at his master's boots.

'In a good hour!' proclaimed Madame Olympe. 'Come in, my dear, and bring your wee lapdog. Will you take some refreshment? You have been hurrying in this heat! I hope you feared no impropriety between your husband and me while Agnes is out of the chamber.' She rose to return Alys's formal curtsy, and gestured her to a backstool. 'There, you may see all respectable.'

'Those were not my anxieties, madame,' said Alys, as Gil seated her. 'My husband's tastes run to other endowments than yours, I believe.' Madame Olympe checked in lifting a filled beaker, then handed it over with another curtsy, her eyes dancing. Before she could embark on a reply, Alys continued, 'But what has been happening?

61

They're saying the burgh clerk is dead, and Gil and your servant witnessed it, or even killed him.'

'My faith, I hope not!' declared Madame. 'Have you been lying to me, maister?'

Gil recounted the tale again; Alys listened attentively, sipping at her cup of fruit vinegar, and said at the end, 'And no sign of the swordsmen now, I suppose?'

'I'd guess they had horses waiting at one of the inns,' Gil said, 'and were across the Clyde by the time the constables began looking for them.'

'It seems only prudent,' agreed Madame Olympe.

'What, you think they planned to kill the man?' Gil asked.

'How should I know?' she parried. 'They came to threaten him, certainly, by what Agnes says.'

'But why was Maister Ballantyne killed?' Alys speculated. 'And why now? Did his household mention enemies? Has he more family?' She set down her empty beaker and took Gil's hand, rather firmly.

'There are two sons,' he said, 'one of them a priest in Edinburgh, the other a notary in Moffat. Three daughters, two wedded about Lanark, one in Edinburgh. He gets on well enough with the sons-in-law. His clerk had a holiday, and had leave to go visit his family at Crossford. That's easy enough to check, but will take time.'

'That seems odd,' said Alys. 'Why would the clerk have the day free? Surely the Lanimer Fair would be a holiday, only last week. He could hardly expect another so soon after.'

'A good point,' concurred Madame Olympe. Socrates crossed to her, and she scratched his ears absently; he laid his head on her lap and blew as he would at a rathole.

'There's more,' said Gil. 'According to his steward, Ballantyne had given out that he planned to spend the day in his closet, dealing with papers and matters of business, and expected no clients. This was unusual, but the steward took it that he was avoiding the upset surrounding the chimney-sweeping. Yet two or three asked for him afore noon, not including the two that Agnes saw. Those two never went near the house door, must have gone straight to the foreshot.'

'And the enquirers were?' Madame Olympe's painted eyebrows rose.

'Aside from Agnes and myself, who were the latest, there was someone from the Provost's house, one of the Franciscans and a man from Maister Vary.'

Alys's hand tightened in Gil's, briefly, though she said nothing. Madame Olympe looked interested.

'He whose wife is missing?' she said. 'That is also a speak for the town, you understand.'

'Aye,' said Gil. The pale blue eyes sharpened under the elaborately folded linen headdress. 'I need to speak to all three of those, and Vary first of all.'

'And did the sweep's boy see nothing?' Alys asked. They both looked blankly at her. 'There would have been a laddie on the roof, to put the fowl down the chimney. He must surely have seen the men running.'

'Another good point,' said Gil. 'I'll mention it to Lockhart. He'll likely know where to find the boy. He must be questioned.'

'But I am curious, madame,' said Alys brightly, 'to know what a lady such as yourself finds to draw her to Lanark.'

'It is a town of the most interesting,' protested madame. 'One may hear the news from all directions. Only yesterday one was telling me how the Commendator of St Johns, what is his name? Noel, Noll? How he is searching for ways to make money. And here you are today, able to bring me all the news of Glasgow.'

63

'Knollys,' said Gil. 'Commendator Knollys.'

'Nevertheless, it hardly seems a likely setting for such a devotee of fashion,' Alys offered.

'I know, my dear,' agreed Madame Olympe. 'But I have sufficient reason, though I appear as a jewel on a midden, a rose upon a dungheap.'

So it's Treasury business, is it, thought Gil. And why does Will Knollys need money?

'A white rose, or a red?' Alys asked.

'Oh, my dear! Virgin white, of course! How could I be other? And yourselves? You visit family in the neighbourhood, I suppose?'

'My mother,' said Gil. 'Who has expressed a desire to meet you. Your fame has spread to Carluke.'

'But of course!' responded madame, alarm flickering briefly in her expression. 'I am overwhelmed with delight at the prospect. And what brings you down into Lanark?' she pursued, as Agnes came quietly back into the chamber. 'Is there not enough in Carluke to entertain you?'

'We are searching for the missing lady, Maister Vary's wife,' said Alys, before Gil could indulge in any more verbal fencing. 'Have you heard anything which might be helpful? I'm told you have become friendly with her mother.'

'No,' said Madame Olympe, becoming serious. 'Mistress Somerville was with me an hour or more, the very day her daughter was found to be missing, but all she spoke of was the coming event.' She leaned back, spread her elbows out, became briefly the image of someone in great pain. Gil saw Alys frown, but madame continued, 'Rather more than I wished to hear, indeed. The lady had no notion at the time, clearly, that her daughter was not safe at home. Have you learned anything?'

64

'Very little,' said Alys. She recounted their discovery of the day before, and the Provost's tale of the caves in the river bank.

Madame Olympe listened, and preserved a thoughtful silence afterwards, saying at length, 'No hint of who the message was from, I suppose.'

'Someone lettered,' said Gil. 'Which would tend to argue against the tinkers and the like gathered for the fair last week. I'd ha said the writing was disguised, myself, to seem clumsier than the scribe's usual hand.'

Madame nodded, one long white finger laid alongside her muscular jaw.

'So someone educated,' she said, 'who reckons Maister Vary can do him a favour, but needs forced into it.'

'We'd got that far ourselves,' said Gil politely.

Madame Olympe flashed him a brief, improbable grin from under the linen headdress, and continued, 'Therefore, someone with plans for the burgh lands, whether within or without the ports.'

'Of course!' said Gil. 'The burgh is the local feu superior,' he explained to Alys. 'In Glasgow, the Council oversees all in the Bishop's name within the ports, but outside them it's a matter for his own men of law to agree to an exchange of sasines or a building work or the like. Lanark is a Royal Burgh and has control over its own lands, which are pretty extensive.'

'Ah,' said Alys. 'I asked the Provost the wrong question.' Gil raised an eyebrow. 'I should have asked about business without the ports as well.'

'Furth of the burgh?' he said in Scots. 'It's possible.'

She shook her head.

'Audrey's friends had heard nothing about works within the burgh,' she said. 'We must look outside. It is inconvenient that the burgh clerk is now slain—'

'Certainly it's inconvenient for him,' observed Madame Olympe, and tittered.

Alys gave her a reproving look and went on, 'But I wonder if we are foolish to assume the death is connected to Audrey's disappearance?'

'Occam's razor,' said Gil. Alys nodded; she knew his views on coincidence.

'Aye, very like,' said Madame Olympe, 'but I've kent stranger things happen myself. As well say the man was slain because I wished a word wi him.'

'I wouldn't dream of saying such a thing,' said Gil.

'What about that bit paper you lifted, Maister Cunningham?' said Agnes. He turned, startled, and discovered her seated near the window with some mending, the image of a good servant observing the proprieties. She was looking hard at him, and now repeated, 'Yon bit paper wi writing, you lifted off the floor afore you called the hue and cry.'

'A paper?' he temporised, his mind working furiously. There had been no chance to look at it, but he would rather not share it with these two, whatever it was.

'You put it in the neck of your doublet.'

'A bit paper?' Madame Olympe joined the discussion. 'How exciting! What does it say?'

'There was a map and all,' Agnes added.

'Oh, that paper,' he said, cornered. He drew the documents out, handed one to Alys, and opened out the other. 'Aye, it's a map – of Lanark, I'd say.'

'Oh, indeed!' Madame Olympe leaned forward, the linen headdress precarious above the paper. 'West Port. That must be north, then. Here is the Gallow Hill, I suppose, and that the Burgh Muir.'

'This mentions the Burgh Muir,' said Alys. She handed the sheet she held to Gil, with a significant look. He gave the map to Madame Olympe and studied the new page.

It was a small sheet, the size of his hand, cut raggedly from something larger, with three lines of writing, two signatures and a mark.

doyg to bere i d to burhmur, it read. *m to ressive s to fee doyg*. Below that was an elaborate notary's mark, of the sort Gil himself used; this one depicted the burgh cross of Lanark, carefully built up in loops of penwork, with the initials GB nestling in their midst, presumably for the newly deceased Maister Ballantyne.

The two signatures were illegible; the mark was inscribed, *wm doyg his mark*. That must have provoked Alys's significant look, Gil considered, recalling his last encounter with Billy Doig, the dwarfish messenger to the politically aware of Scotland, carrier of news and doubtful goods, and sometime dog-breeder. Vary had mentioned such an individual in the marketplace. Could it be the same man?

'And who are S and M?' he said aloud.

'What's that?' Madame Olympe craned to see the scrap. 'Doig to bear – something – to Burgh Muir,' she read. 'M to receive, S to fee Doig. What fortune for M. Agnes, you saw only the two men you described? There was no third?'

'Just the two,' Agnes confirmed. Her mistress shook her head, the towering mass of linen wobbling lightly.

'Doig is conspicuous. And what could he be carrying, that it required a written agreement?'

'Doig might require a written agreement anyway,' Gil observed. 'You know him?'

Madame gave him an expressive glance, but did not answer. Alys retrieved the note and studied it again.

'I D,' she said. 'James, John, Jerome. Davidson, Dalziel, Dempster. It could be anyone.'

'Or maybe five hundreds of something,' Gil suggested. 'Delivering a person to the Burgh Muir sounds like a strange errand even for Billy Doig, more like to be a bill of goods.'

'Bricks, roof-tiles, slates?' Madame Olympe contributed. 'Are they building out there?'

'On the burgh lands?' Gil countered. 'Surely not. The burgesses would have something to say.'

'Five hundred bricks or roof tiles would barely roof a stable. But if it was to be done in secret,' said Alys, 'or at least begun before the burgesses heard of it – could this be what Maister Vary has to consent to?'

'Fencing stobs,' said Gil, his mind working. 'Pit props, some new merchandise, barrels of uncustomed goods.'

'Coin?' said Alys doubtfully. 'No, why carry that out to the muir? Much better take it to Maister S or Maister M for safekeeping.'

'If they trust one another,' said Madame Olympe.

'All this is to assume,' said Gil, 'that the papers have something to do with the matter. They could refer to something else entirely. Ballantyne could have dropped them earlier in the day, they could have blown off his desk when the two men ran out. Doig may be involved in some completely lawful transaction. It might even be a different Doig altogether.'

'Ah, my dear!' said Madame Olympe, one large white hand shading her eyes. 'Such innocence moves me almost to tears.' She lowered the hand, and added in more forthright tones, 'I think you need to speak to Maister Vary, as well as all these others. And that right soon.'

Gil, who had already come to this conclusion, nodded absently, still considering the problem. It seemed more likely that the little document was connected with the death of Maister Ballantyne than with Audrey Madur's disappearance, and the session clerk's violent decease was a matter for the Provost to deal with. But in a quiet town like Lanark, however busy a market it might be, and however recent the Lanimer Fair, two such events this close together seemed likely to be part of some greater action.

'Gil,' said Alys. He looked up, and found all the other occupants of the chamber watching him. 'Shall we go to call on Maister Vary? Now, before the quest on the groom?'

Chapter Four

Gil's first impression was that Vary had not stirred since the previous evening. Seated at his desk, hands knotted white-knuckled on top of the writing-slope, he stared bleakly into the middle distance, and barely looked up when the woman Jessie tapped at the door of his study.

'Has he eaten?' Alys asked softly. Jessie shook her head.

'Nor slept neither,' she said.

'An egg beaten in hot wine,' said Alys decisively. 'With sweet herbs and honey, maybe a drop of rosewater if you have it. Do you know how?'

'The very thing, mem,' said Jessie. 'And the new rosewater's just settling. I'll be right back wi it. Maister,' she said, speaking as to a small child, 'here's Maister Cunningham and his lady come to see you. Sit up nice and talk to them, now.'

'Brosie?' said Gil, though his stomach knotted with pity. 'Bear up, man. Has there been any word the day?'

Vary shrugged, an infinitesimal movement. Socrates padded over and sat down, leaning against his knee, but was ignored.

'There's been all sorts calling, now the word's got round,' said Jessie, pausing in the door on her way out. 'Fro the Provost on down, no to mention Lockhart o the Lee and him fro Jerviswood and others, all wanting to get up a search, but he'll no have it. Our Archie's out looking,' she confided in a hoarse whisper, 'he canny bear it, what wi young Adam lying deid up at the Provost's, and the quest on him called for this afternoon.'

'Come, show me your rosewater,' said Alys. 'Do you distil it yourself, or is it your mistress's work?'

They vanished into the back of the house, terms such as 'double-distilled' floating back. Gil crossed the small chamber to stand by Vary's desk, putting a careful hand on the man's shoulder. Vary convulsed at the touch, flinching away as if Gil had struck him.

'Easy, man!' Gil said. 'I mean you no harm. Has there been no word at all? None o the neighbours has anything useful to say?'

Vary stared blankly at him, apparently parsing this speech syllable by syllable. After a moment he looked down at his knotted hands again. Gil, following his gaze, saw that they rested on a cheap set of tablets, identical to the set Alys had stolen a glimpse of last night.

'Is that the same set?' he asked. 'Or a new one? Is it a message?'

One shoulder stirred in what might have been a shrug.

'Let me see,' Gil coaxed. Vary did not respond, but offered no resistance when Gil slid the tablets out from under his hands. The set was exactly like the previous pair, almost certainly by the same cheap maker, decorated with another woodcut from the same source and painter, this one showing a crowned figure wielding a harp. Inside, dug into the wax, was the grim intimation:

SEIK HIR AND SCHO IS DEID

He closed the tablets and set them down, whistling silently.

'Where did this come from?' he asked. 'Who brought it?'

Vary made another tiny shrug. His lips parted, and he drew a long, shuddering breath and let it out.

'Was there,' he said. 'It. It was there.' He indicated a spot on his desk with a jerky movement of his hand. 'I sat down here. A-aye, I sat down here and, and saw it.' He turned to look at Gil again. 'Wasny there afore,' he said.

'Do you mean it simply appeared on your desk?' Gil asked. Vary considered the question, and after a moment nodded, and went on nodding, frowning.

'Just appeared. Out of nothing. It wasny there, it – it was there.' He turned the hand over wildly to illustrate, narrowly missing the inkpot.

'Was there anyone else here? Your woman said there were callers.'

'Place was full of people.' Vary was still nodding. 'It wasny there. Then it was there.'

'Someone set it down when you wereny looking, maybe,' Gil suggested.

'It just appeared. It wasny there, then it was,' Vary repeated. There was no smell of strong drink about him, or even of small drink, but Gil found himself treating the man like a drunk.

'Can you mind who was here?' he coaxed. 'Who were all the people in the house?'

'Provost,' said Vary after due thought. 'Provost. My brother,' he added in bitter tones.

'Which brother? Gregory?'

That got him a direct look, however brief.

'Jerome. Why would Gregory call? Jerome. Tried to pray wi me.'

'More than that?'

'Half the toun. All her uncles.' Vary fell silent, staring bleakly at the windows, where the burgesses of Lanark

73

went about their business, swimming distorted in the small greenish panes.

'Her uncles? Your wife's uncles?' Gil questioned, but Vary shook his head, another tiny movement. Then with a great effort, he looked round, meeting Gil's eye.

'They tell me Maister Ballantyne's deid, and by violence. Is that right?' he said, quite coherently.

'It is,' said Gil. His friend crossed himself.

'A sad loss to the burgh,' he pronounced. 'He's been an able clerk these ten year, and done well out o't.'

'Was he one of those that called?'

Vary's face closed down, the moment of coherence gone.

'Have you had aught to do wi him lately? In a matter of private business, or Council dealings?'

'No,' said Vary, and swallowed. 'No, I— no.'

'Has he discussed aught about the Burgh Muir wi you? Mentioned it afore you, even?'

'The Burgh Muir?' Vary frowned slightly. 'No, why would he—' He looked at Gil again, and said clearly, 'The Burgh Muir is owned o the Council. There's no private dealings concerning it.' His glance slid away, towards the window again. 'They'd riot,' he added, his voice dropping. 'They'd riot. Break windaes and the like. The burgh folk.'

'I can see that,' Gil agreed. Lanark riots were well known in the county; the burgesses were jealous of their rights. 'So you've no idea what Ballantyne might ha been doing, who he might ha been dealing with?'

Vary crossed himself again and shook his head, but made no other sign that he had heard the question.

Gil watched him for a moment, then left the room to search for Alys. Socrates followed him, his claws clicking on the tiled floor. Gil could hear Alys speaking, and the woman Jessie answering; he found the kitchen by

74

following the sound, and tapped on the doorframe as Jessie turned from the fire, a piggin held in a corner of her apron, towards the dish Alys had set on the wide scrubbed table. Euan, a younger maid and another manservant he had not seen before were leaning against the far wall, talking in low voices.

'There we are,' Jessie said, tilting the piggin over the dish. Socrates watched intently, his nose twitching. 'That's cool enough to eat in a moment, and a few sippets o your toast set about it, it's fit for a king.'

'Indeed,' agreed Alys, smiling quickly at Gil as he entered the room. 'The cinnamon was a good thought. Maybe a rasp of sugar over the top?'

'Oh, aye.' Jessie set down the empty piggin and reached for a fragment of the sugar loaf and its scraper. 'How is he, maister? Did you get any sense o him?'

'Little,' said Gil. 'I need to ken who's called on him. Did you answer the door every time it went?'

'I did,' she agreed. 'Saving any that stepped in by theirsels, I saw all that crossed the door the day. He's no been fit to open the door to Our Lady hersel. I can tell them ower for you.' She considered the dish of rose-coloured custard with its scattering of sugar. 'Now these sippets, mem, and we'll bear it in.'

In a private chamber on the upper floor at the Nicholas Inn, with a view out over the High Street and St Nicholas' kirkyard, they sat round a sturdy cold pie and a dish of new peas with bacon and considered what to do next. Across the chamber pottery rattled on the broad floorboards as Socrates dealt with a bowl of bread and broth. Outside, the inn sign hung unmoving in the still, warm air. It depicted the saint as a bishop, hand raised in blessing, the three purses of gold which were his attribute floating round his haloed mitre as if he were juggling with them. Gil had always appreciated it.

'We need to speak to all these people,' said Alys, dissecting a wedge of pie with the point of her knife. 'Is there time today, do you think?'

'Some of them,' said Gil. 'The Provost again, Brosie's brother the priest – Sir Jerome, is that his name? – and it seems one of the Franciscans asked for Ballantyne. Euan, did you find out if any of Brosie's household went to Ballantyne's door?'

'They did not,' said Euan. 'Unless it was that Archie that's still out searching. Neither Dickon nor the lassie had been across the door the day by what they tellt me, it was the woman Jessie went to the market. Will I serve more peas, mistress?' He spooned peas and bacon onto all three platters without waiting for an answer.

'So I need a word wi Archie.' Gil made a note. 'I wonder what took him there?'

'And we need to ask if anyone has seen Doig,' Alys offered, conveying a morsel of the pie to her mouth with careful fingers.

'Doig? Is that the duarch?' said Euan, swallowing hastily. 'Him that goes about fetching things to folk? Never say it was him slew the clerk!'

'Unlikely,' said Gil. 'Agnes would ha seen him.'

'Agnes would have known him,' said Alys. Gil looked at her, considering this point, while Socrates pursued his bowl into a corner to extract the last of the flavour.

'No,' he said after a moment. 'Even if she failed to mention him, one of the bystanders would have if he was there. They might ha failed to see the two swordsmen, but I think those were local, so it's only a matter of common-sense no to see or name them. Doig's no a Lanark man, he'd ha made a good scapegoat if he was there.'

76

Alys nodded, accepting the argument, but Euan said round another mouthful, 'He could ha hid till the hue and cry was gone elsewhere. Under the clerk's desk, or the like. There's your answer, maister, and I's wager he has the lady and all.'

Gil, recalling another death where Doig had certainly been responsible and had then hidden under the dead man's bed, shook his head.

'That's one thing the constables did,' he said, 'searched the foreshot like the woman wi the lost coin. I've no notion what they were looking for, and I suspect nor had they, but they looked under or inside every stick of furnishing in the place. But that's something you can do after we've eaten, Euan. Ask about the place for the likes of Doig, and if you get any word, find out who he was with, who he spoke to.'

Socrates padded across the chamber to sit down beside Alys, gazing airily into the distance, his soft ears flicking at the little sounds she made dealing with her wedge of pie.

'You should speak with the Provost,' said Alys, not looking at the dog. 'Will I seek out the priest? Which kirk does he serve?'

'One of the altars in St Nicholas,' said Gil.

'Then I could speak to the Franciscans,' she went on, 'and then I think I might return to Belstane, to go study the burgh ledgers further.'

'A good plan. The other men are kicking their heels below stairs, take two of them to attend you. And the dog. I'll send the other fellow up the Burgh Muir to see if there's aught happening up there.'

She cast him a glance which suggested he was stating the obvious, and handed the crust of her pie to Socrates, who accepted it delicately, his tail thumping twice on the floor. Euan rose in a tangle of legs and tablecloth to fetch her the basin of water from the other side of the chamber.

'You could always have a look at the caves by the Mouse,' said Gil, snatching at the cloth to prevent it following the man.

'A bad business, maister,' said Provost Lockhart for the fifth or sixth time, when Gil completed his narrative of the events at the burgh clerk's dwelling. 'It's twenty year or more since any thought they could simply ride into Lanark, slay a man and ride out wi impunity. What the world's coming to I canny think. And Dodie Ballantyne, thrawn auld scunner though he was, will be a sair miss. He's been an able burgh clerk, a good man to keep track o the pence.' He considered Gil, then turned to gaze out of his window again. The sun, pouring through the coloured glass in the main embrasure, cast bright patterns on his face, his velvet bonnet, the close braiding on his brown linen doublet. He had not resumed the mustard-coloured gown; Gil wondered idly whether this was because it was too hot, or because Alys was not present.

'You'd no chance to speak wi him, then,' the Provost continued.

'He was moments from death when I set eyes on him,' Gil replied. 'I'd ha had no answer, even had it seemed the moment.'

'Aye, very wise,' agreed Lockhart abstractedly. He studied the passers-by in the High Street a little longer, then appeared to come to a decision and swung round to face Gil. 'Would you think, maister, this is anything to do wi Vary's lass being stolen away?'

'I don't know your burgh,' Gil said, 'but it seems to me in a place this size, two violent acts so close together are more like to be connected than not.'

78

'Aye.' Lockhart nodded, and paced back to sit down across the empty hearth from Gil. He contemplated the floorboards he had just traversed, and scratched at the rim of one pink ear. 'Madam your wife,' he said after a moment, 'was asking earlier if there was aught due to come afore the Council that Vary might allow or gainsay.'

'She was,' Gil agreed, since some response seemed to be expected.

'Mind, I've no knowledge o this mysel,' the Provost pursued. Gil nodded. 'But I'll tell you this. Dod Ballantyne was hinting lately that he'd some thought o a way to make money, coin that would fall into the burgh coffers. I never jaloused what it might be, and to be honest,' he admitted, 'I never paid much mind. He'd ha told me himsel soon or late.'

'A way to make money,' Gil repeated. 'Within the law?'

'I'd ha thought so. He was a man o law himsel, though he never practised. Made his money in trade, afore he was the burgh custumar, and gey comfortable he was wi't and all.'

'What kind of hints was he putting out? Was it a matter of buying and selling, or a land deal, or a venture abroad? Were there others in it, do you think?'

Lockhart thought about this.

'I doubt he'd be acting his lone,' he said. 'He'd as many contacts, in Leith and Edinburgh and Ayr, I'd ha thought he'd go through one o them at the least.'

Gil tapped his chin, mulling this over in his mind.

'Vary has heard nothing,' he said, 'beyond an order to do someone's bidding.' He described the two sets of tablets with their blunt messages, and Lockhart looked grim.

'Small wonder he's feart for her,' he said. 'And her crying-time as close. She should never ha been abroad, poor lass.'

'Is there any way,' Gil said delicately, 'I could get a look at Ballantyne's papers? I suppose a lot will be confidential, burgh business or the like, but there might be something there that would—'

'That would gie us a hint,' Lockhart finished. 'Aye, and better in some ways the Archbishop's man seeking it than someone from within the burgh.' He pondered a moment. 'It's a good thought, indeed. I'll gie you a line for Dod's steward, he's a capable man and less like to be owerset than his mistress. Did you hear, they'd the sweep in, was why none o the household was aware o what passed.'

'I saw the sweep,' Gil said. 'And his goose. D'you ken where his laddie dwells?'

The steward, the same man who had answered the door to Gil earlier, had assumed more sober state. Earlier, he had appeared in the foreshot to contend with the constables, departed to break the news to his mistress, dealt competently with the bystanders, still in his soot with added bloodstains. Clad now in decent livery and bearing his wand of office, though with a smudge of soot still at the side of his nose, he greeted Gil civilly enough and considered the Provost's request while about him in the hall servants shifted furniture, carried messages to and from the Nicholas Inn, beat wall hangings, and in one case bore a bolt of cloth, still in its canvas casing, down from an upper floor.

'It's the black velvet, Maister Anthony,' said the woman carrying it, on a note of triumph. 'She was right, it was in the wee chamber. Will I take it to Jaikie Wishart the now, or wait till we've found the silk to go wi't?'

'Take it now,' said the steward with decision. 'He can get on wi the cutting while we seek the other. She'll want the gown for the quest, I'll warrant.' He turned back to

Gil. 'I think we can grant this, maister, though I'd as soon owersee the matter myself, if you'll forgive me.' Gil nodded. 'But as you can see it's no that convenient the now.'

'I'd not want long,' Gil said, wondering if this was in fact true. He saw the steward reach a similar conclusion.

After a moment the man said, 'I could spare Auld Henry, I suppose. He's been up and down they stairs ever since— he could do wi a sit-down. You'll no mind if he sits in a corner, rather than stand?'

'Fair enough,' said Gil.

Auld Henry proved to be a wiry ancient with few teeth, who was delighted to have express permission to sit in company with one of the gentry. He unlocked the foreshot with the key Maister Anthony had provided, and led Gil through the little waiting room into Maister Ballantyne's sanctuary, which had been no sanctuary at all.

'And that's where he dee'd,' he pronounced cheerfully if indistinctly, looking at the damp patch on the floor-boards where the bloodstains had already been scrubbed and sanded. 'Aye, aye, we'll no get the mark out, I doubt. And there's his desk, maister. I believe I'm to make you free o't.'

'A moment, man,' said Gil, looking in some dismay at the desk. 'Who's been here? Seems to me it's been searched, and no wi civility.'

'D'ye ken, maister, you're right at that,' declared Auld Henry, bending stiffly to pick up some of the papers on the floor. 'Maybe 'twas the constables,' he suggested. 'They's well enow for dealing wi a stushie in the mercat, but they've no notion o manners wi the gentry.'

'No,' said Gil, 'unless they returned after your maister was borne away. I'll bide here. You go and tell Maister Anthony what's amiss.'

Waiting for the steward, Gil stood without touching anything, considering what he could see. The writing-slope of the desk was tipped back, and the cavity under it had been ransacked; the shelves on the end had been emptied and the four or five ledgers he recalled seeing there were on the floor, two of them lying open on crumpled pages. He had a sudden image of someone shaking the volumes by their boards to free any papers tucked between the leaves, then dropping each to go on to the next. The papers in the rack of pigeonholes beyond the desk had been similarly handled. Someone used to dealing with records had searched the place for a particular document.

The steward, arriving in haste, agreed with Gil.

'We left all straight,' he said. 'Someone's got in, and past that lock. In broad daylight, and all. St Peter's bones, what's the world coming to? And what were they seeking? Their lease?'

'Someone wi a key,' Gil said. 'Take a look – there's no sign it was forced, and no marks from a blade or the like. It's a stout lock.'

'You need a stout lock on a foreshot,' said Maister Anthony, peering at the lock. 'Nobody wi any sense would keep money out here, but they's aye folk willing to take the chance. I've a key, naturally, but I've never had the time to come out here and harrow the place like this. I've all to see to within there. I've no notion who else might have one.'

'Unless they went off wi Maister Ballantyne's,' Gil suggested. 'What key did you use to lock up here when the constables left?'

'My own.' Maister Anthony touched the bunch that hung at his waist, dismay in his face. 'Our Lady save us, I never thought to check. I took it his own was on his bunch, that's on his belt where he keeps— he aye kept it.'

'I'll get a word wi the Provost when I'm done here,' said Gil, 'and find out if it's on his belt now.'

The steward drew a deep breath, nodded, and looked about him at the disorder of the chamber.

'Well, maister, the only man that could tell you if aught's missing, apart from my late maister, is his clerk, Steenie Gardner, that's away to visit his family the day.'

'And that's his employment at an end,' said Auld Henry from the corner, with some relish.

'Will you still be wanting to go through the papers, maister?'

'You never ken your fortune,' said Gil. 'Your house-breaker might no have been seeking the same matters I'd want.' Maister Anthony gave him a sceptical look. 'I'll take the time, if you'll allow it.'

'Maister Anthony!' Another maidservant appeared in the doorway, her arms full of purple velvet trimmed with black silk braid. 'Maister Anthony, what'll I do wi the bere-cloth the now? Only it could do wi airing, there's a couple wee moths been at it.'

The steward departed, muttering distractedly, and Gil, trying to recall whether it classed as housebreaking if the felon had a key, bent to the first bundle of papers.

By the time the Lanark bellman passed down the High Street, Gil had restored a seeming of order to the chamber, and established that there was nothing still in Maister Ballantyne's desk which shed any light on his death. Auld Henry was drowsing on a stool against the wall, which left Gil free to study anything he found, but although the papers in the desk dealt with several ventures into sharp trading, nothing seemed enough to have made a bloody enemy for the trader. More than one docket in the familiar hand of Andrew Halyburton, Scots factor in the Low Countries, detailed barrels containing bolts of cloth, spices, raisins and the like, many annotated with the price the goods had fetched in Lanark and the satisfactory profit they had turned. A small bundle of papers wrapped in one of these appeared to deal with an order for slips of something; Gil frowned at this, trying to decide the nature of the merchandise. Fruit trees? Rose bushes? Samples of paper?

'How big is your maister's garden?' he asked. The old man snorted, jerked awake, straightened himself.

'Gairden?' he repeated. 'No that big. He's biggit a storehouse on the most o the toft, just left a wee kale-yard down the end. Aye, aye, there's the bellman,' he added, as the first clangs resounded off the nearby buildings. 'Are you for the quest, maister? The poor laddie, his mistress has slew him and run off, so they're saying, and where she's away to naeb'dy kens. Are ye about done here, maister?'

'Nothing of the sort,' said Gil briskly to this assertion. The bellman strode past the foreshot, clashing his great bell and crying the quest on the death of Adam Baird, horribly murdered on the road. 'The lass is near her groaning-time, she's no like to run off now. She's been lifted by someone, that's for certain.' He began closing down the desk, and looked about to see that matters were in order.

'So where is she now?' Auld Henry demanded. 'Tell me that, maister. Where is she now?'

'I wish I knew,' said Gil.

The quest on Adam Baird was unsatisfactory. It was held before the Provost's house, with the assize withdrawing into the cooler space of the hall for a refreshment while it deliberated. The conclusion it drew was the right one, so far as it went; when they all filed out again the spokesman pronounced that Adam Baird's death was secret murder, by the same ill-conditioned folk as had lifted Mistress Madur and were holding her prisoner, and the Provost should hunt them down wi all speed, or at the very least learn their names and put them to the horn.

'Aye, aye,' said the Provost testily, hitching up his mustard-coloured velvet. 'If any o ye has ideas how I do that, I'd be glad to hear them.'

However, Gil could see nobody in the crowd whom he wished to question. Most of those he recognised were Lanark burgesses; the young man was identified by two of his fellow-servants from Vary's household, and a weeping girl who must be the sweetheart Mistress Somerville had mentioned was held back with difficulty. The conversation on either side of where he stood was divided between the case under consideration and the death of the burgh clerk. There seemed to be a wide-spread opinion that Maister Ballantyne had come by his deserts.

Gil was considering what to do next when a deep voice by his elbow said, 'Maister Cunningham. I should ha kent I'd find you in the midst o this.'

He looked round, and down, and encountered a hostile dark stare level with his belt.

'Maister Doig,' he said. 'I could say the same. Do you ken aught about the death of this laddie?'

'I do not,' said Doig grimly. 'Neither who nor where.'

'And what brings you into Lanarkshire again? I thought you'd shaken the county's dust fro your feet when you left Glasgow.'

'I get about,' said Doig. 'I get all ower.' He leaned sideways to peer round a stout burgess at the Provost on his steps, dismissing the assize and thanking it for its deliberations. 'If we slipped away now we'd get a seat in Juggling Nick's afore the crowd comes in.'

'True,' said Gil, and turned to follow as Doig made use of his powerful arms and shoulders to apply leverage where nobody expected it, clearing a way for himself through the crowd.

Bessie Dickson, keeper of the Nicholas Inn, a big muscular woman known and feared by drinkers of four parishes, hailed them sourly as the first of the rush, drew them a jug of ale and sent them out into the little garden at the back of the inn.

'For this chamber will be filled elbow to elbow in the space of three Aves,' she forecast, scowling at Doig, 'and I'll no be responsible if you get stepped on.'

'Nor will I, mistress,' said Doig, showing his teeth in a broad, humourless grin.

'That's what I mean,' she said, accepting Gil's coin for the ale, and handed him two leather beakers.

Seated on a bench in the shade, Gil poured ale into the beakers and raised his in a toast.

'Your good health,' he said. 'I hope Mistress Doig is well?'

'Herself? Aye, she's well enow. Still at the dog breeding,' Doig admitted. 'We'd to leave Perth, but she's got a good yard to keep them in at Dundee now, and the merchants' wives o Dundee has taken to her wee spaniels.'

'And you're getting all ower,' Gil said.

'Aye,' said Doig flatly. There was a pause, while he drank deeply of the ale and then considered what remained in his beaker. Gil sat quietly, and eventually the small man said, 'The lass that's missing.'

'Aye,' said Gil.

'It's the speak o the town.'

'Aye.'

'I'm no delicat, you ken that,' said Doig. 'But stealing away a lassie in her condition's what I don't hold wi.' Gil made an agreeing noise. 'I'm no saying it's her uncles has her, mind, but you should speir at them about it.'

'What should I ask of them?'

Doig shrugged his massive shoulders, and slid down off the bench.

'Ask them if they ken where she might be,' he said. 'And keep on asking till you get an answer. Thanks for the drink.'

'Do you ken who has her?'

'If I did, I'd maybe tell you,' Doig flung over his shoulder as he rolled towards the inn door. Gil let him go, and sat back, considering this. It was unlike Doig to volunteer information; he must be deeply offended by Mistress Madur's situation. Which of her uncles did he mean, Gil wondered, and would Michael have learned anything if he had reached them today? And what was Doig's connection to them?

Before he finished the jug he was joined, first by Euan and then by the man he had sent up to the Burgh Muir, one of Henry's henchmen, a huge fellow by the name of Tottie Tammas.

'The man Doig's been all about Lanark,' said Euan triumphantly as he crossed the garden. 'Indeed, maister, I was seeing him myself just the now, coming away from this very place! And he's been seen speaking to all sorts, including the man that's deid, the burgh clerk, though no the day,' he added. 'And they are saying there is a load of gunpowder on the roads of the county, though nobody seems to have seen it hissel, only to have heard of some other body that saw it.'

'Gunpowder,' Gil repeated. 'What on earth for?'

'Och, everyone had a different reason. One fellow was saying, that proves the King will go to war against the English once the harvest is in, for it must be him has sent for it. I am not so sure of that myself,' Euan admitted.

'Nor I, by St Giles. Did you learn how long Doig has been in Lanark?' Gil asked. Euan looked at him, set down his drink, and began to count on his fingers.

'He was first seen on Friday,' he said finally, 'or maybe it was Saturday. But mostly he's been speaking wi strangers, folk in for the fair last week, they say. Been in here and all.'

'I thought he must have,' said Gil, as Tottie Tammas approached them. 'And you, Tammas? Did you have any luck?'

'No what you'd call luck,' said Tammas, sitting down uninvited on the other end of the bench. He raised his beaker to Gil. 'Your good health, maister. You ken the Burgh Muir?'

'I do,' said Gil, 'though no closely.'

'Aye, well.' Tammas took a deep draught of his ale and emerged licking his upper lip. 'You'll ken how it goes up and down, then. There's no place to owersee the hale o't. I'd say it's all as it should be, grazing here, a wee plantation there, the burgh herd and the geese and all where they should be, but there was an odd thing.'

'Odd how?' Gil prompted, as the man took another draught.

'There was someb'dy,' he wiped at his upper lip, 'someb'dy out on the muir taking care I didny see him.'

'How do you ken he was there, then?' asked Euan.

'I got a wee glimp o him now-and-now. Was a fellow in a blue doublet, wi the sleeves off it and his sark sleeves rowed up. Never got a look at his hair, much less his face. If it had been raining, I'd ha understood him keeping his head down, but a day like this, ye'd think he'd ha gied me a wave, maybe come ower to pass the time wi me, acted freendly-like. No pretending I wasny there the way he did.'

'Maybe it was this fellow wi the cartload of gunpowder,' said Euan, and grinned at his own joke.

'No sign of the lads from Kettlands?' Gil asked. 'Did you see where the tinkers had camped?'

'Oh, aye, I seen that. Fires all ower, the gorse hacked down for their horses, broken crocks left where they'd hurt a beast's feet, you could see their spot easy. Never saw the Kettlands men, but.' He tilted his beaker to get the last drops. 'By here, I needed that. Thirsty work, tramping the Burgh Muir in this.'

Taking the hint, Gil dug out a coin and sent him to fetch another jug of ale.

Euan said, 'I suppose the Kettlands men would ha ridden on to track the tinkers by then.'

'Likely,' said Gil. This case seemed to consist of nothing but dead ends; no matter which way they turned he could find no hint of where Audrey Madur might be. The nearest to gossip he had heard was Doig's hint just now; there were many other opinions about her fate but nobody with information to substantiate them.

'Tammas,' he said, as the big man came back with a fresh jug. 'What was in the plantation you saw?'

'Plantation?' the man repeated. He poured ale for the three of them and sat down again. 'Oh, aye, the plantation. I couldny right see, it's ower the far side o the muir, but it's a' fenced wi woven withies, high enow to keep the beasts out and it's fu o what looks like wee trees.'

'Trees?' Gil repeated. 'What d'you mean, trees?'

'Trees,' agreed Tammas, gesturing to describe branches and trunk. 'Wee tottie trees, maybe this big.' He indicated a couple of feet off the ground. 'I never got a look at what sort they were, but someone's growing timber there.'

'On the Burgh Muir,' said Gil. 'Which is common land.'

Chapter Five

'Indeed I did call on my poor brother,' said Maister Jerome Vary primly. 'I offered him the solace of my prayers, for him and for his wife, that she might find forgiveness for her headstrong nature and unbiddable ways. But he turned his head fro me and wouldny speak, so I left him.'

'And you have no notion of where she might be?' Alys prompted, trying to maintain a respectful tone, wondering how Mistress Madur had offended. Vary drew himself up, looking disapprovingly down his long nose at Socrates, who was checking the smells of the kirkyard. The man was very like his brother, a gangling creature with large hands and feet and a narrow face, though his normal expression was as sour as week-old milk.

'My good-sister wouldny hear my considered advice on her household,' he said, 'nor on her deportment neither. And after the business wi the gunpowder we had little to say to one another.'

'Gunpowder?' Alys repeated in astonishment. 'Whatever— I mean, surely not in the midst of the burgh?'

'Indeed it was!' said Maister Jerome, swelling with indignation at the memory. 'A man at my door wi a kinkin-barrel o black powther, saying it was for a Maister Vary, and my good-sister had sent him to me, saying it wasny for her household. The idea! As if a priest would have aught to do wi the nasty stuff, and so I tellt her when I saw her next, and had an earful of impertinence for my pains.'

'How shocking,' said Alys, with all the sympathy she could muster, trying not to think of the replies she would have made to such strictures. 'When was that? What happened to the gunpowder?'

'Oh, a fortnight since or mair. As to what happened wi't, that was none o my concern. Any road, after that we'd little to say to one another. She'd scarce be likely to advise me of her plans.'

'I doubt if she planned to disappear,' said Alys. 'Her groom was slain, she's been carried off, and Maister Vary has had a message threatening her. Her time is very near, no moment to be away from her home and her friends. Is there anybody wi a grudge against you or your brother? Any enemy who might choose this way to get money or cooperation from either of you, or your oldest brother indeed? Gregory, is that his name?'

A flash of dark anger leapt in Maister Jerome's eyes at the mention of the third brother. There was true dislike there, thought Alys.

'A priest has no enemies,' said the priest, his expression inimical. 'If you're looking for enemies to my family, look at my good-sister's uncles. All her kin, indeed. They never cared for the match, as if we wereny good enough for them, and grudged every penny of her dowry. Aye, mistress, look at Somerville or Madur. Question them, no me.'

'And none of the Franciscans neither?' said Henry, as they reached the bridge over the Mouse Water.

'None would admit to having called on Maister Vary,' Alys confirmed. 'Nor could the Prior think of any reason

92

they might have done. I wonder,' she went on, encouraging her horse on to the bridge while Socrates left his mark on the ends of the parapet, 'whether someone went disguised as a friar? Would Jessie not have known him for a stranger, at least?'

'No if he kept his hood down ower his brow,' offered Henry, demonstrating with the floppy crown of his blue bonnet. 'He'd be hid in it. But what would he do that for?'

'Mistress,' said the other groom behind them. 'You were asking about they caves.' Alys turned her head to look at him. 'Just they're in that way.' The man nodded to his left, indicating a stand of trees. He was one of the younger Belstane grooms, and went by the name of Mealsack for no reason Alys could discern. 'Mind, I canny see that anyone's been that way these ten days or mair.'

Alys checked her horse and looked about her. Here, just across the bridge, the road swung to the right, to climb slantwise up the slope past the place where they had found the dead man yesterday evening. Downstream, to their left, the river curled round the low-lying spur on which the trees stood, birch and hazel and a clump of hawthorn. The valley side itself was set back, steep and thick with bushes; further downstream it turned into a cliff of striped rock, grey and red and dark layers dotted with tufts of grass. At the roadside the usual ditch and bank showed a brave display of wildflowers, white campion and yellow trefoil, purple vetch and azure traveller's joy. Bracken and nettles flourished in the ditch itself. As the groom had said, the growing things showed no sign of disturbance.

'Aye,' Henry said, 'it hardly looks as if that's where they're hid. Bide here.' He dismounted, threw the other man his reins, and prowled up and then down the

93

length of the curve in the road while Alys watched, finding no evidence that anything bigger than a fox had crossed the dyke in the past week or so. Socrates, assisting, seemed to come to the same conclusion, and returned to sit beside Alys's horse, his tongue hanging out.

'They're no that big, the caves,' said Mealsack when Henry commented. 'I'd no ha thought they'd be much use as a shelter, mysel.'

'You knew about them?' Alys asked.

'Oh, aye.' Mealsack was a round-faced, fairish fellow with a cheery grin which he displayed now. 'See, I'm fro Lanark town. Henry, he's no, he's a Carluke man. He'd likely no think o the caves, would you, man? They're no that big, mind,' he repeated.

'So I've heard,' said Alys as Henry retrieved his reins, and mounted up again. 'I wonder where they did go. They must have hidden somewhere.'

'Maybe the other cave,' suggested Mealsack. Alys, about to give her horse the office to move on, turned to look at him instead. 'There's another cave, mistress. Upstream,' he waved expansively at the slope ahead of them, 'ayont the old mill, and it's a sight deeper, you could hide a good few folk there if you had to.'

'Show us,' she said.

The path to the old mill took off halfway up the slope. It led down to their right, towards the waterside, slipping unobtrusively between two twisted thorn trees. Its dry and stony entry showed no immediate traces, and when Mealsack pointed to it Alys recognised that even if something large had brushed through the grass and bracken, the fronds would have sprung back long since.

Henry dismounted, and handed his subordinate his reins again, bending to inspect the surface of the path.

'Is there—?' said Alys.

94

'I think so, mistress.' He straightened up. 'How far is this cave, laddie?'

'Maybe better I show you,' said Mealsack. 'But we'd no want to leave the mistress here her lane.'

'Of course not,' said Alys briskly. 'Do we ride, or lead the horses?'

'Best lead them,' said Mealsack.

'Let me go ahead,' said Henry, and drew his whinger.

After a few paces the path became overgrown, with moss and grasses spreading over the stones. Hoofprints and scrapes appeared, all several days old, for the dog to inspect carefully; Henry pointed out more than one animal's tracks, and the marks of two different feet, probably man-sized. It was Alys who found the donkey's little print.

'I've been right,' said Mealsack hopefully.

'They'd hardly stay here, though,' Henry said. 'They'd need provisions, a fire, grazing for the beasts. We'd smell them by now if they'd settled in the cave.'

'I hope so,' said Alys ambiguously.

The path went on slantwise down the bank, towards the remains of a small building which must be the mill. A few balks of timber from its clack-wheel still lay in the river, but of the mill itself only the earthen floor remained, strewn with flotsam from the last high water. Before they reached it, a trampled trail swung off to their left, to go round it and then on upstream among the trees, leaving a sign a child could follow.

'How far from here?' Alys asked quietly.

'Maybe a quarter-mile?' Mealsack offered.

They worked their way along the bank, Alys silent and observant, the two men slowly picking out the marks of individual animals and commenting. One beast had worn down the outer rim on the off fore; one did not lift his near hind properly. One had no burden.

95

In among them, the donkey's little prints were jotted like spatters of ink on a page. One set of hoofprints seemed to have returned, making for the mill and the road with brisk steps as if the animal was moving at a fast walk. It had a nail missing from the off hind; the same beast had made the journey upriver again most recently, heavy-laden, as if it carried two people or some other extra burden.

'The other prints all go one way,' Alys observed.

'Aye, and they're a' several days old,' Henry agreed, 'even these last set.'

'So I suppose they left by a different way. They are not still in this cave.'

'There's six horses and the donkey, I make it,' said Henry, speaking as quietly as she did. 'Yon's too many to dwell in a spot like this for near a week without being noticed.'

'Is there another way out?'

'Aye, the path goes on,' said Mealsack. 'Though it's a scramble to get up to the road, in places. Likely the beasts could do it, but no the lady I'd ha said.'

'I suppose,' Alys said as the thought came to her, 'we should not assume Mistress Madur is held where her captor dwells. She could be anywhere. Any barn or hut or dwelling house, so it's secluded.'

They came out of the trees, to a wide sloping tongue of land where the river took a sharp curve. The horses they were tracking had been tethered, or possibly hobbled, here at the edge of the clearing. Many booted feet had trampled round them, one of the trees at least had been well chewed by whatever beast was nearest, and to judge by the number of heaps of droppings lying about, they had been there for some hours.

Socrates sprang past Alys to range about the open space, sniffing and staring. Grass and wildflowers covered the slope, which rose to another cliff of banded rock; at the further side, near where the land dropped again to the river, was a dark shadow. The dog loped over to this, hackles rising. Alys peered after him.

'Is that the cave? I think there is no one here.'

'Aye, I think you're right,' said Henry, 'but bide here, mistress, till I mak siccar.'

He went cautiously forward. Alys tipped her head up, scenting the warm air the way Gil had shown her, finding only the rich odours of the summer earth, horse-droppings and green growth. There was an elder-bush somewhere near, the last of the May-blossom was fading on a thorn tree, a tangle of brambles spoke of the dark riches of autumn. Nothing more sinister reached her.

Some of the footprints led towards the cave; studying the bruised grasses, she thought that one set of prints was heavier than the rest, as if their maker had been burdened like the late-coming horse. As if perhaps he carried someone.

'None here,' said Henry. 'Here, dog, out o that.'

Alys went forward to join him, while Mealsack busied himself tethering their horses. The cave, just where the valley wall changed from a steep slope clad in bushes to a cliff of that banded rock, was certainly not large, but it would have provided shelter for a number of people if needed, perhaps all those Henry thought had been present. Under a thicker, slanting lintel which she recognised as a good sandstone, the thinner layers had been eaten away, forming a space perhaps four paces across, high enough to stand up in at the higher side. The floor was dry earth, and extended into the shadowy depths, the roof lowering to meet it. She stood in the entry and sniffed again, while Socrates blew hard at one particular patch of the floor, his hackles raised all down his backbone.

'You smell it and a',' said Henry.

'Blood,' she said. 'After this length of time?' She breathed more lightly, testing the faint odours. 'Not just blood. Come out of the light, Henry, I need to see in. Socrates, come away!'

Henry stepped back obediently, and she ducked under the sloping roof, hauled on the dog's collar and looked about her. Socrates, standing obediently, turned and pressed his nose against her skirt, blowing in the same way, and she pushed his head aside.

'It's been protected from the dew, I suppose,' she said after a moment. 'Can you see anything in the floor? Are there prints, other than the dog's? I can see marks, but I can make little sense of them.'

The man crouched to get a better angle, tilting his head to see under the low end of the lintel, and Alys continued to study what she saw. Light and shade were scattered across the dry floor, to no apparent purpose; but after a while she began to see a pattern. Footprints, there and there – and there, smaller ones. Here, where the dog had been sniffing closest, a wider blurred mark as if someone had lain down, two deep marks like heel-prints to one side of it, a complicated mark with two more imprints in it to another side. She looked harder: there was a story in these marks, one she could almost read. And the scents of the place, what were they telling her?

There had been blood shed here, though it was hard to pick out any marks in the dark-coloured floor, but there was another scent mingled with it, faint but particular, which reminded her, reminded her – heat rushed into her face as she realised she was thinking of last night, of Gil's caresses which she had missed so much, of his hands on her back, his kisses on her neck and breasts, her own fingers in the hair on his chest and

98

belly. Gil like Gahmuret in the story, who *never partook of a woman's love without delighting in all her joy.* Why was she thinking of that? And so was the dog, she realised. What had it to do with— Had Mistress Madur been forced, taken by one or more of the men, great with child as she was? Was this a scene of violence? Surely that would— No, from what she had heard of such things, the other men would have gathered round the cave to watch, to wait their, yes, to wait their turn. Indeed, why take her into the cave at all? Instead they had given her what little privacy they could, and then blood had been shed, and that particular scent.

A sudden, overwhelming recollection struck her, of her stepmother's labour, quick and easy and mostly managed in Ersche, the chamber full of strange scents of the charms Ealasaidh had them throw on the fire, but also of this. She had been present, asked to receive her half-brother, to put him in the waiting bath, a great honour and gesture of peace, and he had smelled like this, of blood and waxy stuff and the waters of his mother's womb, as he lay in her arms in the warm towel and screamed with fury.

'Ah, *mon Dieu!*' she breathed. 'The baby. She has— the baby came.'

'What, here?' said Henry. 'Here in a cave like this?'

'Her waters broke,' said Alys. She touched the ground next to the wide mark, and sniffed her fingers. Socrates looked up at her, his tail waving slowly. 'Her time, her crying-time came on her. No wonder, after such an experience, no wonder her pains began.'

She bent her head, closing her eyes, with a fervent prayer to Our Lady for the safety of Audrey and her babe, for her support in their hour of need. To give birth here in the wilderness, like a lady in one of the romances, was not so romantic when you realised there was no other woman present, no help, not even a cloth to wrap the baby in—

'No wonder, then,' said Mealsack cheerfully from across the clearing, 'they's a' the men's prints here where the horses were tied up. They'd no want to be anywhere near her!'

'Did,' said Alys, collecting herself a little but still barely able to assemble the sentence, 'did she survive? Did the bairn—?'

'No sign itherwise,' said Henry, looking about them. 'Unless the bairn dee'd and they threw it in the burn. No sign they've buried aught that size hereabout, let alone the lass hersel.'

'The, the,' she hesitated. Socrates had left her and was casting about near the cave, along the foot of the cliff. What was she saying? What had she meant to ask? Yes, the *secundus*. What was it called in Scots? 'The cleansing. The part that comes away after the bairn. What could they ha done wi that?'

'If they threw that aside,' offered Mealsack, 'likely a fox got it.'

'That's enough of that, laddie,' said Henry sternly. He began to cast about as Socrates was doing, and was just in time to prevent the dog from starting to dig. Brushing the long grasses and bracken aside with his booted foot, he paused, looking down at something. 'I was wrong. They've buried something here.'

Alys stepped out of the little shelter, suddenly needing more air than she could find under the burden of rock and earth. She put her hand against the cliff-face to steady herself, and snapped her fingers weakly at the dog, who came with reluctance to sit at her feet.

'What – what have they buried? Can you tell?'

'I've no spade,' said Henry, drawing the whinger at his side again. 'Depends how deep they— ah!'

100

'No very deep, then,' said Mealsack. Henry, leaning back, free hand over his nose, did not reply but continued to scrape with his whinger at the loose earth he had found. That would do the blade no good at all, thought Alys, hanging onto Socrates' collar. After a moment the man stepped away, his hand still across his nose.

'I'd say it was the cleansing,' he said. 'Looks like a sheep's pluck fro here. No a bairn, any road. Here, mistress, are ye weel?' He stepped quickly to Alys's side. 'It's naught to see, though it stinks like a —'

'Like a charnel-house,' she said, with a slightly hysterical laugh, recovering herself as the new odour reached her. 'That sounds like what we're seeking. Let me look.' She moved over to peer at the mass he had uncovered, keeping the dog away with difficulty. It did indeed resemble a sheep's pluck, nearly a week old and stained greenish by corruption, and with a reassuring absence of small limbs, of hands or feet or a face. 'Aye. Cover it over, Henry, for decency.'

He obliged, making a thorough task of it, then looked intently at her and said,

'Will ye ride for hame, mistress? I canny think ye're weel, sic a colour as ye are.'

'We could get after them,' suggested Mealsack. 'You can see their track fro here, they gaed away up the Mouse.' He pointed across the clearing. Alys peered that way, and made out a swathe of crushed bracken and grass, which led under the trees and up the riverside.

'No,' said Henry, 'no wi a lady to keep safe.'

'Three people and the dog is hardly enough,' said Alys at the same moment, making an effort. 'And only two wi swords. You thought there were five or six of them? I knew I should ha brought my weapon. Better, surely, to go to Kettlands, tell them there and collect

101

more men. Yes, I'm well,' she added inaccurately, while the clearing swung round her, and Socrates leaned anxiously against her knee. 'No, wait, Mistress Somerville was to send her men to hunt for the tinkers. They'll all be fro the place.'

'Come and mount up, lassie,' said Henry, a hand at her elbow. 'We'll see you hame, and then get the countryside raised for a hot trod, catch up wi them wherever they went. I'll wager they've made for Jerviswood.'

'Wrong side the Mouse,' said Mealsack. 'How about Castlehill?'

'How much a start would you say they've got?' Henry asked, bending to offer Alys a knee to mount by. She swung herself into the saddle and arranged her skirts, trying to think clearly about that.

'Mistress Madur left home late in the afternoon. It must have been evening already when they came here,' she realised. 'There's no sign they made camp, or lit a fire, or the like, is there? I've seen none, but I was—' She bit her lip.

'They's been a fire down yonder.' Mealsack had clearly not stood idle while he minded the horses. 'On the sand at the waterside. And you can see where they cut wood to it.' He pointed again, to a series of white cuts in the trees. 'Mind, if they were burning green wood—'

'The smoke would alert the countryside,' Alys said. 'Someone would ha come to see. There's dead wood to burn, though they've had most of what's nearby. I think the green wood was for a litter, a hurdle, to put Mistress Madur on when she was fit to move.'

'And when would that be?' Henry wondered. 'When could they ride on?'

Alys closed her eyes as the images rushed in on her again. The girl alone in the cave, in the twilight, in the dark, fighting to bring her bairn into the world. The

102

men, helpless as most men became at such times (*we cannot blame them*, said a small part of her mind, *we shut them out, small wonder they are no use*) milling about down by the water. What could they do? Heating water was a traditional task, if any had a kettle or pan, but what would they do with it if they did?

'They sent for help,' she said in sudden relief, opening her eyes. 'You mind, we saw one set of prints go out fro here, and return extra-laden. One of the men went for help.'

'Who would they fetch fro here?' Mealsack asked blankly. 'They's no wise-women down the banks o the Mouse, that's for sure.'

'Would they go into Lanark?' Henry wondered, receiving his own reins from his junior. 'More than one howdie in Lanark, I's wager.'

'So they were here,' said Alys, resolutely sticking to the point, 'long enough to fetch help, and then to bring the babe to birth. Maybe a while longer, till Mistress Madur was well enough to be moved. Then they cut withies for a hurdle, and carried her out.'

'They'd no want to take her far like that,' said Henry. He mounted up, and turned his horse to leave the clearing. 'Likely it was dawn or later, they'd be here the maist o that night.'

'I think,' said Alys, 'they were quite close to where they were going, close enough at least for a man to take word that she was captured and well. Well enough,' she amended. 'Maister Vary had word on Friday morning, you mind. They'd at least want to be sure she was taken afore they sent a message, they'd look all kinds of gowks if they threatened him and she'd already come safe into Lanark.'

'So why'd they no go there for help?' Mealsack objected, following on behind Alys.

'Likely there was none to be had,' said Henry. 'It would have to be a woman they could lift and hide away wi the lassie. Whoever they took must be missing like she is, for they'd no be able to set her free, she'd bring the countryside down about their ears.'

'But there's none missing, is there?' objected Mealsack. 'We'd ha heard, surely.'

'Best we start asking,' said Alys.

At Henry's insistence, they rode straight to Belstane, without calling at Kettlands. Alys, sunk in her own thoughts, surfaced long enough to agree with him, but left him to deal with Mealsack's repeated offers to 'jouk up the track and let them ken, afore we ride on'. She saw no point in adding to Mistress Somerville's anxieties about her daughter before they had to. Herself, she was full of turmoil. To her faint relief, uppermost was a similar anxiety for Audrey Madur and her tiny baby, jolted about the Mouse valley on a hurdle, with one woman for company amidst a group of rough men. Surely men who would agree to such an action must be rough and dangerous? At least Audrey was valuable to them, as a playing piece to threaten Vary. But Audrey had a baby, however hard come by, and Alys had none; the familiar, powerful, painful waves of envy and jealousy surged through her, gripping at her belly, biting between her shoulderblades. *Mary, blessed Mother*, she thought, *free me from this sin of envy, help me think as a Christian ought.*

In the hall at Belstane she found not only Lady Egidia but also her youngest daughter. Tib was reclining on a daybed when Alys entered, her pretty face puffy with the effects of her pregnancy, dark curls straggling from beneath her linen hood and clinging damply to her forehead. She was fanning herself with an ivory-mounted goosewing and saying pettishly, 'It wasny as hot when I left the house, Mother, I'll swear it got hotter as I walked. I'll be well enough when I've rested a bit. Alys!' she added, struggling to sit upright, as Socrates padded past her to sprawl by the empty hearth. 'You never came to see me.'

'Gil and I are seeking Audrey Madur,' Alys explained, 'and I think we have found her traces.' She curtsied to Lady Egidia, and crossed the wide chamber to embrace her good-sister. 'No, lie back. How are you? *Madame Mère* is right, you should never have walked this far.'

'It's no more than a mile or two, and Beattie said walking was good exercise. I hoped to see her, but she's from home. Besides, I've been on my own all day.'

'We asked Michael's help,' Alys agreed. She drew a stool close to the daybed, took the fan and began wielding it, and Tib lay back, her face relaxing slightly.

'As to that, anything he can do,' she admitted. 'Did you say you'd found her?'

'No, but her traces,' Alys said. 'We found where the men took her first, and the track leads on up the Mouse Water. Henry wished to bring me home before he started to gather a trod. There were five or six horses. If all those had riders then three of us was never sufficient to approach them.'

'Three?' said Tib drowsily. 'Oh, you and all. I hope you can find her soon. It's a right worry, her being away from her friends this near her time.'

'She'll be safe enow,' Alys said. She watched, still fanning the goosewing, until her good-sister's eyes closed and her breathing grew even. When she was certain Tib was asleep she rose, caught Lady Egidia's eye, and went quietly into the solar.

The older woman followed her, and closed the door behind her, saying, 'What is it? Is Audrey safe, or no?'

105

'She has borne the babe,' Alys said. She was aware of a single swift, concerned look.

'Go on,' said her mother-in-law. 'You found the traces, I take it?'

Alys recounted the afternoon's findings. Lady Egidia listened, stopping her in the middle when Silky mewed at the door. Sitting down with her pet she heard the rest of the tale out, her expression growing grimmer as she listened.

'So on Friday at morn,' she said, 'so far's we ken, Audrey and the bairn were alive, there was a howdie or another woman wi them, and they set off towards Castlehill or further east, wi five or six men for an escort.' Silky nudged her hand, and she caressed the cat's ears, staring at the painted wall-hangings. 'Then whoever ordered this done sent word to Vary. Which message was that?'

'Seik not yir wyf do wir biddign,' Alys quoted. 'That arrived atween Terce and Sext on Friday. Then in the day, a man spoke in his ear, *Tell nobody. No a word to a soul.* And then nothing till this morning, when it was, *Seik hir and scho is deid.'*

'Someone is aware that you and Gil are seeking her,' said Lady Egidia.

'I fear that,' said Alys.

They looked at one another.

'You say Henry is calling a hot trod thegither,' said Lady Egidia. 'If he can take charge, it will go well enow, he's a man of sense. I wish Gil had come back wi you.' Alys nodded, and went to sit down opposite her mother-in-law. 'So what do we ken?' Lady Egidia continued, still stroking the cat. 'What do we ken about who has stolen her, for a start?'

'He can write,' said Alys, 'or at least has someone about him who can write, and he can command silence in his men.'

'He kens the lassie's movements,' observed Lady Egidia. 'This was no deed of impulse; it was planned, in my estimate.'

'So either he dwells close by,' said Alys, 'or he kens her well, and also her mother's household.' They looked at one another again.

'Gil hasny thought of that one,' said Gil's mother. 'How would it work? She guested wi her mother for a few days, wi instruction from Vary to stay till after the fair was over. I'd wager most of Lanark kent that. So the one that ordered it must ha kent when she left, and she only decided to leave that day.'

'No, I think Vary expected her home on Friday, early in the day,' said Alys. 'Their anniversary. They had paid for a Mass, he looked for her to come hear it wi him.'

'So I suppose,' said Lady Egidia slowly, 'they – the ones that took her – could ha watched for her day by day. I suppose they would see her leaving, or maybe arrange a signal, for they could hardly spend the entire day hidden in the branches to wait for her.'

'They might,' said Alys, 'but they'd be gey uncomfortable.' She considered for a moment. 'The road runs near straight from Kettlands road-end to the brow o the brae, at the edge of the valley. Someone could hide under the trees, just by the brow, and see when Mistress Madur set out. A donkey and one of your horses, they'd be easy enough recognised. Then it's a good half-mile from Kettlands to where she was taken. They'd ha near a quarter-hour to get to their positions.'

'It would work,' said Lady Egidia, her fingers stirring in the cat's fur. 'It would work. But it's still worth maybe questioning the folk at Greentower, or Yolande Somerville's own people, come to that, to see if they saw aught that evening or ken anything about signals.'

'Nobody saw anything,' Alys said, then added with guilty reluctance, 'I suppose I should go out and see to that.'

'It's near suppertime,' said her mother-in-law. 'No a good hour to call on folk.' There was a scratching at the door of the solar, and Alan Forrest's voice called. Lady Egidia's elegant brows rose. 'Aye, Alan, what is it?'

'It's that chiel Crombie that used to be at the coal-heugh,' said Alan apologetically, edging round the door. Behind him Tib made muffled, half-waking noises. 'Raffie, or whatever his name is. He's seeking his mither, willny hear me when I say she's no here.'

'Mistress Lithgo's son,' said Alys, opening her eyes wide. 'Seeking his mother?'

'Who is a wise-woman,' said Lady Egidia. 'I'll come down, Alan.'

'No need to disturb yoursel, madam,' said a voice behind Alan. 'Is my mither truly absent? Her house seems as if she's just stepped out.'

Adam Crombie the youngest had improved, Alys thought, in the two years since she had seen him. His manners were nearer to acceptable, and he had lost his air of having a grudge at the world. The family had moved across the Clyde, to another coalheugh somewhere on the banks of the Avon; it seemed as if he must be doing well there, despite his quarrelsome wife. He was covered in dust from the roads, slightly smeared where the cup of ale Alan must have served him had washed his mouth clean, but his clothes, like his hair, were well cut and well kept.

'She was to come to us a few days since,' he was saying. 'It was Bel's birthday on Sunday, we were to have a wee bit feast. She never came, and I took it she'd been called out to a birth, but when she'd never appeared by this morn I thought to ride across and see all was right wi her.'

108

'I've not seen her for a few days,' said Lady Egidia. 'I took it she'd been—'

'But her house,' said young Crombie, in a return to his former manner. 'Have you looked into her house?'

'Indeed no,' said Lady Egidia, in cooler tones.

'It's as if she's just now risen and gone out to the yard.'

'Aye, he's right, madam,' said Alan, still holding the door open. 'I looked in there just the now along wi him.'

'Left all as it stood,' Crombie said, ignoring this. 'She's rose from a meal, I'd say, and taken a cloak about her and left, and no returned. The mice have had the remains o the meal, but I'd say it was several days syne, long enow that if she's called to a birth the whole countryside would ha heard tell of a lassie groaning this long.'

Alys stared at him, recalling with a chill how Gil had told her of a meal similarly abandoned to the vermin, the last time they had dealt with a death out here by Carluke. She shook herself, about to ask if there was any other sign in the house.

'She'd no birth to attend till mine,' said Tib behind him. They all turned to look through the doorway into the hall. She was sitting up on the side of the daybed, rubbing her eyes. 'How long did I sleep, Mammy? No, Beattie's engaged to me for the end of July, and she said the other day she'd no other hereabouts, and she'd need to get the word round.'

'It looks as if it's got round,' said Alys. She looked at Lady Egidia. 'I think we ken who was fetched to Audrey Madur.'

It was not easy to explain to Adam Crombie what they thought had come to his mother. For a start, both he and Tib kept interrupting, asking why this or that other action had not been chosen, asking why Henry had neither followed the trail of Audrey Madur's captors nor alerted Kettlands. Alys found herself becoming sharp with them both. Finally, to her relief, Lady Egidia said firmly, 'Small purpose in quarrelling wi what's done. What we need now is to decide what we do next. Adam, do you want to ride out after Henry and the trod once you've eaten? I can lend you a horse and a helm. Or you could wait till Michael gets back,' she added, with a faint malice which only Alys detected, 'and ride wi him.'

'No, I'll go the now,' said Crombie hastily. 'I'd be glad of the loan of a beast, if you would, madam, for my bay's about done. It's no the distance, it's the hills, this heat.'

Alys hid a smile, recalling how he and Michael had reacted, encountering each other here in the hall; some enmity engendered at the college in Glasgow had followed them out here, never explained. 'I'll come down,' said Lady Egidia, rising, 'and get a word wi whoever's in the stables, since Henry's away out. Come and choose a beast.'

Tib retired to the daybed to put her feet up again, and Socrates never stirred, but Alys followed her good-mother and Adam Crombie down to the door of the tower-house, and out to the stableyard. She was sitting on the mounting-block in the cooler air of the evening, watching Crombie's reaction to the various beasts in their loose-boxes and wondering idly if he had ever won his degree – if he should be called Maister Crombie or not – when there was a clatter of hooves outside. Several of the horses whinnied a greeting to the newcomers, and an ancient groom shuffled out to open the gate to the yard. Michael Douglas rode through it, followed by two of his men on horses Alys recognised. He reined in beside her, and slid from the saddle.

'Where's Gil?' he said abruptly. 'I think there's treason afoot.'

Chapter Six

'Aye, I doubt ye're right, maister,' said Provost Lockhart. He sat back in the saddle, scowling across the Burgh Muir at the fenced-off portion with its neat rows of juvenile trees, and fanned himself with his wide straw hat. Late in the day though it was, the sun was still hot. 'I can see Dod Ballantyne's hand all ower this.'

'Will we get in there and uproot them, Provost?' asked one of the constables hopefully.

'No, we'll leave them the now,' said Lockhart. 'I'll see if I canny turn this to the burgh's advantage first. What are they, Mattha?'

'Larch, I'd say.' Mattha nudged his nag closer and peered over the fence. 'Or maybe Norrowa pine. I've no seen that growin and these areny just like larch. Daft time o year to plant slips, mind you,' he added. 'As hot as it's been, they're like to parch afore they take root.'

'Aye, but if any o them does take root, it's timber for the cutting down, in five or ten year,' said the Provost thoughtfully.

Gil preserved silence, considering the document he had seen in the burgh clerk's chamber, for an order of slips of something. So far as he recalled there had been no name and no other detail.

'Well, well,' said Lockhart, 'I'm right grateful to you, maister, for bringing this to my attention. We'll ha to find out how it was done, when it was done—' He turned to his men. 'Did you lads never notice this when you were clearing the tinkers off the muir?'

'It wasny here, Provost,' said the one who had wanted to uproot the trees. 'We hunted them all across this bit, we'd ha seen them.'

'We'd ha fell ower the fence,' offered another man. 'If it was there, I mean.'

'So it's been done the last two or three days,' said the Provost.

'Or nights,' said Gil. 'It never gets right dark, this time o year.'

'Aye, that's true. Well, lads, we'll away back down to Lanark, and youse can start asking questions. Someone about the burgh must ken how these got here, and by whose order, and when we find him we'll deal wi him. Which reminds me, maister, the sweep's laddie, young Nicol Baillie, he tells us he saw two men running down towards the port. Never recognised them, but gave us a description that accords well wi the one we have a'ready.'

Gil nodded acknowledgement of this.

'There's the matter o the fellow Tammas saw up here,' he said. 'Easy enough to hide here, if you ken the place, I'd ha said, what wi hills and burns and the like, it's a broad muir. What's more,' he added, 'if those trees were brought up the road from Ayr, say, there's no need for them ever to ha entered the burgh.'

'That's true and all,' said Lockhart, staring out towards the Ayr road where it forded the Clyde at Hyndford Lea. 'It could be done in secret right enow.'

They rode back down into Lanark, Gil deep in thought. Descending the High Street, he became aware of Madame Olympe's servant Agnes, standing in the doorway of their lodging above Maister Lightbody's house. She looked at him significantly.

112

Ignoring her, he said clearly to the Provost, 'I'm for collecting my men afore the ports are shut and riding home, maister. I'll be lucky if they've kept supper for me as it is.'

'Aye, the day's wearing on,' agreed Lockhart, as Agnes's good striped kirtle vanished into the lodging. 'I'll send you word out at Belstane if I need you further, or if there's aught you can advise me on.'

'Aye, do that,' Gil agreed, and wished the man a good night. The constables set off to stable their own steeds and the Provost's, Lockhart went into his house, and Gil, dismounting as the street grew steeper, led his beast down to Juggling Nick's. To its evident disapproval, he did not stable it, but tethered it outside. By the time he had extracted Euan and Tammas and seen them mounted, a certain amount of discussion with the gate-ward was needed to get them out of the burgh, but he managed it at length, and they took the road home with some relief.

'Well, that was a wasted day,' observed Euan, as they crossed the bridge. 'It's still a great mystery where the lady might ha vanished away to.'

'It's a worry,' said Tammas. 'I doubt we'll never find her alive now. She'll be under a dyke or floating in the Mouse somewhere.'

'Never say it!' exclaimed Euan, crossing himself. 'Our Lady send her safe, and her bairn too!'

'Hold up a moment,' said Gil. 'I've heard there are caves down here, along the waterside. If they took her there, they'd ha left the road about here.'

All three men scouted up and down the roadside, but could see no sign that anyone, let alone a group of men or horses, had crossed the bank at the roadside.

'Is there no other caves?' Euan wondered. 'Maybe up the river instead of down?'

'I've heard o none,' said Gil, 'and I don't intend to go seeking them this evening. I want my supper.'

'Maister,' said Tammas, looking back the way they had come. 'Is that someone on the road?'

'One horse,' said Euan, turning his head likewise. 'Making a good speed, so it is.'

'There's three of us,' said Gil, swinging his beast round to face the sound of hoofbeats. All three animals had their ears pricked, and Tammas's horse produced a soft whicker.

The steed which came round the curve in the road, slowing as the gradient steepened, was a handsome creature, broad-chested, deep in the barrel. Gil was completely unsurprised to see that its rider was his cousin Sandy Boyd, pale hair blowing in the air of his movement, shirt neck open and sleeves rolled up, a beribboned black velvet doublet gathering dust. He was more taken aback to realise, as his kinsman drew abreast of them, that Billy Doig was perched uncomfortably on the pillion, clinging to Boyd's belt.

'In a good hour!' said Boyd happily. 'I hoped I'd find you.'

'Oh, you did?' said Gil, misliking the omen in these words. 'So you came after me *from the cyte of Camelot on horsbak as moche as ye myght,* and to what end?'

'I'll ride on wi you,' said his cousin, grinning as he placed the quotation. 'We've news.' He flicked a glance at Gil's men.

'News,' said Gil flatly.

He sent Euan and Tammas ahead, far enough to be out of earshot, and turned his beast for Belstane. His kinsman fell in alongside, and Doig said, 'Guid e'en to ye, Maister Cunningham.'

'Have you news and all?' Gil asked him pointedly. His cousin laughed.

114

'No need to be so suspicious. My aunt would ha my guts to stuff cushions wi if I brought harm to you. No to mention your bonnie wee wife,' he added.

'So what's this news?' Gil prompted, unconvinced. 'Does it concern Mistress Madur?'

'No,' said Boyd. 'At least, I think not. It concerns the burgh clerk, Maister Ballantyne.'

'Aye?' said Gil. 'It was you delivered the trees, was it, Maister Doig?'

Under the trees which shadowed the road he could not be certain, but he thought surprise flickered in both faces.

'It was,' said Doig. 'Took them out the Burgh Muir on Saturday. The tinkers put them in the ground, Saturday and Sunday nights, and fenced them away from the burgh herd.'

'Fast work,' commented Boyd. 'How many, five hundred wee trees?'

'A whole tribe o tinkers,' countered Doig. 'Even the bairns. They were well enough paid, though no by me.'

'Who by?' asked Gil.

'Aye, that's the point,' said Boyd. 'He never kent their names.'

'I recognised the burgh clerk's house, where I met them,' said Doig, 'and got his name that way, but seeing he's deid, I'll never get my fee from him now. He paid the tinkers in coin, or he'd never ha got the work done, but like a fool I allowed him the account.'

'So what's the plan?' Gil asked after a moment. 'What do you intend, and why are you telling me this?'

'Thought you might find it useful,' said Boyd innocently.

'Thought you might be able to help,' said Doig at the same moment. 'Scratch my back, I'll scratch yours.'

'And if I'm not wanting my back scratched?'

Boyd shrugged. 'We go back to Lanark.'

'What, at this hour? How will you get in? They've shut the ports.'

'Same way we got out,' said Boyd, but did not elaborate.

Gil looked from Boyd to his passenger, considering.

'You could describe them, I suppose? How many were there in the venture?'

'The late Maister Ballantyne,' said Doig, 'and two more. Aye, I can describe them well. One about our freen's height,' he nodded at Boyd's back where his big hands still clutched at the belt, 'short hair, fairish, thin face, showy dresser. Aye a feather in his hat and a swagger to him. The other, that was to fee me, maybe a handspan shorter, longer hair o a light brown colour, heavier built, left-handed and a neb like a Kerr's.'

'That is interesting,' said Gil slowly. And the shorter man's initial was M, he thought. The other, presumably, was S. Muir, Mowatt, Marr, even Murray? Scott or Steel? Or were they Madur and Somerville?

'Isn't it?' said Boyd happily. 'D'you ken either man?'

'No so as to name or accuse them,' Gil admitted, 'but I tell you what, Michael Douglas was to go all about the neighbourhood asking for Audrey Madur the day. If you came back to Belstane wi me you could get a word wi him. He kens the neighbourhood and who dwells in it better than I do.'

'Ah, your good-brother,' said Boyd. 'And is madam your mother at home?'

'She is,' said Gil. There was a short pause, while the horses clopped onwards.

'I'd like fine to put names to them, I'll admit,' said Doig in his deep voice. 'You still have that wolfhound, Maister Cunningham?'

116

'I've no doubt o that, Billy,' said Boyd. 'Aye, we'll call on my aunt, Gil, and thanks for the offer.' He gathered up his reins. 'Will we make more haste? I'd as soon be back in Lanark afore first light.'

'I'm surprised you never met Crombie on the road,' said Michael Douglas. 'It's no an hour since he left here.'

'Likely he went round the other side o Kettland Muir,' said Gil, 'if he thought he was seeking the trod further up the Mouse Water. He knows these parts well, after all. So Mistress Lithgo's missing, my wife thinks Audrey Madur's bairn is born, and Henry's leading a hot trod through Lanarkshire after them, wi Adam Crombie in pursuit.'

'That's about the size o't,' said Michael. He lifted the jug and poured more of the vinegar-and-water mix into everyone's cups. They were in the steward's room, where Alan had set out a generous supper of leftovers and cold cuts which, as he said, ought to be ate up afore they were much older. 'No, I'd my supper wi the ladies, help yoursel,' he went on as Gil offered him a slice of pie. 'Tib couldny wait for her vitals, though she doesny eat that much at a time the now. I'd as soon tell you what I learned, Gil, and get her away back to the Pow Burn.'

'I can see that,' said Gil. 'But Sandy, here, wants to learn if you ken these two men he and Maister Doig have had dealings wi.'

'It's Billy that's had dealings wi them,' said Boyd. 'I prefer no to niffer wi the nameless.'

Doig threw him a black look from under his heavy brows, but obliged with the two descriptions he had already given Gil. Michael heard him in silence, looking into his cup.

'Left-handed,' he said at length, 'and a neb like a Kerr. Old man Madur, from my grandsire's day, that would be Audrey's grandsire, was wedded to a Kerr. She'd be mother to Henry and Jocelyn, I suppose, and Jocelyn Madur certainly has her neb, though I couldny tell you offhand if he's corrie-fisted or no, I'm no that well acquaint wi the man. There's James Mowat down by Braidwood, that's left-handed, I chanced to notice it the day, but he's clippit short as a priest. But the ither sounds gey like Robert Somerville, wi the swashing and the feather in his hat. For all he's short o money, he's aye well turned out.'

'Terrible,' said Boyd, straight-faced. 'How ever does he do it?'

Michael shot him a glance, decided he was joking, and went on without comment, 'Mind, Somerville's no the only one takes pride in his appearance. There's a few more it could be.'

'I can see that,' said Boyd, still straight-faced.

Michael, who had been riding about Lanarkshire in a red leather doublet of complex cut and even more complex braiding, gave him an exasperated look, and Doig said to Boyd, 'You're no help, ken that?' He paused as Socrates nudged the door open and swaggered in, grinning, to greet him with delight. 'Get aff, ye daft dug,' he said, pushing at the shaggy grey head with scarcely hidden pleasure. 'Aye, ye've a good memory, I can tell. I seen that fellow, one time,' he added to Michael, 'in a short gown o tawny satin, faced wi crimson silk. Fair made yir een water, it did. That any help?'

'Tawny satin faced wi crimson silk,' Michael repeated. 'Oh, aye, that's Rab Somerville. There canny be two short gowns in the country like it.'

'Right,' said Gil. 'That's one o them named, anyway.'

'And where does he dwell?' asked Doig grimly. Socrates, deserting him, went to greet first Gil and then his cousin. 'I'm no a local man, and it seems to me I'm as

118

well no asking a' that passes by for directions to his lodging.'

'Up ayont Forth,' said Michael. 'It's a fair ride fro here. You'll no want to set out now, surely?'

'Eight or ten mile from here,' said Gil. He found his cousin eyeing him speculatively, and sat back, raising a hand, palm out. 'Oh, no, Sandy. Count me out o this one. I'm doing no more housebreaking wi you or any other.'

'Housebreaking?' said Michael, startled, and went red. 'I mean—'

'What, are you feart?' challenged Boyd. The dog, abandoning hope of attention, padded back to Doig and sat down, leaning heavily against him.

'I could do wi getting my wife home,' said Michael with determination, 'and there's a day's findings to report. Will you hear me now, Gil, or will I come back the morn?'

'I'll hear it now,' Gil said, aware of gratitude. 'Sandy might as well hear it and all.'

'Oh, a tale!' said Boyd eagerly. 'Tell on, tell on, bold Douglas.'

'I made a note,' said Michael, drawing his tablets from his purse, 'seeing I wasny sure how far I'd get. Lockhart at the Lee, Waygateshaw, Braidwood, Nellfield, none o those had any word o the lassie and all seemed genuine in their concern when I told them the tale. Though some o them,' he grinned at his notes, 'were certain at first I was seeking a load of gunpowder. Seems there's a tale of a cartload of the stuff going about Lanarkshire. And at Nellfield,' he added, 'it was guns I must be seeking. A whole batch of guns brought in from Portingal, said the steward, though he'd seen not a whisker of sic a thing, and couldny mind where he had the tale from. Any road, I had Attie scout all their stables for me, no sign of a jennet or one o Bluebell's get at any house, though

119

there was other Belstane beasts to be found a plenty. So then, sooner than cross the Mouse I stayed this side and went on to Drums and Foulwood, and then to Castlehill.'

'Who holds Castlehill again?' Gil asked.

'That's Henry Madur,' said Michael.

'Henry? No Jocelyn?'

'Aye. Though he doesny dwell there, it's a man Lindsay he's put in it. Civil enough fellow.'

'William Lindsay,' said Boyd. 'The Lindsays are sweetly perfumed in the King's sight, well in wi the court. William's some kind of a third cousin to Montrose, is that right? Davie Lindsay, I mean.'

'That's the one,' Michael agreed. 'His grandsire and Lindsay of Montrose's were brothers. Or maybe cousins.'

'There's a lot o it about,' said Boyd, not looking at Gil. 'Go on.'

'Naught to see at Castlehill,' said Michael, 'though I kinna wondered if the steward kent more than he let on. When I said I was seeking Mistress Madur he looked round sharpish from what he was at, just about dropped the jug of ale. Lindsay never noticed, he'd his back to him, and by the time I got to ask the man he'd a smooth tale that his wife had mentioned the lassie that morning, saying her groaning-time was near, wondering how she did in this heat.'

'Plausible,' said Gil.

'Aye.' Michael emptied his cup, and referred to his tablets while Gil refilled it. 'So I rade on, Cleghorn, Ravenstruther, where they fed me, Mossplatt, Hyndshelwood, Throwburn, which is Henry Madur's and the steward had the exact same tale—'

'Did he now?' said Gil. 'Did he seem surprised to be asked for the lassie?'

'Seemed to me he was waiting on the question,' said Michael.

'How long were you at Ravenstruther?' Gil asked.

'More than an hour,' said Michael. 'Plenty time for anyone to ha rid past me, by the back roads up to Throwburn or even across the muir.'

'Did you check the stables?'

'Attie did. No sign o the beasts, but he spied a jennet's bridle at the back o an empty loosebox when the Throwburn lad went out for a driddle. The wee thing could ha been hid in a far field, or in one o the barns, or the like.'

'So she's been as far as Throwburn,' Gil said thoughtfully, 'or at least her jennet has, and likely Madur's men at the least know about it.'

'Aye, but there's more. Ayont Throwburn I called on both the Forth houses, east and west, and then on to The Cleuch. Rab Somerville holds that,' he said to Doig, who was watching him intently. 'D'ye ken the house, Gil?'

'No,' said Gil after brief thought. 'Never been there.'

'They've built new, abandoned the tower-house, though I think they use it yet for storage. The new house is a hall wi two wings, a bit like our house at the heugh, though a sight bigger. The wings are two floors and an attic, a right warren it must be. So I got there, and the steward welcomed me, offered me a seat in the garden in the shade, and a refreshment, while he sought out his maister. I accepted, seeing the garden's on the north o the house.' He glanced from Gil to Boyd, to see if he was understood. 'I'm seated there, enjoying a draught o some very good ale, and I hear voices. Ower my head, they were, as if they cam from an upper floor of the house. *I lost my temper*, says one of them, *what's done's done, so let's ha an end o't*. And another says, *That's no my concern, my dear. It's none o my problem if you wish to go about slaying clerks or stealing away ladies —*'

'Ah!' said Gil. Michael nodded, but went on, '*It's on your head*, he says, *I'm here to discuss another matter entirely*. And the odd thing was,' said Michael, 'the first voice, the one that lost his temper, sounded like Rab Somerville right enow, but the second voice was Irish.'

'Irish,' Gil said flatly, aware of Boyd beside him intently saying nothing whatever. Across the table, he realised, Doig was equally intent, though his strong fingers worked in Socrates' shaggy ruff so that the dog groaned faintly in pleasure.

'Aye. Irish out of Ireland, I mean, no an Erscheman. You can tell. So I moved, quiet-like,' said Michael, 'to a bench against the house wall, under the window that was open. One o the attic chambers, it was, no wonder they'd both the shutters set wide, it would be stifling hot up there.'

'A kind thought,' said Boyd lightly. 'You'd no want them to be embarrassed, thinking they were overheard.'

Michael, recognising this joke, acknowledged it with a flick of his brows and went on.

'So they fenced about a bit, neither o them willing to name what they'd to discuss, but at length it cam clear, that the Irishman's negotiating for Somerville and his marrows to slay somebody, here in Scotland. You can be sure I cockit my lugs at that,' he said grimly, 'trying after a name I could report or warn. But all they said was, *The boy, the stocach, the gossoon*. Never a name used.' He looked about the table, seeming a little thrown off his stride by the expressionless stares of two of his hearers.

'Those all mean the same thing,' Gil observed encouragingly.

'I ken that,' said Michael. 'There was one or two black Irish at the college in my time. So as far's I could collect, the *gossoon* they're after isny in Scotland the now, but he's expected any time, as a guest o James Stewart. The Gordons were mentioned and all, Lady Katherine in especial, you ken, Huntly's third lassie. Whether they're in the plot or they're a' to be slain wi the gossoon I couldny make out. I think the Irishman was stepping back and forth fro the window, the way his voice came and went. Somerville was reluctant, to gie him credit, though I suspect it was as much because he doubted being able to do the deed without being recognised. He said a time or two he'd no wish for the attention o the Crown.'

'Dear, dear,' said Boyd.

'The Irishman pressed him a bit,' Michael continued, 'mentioned a price though I never caught what it was, said if he wouldny do it he'd find another. Then the steward interrupted them.' He spread his hands. 'That's about all I got.'

'You got a good deal,' said Boyd at last. 'Dates? Places?'

'No,' said Michael with regret. 'Save that he's no in Scotland yet, as I said. Oh, a Maximilian was mentioned. That's no a Scots name, nor yet an Irish one.'

'No,' said Boyd.

'I hesitate to ask it,' said Gil, 'but did you see any sign of Mistress Madur? Any word from the steward – or Somerville himself, for that?'

'Oh!' said Michael, and swallowed another gulp of ale. 'As well you asked, I near forgot. Attie said he saw one o Bluebell's get in the stables, about five year old wi a sock and a star. Somerville denied all knowledge o the lassie, but then he'd had a chance to think about it. I heard the steward tell him what I was asking when he finally chapped at the closet door where they were talking. Or at least,' he said scrupulously, 'I heard Somerville saying, *Michael Douglas? Asking for who? Oh, the deil take him, I'd better ha a word*. So he'd time to get his tale

123

straight, saying he'd no notion she was from hame. I never got round to telling Crombie that,' he added, 'So I hope the trod's no all ower the countryside on a false trail, if he did catch up wi them.'

'You never had a sight of the Irishman?' Boyd asked casually.

'No, I never. Somerville cam down to the garden himsel to speak wi me, expressed concern for his niece, said he hoped she was safe.' He grunted sceptically, and fell silent.

'You're right,' said Gil after a moment. 'There's treason afoot, and we need to inform on it. Will you scribe it, or will I? Then we can get it sent to,' he paused again, considering. 'I'm inclined to send it to Blacader, making it clear who got the information.' He met his cousin's eye across the table, and got a tiny nod in acknowledgement.

'I can scribe it,' said Michael reluctantly. 'I think maybe you're like to be busy.'

'Good man,' said Boyd, and pushed his stool back from the table. 'Now, shall we go up and greet my aunt? Then you can collect Lady Tib and get away home.'

'I'll bide here,' said Doig hastily. 'No need for me to disturb her ladyship.' He reached for the final wedge of the pie, and nodded dismissal.

The three ladies were in the solar, with the last of the sunlight still sloping in at the north windows, warming the white sandstone of the empty fireplace. Tib was drowsing on the daybed, Alys and her mother-in-law were talking softly, and Lady Egidia's cat was curled on her knee, its kitten sound asleep in the basket. Socrates bounded in ahead of Gil, waving his tail at Alys, and the cat looked up, flattened its ears and glared, but stayed where it was. Lady Egidia stroked the grey fur and smiled at her kinsman.

'Come in, Maister Boyd,' she said. 'I've been waiting for you.'

Boyd made her a deep bow, flourishing his felt hat.

'Forgive me, madam!' he said, pressing the other hand to his heart. 'Though I may never forgive mysel for keeping sic a one waiting, *more decore than of before And swetar be sic sevyne.*'

Her eyebrows went up.

'You suggest I am *indeflore*?' she asked.

'I need to get Tib home,' said Michael, crossing the chamber to take his wife's hand. 'It's high time she was back in her own place.'

In the bustle of rousing Tib, ordering horses and a suitable saddle, bidding farewell, Gil managed to draw Alys aside and exchange a summary of what they had both discovered after they parted in the afternoon, though hers differed only in the greater detail from Michael's earlier report.

'That poor girl,' she said, 'in such a plight. I hope they are keeping her safe. Gil, do you really think she is at The Cleuch?'

'I think she's been taken there,' he said cautiously. 'I don't know if she's still there. If they work out that Michael could have overheard them, they'll move her. They might move her anyway, merely because he asked after her.'

The travellers finally waved off from the gate, Tib's plaintive tones dwindling into the warm evening, the remaining party retreated to the solar again.

'Now,' said Lady Egidia, sitting down and lifting her cat, 'what are you after, Alexander? How is your sister, by the way? And her bairn? The new marriage goes well?'

'It does,' admitted Boyd with a grimace. 'He's no at all to my taste, nor I'd think to yours, madam, but Maidie

125

has John Sempill well in hand, and the boy is shaping better than I feared. He's more a Boyd than a Sempill.'

'Our Lady be praised for that,' said Lady Egidia. 'And what is it you want wi my son?'

'Guidance,' he said promptly. 'I need to find my way to The Cleuch this night.'

'The night?' she said, raising her eyebrows. 'It's no that far, a course, but need it be the night?'

'It must,' he said. 'I need to be in Lanark by daylight. Besides, if Mistress Madur's there, as we think she might be, the sooner we fetch her away the better.'

'You'd need men for that,' she said briskly, 'and Henry's taken the most of our fellows for a trod. How certain are you she's there? I'd ha thought they'd move her again after Michael was there. After all, they seem to be waiting for Vary to do something for them, so they'll no want her rescued yet awhile. Will you and Gil be enough on your own?'

'Mother,' said Gil, aware of fighting a losing battle, 'last time I went out after dark wi Sandy Boyd I was near being arrested for housebreaking.'

'Surely no, dear,' she said. Alys caught Gil's eye, looking anxious. 'Sandy, you'd never lead your cousin into anything like that, would you?'

'Oh, wouldn't he?' said Gil, before Boyd could answer. 'What are you planning at The Cleuch, anyway, Sandy? Tell us. The truth, mind. Audrey Madur's nothing to do wi't, is she? She's no more than a pretext.'

'Oh, the truth?' said his kinsman, waving one large white hand so that for those who knew her Madame Olympe was suddenly in the chamber. 'What's truth but a naked lassie at a well? She aye needs covered up in some way. I want to be at The Cleuch,' he said, reverting to Sandy Boyd, 'for a word wi Robert Somerville, who I think kens more than a wee bit about something

126

I'm concerned wi. I'd be right glad o a word wi his guest and all, if he's still about, but I'm less hopeful o that. And as I say, if this lassie's there we can bring her away. Maybe.'

'Michael kens the house better than I,' said Gil. 'You'd be better waiting till the morn.'

'And your word won't wait?' said his mother, ignoring this. 'Come, Gil, don't be so misobliging. I'm sure Sandy willny lead you into more housebreaking the night, will you, dear? Or anything else of the sort?'

Alys was biting her lip, but Boyd gave her a gleaming smile, then turned the same on Lady Egidia.

'He'll be as safe as if he rode in my purse,' he assured her, patting the item.

'I wouldny fit,' said Gil. Boyd flicked his eyebrows at him, but the smile did not waver.

'I think you should find your father's helm, Gil,' said Lady Egidia. 'It's in the great kist in my chamber, along wi his good jack.'

'Madame—' began Alys. Lady Egidia turned; they exchanged a long look. Then Alys dropped her eyes. 'I suppose,' she said quietly. Gil looked from one to the other, frowning. What were they about?

'Well, if that's settled,' said Boyd. 'Away and find your helm, Gil, and we'll be off. Ten mile, did you say, and the light going?'

'There's a moon,' said Alys, apparently accepting the situation.

'In the house o the Ram,' said Boyd, 'so it rises at midnight.'

'Aye, but it's the third quarter,' said Gil gloomily. 'It'll no be much help.' He got to his feet, and laughed suddenly, without humour. 'I recall Pierre complaining that Scotland is by far too full of strong-minded women. He was right there.'

127

'Well, I canny think of any here,' said his mother. 'I've no notion who you'd mean.'

Lying on a dark hillside, peering down at the policies of The Cleuch, the groom Steenie said, 'You see, maisters, I was right to come round this way.'

'Agreed,' said Gil. 'I shouldny ha doubted you.'

The man had been a last-minute addition to the party, when Lady Egidia had accompanied them all down to the stableyard and found him the only stablehand still about, having been home at his supper when the trod set out.

'Ah, Steenie,' she had said, and even in the failing light Gil had seen on Steenie's scarred face the expression most men wore when addressed by Lady Egidia in that tone. 'You ken Forth and the lands about it, I think.'

'Aye, mistress,' he acknowledged, looking at the rest of the group rather than meet her eye, a flicker of recognition in his face as he saw Doig.

'Fine,' she said. 'Saddle up for yoursel and Maister Gil, as well as my cousin and his man here. They're wanting to be at The Cleuch by moonrise.'

Alys's hand slid into Gil's; he looked down at her, grimacing, and she tightened her clasp, and stroked the moth-eaten velvet of his father's good jack with her other hand.

'You'll be careful,' she said.

'If I can.' He raised the hand in his and kissed it. 'Don't wake for me, sweetheart.'

'What, you think I can sleep?'

'Gil, are you coming or no?' demanded his cousin.

'And Sandy,' said Lady Egidia, as Boyd swung himself into the saddle. He gave her another gleaming smile and she switched to French. 'When you come into

Lanark, if you should encounter this Madame Olympe of whom I hear so much.'

'Aye?' he said, the gleam fading a trifle.

'Give her my good greetings and tell her how greatly I long to meet her. She must be a personage of the most remarkable.'

'I'll do that, madam,' said Boyd, maintaining the smile resolutely, then bent to assist Doig to scramble up behind him, his mount flattening its ears at the unexpected movements. Gil grinned at his horse's flanks as he checked the girth, then took his reins from Steenie and mounted up.

'Let's away, then,' he said, 'afore the night's wasted.'

Now, studying the scene before them in the light summer night, he reckoned it was no more than an hour past midnight. The moon was up, but still low in a clear sky, silvering the hills about them; the cottages of Forth were shadows against the white ribbon of the road half a mile away, and an owl crossed soundlessly before them, silencing the tiny squeaks and rustles of the night. All was peaceful, except around the house itself.

'What are they at?' Steenie wondered. 'The place is beelin!'

'That could be in our favour,' said Boyd thoughtfully. Below them the torches hurried to and fro in the yards, lights moved from one window of the house to another, alarmed shouting rose up to them clearly on the warm night air. 'What are they saying?'

'Someone's deid,' said Gil, catching the word. Doig swore.

'So what is it ye're wanting?' Steenie asked. 'Was it just a look at the house, or are ye for calling on them, or what? Will we go down and chap the door?'

'I'm wanting a word wi Robert Somerville,' growled Doig, 'whether he's deid or no.'

129

'You're seeking the lassie Madur, Gil, are you no?' said Boyd without looking round. 'House or outhouses, or the tower-house?'

'No saying,' said Gil. 'If we get closer, I might make it out. And you?'

He felt rather than saw his cousin's shrug beside him.

'I'm here to speak wi Rab Somerville, like Billy,' he said. 'And I'm planning to kill his house-guest, forbye.'

'Right,' said Steenie. 'So you'll be wanting to get closer, then?'

The house, a generous edifice much as Michael had described it, of two timber-framed wings on either end of a high-windowed stone hall, was perched on the edge of a steep-sided river valley, one short wing facing the thickly tree-clad slope. Gil realised with slight surprise that it was the Mouse Water which ran there.

'If I dwelt there, I'd ha cleared the glen,' he said critically. 'Too much cover.'

'They've a stout wall,' said Steenie. 'And clear ground atween that and the house. It's no a strong place, but Somerville's no daft. And they've the tower-house yet, if they'd the time to retreat to it. I's wager the lassie's in there, maister.'

'I see that,' said Gil. 'I'd say you were right.'

The tower-house, an old-fashioned solid structure, lay south-east of the main house, at the other side of a complex of outhouses and stables. It would have been invisible, Gil saw, from the north side of the house where Michael had been put to wait.

'The trees are still too far away to be any help,' said Sandy Boyd. 'Maybe we should just throw you ower the wall, Billy.'

Doig growled at him.

'I'm inclined to try the main yett, here at the south side,' said Gil. 'D'ye see, it's ajar. I can see torchlight in the gap by times. That gets us into the yard where all the stir's happening, and we can plan from there.'

'Well seen,' said Boyd. 'Right, who's wi us? Billy, you're wi me, I take it.'

'I'm wi Maister Gil,' said Steenie firmly.

'Signals,' said Gil.

'Oh, if you hear me scream, run like lightning,' said Boyd cheerfully.

'I can do a peesweep,' said Doig improbably. 'If I'm leaving, I'll cry like a peesweep, three times, and make for where we left the horses.'

Gil settled his father's helm more firmly on his head, wishing yet again that the brim was narrower like that of his own helm, and tightened the chinstrap.

'Let's go,' he said.

Whatever had happened within the high wall, it had overset the household completely. There seemed to be no watch being kept; they approached the main gate of the place with caution but were not challenged, and the shouting they could hear made it plain that someone was dead, that another man who might have had authority had left the house in the afternoon, and someone they only called *him* was nowhere to be found. Gil paused by the gates and held up a hand, listening.

After a moment he braced himself, pushed the gate wider and stepped inside, aware of the other men following him.

'What's afoot here?' he demanded in carrying tones. 'What way's this for a baron's household to be behaving at this hour?'

Behind him, his cousin stifled a laugh. Two, then three, then half a dozen men in the yard stopped their running about, stared at him for a moment and then approached slowly, the torches illuminating a dawning hope in their expressions.

'Maister? Somerville's deid,' said the one nearest him bluntly. 'Somerville's deid, knifed in his closet, and we dinna ken what to do!'

Doig snarled. Sandy Boyd said, expressionless, 'Oh, my. What a pity.'

Chapter Seven

'Who's your steward?' Gil asked. 'Who's in charge?'

'Naeb'dy,' said the same man. 'We've no— he sent the maist o them out an errand afore suppertime, and the steward wi them; they's just us here. We've no instructions.'

Clearly, the more reliable men had gone with the errand, Gil thought.

'Right,' he said decisively. 'I want the whole of you that's left here to stop running about like hens wi the fox in the yard, and get assembled here in yon corner. Steenie, you can owersee that. And I want a look at Somerville first. You,' he pointed to the spokesman, 'take us up to where he lies.'

'Me?' said the man in alarm. 'I'm an outside man, I'm no used wi the house.'

'I'll tak ye, maister,' said another man, stepping forward. 'I'll no look at him, mind, he's all ower blood, I seen him already, but I'll tak ye up the stair.'

'Here,' said the man who said he was an outdoor man, 'is he to go in and all? The duarch?' He was making signs against evil with his free hand. Doig grinned his humourless grin at him, showing white teeth, and stropped his knife on his hard palm.

'He is,' said Gil curtly.

Finding the usual collection of lanterns set on a kist just inside the great door of the house, he made their guide wait while he lit one for himself, and watched Boyd and Doig do likewise. After a little thought the man lifted a fourth and put fire to the candle inside.

'It's this way,' he said, looking warily about him at the shadowed hall. 'And he's— we dinna ken where the man that did it's gone. If he's in the house yet or no. He could be anywhere, maister, just waiting to slit all our throats!'

He took a deep breath, as one going to his execution, and set off for a doorway at the far end of the hall. Gil, keeping a reckoning in his head, recognised that they were going into the western wing of the house, the one which overlooked the river.

Beyond the doorway was a well-furnished chamber, with new, pale oak furniture mixed with older, darker pieces, cushions of brocade scattered on the settle to gleam in the lantern-light. Their guide crossed this chamber and the next, paused to listen carefully, and stepped onto a newel stair.

At Gil's back, Boyd murmured, 'If we come on the Irishman, he's mine.'

'Wi pleasure,' said Gil, following the manservant.

They climbed that stair, crossed two more chambers where the windows showed palely against the dark walls, found another stair which Gil reckoned must be above the doorway by which they had left the hall. Whoever built this house, though he had not fortified it, had kept its defence in mind. Ascending this second stair on to the attic floor they traversed more small chambers, furnished under their slanted roof-beams apparently at random.

'Who needs this many chambers?' wondered Doig at the rear of their little procession. 'Even the King hasny this many chambers at Stirling.'

'What makes you think you've seen the whole o his lodging?' asked Boyd.

'Wheesht!' said the manservant, then realised what he was doing. 'Yir forgiveness, maisters, but we dinna ken where he's got to. He could be hearkening to us the now, waiting to spring on us out the shadows.'

'Where are we headed for?' Gil asked.

'We're here, maisters.' The man stopped at the further side of the chamber they had just crossed, before another doorway. 'He's in yonder, in his closet. I'll no venture in, I seen him once and that's enough.'

Hand on his whinger, lantern held high in the other hand, Gil stepped into the closet.

It was a chamber of some size, certainly twice the size of Gil's own closet at home in the house on the Drygate. To the right of the door stood a cabinet of little drawers like an overgrown spice-kist, the kind of thing collectors kept to hold their curiosities; to the left a writing-desk, with an inkstand and pen-rest at the top of the slope and nothing else on its surface. Across the chamber, between two windows, a great chair with a shelf of books above it, two backstools standing near it as if there had been a conversation, a meeting of some sort. Three people, thought Gil, Somerville and the Irish visitor and who else? To left and right between these walls the roof had been lined with planks, forming a ceiling which came down low, so that the side walls of the chamber were no more than three feet high.

Resisting the temptation to go and study the books on the shelf, Gil turned his attention to the corpse, which was hard to ignore.

Robert Somerville lay between the writing-desk and the great chair, his hands tethered to the chair-legs, his feet to the desk. He lay stretched in his flamboyant,

135

ruined clothes, bright between the bloodstains even in the lantern-light, surrounded by a black pool of blood as Maister Ballantyne the burgh clerk had been. The resemblance ended there: this man was younger, perhaps in his fifties, and beardless, and had died in a different way, not by a single thrust through the breast but by many cuts, many blows, small acts of damage and harm which had—

'Them's his fingers,' said Doig. 'Four, five – all ten o them. And his ears and his nose. Christ aid, he's been hackit in wee collops.'

'And all laid out very neat,' said Boyd. 'Just where he could see them. How thoughtful.'

'Somebody must ha heard this going on,' said Gil grimly, looking at the expression on the dead man's bloody face. 'He'd never ha taken sic abuse in silence. Why did none of them come to his aid?' He bent to close the staring, horrified eyes, then turned to speak to their guide, and discovered the man had vanished. 'Confound it, where the deil has the fellow got to? I never said he could leave.'

'You might ask,' said Doig ambiguously. He stepped past Gil into the chamber and bent over the corpse, carefully avoiding the pool of blood, to pat the dead man's purse where it hung at his belt. 'Nah. No much in there. I wonder where he's got it hid?'

'Got what hid, Billy?' asked Boyd.

'His coin. He owes me fifty merks, and I'll have it the nicht, if I've to search this house to get it.'

'Likely in that cabinet.' Boyd jerked his head towards the handsome piece in the other corner. 'You'll want a stool to get at the drawers.'

Gil opened his mouth to object, and decided against it. Instead he said, 'He never told.'

'Agreed,' said Boyd after a moment.

136

'How d'ye make that out?' said Doig, pausing in dragging one of the backstools across the chamber. 'Oh, aye. He's no had his throat or his wame slit. He's just dee'd on him, likely bled to death, no had to be slain at the end.'

'I wonder what it was he kent,' said Gil thoughtfully.

'I hope, for her sake,' said Boyd, 'it was the whereabouts of the lassie Madur that he didny tell.'

Gil moved past the dead man, stepping over the neatly arranged trimmings of the corpse, and looked out of a window. As he had surmised, he found himself looking down into a little knot-garden, its further section brightly lit by the moon, the nearer in dark shadow. This chamber was almost certainly where the conversation Michael had overheard had taken place.

'Well,' he said. 'There's naught we can do for Somerville but set up the hue and cry, and search this house to find if his killer's still on the premises.'

'He'll ha made off, if he's any sense,' said Doig, slamming a small drawer shut with a resounding clack and opening another. 'Ah, what's this? That's more like.' He drew a purse from the little cavity and weighed it in his hand speculatively. 'Could be, could be. Let's have a look.'

'Is the man married?' Gil asked. 'Had he family? Kin? I ken very little o him.'

'Widowed,' said Boyd. 'Two sons, I think, one at the college at St Andrews, though I'm no certain where the other dwells.'

'And maybe recruited to slay the Duke o York if he comes to Scotland,' said Gil.

'You heard that,' said Boyd.

'I did. Will they really gie him Katherine Gordon? The Duke o York, I mean, or whoever he is. The Fleming fisher's son.'

137

Boyd shrugged. 'No saying. He might no come to Scotland, though he's long invited. Maximilian's fitting out a fleet for him to invade England the now, but none of us think that will come to aught. His next road would be Ireland, but the Irish have done all they're going to do for him. They'll likely pass him on here as soon as they can. The O'Neill has been speaking to James Stewart already, and the fellow's writ a touching letter to Kate Gordon and all.'

'Right.' Gil took a final look at the corpse, holding his lantern low to study the shredded countenance, noting the cuts about the mouth and other sensitive parts of the face under the sticky layer of blood. 'I tell you, if Somerville concealed Audrey Madur's whereabouts from the fellow that did this, he's won absolution for aught else he's done.'

'Amen,' said Doig. He had been counting the coins in the velvet purse he had found, and now jerked the strings tight and tucked the object into the breast of his doublet. He closed the little drawer with a slither and clack of wood. 'I'm happy to leave, maisters, if you've seen enough.'

'Sandy?' said Gil.

'I need a bit time alone wi the deceased,' said Boyd. 'God ha mercy on him.'

'It doesny just seem right to leave him here, mind,' said Doig. He retrieved his lantern from the top of the cabinet, and slid down from the backstool where he had been perched.

'The Sheriff will need to see him,' said Gil, 'or whoever he sends. I've no powers out here, save Blacader sends me in himsel. We shouldny interfere wi the corp.'

'Oh, indeed,' said Boyd lightly. 'Away down and see if your man's got the servants thegither, Gil. And you, Billy.'

138

Gil, deciding he had no wish to know what his cousin was about, set off into the enfilade of dark chambers, Doig rolling along at his side like a ship in a high sea.

They found the man who had guided them collapsed at the foot of the first newel stair, his lantern missing. Gil swore at the sight of him, lying where he had fallen, yet more blood dark and shiny about his head.

'Throat cut,' said Doig, bending to see closer. 'No a quarter-hour syne, at that.'

'Sweet St Giles,' said Gil. 'I heard naught. Did you?'

'No me. Must ha been quick, likely took him from ahint.'

Doig gingerly flicked open the door of his lantern, blew the candle out, and moved nimbly away from the corpse. Gil did likewise; there was enough light to see by, once his eyes grew accustomed, from the glazed upper portions of the two big windows of the chamber.

'He'd ha done better staying wi us, poor devil.' He muttered a prayer and crossed himself, then looked back up the stair, wondering whether he should return to his cousin, whether this killer in the dark would be waiting above them or below or elsewhere in the shadowed house.

'I'd back Sandy against any four you care to name,' said Doig, correctly interpreting his silence. 'We're warned, any road.'

'Aye,' said Gil. 'We'll need to leave this fellow here the now, it'll take more than the two o us to get him down the stair. None o this seems right, but our first task's to find the fellow wi the knife.' He tipped his head back and called, 'Sandy!'

There was a distant slither and a wooden clack which resounded in the silent chambers.

'Ah, the voice of the turtle!' responded his cousin. *'Garde à toi! Y a ici un autr'homme mort.'*

'Ah. Notr'homme?'
'Le valet de maison, oui.'
'Entendu.'

Satisfied that Boyd was warned, Gil drew his whinger, heard Doig draw his own weapon, and paced carefully forward into the dark chambers between him and the next set of stairs, ears at the stretch, aware of Doig at his hip.

They reached the hall without encountering anyone. The great door stood ajar, a shaft of moonlight lying across the polished floorboards and darkening the rest of the chamber, and voices from outside suggested Steenie had obeyed instructions and gathered the servants together. Gil stepped into the high, shadowy space and immediately sideways, back against the wall. Doig moved with him, and over the sounds from outside Gil thought he heard a door close, at the other side of the hall. He froze.

'I hear him,' Doig whispered.

They waited, but there seemed to be no further movement inside the house. After a little, Gil, trying to breathe silently, nudged his companion towards the great door and that spear of moonlight. This must be how a mouse felt, he thought, with the cat in the same chamber. Moving cautiously sideways, listening to the panicky tone of the voices out in the yard, they achieved the door and sprang through it, Gil flinging it wide open behind him.

'What's he after?' Doig wondered as they crossed the yard to the group of men huddled in the far corner. 'Him wi the knife, I mean. Why's he still in the house?'

'Had that cabinet been searched? Afore you got to it, I mean.'

'I'd say no. You could be right, he's after a chance at that.' Doig showed his teeth again. 'Well, if he tries the now he'll meet our Sandy.'

140

Steenie was facing the gathered servants like a sheep-dog with a penned flock, his hand suggestively near his whinger, the tight glossy scars on his face shining in the moonlight. As Gil approached, the man said, apparently in answer to somebody, 'Well, if none here's willing to take charge, you'll just need to do what Maister Cunningham orders. Aye, Maister Gil,' he went on smoothly, hearing Gil's booted feet on the flagstones, 'so what did ye find?'

'Aye, and where's Davie? What have ye done wi him?' demanded somebody at the back. Gil looked over the heads and identified the outdoor man who had refused to guide them. Like the rest of the group, he seemed very young; few of them were past twenty, he estimated.

'Davie's deid,' he said bluntly, at which his questioner cried out. 'He wouldny stay wi us, set off on his own, and we found him the now wi his throat cut.'

'Christ ha mercy on us!' said someone else, and they all crossed themselves in a ragged movement. 'Are we to be picked off one by one?'

'No if you stay thegither,' said Gil. 'I want the house searched, for the man that killed Davie and likely killed Somerville is still within doors.'

'Maister, no!' said the nearest man. 'You canny make us!'

'If we go by fours,' said Gil, 'wi torches or lanterns, we'll be safe enough. It's only the one man we're seeking. What weapons have you?'

'Aye, but he's naught to lose,' said someone. 'He's wanted for murder a'ready, he can only hang the once.'

'Are ye men or mice?' demanded Steenie. 'It's nae wonder your maister's lying deid up the stair, if this is the likes of what's served him! You, you and you,' he pointed, 'you're wi me. Get fresh torches, get them lit. How will we work this, Maister Gil?'

141

'Doig's group secures the hall.' Gil picked out another five men. 'You've more than one door to watch, so keep awake. Take orders from Billy, he's fought more battles than you've had hot dinners, any o you. Steenie, when the hall's secure, you clear the chambers ayont it, that end o the building,' he waved at the eastern wing, 'and shout when you're done, and I'll take you three,' he pointed to the last group, 'and get up the stair. And if any o you kens o closets or side-chambers where our handy friend might be hid, he's to say it.'

Waiting on the steps for Doig's group to declare the hall clear of mysterious men with knives, Gil said quietly to the man beside him, whose name seemed to be Doddie, 'Where did they move the lassie to?'

'Och, I wouldny ken,' said the man. Gil turned to the other two, but they shook their heads blankly.

'I hope they took her in a litter,' he said conversationally.

'There was nae lassie,' said one of Steenie's group firmly. 'Nae women in the house.'

'Aye, there was!' said Doddie. 'And the auld wife and all, wi a tongue to flay a bullock! Well, she wasny in the house,' he qualified, 'she was in the tower, but I'd to carry her food.'

'Hall's clear!' said Doig at the doorway.

'Right, lads,' said Steenie.

'There was nae lassie, d'ye hear me, Doddie Allen?' said the man who had intervened. 'Mind what Somerville said!' He turned to follow Steenie into the house.

'Aye, weel, Somerville's deid. And there was so a lassie!' said Doddie. 'And the wean and all. It was a bonnie wee thing, so it was, no longer than my airm.' He measured fingertip to elbow, and nodded defiantly at

142

Gil in the torchlight. 'It was sucking weel,' he added. 'She'd plenty for it.'

'But you've no notion where they took her,' Gil prodded.

'Might ha been Hyndshelwood,' offered one of the other men. 'Or Castlehill, maybe.'

'Castlehill's no Somerville's land,' said the third. 'Nor Eastshiel's neither.'

'Aye, but Richie Thomson's the steward there, he'd find a chamber for them gin he was asked. He'd do aught for Jocelyn Madur o Eastshiel, so my Da says.'

They continued to discuss this in low tones while they waited, but had produced no other useful suggestions when Steenie's call told Gil the ground floor was clear.

'Come on, then,' he said. 'And keep it quiet, men.'

Doddie took a firmer grip on the kitchen cleaver he was armed with; the other two raised their garden forks; and all three followed him with visible reluctance into the hall, which was now brightly lit by half a dozen torches, and into the east wing.

'Never a sign, Maister Gil,' Steenie reported, waving at the row of lit chambers. 'Save that one o the windows was standing open.'

'Show me,' said Gil.

'This one.' Steenie led him into the middle chamber of the three, and pointed to a shutter, unfastened and standing ajar. Gil stepped over to it and looked out cautiously.

'What's out this way?' he asked.

'Danny here tells me it's the stables this side, and the old tower ayont them.'

'Well, if he went that way, he's had the most o half an hour already,' Gil said. 'I'll go secure the upper floors here, and then we'll check the stables. How many horses would there be?' he asked Danny, who seemed to be the man who had argued with Doddie.

'Four,' said Danny. 'No the best he's kept, save one o them.'

'The rest would have gone wi this lassie that's no here,' speculated Gil. Danny gave him a resentful glance, and said nothing. 'Keep an eye out this window, Steenie, and I'll go clear the upper floors. Wi me, you three.'

Whinger in hand, his reluctant cohort behind him, he took the stairs at a run, sprang out into the chamber at the top whirling as he went, the flames of his torch streaming. The corners of this chamber were empty, nobody lurked behind the few pieces of furniture which stood about, there were no hangings to hide a—

'That's an orra thing,' said one of the fork-bearers, staring about him at the shadows jumping up the walls by torchlight.

'What is?' Gil said, making for the door to the next chamber.

'Where's the hangings? This chamber's got right bonnie ones, in pictures.'

'Is that smoke I smell?' demanded Doddie. 'Maister, is that smoke? What's burning?' He turned his head about, sniffing.

'It's your torch, you loon!' said the other fork-bearer. Gil looked about him, made hastily for the next chamber where the stair was, and looked upwards. In the gaps between the boards which floored the chamber above and ceiled this one, red light glowed and flickered. A crackling met his ears.

'Fire!' he said. And like an echo, from below came Steenie's shout.

'Fire! Fire, maister! The stables are afire!'

'The beasts!' said Doddie. He turned and fled towards the stairs, the other two men after him. Gil followed in some haste.

144

'Six men to the stables,' he ordered, 'you three and the three that was wi Steenie. The rest o you, wi me. We need buckets, we need brooms. Where's the well?'

'I shouldny worry,' said his cousin's voice in his ear as the men pounded past him. 'The other attic's caught and all, and the thatch. We'll no save the house.'

Gil turned to stare at him.

'What, both wings at once? How did that happen?' he asked.

Boyd shrugged. 'Who can tell? Come on, we need to get out o here.'

'Anything else we need to get out?'

'The two corps are in the yard.'

'What about Somerville's kist, any valuables—'

'Oh, the fire's dealt wi all that.'

'You're a wonder o the age,' Gil said, dragging the great door shut behind him.

'Run!' said his cousin. Gil put on an extra burst of speed, and a flake of flaming thatch narrowly missed his shoulder.

'Sweet St Giles preserve us!' he said, looking back at the house. 'It's thoroughly caught and all!'

'That's what I said.' Boyd looked about him. 'Where are the men? Are they all gone to the stables?'

'Aye, they are.' Doig appeared out of the darkness. 'I think they've got the beasts out, I could hear them skreeling and they've stopped now. Will we just get away back to Lanark, Sandy?'

'Aye, we'd best,' said Boyd, glancing at where the Lothian hills showed up black against the paling north-eastern sky. 'We're cutting it fine as it is.'

'Can you find your way?' Gil asked.

'Over the river to Forth and then down the road to Lanark,' said Boyd confidently. 'Call on me the morn if you're in the burgh. Or your bonnie wee wife,' he added, clapped Gil on the shoulder and vanished into the night, Doig after him.

'Is that them away?' Steenie said at Gil's elbow. 'Is that the duarch that was in Perthshire yon time, and all?'

'It is.' Gil looked up at the burning roofline of The Cleuch, and then down at the two corpses, laid carefully at the far side of the yard. Had Sandy got them out of the building on his own? No, surely he had made the men help. Why had he done so? For the sake of justice? It hardly seemed necessary, given that both Somerville and his servant were dead already and their killer was known.

'I came to tell you, maister,' said Steenie, as a window burst out in a spray of shattering glass, and flames roared out and up the side of the building. 'You're needed in the stableyard.'

As Doig had said, the horses had been got out of the stable, which was blazing merrily at one end. Three, an elderly gelding and two stout ponies, were now galloping and snorting round the nearest fenced grazing, much alarmed by the situation. A fourth appeared to be tied at the far side of the patch of grazing, tossing its head and tugging at the rope, squealing with rage or fright. The Cleuch servants were running to and from the well with buckets, attempting to control the fire, though Gil suspected they had as little hope of saving this building as the main house, and smoke and sparks were drifting everywhere, rising with the roar of the flames and all falling across the yard.

'Three was in the stable,' said Steenie, 'and they got them out, cleverly done it was, wi sacks ower their een, though one lad was kicked, and put them in the parrock here. But that fellow was tied there a'ready.'

Gil peered through the grey dawnlight at the distant animal, which whinnied and tossed its head, trampling with its forefeet again as he watched.

'Is he saddled?' he asked.

'He is,' said Steenie. 'I could do wi a hand. Come and look.'

He led Gil round the outside of the fence and in at the gate, fastening it carefully behind them with the loop of rope over the gatepost. The gelding galloped up to them, snorting, and swerved away at the last moment, the ponies thundering after it.

'It's no just the fire,' said Steenie. 'They've company in here, and they're no liking it.' He whacked a speeding pony on the rump as it passed him, neatly dodged the flying heels, and set off along the fence, keeping close to the planks.

'Company?'

Gil, sniffing cautiously as he followed, realised he could smell something other than the smoke and the sweating horses, something unpleasantly familiar. Not just blood, but the extra stink of death, of loosed bowels and bladder. The tethered horse was tied to an over-hanging branch, and the dark patch beneath him was not simply the shadow of the branch and his muscular barrel in the leaping light. Nor were the dark markings on his forelegs the colouring of a bay horse, because the rest of the animal was chestnut.

'Watch him, maister,' warned Steenie. 'He's in a right passion, poor brute. What this fellow did to him, to make him hammer him like that, I canny tell.' He moved slowly forward, a hand out, chirruping to the stallion, then switched to hissing between his teeth as one did while rubbing a horse down. The animal tossed his head, whinnied loudly, stamped with those dreadful stained forefeet, but swung his hindquarters away from Steenie, watching him warily. 'If I can get his tether,' Steenie said quietly, 'can you get the corp, maister? Siss-siss-siss, clever lad, good lad.'

147

'What's left o't,' Gil said sombrely, looking at the pulped and hideous object under the stallion's hooves.

'Aye, poor brute,' said Steenie again, 'tethered next to that. Good lad, good lad. You're tired, are you no? Come and we'll find you a better place to stand. Siss-siss-siss . . .' Still talking soothing nonsense, he reached out, lifted the knotted reins from the beast's neck and looped them over his arm, then drew his knife. A quick slash, a calming word when the stallion threw his head up, and the tether was severed. 'Come up, lad. Back up. Back up,' Steenie coaxed, turning the handsome chestnut head so the thing on the ground was hidden. 'Come and we'll wash you clean, get the stink off you.'

The chestnut drew a deep shuddering breath, blew it out, and dropped his head against Steenie's chest, his proud stance relaxing. Steenie caressed the muscular neck, and Gil bent and seized the corpse's boots, admiring the man's skill. He could have attempted the like with a dog, but he had not Steenie's knack with horses.

The gelding and the two stout ponies had calmed now that the stallion was quieter. They stood at the far end of the little field, watching intently as Gil dragged the battered corpse towards the gate. The head and one arm had taken most of the damage; it was difficult even to see what colour the man's hair had been let alone identify him, even in the growing light of the new morning.

Achieving the gate, he opened it and dragged the corpse through, then dealt with the rudimentary fastening. As soon as the gate was shut the gelding dropped its head and began grazing, and shortly the ponies followed its example. Steenie had retreated to the far end of the paddock, beside the other beasts, and appeared to be washing the stallion's forelegs with handfuls of grass dipped into the water-trough which stood there. In the stableyard, smoke still poured from the stable building, though there were no flames visible; beyond that range the house was burning furiously, black and grey smoke towering into the brightening sky, flames leaping through it. There was the occasional crash and burst of sparks as a section collapsed.

Somerville's remaining household were still wearily throwing bucketfuls of water on the stable building. Each still raised a hiss and gout of steam, and they seemed to have the sense to carry on meantime. Gil looked at the corpse at his feet, and hunkered down for a closer look. Who was this, and more to the point what was he doing dead in the Cleuch paddock? Was it the Irishman Sandy Boyd was so intent on killing, or another?

The man was shorter than Gil by a handspan, and much wider in the girth, almost stout. Was he a priest, Gil wondered. His clothing was sober enough, doublet and hose of good plain stuff in a dark tawny, and a short gown which was now very muddy but had begun yesterday as a pale brown colour. His hat was not visible, likely pounded into the bloody mire where the stallion had been tethered. The neck and jaw, which would stiffen first, were badly mangled by the shod hooves,but seemed to be hardening; the man must be dead at least a couple of hours, maybe nearer four, he reckoned. If this was the Irishman's doing, likely he had killed this man first, perhaps pursuing him when he set out from the house, and then returning to attend to Somerville.

The purse at the dead man's belt yielded only a pair of beads, a few coins and a set of tablets in a velvet pouch. Gil loosened the cord and slid the tablets out; the covers were carved wood, with hunting scenes, deer on one, a smaller scene of hawking on the other. Not cheap, he considered. He opened the cover, and studied the

149

leaves within by the dawnlight. Some scrawled numbers, apparently an attempt at working out an account; a note of today's date, no, yesterday's, *xvi iunii cluch*, and a list of places. *Ayer, irving, dowglass, lanrik,* it read.

'Ayr, Irvine, Douglas, Lanark,' he said aloud. 'Progress towards Edinburgh?'

He looked down at the tablets again. The next line said *Nott glassgowe. I'm glad to hear it*, he thought, and wondered what was wrong with what he was looking at. The writing was clumsy, but many people sufficiently well-to-do to possess a set of tablets like this were still unaccustomed to using them. He flipped the covers shut, to admire the carving, which must have been custom-made, and then open again.

That was it. They opened on the wrong side. His own set, Alys's, every set he was familiar with, even the cheap ones which were used to send word to Maister Vary, opened at the right-hand edge like a book. This set opened at the left edge, with the silk cord hinge at the right side of the principal carving, the deerhunt which covered the whole surface.

'Corrie-fisted,' he said aloud. 'We've found our left-handed man.'

He put the tablets back in their pouch, stowed that in the man's purse, and began to check the rest of his clothing. There was nothing in the sleeves of the short gown, nor in its collar or wide lapels, but something which crackled, and something with sharp corners, lay within the blood-stiffened breast of the tawny doublet. He was unlacing the doublet to find the items when a sword-blade inserted itself between him and the corpse.

'Back away,' said a voice calmly. 'Back away now, you villain. Robbing a corp, are you— Gil Cunningham!'

He sat back on his heels, looking up at the wielder of the sword from under the wide brim of his father's helm.

'Robert Hamilton,' he said. 'Good day to you.'

Robert Hamilton of Lockharthill, youngest son of Hamilton of Avondale and the Sheriff's depute in this part of Lanarkshire, put up the sword, and gestured to the devastation about him.

'What's ado here?' he asked. 'I can get nothing from that bunch o daft laddies, but Somerville's lying deid and mutilat' at his own front door, and now I find you despoiling another— St Peter's balls, what's come to him?' he demanded, getting a clearer look at the state of the corpse.

'I suspect,' said Gil, going back to his task, 'that we were meant to think yon chestnut trampled him to death.'

'But?' prompted Hamilton intelligently. Gil pushed aside the fronts of the doublet, revealing a great blood-stain on the shirt beneath, with a slit at the centre.

'If he was slain,' he speculated, 'or at least knifed like this, and then thrown under the beast's feet where it was tethered, it would be rearing and trampling, trying to get away from the smell of blood. And a course the more it trampled, the worse the smell of blood would get. My man's soothing the beast now,' he added. 'He kens a good horse tonic wi hemp in it, will calm him down.'

'St Peter's balls,' said Hamilton again. 'The poor brute!' He took a step back. 'Get on and examine him, Gil. Did I no hear you're Blacader's quaestor now? Is that what's brought you here? I came to see what the smoke was about, for you can see it from here to Edinburgh I'd wager. We saw the flames afore the sun rose.'

'In a way,' said Gil carefully. 'I'd come up here wanting a word wi Robert Somerville, and encountered the household at a loss, for they'd newly found him deid. It was while I was viewing the corp that the house took

151

fire, in more than one place at once, and the stables at the same time.'

'Arson,' said Hamilton.

'It seems like.'

'Hmph,' said Hamilton. 'Right. Get on and examine him,' he said again, 'and come up to the house and tell me what's what. I need to question these fellows. Is this all Somerville had about him, a cartload of daft laddies?'

'I think he'd sent the best of the household out an errand,' said Gil drily. 'It's cost him his life, and his house, and a deal of pain aforehand. I'm glad I'm no his heir.'

'*Et moi aussi*,' said Hamilton, and strode off out of the stableyard. Gil grinned, recalling that the phrase had been about all the French Hamilton had acquired in their time in Paris, that and the more useful, '*Une grande carafe de vin, ma belle.*'

As soon as the other man was out of sight, he fished inside the breast of the corpse's doublet, and extracted a folded bundle of papers and another set of tablets. Without surprise, he saw that these were a match for the two sets already delivered to Maister Vary, this one decorated with a bright woodcut of the Last Trump. Opening them, he found the stark message: *CEIS TO SEIK HIR*. Cease to seek her; abandon the search. This must be M, as he had feared.

Setting this aside, he opened out the bundle of papers. After a brief scrutiny he folded them down again and stowed them, as the corpse had, in the breast of his doublet. The sheet on the top was a letter introducing a man called Felim O Flaherty, and begging the recipient to hear his words. It seemed likely to Gil that his cousin Sandy was the best person to deal with this.

He got to his feet, stretching the cramp out of his legs, and called to Steenie, who had finished washing the stallion and was now petting the creature while it grazed warily, making much of it with sympathetic tone and words. Steenie led the beast over to the fence, and Gil said quietly, 'Is he up to the journey home to Belstane?'

'If we take it slow,' said Steenie. 'He could do wi a feed, but he's had a bite o grass while we been stretching his legs. He'll manage for a bit.'

'Get away the now,' Gil said, 'you should find another gate in the wall out ayont the tower-house, and wait for me where we left the horses. We'll take him to my mother. I've no notion who he belongs to, but one of her mares must be ready the now. She'll kill me if I pass up the chance o his get, and it'll take his mind off this.' He gestured at the corpse, and the horse startled away from him.

Steenie grinned broadly, touched his blue bonnet and began to coax the stallion towards the gate. Gil watched them go, as did the gelding and the two ponies, and then turned away to go up to the house.

It was a dismal sight. The two end wings had fallen in, the timbers of its frame black against the early-morning sky, smoke still drifting up from the interior. The hall, its limestone walls blackened, had survived for the most part and stood roofless and elegant, some of the glass still in the windows catching the sun. The bonfire smell clung to everything, and in the courtyard before the smouldering ruins, Robert Hamilton of Lockharthill was attempting to question the remaining household.

He was not having a lot of success, at least partly because the young men were exhausted, hungry and half-asleep. He was further distracted by most of the men of Forth who had arrived to lend a hand now it was daylight, wishing to question their various sons or nephews among the group and bear them home to be fed, washed and put to bed. When Gil arrived,

153

Hamilton was engrossed with Doddie Allen's account of the night.

'And Maister Cunningham seen it was on fire,' the lad was saying, 'and his man seen the stables was on fire, and we all ran to get the beasts out the stables, so we couldny put out the fire in the house, and any road the house was on fire both sides and the hall and all, we'd never ha got enough water out the well, it was running dry afore we put the stables out.' He paused to yawn enormously. 'Maister, can I get gaun hame? I'm that weary.'

'D'you ken what happened to Somerville?' demanded Hamilton. Doddie shook his head.

'No me, maister. I never seen him till he was lying here in the yard, I'd ha boaked at the sight o him, I'd surely mind. It's no right what was done to him, nor to Davie.'

'Away hame, lad,' said Hamilton, not unkindly. 'Aye, Gil. Come and tell me what you ken.'

Gil, trying not to yawn as Doddie had done, delivered an elisive summary of the events of the night, feeling that his cousin and Doig were distractions better omitted. Hamilton heard him out, frowning.

'You found Somerville like this,' he said, nodding at the man's ruined countenance. 'Did you no attempt to find the man responsible?'

'I did,' Gil responded. 'That's who I was seeking when I realised the house was alight. It's my belief he got away.'

'Is it?' Hamilton eyed him, frowning again. 'How d'ye make that out?'

'We found a window open, and I'd say it was the same man that thought o knifing another fellow and throwing him under the stallion's feet, though that's likely been an hour or two earlier.'

'Aye.' Hamilton turned this over. 'Aye, you could be right. The way he's hacked wee bits off Somerville, it fair turns yir belly. Do we ken who he is?'

'I've never a notion. I wish I did,' said Gil, with partial truth. 'Maybe these fellows could gie you a description. Him or his horse,' he added on an inspiration.

'And the same fellow slit this lad's throat,' said Hamilton, looking at the second body. One of the older men who had arrived knelt by it, blue bonnet in hand, head bent. 'How'd that come about? Oh, aye, you said, he wouldny stay wi you, he gaed off on his own and the fellow took him in the dark. Somerville should ha stayed in his tower-house,' he added. 'He'd ha been a sight better defended. I'll wager the heir will move back in there.'

'And there's a hot trod going about the Upper Ward,' Gil remembered. 'If you come across them, send them hame to Belstane.'

'A hot trod?' repeated Hamilton incredulously. 'What, for this?'

'No, for the lassie Madur that's missing from Lanark. That's what brought me up here,' Gil admitted. As he guessed it might, this led to another long explanation. Hamilton heard him out, shaking his head.

'I knew of this: Provost Lockhart sent word. You'd think we dwelt in the Marches. So have you any notion who the corp in the stableyard might be? Or where the lassie is?'

'None,' said Gil, again with partial truth. 'You're as done as the men,' said Hamilton eyeing him.

'I could do wi asking some questions, just the same,' said Gil. Hamilton nodded, and waved the last of Somerville's household forward. It was the man Danny, who had insisted there was no lassie present at The Cleuch. In answer to Hamilton's questions, he gave the

155

same account as his fellow, that he had never seen Somerville dead till his corpse appeared in the yard, that he had been searching the house when the cry of fire went up.

'Who was at the house afore that?' Gil asked. Danny looked at him sharply, startled by the change of subject. 'There was Somerville himself, but who else was here?'

'There was Madur o Eastshiel.'

'Of Eastshiel?' Gil repeated. 'That's Jocelyn? No Henry?'

'I couldny say, maister,' said Danny, becoming sulky. 'No having been presentit. Our steward cried him Eastshiel, is all I ken.'

'Mind your tone, man,' said Hamilton.

'Was that all?' Gil asked quickly. 'Somerville, and Madur of Eastshiel?'

'There was—' Danny hesitated, and looked about him warily, as if expecting someone to leap over the wall, knife in hand. 'There was,' he said again, and swallowed. 'It's an Irishman, see, that's been here two-three days. I never heard his name.'

'Describe him,' said Hamilton.

'Well, he's Irish,' said Danny, as if that was sufficient. Under patient questioning, he divulged that the Irishman was of great height, black-haired and black-bearded, 'wi manners like the gentry though he doesny look it', and his horse was no longer on the premises, being a piebald, hogged and docked and fifteen hands in height wi a great black stripe down his brow and a black mark on his quarters like a cat's face.

'We should be able to find that,' said Hamilton in satisfaction. 'Have you more questions, Gil?'

'Aye,' said Gil. 'When did the steward go out fro here, Danny? And what's his name?'

'He's a Somerville and all,' said Danny cautiously. 'Jackie. He's a second cousin, I think.'

'And he left?' Gil pressed.

'Afore supper, it was. Maybe four o the clock?'

'Was he no expected back the night?' Hamilton asked.

Danny shrugged. 'They never tellt me. Nor where he went,' he added, anticipating the next question. 'Just it was him and all the other men rode out, and left us to mind the house, and then Davie,' his voice cracked and his face crumpled, 'Davie found Somerville deid and we none o us kent where Eastshiel was nor the Irishman, and then it came dark, and there was naeb'dy to order us, till Maister Cunningham came. Can I go to my Da, maister?' He scrubbed at his eyes with one hand, and waved the other at the man kneeling by the side of the dead boy.

'Aye,' said Hamilton, sighing. 'And I still canny learn how these two corps came down into the yard. It wasny you, was it, Gil?'

'No,' said Gil.

'They must ha flown.' Hamilton eyed Gil in the morning light. 'You're as beat as the men. Get away home wi ye, if ye will. I'll be in touch.'

Chapter Eight

Alys helped herself to more porridge, reflecting that breaking one's fast to the sound of argument was never a good beginning to the day.

'You're telling me,' said Adam Crombie explosively, 'that he found where my mother's been till yesterday afore suppertime, and never followed on to where she's been taken now? I've a mind to go and waken him—'

'You'll not bother, maister,' said Lady Egidia from her great chair by the empty fireplace. 'You've had a night's sleep, my son hasny, since he was putting out fires until after sunrise. Besides, we've no idea where she's been taken.'

'One o Madur's houses, one o Somerville's,' said Crombie. 'That's none so many, he'd just to go round and ask.'

'Fetching up at the door and shouting isny maybe the best way to win her free,' offered Michael. Crombie glared at him. Ignoring this, Michael put his empty porridge bowl on the plate-cupboard, to the visible disappointment of Socrates, and began to smear butter on a wedge of bread. 'I think it's time we spoke wi the Depute.'

'He was up at The Cleuch at dawn, by what Gil said,' Alys offered.

'How would they move two women and a baby about Lanarkshire,' Lady Egidia wondered suddenly, 'without it being noticed? They'd ha recognised Beattie Lithgo at Forth as soon as set eyes on her, let alone down by Castlehill. She lived in your house, after all, and went all across there wi her herbs and her wisdom.'

'Maybe inside a litter?' Michael suggested. 'If the curtains were down and they were threatened no to speak out, none would ken who was inside. Or what.'

'There's no that many folk go about in a horse-litter,' said Lady Egidia, frowning. 'It's the likeliest answer, but it would still be noticed. Worth questioning the folk at Forth, I'd ha thought.'

'Aye, and why did Cunningham no do that while he was there?' demanded Crombie.

'I'll ride to Lockharthill wi you,' said Michael reluctantly, 'and we'll talk to Robert Hamilton. I think it would take the Depute's word, and some o his men and all, to get cooperation at some o these houses, given that Somerville and Madur the younger are deid.'

Or even more than that, thought Alys, but said nothing.

'Thank you, Michael,' said Lady Egidia. He reddened.

'Aye, well, Tib's in a right tirravee about this. She's bade me do all I can.'

'I'll ride for Lanark,' Alys said. 'May I take Henry, madam?'

Her mother-in-law looked closely at her, eyebrows raised, and finally nodded.

'A good idea,' she said. 'Take your man Euan and another and all.'

Alys pulled a face, but agreed. Gil would be in no mood when he woke for Euan's insouciant approach to life; better to get the man out of his way.

'I still canny see,' said Crombie, 'why it's taken this long to get this little. You'd think as many men searching Lanarkshire would ha turned something up afore now.'

'If only this cartload of gunpowder,' agreed Michael.

'It's a big county, maister,' Lady Egidia reminded him pointedly. 'Now if you're to reach Lockharthill wi time enough to ride on, you'd best get moving.'

When the two young men had left the hall, she looked at Alys, eyebrows raised again.

'I thought to call on, on, on Madame Olympe,' Alys said. 'Her maid will be present,' she added. 'And on the way, I shall go into St Andrew's kirk and get another word with St Malessock. He should have a care to Mistress Lithgo, after all.'

'A good notion,' agreed Lady Egidia, with some ambiguity. 'There's a lot you could ask.'

'So I thought,' said Alys. She set her bowl down for the dog, and caught her breath as the kitten scampered out from under the plate-cupboard to investigate. Socrates, finding a morsel of grey striped fur climbing into the bowl, lifted his head, staring down at the little creature, then waited carefully until it had had its fill before he continued to lick out the dish. Alys made no comment, but bent to pat his head as she passed him, and he wagged his tail briefly.

'Silky's dam was the same,' said Lady Egidia reminiscently. 'She had my lord's dogs cowed before she was three months.'

St Andrew's kirk was busy, at this early hour in the day. Many in the village had called in to pay their respects before one altar or another, Sir John and his clerk were singing Terce in the chancel, a group of elderly women were in avid discussion near the south door, and St Malessock's side-chapel blazed with lights. Clearly he was popular in the parish he protected. Alys, putting

161

some coins in the offertory box, selected a candle, lit it from another and fixed it on the pricket-stand next to the altar-rail, curtsying to the painted wooden box on the altar where St Malessock rested. Then she knelt on the folds of her skirt and drew out her beads, not the Sunday set of red glass with her mother's little cross and her grandfather's carved cockleshell on it, but the every-day wooden ones with the St Elizabeth medal, just as eloquent under her fingers.

Drawing a breath, she turned her mind to the battered figure she had seen raised from the peat, two years since, when Beatrice Lithgo had been accused of murder. Naked but for a fox-skin girdle, slain in three ways and drowned in the bog, the man had lain there for who knew how long, but Sir John had decided he knew his name and translated him to the kirk, and the small healings had begun almost immediately. *Blessed Malessock*, thought Alys, *if that is your name; there is one of your subjects missing, a wise-woman who uses her gifts for good, and a young woman taken for her harm. Show me how to find them, how to rescue them. You are the guardian of your people,* she thought, *use me as your shield. And Gil as well,* she added hastily, and was suddenly aware of a ripple of – was it amusement? Her eyes flew open, but there was nothing to see.

And why did I call Mistress Lithgo his subject? she wondered. Saints don't have subjects.

'Is that yourself, Mistress Mason?' said an aged voice nearby. She turned her head, to find a pair of old women watching her with beady eyes. Searching memory, she found their names, and jumped to her feet, hands out to clasp theirs in greeting.

'Mistress Mally, Mistress Isa,' she said. 'Forgive me, I never learned your surnames. Are you both well?'

Both were well enough, though she had to hear all the detail of what had ailed them the past winter. She coaxed them to the bench at the wall-foot, thinking they should not stand so long, and heard them out politely.

'And yoursel, mistress?' said Isa, the small spare one with the claw-like hands. 'I've no heard any news o ye this last year or so?' She cocked her head enquiringly.

'No,' she said, aware that her colour was rising. 'I'm well enough.'

'Hmph. And is that right,' said Isa, cutting across something her stouter friend was about to say, 'that your man's trying to find the lassie Madur that's gone missing?'

'It is,' Alys agreed. Their eyes brightened, and she settled down to tell them as much as she felt was wise. They listened eagerly, with occasional glances at one another, much nodding and significant *Mphm* sounds.

'And still no sign o her,' said Isa when she finished. 'Taken fro The Cleuch afore supper last night, and vanished again.'

'They might ha seen her go down through Forth,' said Mally.

'They might,' said Isa. 'But it's in my mind Rab Somerville had a place ower towards Lothian.'

'Did he, now?' said Alys. 'Where would that be?'

'Oh, I've no notion,' said the old woman, her gaze raking Alys's face. 'I was never out o Carluke, save to the Lanimer Fair once when I was a lassie, I couldny say where it is. But it's up in the hills ahint The Cleuch, by what I heard.' She paused, thinking.

'It's Tanbrack, isn't it no, Isa,' said Mally.

'No,' said Mally decisively. 'That's no the name.' She considered again. 'Tarbrax. Aye, Tarbrax, that's it.'

'Tarbrax,' repeated Alys. 'I will tell my husband.'

'Will ye, now?' said Isa, the bright eyes gleaming. 'Here, Mally, we'd best get on. That's Sir John done wi Terce, we've a kirk to clean here.'

163

'Oh, aye,' said Mally with reluctance. She rose, lifting a bundle of cloths from the bench beside her. Isa watched her bustle off, then turned to Alys, putting a hand on her arm.

'Listen, my pet,' she said quietly. Alys stared into the wrinkled face. 'I was four year waiting for my first. Then we did it, ye ken? we did it in the orchard, under the apple trees, at the new moon. I'm no saying that's the answer, but it's aye worth a try.'

Alys, anchored by those bright eyes while the church swung round her, nodded. The old woman patted her arm, and got to her feet. Alys found enough voice to say, 'Thank you!'

Isa waved a clawed hand, and trotted off after her friend, leaving Alys staring. In the orchard, at new moon. And how would she persuade Gil – *could* she persuade Gil? Would she have to behave like, well, like a—

'Mistress?' Henry was beside her. 'The day's wearing on. Are ye for Lanark, indeed?'

'Aye, very true, madam,' said Mistress Whitehead. 'It's a sad tale, and I canny see that it'll end well.' She arranged her mustard-coloured velvet sleeves, which Alys reckoned must have come off the same bolt as her husband's best gown, and fanned herself happily. 'And you, Mistress Mason,' she added, turning from Madame Olympe to Alys. 'Did I hear you say your man's hunting for the lassie?'

'He is,' Alys agreed. 'He's had no luck so far, though he was out all last night.'

'Oh, he was, was he?' Mistress Whitehead's tone altered to a prurient sympathy. 'All night?'

'He was at The Cleuch when it burned down,' Alys said innocently. 'Robert Somerville's house.'

164

Beyond the Provost's wife, Madame Olympe hid a smile in her silken sleeve and said in shocked tones, 'Burned down? *Ma foi*, what is this? I had thought Lanark a peaceable place, and are people burning one another's houses down?'

'I heard about that and all!' exclaimed Mistress Whitehead. 'What happened, mistress? Was it fire-raising, or a candle owerset, or what? Your man was up at the very house? Did he see how it begun?'

'Nobody kens how the fire started,' said Alys. 'It's sad, Somerville died, and one of his men.'

'Well!' said Mistress Whitehead. 'And is that right, that there was none o his household there, so the house and stables burned to the ground, and all in it?'

'Few of the household were present. They got the beasts out,' said Alys, 'but the house was lost while they did that. My husband was directing the men, and said the well ran dry afore the fire was out.'

'Well!' said Mistress Whitehead again, in suppressed excitement. As Alys had hoped, after a very short while she excused herself, on the grounds of a press of household duties, and left Madame Olympe's lodging, calling to her groom. Alys, peering circumspectly from the window a moment later, saw her hurrying, not towards her own house, but across the wide street, to order her man to rattle at another wide door.

'She'll have that spread round the town by dinner-time,' surmised Madame Olympe in French. 'Cleverly done, cousin. Enough to keep her happy, nothing to endanger her.'

'She's fly, this one,' observed Agnes in Scots, coming into the chamber with a tray. 'Here's a wee refreshment, mistress, you'll be dry after the ride from Carluke.' She set the tray down on a kist and poured something with leaves in it from the jug.

'And how did you leave them all?' Madame Olympe enquired, passing a beaker as Alys thanked the woman.

'Madame Mère is in excellent health,' Alys replied, sniffing the drink. Recognising a honeyed infusion of garden mint and thyme, she drank gratefully. 'My husband still slept when I left, and the two guests we had last night had departed to find the Depute.' Were they likely to be overheard, she wondered. Did she need to be cautious in naming people?

'And what brings you into Lanark by yourself?' Those pale eyes were studying her. Today Madame was gowned in a screaming green brocade faced with carnation-coloured silk, worn over a kirtle of red and white stripes. The result could do no favours to the natural colours of the fair skin and pale brows, but these were painted in such high contrast, Alys found she could hardly pick out the lineaments of the man who had coaxed Lady Egidia into lending him Gil yesterday evening. This was the reason for the paint, she recognised.

'Two reasons,' she said, smiling sweetly. 'I was to give you these.' She reached into her sleeve and drew out the wad of papers Gil had showed her last night. 'Madur of Eastshiel had them on his person.'

Madame took the papers in one large white hand, unfolded them, and froze briefly.

'Where did you— how did you come by these?'

Alys relayed Gil's account of the trampled corpse, its retrieval, and his discovery of the papers and the tablets with the undelivered message. Madame Olympe listened, skimming the papers meantime, then sat back and smiled.

'What a gift he has sent me!' she pronounced. 'This is as a ruby of great price, and I thank you for bringing it to me.'

166

'*De rien*,' said Alys. Madame looked from the papers to her face.

'And your second reason? You said you had two reasons.'

Alys looked her in the eye. 'I need answers from you,' she said bluntly.

Madame tittered, and raised a hand in assumed surprise. '*You* need—?'

'Yes.' She met the pale, challenging stare. 'If my husband goes into danger, I wish to know why.' Madame made no answer. 'There is more at stake here than one young wife and her baby. I've read those papers, madame. What was Somerville playing for?'

'Oh, my dear, how should I know?'

'No,' she said, 'I won't accept that. The day you don't know what the stakes are in any game you're in is the day you will lose it.'

'I tellt ye she was fly, this one,' said Agnes. She had lifted some mending and seated herself by the window, with an excellent view of the street.

'Agnes,' said Madame, in warning tones.

'So what was Somerville entangled in?' Alys pressed. 'Who is the man who rode away on the pied horse, and why did he question his hosts *à l'outrance* before he left, and then fire the house and stables? I assume, whatever his name is, it isn't Felim O Flaherty.'

'Is that all you want to know?' asked Madame, an edge in her voice.

'By no means, but it's a start.' Alys smiled at the pale eyes set in their bright paint. 'Come, we are on the same side, and I am used to keeping counsel. Oh, and what do you know about the gunpowder?'

After a moment Madame's tinted mouth twisted.

'I am not certain, you understand.' Alys nodded, but kept her disbelief to herself. 'The man on the pied horse

167

is Irish. He seeks those willing to,' Madame paused, selecting a word. 'To eliminate a certain person at a time when he is a guest of the Scottish Crown.'

'At whose behest?'

Madame shrugged, with a rustle of brilliant green silk.

'The Tudor, I imagine, though more than he would like to see the boy vanish from the board.'

'Not an Irish— not anyone in Ireland?'

'There are some who have lands in Ireland and in the Isles as well. Those who disapprove of offers which have been made already to the boy.'

'Offers of friendship and support,' Alys stated. 'An offer of marriage.' She smiled again into the painted face. 'Gil told me this last night. Come, there is more. This name, for a start, O Flaherty. What does that tell you?'

'It isn't his name, of course. As you said.'

'We have a description, of sorts.' Alys relayed what Gil had told her. Madame Olympe nodded, as if she had expected it, and Alys added, 'I have set Euan to ask about Lanark for the pied horse. The markings sound distinctive.'

'Ah, the egregious Euan Campbell. He won't find the beast, our man won't risk Lanark.'

'Further, he has only to shave to change his appearance mightily,' Alys said.

'As a final recourse only. They are much attached to their beards, these Irish.' Madame tittered. The sound had not changed, Alys thought, since they first met.

'*Eh bien*, tell me about him! How dangerous is he? Why does he want to find Audrey Madur?'

'Why should he?' countered Madame Olympe. 'She's surely no great prize.'

'Why then did he question his hosts?' Alys said again. 'What other matter could they have had or known, that he wanted?'

'Did they have aught that he'd want?' put in Agnes in Scots. 'A jewel, a paper? Could they ha hid something in the bairn's wrappings, or the like?'

'Heavens, I hope not!' said Alys.

'*Qui peut dîre?*'

Madame shrugged dramatically, spreading her white hands.

'Sandy,' said Alys crossly, 'we already know you are a *solsecle of swetnesse and lady of lealte*. Now will you stop fencing like this and answer me direct? I'm concerned for Gil, and for Audrey Madur, before anything else, but I'll serve the Crown so well as I may after that. Now tell me about the Irishman. Or begin at the other end: what could Audrey's uncles know or hold that he would want? What were they doing? Where did they get the money for this venture, whatever it is?'

'Money?' said Madame warily.

'My good-mother says both are perpetually short of money,' said Alys, 'but Gil has described The Cleuch to me. Even by lantern-light, it was a handsome house, well appointed and quite new built. I could make a good guess at how much Somerville paid for it, first and last. What has he been at?'

Madame Olympe sat back and began to laugh, dropping the elaborate manner so that Sandy Boyd surfaced.

'It bites!' he said. 'I'm sorry, cousin, I do you an injustice. I should remember you took a wanted murderer on your own the last time we met.' Alys maintained her quelling stare. 'Very well.' He crossed long legs under the gaudy silks, displaying one large, elegant leather shoe. 'So far as I know, Jocelyn Madur and Somerville hatched a plan with the late burgh clerk to plant out timber on the Burgh Muir, which is like to cause a riot when the burgesses get to know of it. I do not know whence came the funding, though I suspect not from Ballantyne. They stole away Mistress Audrey to use as a bargaining token with her man, to get them permission before the Council to use part of the common land.'

'That would not be lawful,' Alys objected. Boyd shrugged one shoulder.

'*Une bagatelle*. Our good friend William brought the little trees from Ireland. I am not certain how much more he carried, but there was certainly a cartload of trees.'

'Ah.'

Boyd nodded, and continued, 'He tells me, and who am I to doubt him, that he took exception to the use of a lady in Audrey's state, and demanded his due payment from Ballantyne, who laughed at him. Then Ballantyne was slain, not by Billy, I suppose by Somerville from what your good-brother had to report, and so we come to what you know already.'

Not entirely, thought Alys, but close enough. What has he left out?

'Do you know where Tarbrax is?' she asked. Boyd blinked in startlement.

'No,' he said.

'I was told Somerville has a place there.' She considered him. 'I want to ride up to Forth and question them there, to see if they saw Audrey being moved. Even shut into a horse-litter, she'd be noticed, I'd have thought.'

'True,' agreed Boyd.

'Will you ride with me?'

He looked even more startled, and Agnes raised her head from her mending, looking from one to the other.

'I think you should, madam,' she said in Scots. 'Mistress Mason has her men wi her, it's no as if you'd be

170

riding out your lone. You've the blue worsted riding-dress,' she added.

Getting Madame Olympe apparelled for riding and on horseback was less than straightforward. The blue worsted riding-dress, braided on body and sleeves with enough red and green silkwork, Alys estimated, to trim any three of her gowns, was not easily assumed, given how many parts must be laced, buckled, strapped and tied on. The headdress which went with it was similarly secured by two separate gilded leather straps. Certainly, Alys reflected, if Madame took a tumble from her horse, she would not wish her headdress to come off. Over that went a wide-brimmed straw hat. Then a pair of red leather boots must be introduced on to Madame's large feet and shapely legs.

'*Mon Dieu*, what a labour of Hercules!' exclaimed Madame, as Agnes fastened the buckles on these. 'We must take food with us, or I shall faint with exhaustion!'

Agnes, rolling her eyes, set out to the Nicholas Inn to order matters, and shortly returned with Alys's men, who were leading the Belstane horses and a sturdy bay with a wall eye.

Henry, assessing the two figures on Maister Lightbody's doorstep, said only, 'Where are we for, mistress?'

'Forth,' said Alys crisply as he put her up into the saddle of her own beast. 'Is it far?'

He thought briefly, watching Euan attempting to offer Madame Olympe a knee to mount by while the third man, a garrulous fellow called Patey, held the bay's bridle.

'Eight mile or so. No that bad. I wondered why she,' he jerked his head at Agnes, 'wantit bread and cheese in the saddlebags.'

171

Riding through Lanark in company with Madame Olympe was an experience Alys felt she would rather not repeat. People turned to look, many ladies curtsied and waved, small boys ran alongside the horses until Henry threatened them with his whip.

'You never do anything unobtrusively, do you?' she said.

'Oh, my dear, why would I do that?' returned Madame, with a hand at her jaw. 'One must always be observed. Why else were we given clothes to wear?'

'For modesty?' Alys offered, thinking of Mère Isabelle's strictures.

'Modesty,' pronounced Madame, 'is for those who have that concerning which to feel modest. You, for instance, my dear. The rest of us must make do with being noticed.' She waved and bowed to the gate-ward on the North Port, while Alys tasted this remark, coming to the conclusion that it was a compliment.

It was another hot day, and nearing noon. About them the fields lay peaceful, the grain ripening, the second crop of hay rising almost while one watched. Larks sang overhead, small brown birds whirred back and forward between the grassy banks on either side of the road, a kestrel hovered on their right. A straw hat like Madame's might have been a good idea, Alys thought.

'Where is this Forth?' Euan asked behind her. 'I was thinking it is the river where Linlithgow is, but we will not be riding so far the day, surely?'

'It's a wee toun up yonder,' said Patey, waving an arm at the hills which rose purple ahead of them. 'Aye windy up there, the folks a' grow sideyways like trees.'

'These hills are very different from Ardnamurchan,' said Euan, his tone disapproving. 'Barely they deserve to be called hills.'

172

'Still kill you if you get lost out here in bad weather,' said Henry.

'What did you find when you led the trod to Castlehill?' Alys asked Henry. He shook his head.

'That was a waste o time. I'd my doubts the hale time we was there,' he admitted, 'but what wi young Crombie shouting about his mammy, and Richie Thomson the steward going on about how affrontit he was, what an inconvenience and offence this was for his tenant, which is a William Lindsay that's a cousin to Montrose, it was kinna hard to keep my mind on what I was at.'

'So what made you doubt them?' Alys asked, aware of Madame Olympe listening.

'For a start, the trail led straight there. You'll no ken the house, mistress?' Alys shook her head. 'It's on a spur atween two burnies where they run into the Mouse, high up, a good spot to defend. They's no other spot they could ha been headed, the way they climbed up out the glen. So claiming he'd never set eyes on the lassie or on Mistress Lithgo, well, it didny hold water. I'd wager Lindsay had no notion o what we asked about,' he added thoughtfully, 'but Thomson kent a lot more than he was saying, for all young Crombie's flyting at him.'

'And you searched the barns,' said Alys.

'I did, mistress, and the outhouses and all. I couldny see any sign there'd been two women and a bairn in any o them. I wished I'd thought to take the dog wi me.'

'He was asleep and snoring,' said Alys. 'You'd ha needed to carry him.'

'Maister Gil said when he cam home, he thought the women had been there for a while and moved on, perhaps direct to The Cleuch. And then moved again last night.' He grinned sourly. 'Ye'd think they'd be seen, all this riding about Lanarkshire by night, and the nights as short the now.'

173

Forth was an unprepossessing village, a huddle of little houses each in its toft, perched on the bare hillside below a tiny church, surrounded by bent trees and ripening crops in the striped fields. The crops, Alys noted, were nowhere near so far on as the grain around Lanark. Several dogs ran out as they approached, barking a warning; they included a couple of shaggy grey creatures with long legs at which Alys stared, frowning. Several children appeared to shout at the dogs and watch, round-eyed, as the travellers rode into the hollowed-out street of the village and halted, looking about them. Somebody ran into one of the low houses, and a couple of men emerged, dressed in patched homespun and peering under their hands at the travellers. One of these came forward, ducking in an awkward bow, blue bonnet in hand revealing a balding pate.

'What's your will, ladies?' he said politely enough. 'Are ye seeking somebody here in Forth? I'm Martin Burns, see, I'm the clerk,' he nodded at the diminutive church further up the hill, 'if there's aught I can do for ye—?'

Alys, finding both Henry and Madame Olympe looking at her, realised she had not completely thought this visit out. She swallowed, and composed her mind.

'I think there was a fire up at the house last night,' she said.

'Aye, there was, mistress.' The clerk bent his head and crossed himself.

'I should like to speak to those who were there.'

'At the fire, mem?' he said, startled.

'I'm Alys Mason. My husband was there,' she said reassuringly, not looking at Madame Olympe. 'Maister Cunningham. He helped the household, and spoke with the Depute after.'

Enlightenment came to his face.

174

'Och, him!' he said. 'Aye, we've cause to be grateful to him right enough. Would ye maybe step inside, mistress, out the sun, and take a drop o Ellen Brewster's ale? Tammas, run to your mammy,' he said to one of the children. 'Bid her bring a couple jugs o ale to my bit.'

'That grey dug wi the long legs,' said Henry, catching Alys as she slid from the saddle, 'it's the image o our Socrates, in't it no? And the other one and all.'

'How could that be possible?' she asked, looking him in the eye. He grinned and gave her a tiny nod. Alys looked about, and found that Madame Olympe, elbows out, her wide skirts held up out of the dust on either side, was already picking her way towards the house Martin the clerk had indicated. Alys followed her, working out what she wanted to ask.

Inside the clerk's house it was dim, and smoky, but there were several stools, two kists and a settle, and a box bed lurked in the shadows at the back of the single chamber. The peat fire glowed red on the central hearth, with a stewpot bubbling quietly above it on a tripod. A woman in a faded red kirtle appeared almost on her heels with a jug of ale slopping over in each hand, eager to pour for Martin Clerk's guests and find out what brought them to Forth. She was a sturdy woman, with bare muscular forearms and a generous bosom, and she lost no time in extracting beakers from a shelf near the door, wiping them carefully with her sacking apron, and filling them with ale, while Burns himself placed seats for his guests. Outside, beyond the open door, Alys was aware of the horses being moved into a shady spot, of another jug of ale being carried for the men.

'And ye're wanting to speak to those that were at the fire,' said Burns, after suitable healths had been drunk. 'Ye'll ken we lost one o the laddies. A sad thing, very sad.'

'I do,' agreed Alys, aware of her companion's silence. 'Our Lady bring him safely from Purgatory.'

'Amen,' agreed Burns, crossing himself again.

'How do the others do the day? I hope they've no trouble wi their breathing.'

'One or two,' he admitted. 'Coughing, pains in the chest, and the like.'

'I can recommend an elixir will help that; we found it a useful thing when I witnessed a great fire at the Blackfriars in Perth. And I suppose there's little work at the house meantime,' she went on. 'That's, is it five households? that have lost earnings, and no saying when Somerville's heir will fee them again.' He nodded. 'I'd like a word wi the mistresses o those households and all.' Madame Olympe looked sharply at her, but remained silent. 'Have you heard aught from the Depute the day, or from the heir?'

'No from the heir, it's ower soon,' said Burns. 'The Depute was in the toun this morn, asking who kent aught, but there was none o our laddies kent nor buff nor stye as to who set the fire nor how it spread, nor where the man might be that rid the pied horse.'

'And Somerville's steward has never shown?'

'Jackie Somerville? No him,' said Burns witheringly. 'If he's heard the word, I's wager he's—' He bit off what he was about to say. Heading for Leith? Alys speculated. Filling his purse? Nothing complimentary, at all events. 'As to the way Somerville was treated,' Burns went on, 'no to mention Eastshiel found deid in the paddock, it's been a dreadful day for The Cleuch yestreen, mistress, a dreadful day.'

'Indeed it has,' she agreed. 'And to think that if Somerville hadny sent half his men away after suppertime, the house might ha been saved.'

'So they say,' he said, eyeing her in the dimness. 'I never seen them go, myself, but the laddies tellt me.'

'What, they never came through Forth?' Alys said, and took another mouthful of the thin, sour ale. 'I'd ha thought they'd ride through here whatever road they took.'

'Aye, well, maybe no if they went the other way,' said Burns. 'If they went to Tarbrax, or the like.'

'Tarbrax?' she asked innocently. 'What's that?'

'Another o Somerville's places. Seven or eight mile east fro here, it is. He doesny— he never dwelt there much, the tower's no in good repair, but there's sheep and a bit barley, and the ferm-toun. They might ha went there.'

'They did,' said Mistress Brewster. 'I seen them.'

'What, are you here yet, Ellen?' said Burns, startled.

'You saw them, mistress?' said Alys. 'How was that?'

She moved forward out of the shadows at the back of the chamber, nodding to Alys, trying unsuccessfully not to stare at Madame Olympe's painted face.

'I was out at the midden after supper,' she said. 'I looked up the hill, and I seen them on the road, gaun away from The Cleuch, up past the ewe-buchts, ye ken? That's the road to Tarbrax, right enough.'

'There's other houses that road,' said Burns dubiously. 'Will ye tak more ale, mistress?'

'I'll take more, wi pleasure,' said Madame Olympe, holding out her beaker, her French accent much moderated. 'Is it your own brew, mistress? I never tasted the like, in Scotland or France.' *A true word*, thought Alys. 'What do you place to the wort? Will you not sit a moment and let me know?'

'Aye, sit, Ellen,' said Burns, getting to his feet, 'while I tak Mistress Mason to speak wi them that was at the house.'

He led Alys out into the street, where Henry and the other two men, in the shade by one of the gable-ends, looked up alertly from the jug of ale. She gestured to them to stay where they were, and followed the clerk to the next house down the hill, away from the little church.

'This is Eck Smellie's house,' he said quietly. 'Danny cam home fro the fire, but Davie didny. Their mother dee'd last Yule, o the chin-cough; there's four more weans after Davie. The neighbours will be in, for the wake.'

She nodded, recognising this for what it was: the priest's recommendation, or that of his delegate, to the giver of charity. Grateful for the preparations she had made before leaving Belstane, she delved for her purse under the wide skirts of her riding-dress, extracted the largest of the small bundles in it, and tucked it into her sleeve.

The house was quiet when she stepped inside, and it took her some moments to realise that the neighbours were indeed present, as many as a dozen people sitting around on stools, on a settle, on the side of the wide bed, some murmuring over their beads, some silent. In the centre of the room, on a board balanced across two more stools, a very young man was laid out, shrouded and draped in a mended blanket by way of a pall. On the floor beside the board two little girls sat, sniffling.

'Madam,' said a voice, and she realised that an older girl was approaching, curtsying awkwardly. 'Forgive us, mem, it's no—'

'Chrissie, away and sit down.' This must be Chrissie's father, stepping in front of the girl, drawing off his bonnet civilly enough. Alys put a hand out to him.

'I'm right sorry for your loss,' she said. 'Our Lady see him safe from Purgatory. I'm— that was my man that was at the house yestreen. I came to see if I could help.'

'Help?' said the father. 'What way could you help? My boy's deid.'

'Now, Eck,' said Burns in a tone of rebuke.

'My husband's seeking the man that set the fire and killed Davie,' Alys said. 'The Irishman. I hoped Danny or the other lads might ha seen something that would help him.'

He stared at her, his expression not entirely friendly. After a moment he turned, jerked his head at one of the seated figures, and said gruffly, 'Danny. Away out and talk to the leddy.'

'And maybe,' Alys added softly, putting the little bundle of coin on one of the shelves near the door, 'this would help tide you over till there's more work.'

Danny, out in the daylight, eyed her in puzzlement.

'I tellt your man all I kent,' he said hoarsely. 'And Hamilton the Depute and all.'

'I might have some other questions,' she said. He was a sturdy young man, slow-moving but apparently rather quicker of thought, with a broad open face and a thatch of mouse-brown hair. 'Tell me, did Somerville ever have any gunpowder at the house?'

'No,' he said, shaking his head blankly. 'What way would he have gunpowder? They's no guns at the house, nor yet cannons nor the like.'

'And how long had the Irishman been at the house?'

'Two-three days,' he said. 'I tellt them that.'

With a little coaxing, he decided that the man had arrived on Saturday, that his horse had been fresh enow, it had likely not been rid far that day. He had never heard the Irishman's name nor heard him speak, it was just that the house servants called him that. Nor had he seen the man leave, but his beast wasny in the stables when they got the horses out from the fire.

'And when the steward left after supper,' Alys said, nodding approval of this conclusion, 'who carried the baby?'

'Oh, that was Tammas Lockhart,' Danny said confidently, barely noticing the change of subject. 'In a kinna sling about his breast.'

'And threatened its mammy not to speak,' she proposed. He took a breath as if to deny it, and doubled over coughing. Alys thumped him firmly on the back, and eventually the spasm passed.

'Aye,' he said, wiping sooty phlegm off his chin. 'Aye, he said that. Or he'd put a knife in its wame. That's no right,' he said, breathing heavily. 'They tellt us no to say aught about it, no to mention it, pain o losing our places, but.' He paused, catching his breath again. 'Seems to me I've lost my place any road. And Doddie's right, it's no a right thing to talk like that to a lassie wi a new bairn.' He drew another difficult breath.

'You must stop speaking,' said Alys. 'Go back in and sit down. This will pass after a few days, but until then you must take care. It's the smoke,' she said reassuringly. 'It does that when it gets into your chest, so you need to cough up the soot.'

The young man went willingly, replacing his blue bonnet as he went, and sat down limply just inside the house door. Alys looked round, and found Martin Burns the clerk at her shoulder.

'Is any here herbwise?' she asked him. 'I'd brew up the elixir I know of, if I could put my hand on the ingredients.'

Maggie Inglis, it seemed, was herbwise, so far as any was in the place.

'That's Will Allen's wife, ye ken,' said Burns. 'This house ower yonder.' He gestured to another tiny cottage set in a well-tended garden, with a fence of woven hazel and more low partitions of sticks and woven rushes, to protect the plants from the searing winds.

'Doddie's mother,' said Alys, calling up the surname

from Gil's account of the night. He stopped to stare at her, hand on the gate.

'Aye, it is, mistress. A good laddie,' he confided, 'but a wee bit saft. Ye ken?'

Mistress Inglis met them at her house door, still pinning on her kurtch, curtsying at the same time, clearly in a state she would herself have called *all of a flither*.

'Mistress!' she said, smiling uncertainly at Alys. 'Was ye wanting a word wi us?'

'With yoursel, mistress. I hoped you might have sage and thyme,' said Alys. 'Maister Burns here tells me you are herbwise. And pepper as well, maybe?' Celery seed would be too much to hope for, she was thinking.

'I've no a lot o pepper,' said Mistress Inglis doubtfully. 'But I've the others growing fresh in the yard here, you can see for yoursel.'

'And honey?' Alys said hopefully.

'Oh, aye, I've that.'

This house, like the others, had one chamber only, but held two box beds and a truckle bed slid under one of them, and not only stools and a settle but a great chair as well. This was offered to Alys, but she refused it, and set about explaining the elixir she wished to concoct. Her hostess heard her out, listening intently in the light from the open door.

'I've never brewed that one,' she admitted, 'but I've heard o all those as sovereign for coughs and chest troubles. It's well worth it, mem, if it helps the laddies, for all five that came home – poor Davie,' she said, dabbing at her eyes, 'all the five has terrible coughs. I'll send the bairn round, see if any o the neighbours has pepper.'

Stepping to the door, she summoned one of the children in the street, and sent him out again with brief instructions, then began to denude her herb-plot of thyme and sage, stripping the leaves into her apron with swift movements. Alys, left inside the house, looked about her and found a young man of much the same age as Danny sitting quietly in a corner.

'Doddie?' she said. He straightened up with a start.

'Aye, mistress?'

She considered, briefly, what she knew already. Best not to make the young man talk too much, after Danny's coughing fit. She did not wish to be accused of making all the Cleuch servants worse.

'Can you tell me, who else has visited the house lately?' she asked. 'I know of Madur of Eastshiel, and the Irishman. Have there been other guests to the house? Other folk that came to speak with Somerville?'

'To the house?' he asked wonderingly. 'I'm no an inside man, I wouldny ken about that.'

'But you hear things,' she said. 'You've the horses to stable, you meet the other servants that ride with the guests. Who else has been to call?'

'I wouldny ken who comes visiting Somerville's other houses,' he said, his voice troubled.

'Of course not, if you were never there.'

'There was Maister Hamilton the Depute,' he offered.

'When was he there?'

'Just yestreen, mistress.'

'Very good,' she said, restraining her impatience. 'That's very good.'

'And there was the lassie that had a bairn, and the auld wife wi her. And the wee bairn.' She could hear in his voice that he was smiling. 'It was a bonnie wee bairn, even if it wasny all in clean linen.'

'All bairns are bonnie,' she agreed, the familiar knot of envy twisting in her stomach. 'Was there anyone else, can you mind?'

182

'I mind,' he said after a moment. 'There was someone last week. More than a week syne.'

'What's this about a bairn, Doddie Allen?' demanded his mother from the doorway. 'There never was a lassie wi a bairn up at The Cleuch! You're telling stories!'

'No, I'm no!' he said indignantly, and began to cough. 'She was there!' he added through the paroxysms. 'She was!'

'Have you a drink of water for him, mistress? It will help,' said Alys, still restraining impatience.

'There,' said Mistress Allen, her hands full of her bundled apron. 'The tub by the door, mem, if you would, and a beaker beside it.'

She fetched water to the young man, and stood over him while he sipped at it, his chest still convulsing. When the coughing stopped, she closed his hand round the beaker. 'Bide quiet till you can speak,' she said, 'and then tell me who came to the house last week.'

'And no more o your stories, my lad,' said his mother roundly.

'There was a bairn up at the house,' said Alys. 'He's not making it up. I need to find the lassie that bore it.'

'Never!' said Mistress Allen, staring at her. 'Who was it? What bairn? Who's the faither?'

'Let me give you a hand with this elixir,' said Alys, 'and I'll tell you, while Doddie gets his breath back.'

By the time the boy could speak, the two women had the herbs chopped and packed into a pipkin and set by the fire, and the child from outside had returned with a handful of peppercorns in a twist of linen cloth from his Auntie Jess, saying she wanted the bit cloth back and the return of the peppercorns when his mammy got the chance.

Mistress Allen, still amazed by what Alys had told her, rewarded the boy with an oatcake and green cheese and went back to speculating on what had made Somerville steal away a respectable lassie, and why. Alys had begun to grind the pepper in Mistress Allen's little mortar when Doddie finally set down the wooden beaker. 'Mistress? 'he said tentatively. 'I minded who it was, right enough.'

'Tell me, then?' she said hopefully. His mother drew breath for more exhortations to tell the truth, and Alys reached out to put a hand on the woman's arm. 'Who was it?'

'Jackie Somerville cried him Maister Vary.'

Chapter Nine

'I don't see why you just let him get away,' said Lady Egidia.

'Mother, I'd little choice,' said Gil. 'I've no authority over Doig, and he's a bonnie fighter forbye, and you canny keep Sandy in one place any more than the smoke from the fire.' And that was a badly chosen word, he realised, as the image of the smouldering house at The Cleuch rose in his mind's eye. 'What did you tell me about Michael and young Crombie?'

'They've gone seeking the Depute,' said his mother, passing the platter of sliced mutton. 'I think Crombie hopes he'll send an armed band and a warrant of some sort to let them search all Somerville's houses.'

'Right.' Gil laid a slice of meat on the wedge of bread he had just buttered, and bit into the result, considering this. 'And Alys is gone to Lanark.'

He had reached home some time after Prime, with Steenie leading the weary chestnut. There had been a great bustle of interest in the beast when they rode into the stableyard, but Gil had left this behind and slipped into the house to encounter his mother and his wife, report briefly, wash and fall into bed. Now, too near noon and with a few hours' sleep behind him, he was seated in the solar, consuming a quantity of food and small ale and describing his night's work in more detail.

'You should call on Mistress Somerville,' said his mother. He pulled a face, but nodded acknowledgement of this. 'I've no idea whether she's had word of what Alys found, that it seemed as if the girl was brought to bed in a cave like someone in a romance. We sent no word last night. Alys wasny right certain, and we thought it better to wait till there was definite news.' Gil nodded again in agreement. 'I wonder if she kent what her brother was at?' she added.

'What I wonder,' he said, swallowing the mouthful he was chewing, 'is where Somerville got all the coin he's been spending.' She raised her eyebrows. 'You described him as *aye short of money*, but he's lately built that great house that's just gone up in smoke, Michael reckons him for a showy dresser, either he or Madur had that bonnie chestnut we brought in this morning—'

'Indeed!' agreed his mother. 'How did you come by him, Gil? Such a handsome beast! And such bone about him, such proud bearing.'

'He's killed a man,' Gil warned, 'or at the least, trampled him after he was dead.' He explained, briefly. 'Steenie managed to gentle him, so he may get over it, but he'd had a bad fright, poor brute.'

'It's a chestnut,' said Lady Egidia, as if that explained everything. Perhaps it did, Gil thought, recalling an overbred chestnut his father had once owned.

'I've no notion who he belongs to. You'll likely need to hand him back.'

'Aye, but until then there's two of the mares at least . . .' Her voice trailed off. He grinned, and helped himself to more bread and meat.

'I still have to track down Audrey and Mistress Lithgo,' he said, adding a spoonful of pickled turnips to the assemblage. 'Unless Michael and Crombie find them first. I need to locate Somerville's steward, I need to find this Irishman, I need to go into Lanark and report to Lockhart and to Brosie Vary, who must be near out of his mind by now. I wonder if Mistress Somerville's men found the tinkers? Doig said they only left Lanark Muir on Sunday, they should ha been easy enough to find. You're right, I should call there, speak to the men as well as herself.'

'But why have you no found her, maister?' demanded Mistress Somerville. 'If you ken who's got her held fast, why have you no led an armed band to free her out their grasp? And who is it's got her anyway? Is it no the tinkers?'

'It seems,' said Gil cautiously, 'as if it's your brother Robert was holding her.'

She stared at him, her eyes growing round with shock and the high colour ebbing from her padded cheeks. She was more plainly attired today, but had assumed the pleated barbe and draped veil to receive him, and against the white linen her face had turned a yellowish grey.

'My – my brother Robert?' she repeated. The maid-servant at her side shook her head.

'Surely no, mem,' she said. 'He's mistaken, for certain.'

'Aye.' Mistress Somerville swallowed. 'Aye, you must be mistaken. What would— why would Robert do that? Her own uncle? You're mistaken, maister, and it's no kind in you to – to persist in it, now when he's deid, burnt up in his own house!' She sat back on the upholstered daybed, dabbed at her eyes with a handkerchief, and glared at him from behind the fine linen folds. Socrates rose from his seat at Gil's side and went to nudge her hand with his long nose, but she pushed him away. Offended, he resumed his place.

'I think,' said Gil, still choosing his words with care, 'he stole her away to use her as a bargaining token, to persuade Vary to do something to his advantage.'

'Vary!' she snorted contemptuously. 'He aye acts to his own advantage. I tell you, I'll no forgive him for concealing it from me that my lassie was lost!'

'To your brother's advantage,' Gil said patiently. 'It seems as Robert Somerville was involved in something that would have made him money, but he needed Vary to persuade the Burgh Council to agree to it.'

'Money?' she said sharply. 'Robert never had money. It aye ran through his fingers like sand.'

'He'd built a handsome house up at The Cleuch,' Gil observed. 'Do you ken where he got the coin for that, mistress?'

'I'd heard he was building,' she said, staring at him. 'They said it was a right palace, fit to be at Linlithgow, but I took it that was just country folk talking.'

'A hall and two wings, of two storeys and the attics,' Gil said. 'The timber alone must ha cost a pretty sum, no to mention carting it across the hills from Leith.'

'Ha!' she said bitterly. 'Never tellt me a word o that. Last I seen him, it would be,' she paused to reckon on her fingers, 'Candlemas likely, he never said a word o that.' She stared at Gil again, obviously thinking hard.

'So he never mentioned guns to you?'

'Guns?' she said in astonishment. 'What would he ha anything to do wi guns for? Nasty things they are, kill you as soon as look at you.'

'Maybe he's found coal or the like,' suggested the maidservant helpfully, 'like the Douglas ower at Cauldhope.'

'The whole county would ken if he'd found coal,' said her mistress. 'Where would our Robert get money from, that he'd keep it a secret?'

'Embra?' offered the woman. 'Commendator Noll, or whatever his name is?'

'Och, you're a fool, Christian,' said Mistress Somerville. 'Where would he get money at Edinburgh, tell me that?'

'It seems,' said Gil, 'as if he was in some kind of a bond wi Madur of Eastshiel and Ballantyne the burgh clerk in Lanark.'

'Ah-huh!' she said, as if he had confirmed something for her. 'That would be it. My good-brother o Eastshiel has aye had sticky fingers, he'd cheat Our Lady hersel if he'd the chance.' Gil preserved his countenance carefully, reflecting that though the Cunninghams had backed the wrong side at Sauchieburn he had no relations, even by marriage, who deserved such an encomium. 'Ask at him,' Mistress Somerville was saying. 'Ask at Madur o Eastshiel what he's been about wi my brother Robert.'

'We can't,' said Gil. 'He died up at The Cleuch last night and all. And Ballantyne was killed yesterday.'

'Christ aid us all!' said the maidservant, crossing herself energetically. 'You'd think the English was invading, the way folks keeps getting killed.'

'Have you any idea what they might have been about?' asked Gil, and decided against explaining that it was probably either Somerville or Madur who had killed Ballantyne. 'It might help us to track down where they have Mistress Madur hidden away.'

'Can you no ask Jackie Somerville,' said Mistress Somerville, 'that's my brother's steward?'

'I would if I could find him,' said Gil. 'Where might he have gone?'

'Oh, never ask me!' said Mistress Somerville, suddenly losing patience with the interview. 'I've tellt you all I can, maister. You'll need to go now, I – I have to think on

189

all this you've let me hear. It takes some getting used wi, when all I want's to see my lassie safe in her own home!'

The maidservant murmured something comforting and patted her mistress's shoulder. Gil took his leave, with mingled relief and reluctance; he was certain Mistress Somerville could tell him more, but the right questions would not come to his mind, and talking to her was not easy. Socrates seemed to agree, to judge by his bearing as they left the house.

Down in the stableyard Tottie Tammas was deep in conversation with Billy, the man who had ridden with them on the first search on Monday evening, and another of the Kettlands men. They seemed to be agreeing on the difficulty of searching Lanark Muir in this heat, but fell silent as Gil approached.

'Maister,' said Billy, pulling off his bonnet. 'I take it there's no good word.'

'None yet,' said Gil. 'It seems as if she was still alive yestreen.'

'And ye'd traced her up at The Cleuch! Robert Somerville's house!' marvelled Billy. 'And then it burned down.'

'She'd been moved by then,' Gil said, 'but we've not learned yet where she's been taken.'

'Just as well they moved her, maybe,' offered the other man, 'if the house went on fire.'

'Did you track down the tinkers?' Gil asked, ignoring this.

'No, we never,' said Billy, pulling a face, 'though it seems as if it's no matter, if you ken where she is now. We tracked them the length o Thankerton, but they just vanished into the heather ayont that, no sign at all.'

'Was surprising we found that much,' commented the other man. 'You canny see where they've went, for the maist part, they come and go like smoke.'

190

'They'd left plenty sign on the Muir,' said Tammas.

'Aye, but where they've camped it's a different matter,' said Billy. 'Ned's right, it's no that usual to see where they've went.'

Riding into Lanark, Gil looked about him, hoping to see Alys. His mother had been vague about her errand, though it seemed as if a visit to Madame Olympe was involved. He was in more than one mind about this; while he was certain Sandy's tastes ran to other temptations than Alys offered, and he knew that Agnes would be present at any interview, he was concerned about what his cousin might persuade Alys to by way of searching for Mistress Madur, or worse, for the Irishman. The absence of any of the Belstane horses in the stables at the Nicholas Inn strengthened his doubts.

'Aye, they was here,' said the aged ostler as he took the reins of Gil's horse. 'But they rade out again afore noon, wi a bite bread and cheese bespoke for the saddlebags. No, I never seen the young lady, but your men said she was wanting her beast, I take it she rade out and all. And would you be willing to gie me a hand wi these fellows, young sir?' he added to Tammas, with an ingratiating grin.

'You never heard where they were off to?' Gil prompted hopefully.

'No me, maister. I deal wi the beasts when they come in here, I'm no concerned where they come and go to when they're no in my yard.' The old man set off ploddingly towards the stables, with Gil's beast following eagerly, clearly expecting a bundle of hay at the very least.

Leaving Tammas, who had his instructions already, Gil went out through the arch of the stableyard and into Lanark. An attempt to call at Madame Olympe's lodging was fruitless; nobody answered his rattling at the door, but after a while an elderly maidservant stuck her head out of a window of Maister Lightbody's house. She peered up at him where he stood on the forestair, shading her eyes against the bright sunlight in the street. 'She's away out, and Agnes and all,' she advised him.

'D'you ken where they went?' Gil asked her.

'No me. Madam went off on a powny – mind you, it was a sight to see her getting mounted up on its back – but I think Agnes is went to the market, just.' She eyed him assessingly, and glanced at Socrates who was waving his tail at her. 'Did I no see you here the ither day? And that dog, and you'd your wife wi you, maybe? For I think it's your wife that madam's rade out wi.'

'You've no idea where they went?'

'No me,' said the woman, as the ostler had done. She withdrew into the house, and Gil descended the stair and made his way to the Provost's lodging, in some concern. Alys was less wary of his cousin than he was, and more inclined to listen to his blandishments, he felt. What could Sandy have cozened her into, riding out of Lanark in this heat?

Provost Lockhart had also taken refuge from the heat, in a pleasant little arbour in the garden at the back of his big house. Seated in the shade, stripped to sleeveless doublet and with his shirtsleeves rolled up, his writing-slope on a little table before him, he was dealing with what appeared to be Council papers. When Gil appeared he gathered these up and set them aside.

'Maister Cunningham,' he said, rising to bow to the visitor. 'Aye, John, fetch another jug and a glass for Maister Cunningham, and a stool forbye. Come in out the sun, maister, it's another parched day, and tell me all what went on up at The Cleuch. A bad business, a very bad business.'

He heard Gil's account of the fire and the discovery of the two bodies with much head-shaking, wiping his perspiring pink brow with a handkerchief and exclaiming, 'Christ aid us! What's the world coming to?' at frequent intervals. When the tale was done he sat for a little, gazing at Socrates, who was inspecting the clipped box hedge outlining the nearest flowerbed.

'I'd never ha thought it o Somerville,' he said eventually. 'Madur o Eastshiel, now, he's aye been a chancer, but no Somerville, no him. What's he got mixed up in, maister, can you tell me that? First he's plotting to plant trees on the Burgh's land, and stealing away Vary's wife to get him to consent to it, and now here he's tortured to death in his own house, poor deil, and Madur deid and all. Unless it was Madur that slew him?' he added hopefully.

'I'd say not,' said Gil. 'Someone else had stabbed Madur and then thrown him where the chestnut could trample him. We're seeking whoever did that, and it's as like as no he slew Somerville and all. But it's the Depute's business to find him, no yours, seeing it happened outside the burgh.'

'Our Lady be thanked for that,' agreed Lockhart. 'I've all to do a'ready, what wi Dod Ballantyne deid in his foreshot, and another Burgh clerk to find and get sworn in. I'd the Depute here the morn, I'll no conceal from you, but he'd little he could tell me. You've let me hear a deal more o the situation.'

'What I'd hoped from you in return,' said Gil, acknowledging this, 'is maybe a wee bit help in seeking this man we think slew Somerville. I ken he's the Depute's concern, but it's tied up some way wi the matter of Mistress Madur.'

'Aye?' said Lockhart warily. 'Is it the loan o the constables you're after? For they've enough to do within the burgh, maister.'

'No, no,' said Gil hastily. 'They've enough to do, as you say. No, I hoped maybe the bellman could cry this horse the laddies at The Cleuch described to me, to ask if anyone's seen him.'

'No the Irishman?'

'No the Irishman,' Gil confirmed. 'I want to fright him, no to panic him.'

'Aye, we could do that,' said Lockhart. 'Gie me the description again, and we'll summon Geordie and his bell.'

Leaving the Provost's house, Gil could hear a group of horses approaching the High Street from the Edinburgh road. Socrates suddenly produced the soft bark he used as a greeting and sprang away across the street, and a moment later Gil realised he could hear a brisk argument in French over the walking bass of the hoofbeats. As the group emerged into the wide marketplace, Socrates dancing round one of the lead horses, he recognised the riders, and made out words.

'And I say we must confront him first! The man is paralysed by fear and shock, he has no connection to the plot other than to be afflicted by it.'

'Caution is needed, I told you. If we alert my quarry, we could lose him.'

'And if we wait, we could lose *my* quarry, and I will not permit that! Her life is in danger the longer we delay.'

'Oh!' said Madame Olympe, reverting to Scots. 'Here's your wee lapdog! Is your man in Lanark, then?'

'Yes,' said Alys. She paused to pet Socrates where he stood up grinning and pawing at her knee, then slid down from her horse before Madame's lodging and put her hand in Gil's as he reached her side. 'We need to talk,' she said.

'*Assurément*, we must talk,' agreed Madame Olympe, descending more ceremoniously from her saddle, with Henry and Euan to hold her elegantly gloved hands. 'But should we not retire to my lodging first? One would not wish to affright the citizens of this town.'

'Nor the horses,' agreed Gil. She cast him a sharp glance, but inclined her head in thanks to Henry, waved graciously to the maidservant who was watching with interest from Maister Lightbody's house, caught up the tail of her blue riding-dress to reveal red boots with black straps, and led the way up the forestair.

As Agnes shut the door behind them, Alys tugged at Gil's hand, drawing him into the main chamber, patting the dog with her other hand as he danced at her side, nudging her with his long nose.

'Socrates, *sit!* Mistress Madur may be at Tarbrax,' she said. 'It seems as if that was where the convoy was headed. Henry would not ride there with us, he wished to wait for you. And Maister Vary has visited The Cleuch.'

'Vary?' he repeated in astonishment. She nodded.

'We must speak to him, Gil, at once, before we ride to Tarbrax. I am certain there is some explanation.'

'We can't afford to alert him!' said Madame Olympe, turning in a swirl of wide skirts. 'I need to find the Irishman, or learn that he is left the country. I can't risk Vary passing word to him—'

'You have not seen Maister Vary,' Alys retorted. 'I tell you, he is not capable of plotting as you suspect.' Socrates, looking from Alys to Madame, rumbled a faint growl deep in his chest.

'Quiet, Socrates. You had best tell me,' said Gil, as Agnes set out beakers and a jug of ale. Alys succinctly reported her findings at Forth while Madame, with a tight expression that threatened her face-paint, divested

195

herself of her straw hat and unbuckled the straps of her headdress.

'I had already been told,' Alys went on, going unaccountably pink, 'that Somerville had a house at Tarbrax. It seems he never lives there – lived there,' she corrected herself, 'which I suppose is why nobody has mentioned it before. And,' she glanced at Madame, who was now draining a beaker of ale, 'we have word that there was a horse-litter with the party that rode out that way from The Cleuch. Mistress Brewster told Sandy of seeing it, with – was it a half-dozen riders, Sandy?'

'Aye,' Madame said curtly, setting the beaker down long enough to refill it.

'And then Doddie recalled another man visiting, apart from the Irishman and Madur of Eastshiel, and swore the steward called him Maister Vary.'

'Sweet St Giles!' said Gil. He took possession of the jug and poured ale for Alys and then for himself, considering. 'This changes matters. The boy is certain?'

'I believe him to be sure of what he says,' she stated. 'I think we must confront Maister Ambrose Vary,' she went on earnestly, and took a grateful gulp of the ale. 'I cannot believe he has plotted this. He is in such despair, Gil, you saw it too!'

'It's hard to credit,' he said slowly. 'I'm agreed, I'd sooner speak wi him afore we run mad wi the notion, but I think it might be wiser to ride to Tarbrax first, and preferably wi a writ from the Depute and an armed band at our backs.' He glanced at his cousin, who was still wearing that grim look. 'Sandy, do we think the Irishman's at Tarbrax and all?'

'Could be anywhere,' said Sandy, suddenly dropping Madame's manner. 'They'd no notion when he'd left The Cleuch, let alone what direction he took. I need to check the information I have, see where he might ha moved on to or taken refuge.'

'Doig's friends the tinkers?' Gil suggested. 'The Kettlands men tracked them as far as Thankerton, and then lost the trail, which gars me think they might be found in any direction other than that.'

'Aye.' The other tilted his head, considering, and just as suddenly Madame Olympe was back. 'Ah, my dears, I must chase you away! I find myself *un peu fatiguée* after such exertions. I must rest, and give myself up to thought. Call on me the morn's morn, if you have news.'

'Well!' said Alys as they stepped out into the street. 'Do you think I have offended him?'

'Undoubtedly,' said Gil, offering her his arm. 'But that's no excuse for discourtesy. Are you still thirsty?'

'A little,' she admitted.

'Vary's servants would offer us refreshment.' He snapped his fingers at the dog and set off down the hill. She looked up at him in surprise.

'I thought you were against speaking to him?'

'I have changed my mind. But we must be cautious,' he counselled.

Vary was not at his desk today. Jessie greeted them with relief, drew them into the dark hall of the house and said, half-weeping with anxiety, 'He's out the back, away down the garden. He's been walking up and down the whole day in that sun, talking to himself. I canny make sense of what he's saying. He's no eaten, he's no slept, for I could hear him tramping up and down in his chamber every time I wakened mysel. He'll be into his grave afore we get word o the mistress if this goes on. Have ye no found her yet, maister?'

'No yet,' said Gil, before Alys could speak. 'Has he spoken to anyone?'

197

'His brother fro the kirk called,' said Jessie in dry tones. 'Would pray wi him, preaching at him about how it's the mistress's reward for her wilful behaviour and the like. My mistress!' she exclaimed indignantly. 'As merry a lass as there's been in this house since his first wife! I can tell ye, maister, they've a true regard one for the other, my maister and mistress, for all it wasny a love match, ye've only to watch them day by day as I do, and it's my belief it's that his brothers canny stand.' She paused to think a moment, and sighed. 'There's been no other callers that I mind; he sent as many away yesterday and they wouldny call again the day.'

'Gil,' said Alys, 'you should go out and speak to Maister Vary. If Jessie will let me into her kitchen again, maybe we can put up something to tempt him to eat.'

'Oh, aye, and welcome, mem,' said Jessie.

Wondering what Alys was planning, Gil took the dog and went out into the garden. It was not as large as Maister Lockhart's, but long and narrow, with a pleached alley of hazels to one side, the growing clusters of nuts showing like ruffled green flowers among the thick leaves. Vary was not in its shade, but pacing away along one of the little paths between clipped lavender hedges, his head and arms moving jerkily as if he was arguing a point with some invisible interlocutor. Socrates bounded down the garden to greet him, by thrusting his head against the man's hip and gazing up at him, tail waving. Vary stopped, and looked down at the dog for a moment as if he had never seen one before, then turned and saw Gil.

'Oh! It's you, Gil!' He stared hard at Gil's face. 'Have you— is there any word?'

'Very little,' said Gil.

'But some? What? What have you found?' The man was braced, trembling.

'We found their trail, away from the place where they captured her. Alys found it, wi some of my mother's men,' Gil corrected himself. 'They headed up the Mouse, and made for Castlehill, but there's no sign of her at Castlehill, though we searched the place. We've not found yet where she might be now.'

'Castlehill?' Vary repeated, his eyes widening. 'That's—' He swayed, and Gil seized his elbow to steady him. 'That's Somerville's place. Is it her uncles? Her family, that's stolen her away? Put her in danger, and the bairn and all?' He pulled himself upright. 'Where are they? Which of them is it? By Our Lady, I'll kill them! I'll have them at the law!'

'You may be too late,' Gil said, in some amazement at this transformation. 'Rab Somerville and Jocelyn Madur both are deid in a fire at The Cleuch last night.'

'A fire?' Vary repeated, in that more vigorous tone. 'A *fire*? She wasny there, was she? Tell me she wasny there!'

'So far as we can make out,' Gil assured him, 'she wasny there. Come, sit down in the shade and I'll tell you what we've learned.'

Vary looked about in blank surprise, as if he had not been aware of where he was, but allowed himself to be drawn into the hazel alley, where he sat obediently on the slightly mossy bench, listening intently to Gil's carefully edited account of the hunt for Mistress Vary and the fire at The Cleuch. He was shocked by the manner of the two deaths.

'I never had time for either man,' he said, crossing himself, 'pair o chancers both o them, and Henry Madur's no a lot better, but there's none deserves that kind of an end.'

'Have you any idea what this might all be about?' said Gil, still adjusting his mind to this revived Vary.

'No,' said Vary firmly. He stared at the dancing light which fell between the hazel leaves, and after a moment

199

said, 'I suppose they wanted to bring me to consent to one o their daft schemes, but I've no notion what it might be. It could be what you found on the Burgh Muir, indeed – and the idea, setting up a plantation o timber up there, on Burgh land! – but it seems to me it might be more than that, something greater than that.'

'Such as what?' Gil asked hopefully, but the man shook his head.

'I need to think on it. There might be some hint they've dropped, some mention – did you say Dod Ballantyne was in it and all? I wonder if it's something he was after? And my head's still all tapsalteerie wi this.' He clenched his fists, suddenly overcome again. 'Oh, my lassie! Our Lady send she's safe! Her own kin, to do sic a thing!'

Gil clapped him on the shoulder.

'Try what you can call to mind,' he said. 'Anything at all. You never ken what could lead us to the right answer. Has Ballantyne maybe said aught at a Council meeting lately? Has either of your wife's uncles mentioned any plans?'

'I never speak wi them if I can avoid it,' Vary said, staring at his clenched fists. 'They're – they were aye full o daft notions, horse breeding, growing timber, importing espinyards from Spain – it's a kinna portable cannon, something like a harquebus,' he added, glancing at Gil. 'Ye ken there's talk o seeking a Spanish bride for James Stewart? Lindsay of Pettinain's youngest, James, was wi the party that travelled there in the spring to spy out the situation, afore the first embassage sails, and he brought one o the things back wi him, and a couple men to work it and all. Rab Somerville got to see it and ran off wi the idea to import and sell the things to the Crown. I don't see that can be it,' he said thoughtfully. 'No unless he wished to build a gunpowder store in the burgh, or the like, which I'd never permit.'

Could that be what interested the Irishman, Gil wondered. But surely the Irish could import such things direct from Spain if they could afford to.

'Maister? Are ye there, maister?' called Jessie, out in the garden.

'We're here in the alley,' Gil called back. In a moment she appeared at the end of the green tunnel, bearing a tray, with Alys behind her.

'Would ye maybe tak a wee drop broth—' she began, and checked in amazement at the sight of her master sitting making lucid conversation. She glanced quickly at Gil, smiled, and then continued without giving any other sign, 'Mistress Mason made the wee sippets o toast for it wi her own hands, and spread them wi the new butter. See, I'll put it here on the bench at your side.'

Vary looked down at the tray as she set it beside him, and then up at her face.

'Jess,' he said, and put a hand on her arm. 'Jessie, I think you and the rest o the household's been,' he swallowed, 'unco guid to me these last days, unco patient. I thank you.'

Even in the shade of the alley, Gil could see the woman redden.

'Och, maister!' she said, and patted the hand. 'Och, maister!' she said again. Her mouth quivered, and she turned and hurried away, pulling her apron up to cover her face. Vary watched her go, and turned to Gil.

'I never meant,' he said, vexed. 'Och, Mistress Mason, I never saw you there. I hope you're well, mistress? Will you have a seat, please, it's no—'

'Sup your broth, maister, before it cools,' said Alys, sitting down beside him. He took a spoonful obediently, and then one of the sippets of toast. Then, clearly, he realised how hungry he was, and started spooning the broth, a richly scented brew of chopped roots and dried pulses with pieces of ham quite visible. Alys looked on approvingly, and slid a glance sideways at Gil under the narrow brim of her hat. He watched, slightly apprehensive. What was she about to say?

'Maister Vary,' she said, 'tell me about your brothers.'

'My brothers?' he repeated, startled. 'We don't— I keep away from them. When I can.' His gaze sharpened. 'What, you think it's one o them's stolen my lassie?'

'No, no, I don't think that. One of them's a priest, am I right?'

'Aye.' His face tightened. 'Jerome. Round here day by day, offering to pray for us, aye preaching at me about how it's a judgement on me, how I should ha kept her closer, lessoned her in obedience. Hah!'

'Has he interests outside the burgh?'

'Jerome? He's a benefice, somewhere in the Lothians I believe. I'm no that interested.' He thought briefly. 'And he's property in the burgh. I'd to stop him putting a potter in there, wi the kiln and all, like to burn down that end o the town.'

'And your other brother, Gregor is it? Where does he dwell?'

'Gregory,' Vary corrected, as if the word smelled bad. 'He has the family lands by Carnwath, seeing as he's the older. By the half o an hour, as he's never ceased to remind me, all our lives.'

'I've never met him, I think,' said Gil.

'He went to St Andrews. Being the older foundation, you ken,' said Vary, much as Lockhart had done.

'And he has a family? An heir?' asked Alys innocently.

'No him. He's had no better fortune that way than I have,' Vary told her. 'Though I hope mine—' He bit off the words, clearly reluctant to tempt fate. 'He's no wife the now.'

'He must deal wi the Court,' said Alys, still in that innocent tone, 'as handy as he is for Edinburgh or Stirling. I suppose he's in touch wi all that goes on.'

'Aye, now-and-now,' agreed Vary. 'Why?'

'No reason.' She smiled at him. 'I'd like to live in Edinburgh, and see the King come and go.'

'The King's here often enough,' Vary observed. 'He rests at Lanark on the road to Whithorn now and then. He was here only last quarter indeed, and half the Court wi him.' He grunted. 'Sic a to-do there was about Dod Ballantyne's house, where he lodges ordinar. The chimney was blocked in the great chamber, smoking like to kipper the whole Court. We'd to hunt all round Lanark for braziers and footwarmers and the like. Seems daft to think on it in this weather.' He turned his head to look at Gil. 'What must we do to seek Mistress Madur? I've no notion where to begin. We should ride to Lockharthill, I'd reckon, speak to the Depute.'

'That would be a good start,' said Gil cautiously.

'I'll away in and get my boots on,' said Vary with decision. 'Your servant, Mistress Mason.'

He strode off out of the alley and towards the house, leaving Gil and Alys staring after him.

'What roused him?' Alys asked after a moment.

'Learning who stole Mistress Madur away,' said Gil. 'I suppose knowing who he should hunt down makes all the difference.'

'I have been speaking to the household,' she said quietly. 'When their maister rides out of Lanark, the man Archie rides with him, to help with the instruments and hold the end of the chain for measuring. Vary's been nowhere near any of his wife's uncles these past two months, and nor has he ridden out without an attendant, nor been away from home alone long enough to

203

get to The Cleuch and back. Whoever the laddie saw at The Cleuch, it was not this man.'

'Good work,' said Gil, turning this over in his mind. 'The older brother?'

'So I thought,' she agreed. 'Should we tell Madame Olympe?'

'We ought to,' he said reluctantly, beginning to move towards the house. 'It may have some bearing on the search for the Irishman.'

'How far away is Carnwath?' she asked. 'What is his house called? Do you know where it lies?'

'Kersewell. I'd need to enquire,' he said. 'Lockhart would tell me, I've no doubt. Carnwath itself is seven mile or so from Lanark, but it's a broad parish – the biggest in Lanarkshire I believe – so we'd need the directions afore we set out.'

The kitchen door opened as they approached it, and Jessie stepped out, holding something which she eyed warily.

'Maister?' she said, and looked about the garden. 'Where is he?'

'He went to put his boots on,' Alys said. 'What have you there?'

'I've just the now found this at the door,' she said. 'I thought someone tirled at the pin, so I went, but there was naeb'dy there, only this lying on the step.' She held out a set of cheap tablets. 'Is it – is it maybe another message? Should I gie it to him, or would you take it, maister?'

Gil looked at the object in some dismay.

'On the doorstep?' he repeated. 'And no sign of whoever left it there?'

'No sign.' She shook her head. 'Two-three laddies passing, but they'd not seen anyb'dy at the door, I asked them.'

'Maybe we should,' said Alys. 'Should look at it.'

'Look at what?' said Vary, emerging from the door behind his servant. 'Gil, will we— what have you there, Jessie?'

Wordlessly she held the tablets out to him. He stared at them, as if at an adder, and slowly put out his hand and took them. He turned them over once or twice, then visibly braced himself, unwound the string and opened the leaves. The colour left his face.

'Gil,' he said. 'Gil. It's a, it's a, it's ransom. They want a ransom.'

'*Ransom?*' echoed Alys. 'But how? How do you pay ransom to the dead?'

'Oh, maister!' wailed Jessie. 'Just when we thocht—'

Gil extracted the tablets from Vary's unresisting grasp, and turned them to read the message scrawled on the wax.

V HUNERT MERK, it read, *TO HENFFORTH LIE ATT MUNES RISE.*

'Five hundred marks!' he said. 'Ambitious. To Hyndford Lea at moonrise.'

'How?' said Vary. 'I thought you said they were deid, Gil. How are they sending like this if they're deid?'

Chapter Ten

Gil turned the set of tablets over, studying it.

'This is not the same as the other two messages you've had,' he said. 'It's by a different maker, I'd say, and the wood-cut is from a different set, not a saint's image at any rate.'

'Aesop,' said Alys, looking over his arm. 'I think it's the fox and the crow.'

'And the writing is different. There's no attempt to make it look unpractised.'

'What's that mean, maister?' asked Jessie, staring at the tablets. Socrates paced up the garden and raised his head to sniff at the tablets' wooden backing.

'Gil, what do we do now?' said Vary. He was shivering, despite the heat of the day. 'How can— what— how do we tell where to seek her? Who sent this? Who's holding her now? What can we *do?*'

'What are the choices?' Alys asked.

'We could ask Lockhart for help,' Gil said. 'Though I don't know how many men he has to command. It might end wi half the Burgh Council a-horseback, the Host of Lanark so to speak. We could send to the Depute, or better still ride there as we planned to just the now, and see if he can help.'

'Aye, but what's all these men to do?' asked Jessie. 'Ride hither and yon about the county seeking the mistress, and the man that sent this message?'

'That's the question.'

'If Mistress Madur is really at Tarbrax,' Alys began.

'Tarbrax?' said Vary sharply. 'How— is that where— how d'ye ken?'

'We think she was moved there just afore the fire at The Cleuch,' Alys explained.

Gil stepped away from the little group, the better to pace while he thought.

'If she's at Tarbrax,' he said after a moment, 'this,' he waved the tablets, 'may ha come from the men who hold her there, the men Somerville sent there wi her.'

'Aye, who else?' said Jessie.

'Hyndford Lea is the other side of Lanark from Tarbrax, though I suppose it's straight down the Ayr road from where they are. She could still be up at Tarbrax. They'll no be planning to bring her to the ford, too easy for us to snatch her back and then they've lost all.'

'And easy for them to snatch the money,' observed Alys, 'and then we've lost all.'

'We need to start wi Tarbrax,' said Gil. 'The question is, whether to speak to the Depute and get men and a warrant, go in force to demand her, or to go in quiet, just a few of us.' He glanced at the sky, still a brilliant blue. 'It's no more than five of the clock, there's plenty daylight left. It's only a couple of hours' ride from here.'

'Could go by Lockharthill on the way to Tarbrax,' said Vary. 'Come ben the house, Gil. We need to, to sit down, plan this properly.'

'Do you know the house at Tarbrax, maister?' Alys asked.

'I was, I was, I was there once,' said Vary with an effort. He turned and led the way through the kitchen, where the other servants stood hastily as they passed. 'Must be ten year since. I canny mind aught about it.'

'What like is the place?' Gil asked, following him into his closet. He seated Alys, and took the stool Vary waved him to. 'Is it stone, or timber? Is it defended?'

'It's old.' Vary thought deeply. 'Timber over stone, three storeys, outhouses. Drystone barmekin, no very sound. No what you'd call secure, far's I can mind, for all it's so isolate.'

'We have four men wi us,' said Alys. 'Your Archie would ride out, and Nicol as well I think.' He nodded. 'That makes nine of us and the dog, even without asking help from the Provost or the Depute. Gil,' she gave him a significant look, 'do you think your cousin Sandy would come too?'

'Worth a try,' he said, considering it.

'Sandy? What Sandy?'

'Sandy Boyd,' said Gil. 'He's, er, in the area.'

There was a rattling outside as someone tirled at the pin. They heard one of the servants go through the hall to answer the door; indistinct voices exchanged a few words. Gil got to his feet, recognising the deep tones.

'Forgive me, Brosie,' he said briefly, and went out into the hall. The younger manservant, Nicol, was arguing a point with the visitor; Gil, approaching, saw that it was indeed William Doig on the doorstep.

'You'll no get in!' said Nicol. 'There's enough ill luck in the house a'ready, we're no needing the likes o you adding to't!'

'You gomeril, I'm trying to turn that! Maister Cunningham!' said Doig, spying Gil under Nicol's arm where he held the door against him. 'I've a word for ye!'

'And what would that be?' Gil asked. 'Aye, let him in, man, he's known to me. What is it, Maister Doig?'

'You'd a wee message at this door, a half hour or so since,' stated Doig, making his way into the house with his rolling gait.

'Aye?'

'I seen the laddie that left it.' Doig followed Gil into the closet, nodded to Alys, ducked his head in a sort of bow to Vary and drew off his blue bonnet. 'I kent him, see, one o that clan o tinkers I spoke o afore this.'

'The ones that were on the Burgh Muir?' Gil said.

'Aye, them. Laddie about twelve year old, dropped the thing on the step, tirled at the pin, and made off up the town.'

'Up the town?' said Alys, while Vary stared open-mouthed at this exchange. 'So he was making for,' she closed her eyes, moving one finger in different directions, 'making away from Carluke.'

'Towards Hyndford Lea,' said Gil. 'Though that might mean nothing.'

Doig nodded approvingly at this.

'Ransom demand, was it?' he speculated.

'It was.'

'Aye. Someone's chancing it.'

'So I thought,' said Alys. He gave her an even more approving look. 'Do you ken where he is, maister?'

'No me,' he said with regret. 'If I did, I ken who'd be after him like a shot. No, I think he's hid wi the tinkers, wherever they've got to. That horse o his would disappear among theirn.'

'Of course!' said Gil, catching up with the conversation. Vary was still gaping. 'He's asking five hundred marks, to be at Hyndford Lea at moonrise.'

'Well, wherever your wife is, maister,' said Doig to Vary with rough sympathy, 'she'll no be there.'

Vary closed his mouth, swallowed, and said, 'Who – who are you? *What* are you—?'

'A friend, maister,' said Alys soothingly. *For the moment*, thought Gil, but said nothing.

210

'Right,' said Vary, with sudden decision. 'I want— I'll ride to Tarbrax. If there's a chance she's there— Are you wi me, Gil? And you, mistress, what will you do while we're— should we maybe see you back to Carluke first?'

'I'll ride wi you,' said Alys. 'Though we must hire fresh horses, Gil. The Belstane beasts will be tired.'

'Oh, mistress, I hardly think,' began Vary, but Gil said, 'So's you keep back if there's trouble, given that we've no armour for you.'

She glanced at him, but made no answer.

Doig resumed his blue bonnet, tugging it to its usual jaunty angle, and said, 'I'll away then, maisters, and I wish you good fortune.'

Gil, accompanying him to the door, said quietly, 'Can you let Sandy hear this? If he can find the tinkers—'

'Aye,' said Doig, stepping down into the street. 'I might do that.'

Gil felt he would have been happier with the cavalcade that left Lanark if it had been better armed. Vary and his men were suitably apparelled, and had lent Henry a jack belonging to the dead groom Adam, but none of the other Belstane riders had any armour, though all except Alys wore swords. They clopped and clattered out of the burgh by the Edinburgh road, and made good speed eastward, moving briskly on the dry, dusty roads. Vary rode in the lead, tense and white-faced, his mount tossing its head and mouthing at the bit as it recognised his unease. Gil rode just behind him, thinking about what lay ahead, trying out various strategies, Socrates sprawled across his knees with his head up drinking in the scents in the wind of their going. At his side Alys was also silent, until she spoke suddenly.

'The Irishman might be there.'

'But you think not,' he said, interpreting her tone. 'Nor do I. I'd wager Doig's right, he's joined that tribe of tinkers along with his horse.'

'Perhaps your cousin will find him at the bridge.' She bit her lip, as the party slowed to pass a pair of lumbering tilt-carts which occupied most of the width of the road. 'I wish we could do that too, but there's no way to be in both places.'

The road lifted up out of the wide, flat lands by the Clyde, through Carnwath with its handsome church, and swung northward to climb up the western flank of the Pentlands. They crossed another river by a ford, 'The Medwin,' said Vary briefly, and worked their way up its valley, still climbing. When they stopped to breathe the horses, Socrates leapt down to check the path. Gil turned and looked back through the cloud of dust they had raised, and found the whole of the upper Clyde valley laid out in the sunshine, the river coiling and glinting among the fields, the purple mass of Tinto Hill in the midst of the scene, and beyond it a vista of more round-headed hills, blue into the distance, like the landscapes in Alys's prayer book.

'Ride on,' said Vary, and they spurred the reluctant horses. Socrates, taken by surprise, galloped after them and sprang up to Gil's saddlebow.

'What's the approach to the house like?' Gil asked Vary. He shook his head.

'I canny mind. There's a track goes off this road, that much I do mind, but how you come on the house—' He chewed at his finger, staring into the distance.

'Is it Tarbrax we're for, maisters?' asked Henry, urging his beast up behind Gil's. 'I was there once wi Cunningham, God rest his soul.'

'Amen,' Gil said, crossing himself at the mention of his father. 'What d'you mind, then?'

212

'It's on the side o the valley,' Henry tucked his reins under his thigh, the better to demonstrate the slope of the land, 'a bit back fro the burn, see, wi a wide-open prospect to the west, and there's a kinna spur o the hills to the south that the track goes over, so you kinna come on it unexpected-like.'

'And the house?'

Henry shook his head.

'No that good in eighty-eight, the Deil kens what it's like by now. I'd ha said Somerville didny use it, and he didny put aught into its upkeep. The stables were like to fall down, I couldny put the beasts into them, we'd to hobble them on the muir to get what grazing they could.'

'Right,' said Gil. 'We'll halt this side of this spur of the hill, and I'll go forward on my own to spy out the place, see what I can learn.'

'No, I'll go—' said Vary.

Euan Campbell spoke up from the back of the ride: 'Will I no be going forward my lone, Maister Gil? I am the best stalker after deer in Ardnamurchan. I can be learning all there is to ken about the place and never be seen.'

'Aye, but this isny Ardnamurchan,' said one of the other men.

'A hillside is a hillside,' said Euan obstinately.

'That's no what you said the morn,' said someone else.

'Euan will go forward,' said Gil, putting a stop to this, 'to learn what he can.'

By the time Henry called a halt it was beginning to be evening. The day was still warm, but the sun was visibly dipping towards the horizon, away round to the northwest. Larks sang in the blue depths above them, a hunting buzzard quartered the hillside, and Gil could hear a wheatear's alarm call from a pile of rocks uphill from

213

them. They had left the Edinburgh road and cut in through the hills, forded a burn whose peat-brown waters, the colour of Alys's eyes, ran lazily in a deep-cut bed which spoke of winter spates, and now faced a climb to a low saddle over the spur of the hill Henry had described.

'It's just ower there,' he said, 'as far's I can mind. Only thing is, I'd ha thought we'd see smoke by now. They'll need the fire going if they're cooking.'

'Odd,' said Gil, frowning. 'Unless they brought bread and cheese and the like wi them.'

'Wish we'd brought the like,' muttered someone at the back. 'My belly's flapping.'

'Quiet!' said Gil, as Euan slid from his horse, giving his reins to Tottie Tammas.

'I should go too,' said Vary, watching the man go forward at a crouch, then on his belly in the rough grass of the hillside. Socrates jumped down to follow him, much interested, and Alys called him back.

'Euan's good,' said Gil. 'He'll bring back word, sure enough.'

They sat their horses, watching as Euan melted into the landscape. The wheatear had flown off in alarm, though the buzzard still sailed above them, mewing; Gil, catching a small movement out of the tail of his eye, thought at first he had found the buzzard's prey. Watching without looking at it directly he realised that whatever was moving was much bigger than a hare or rabbit, and gradually made it out to be a human figure, not full-grown. A boy, to judge by the short hair, perhaps eleven or twelve. The dog had not noticed him yet.

'Good evening to you,' he called softly, turning his head to look straight at the youngster. There was a pause, and a muffled curse, and the boy stood upright, grinning. Several of the men at Gil's back exclaimed,

214

and Socrates growled at this sudden appearance out of the long grass.

'It's your lordship has the sharp eyesight, sharp as a needle,' said the ragged figure, touching his brow to Gil. 'And were you seeking the house o Tarbrax, your lordships?'

'We are,' said Gil, studying the boy. He was thin, with bare brown arms and legs, a tattered and very dirty shirt belted about his waist with a length of cord, dark hair straggling about his face. He wore an expression of innocent candour which Gil assumed must be entirely spurious. Now he shook his shaggy head.

'No use, my lords, no use to go there. Your errand's wasted, so 'tis.'

'Why?' asked Vary sharply. 'How so?'

'Why, they's all left. Left the morn, so they did,' the boy assured them, nodding at the track behind them. 'I seen them myself, my lords, wi these eyes.' He cast Gil a sidelong look with the eyes in question. 'They took all the horses away down this track, they did indeed.'

'That could be why they's no smoke,' said Tottie Tammas. 'If the house is empty.'

'Did they have a horse-litter wi them?' Gil asked.

'I never saw it,' said the boy. His Scots was rapid, and his accent was strange, a kind of lilting, singing intonation. At Gil's expression, he added, 'If I had I'd tell you, so I would, I'd no conceal it from your lordship. No horse-litter went down this road.'

'Did it go the other way?' Gil asked. 'Any other way from the house?'

'Ah, you're a wise one, your lordship! No, never a horse-litter left the house o Tarbrax the day.'

'And why have you sprung up out the heather,' said Henry inaccurately, 'to tell us this? What reason have you?'

'That's no very friendly,' objected the boy. 'Here I'm telling you this out the goodness o my heart, and you ask my reasons? Would I have to have a reason to do a passer-by a good turn? And you, bonnie lady,' he added to Alys, 'that was a true word you were given this day, you should remember it well.'

'He's full o nonsense,' growled Vary's man Archie. 'Gie him the flat o your whinger, maister, or we'll be here a' nicht hearing him.'

'Hey, here's that Euan,' said Henry, as the gallowglass appeared over the brow of the rise. 'He's ganging quite open, no hiding in the grass. I doubt this wee limmer's right, the house is empty.'

Gil watched Euan for a moment, then turned back to speak to the boy, only to find he had vanished. There was not a sign of his going, no movement among the tussocks of grass and clumps of reed. Alys, rather pink across the cheekbones under her layer of dust, was staring at the place where he had been.

'I have no certainty,' said Euan when he reached them. 'The house is silent, the gate is wide open, you would be thinking nothing breathes there.'

'But?' said Gil. The man gave him a sideways look, suddenly very like the vanished laddie.

'You ken that thing,' he said diffidently, 'where you are looking down into a corrie, and nothing is moving, but you are certain as salvation there is deer down there? You ken that, maister?' Gil nodded. He had little experience of red deer, but he had felt the same thing on other hunts. 'It is like that, maister. I am certain as could be there is someone in the house, though it is seeming empty.'

'Sounds like a waste o time,' said someone.

'We are come this far,' said Alys. 'We might as well mak siccar.'

'Vary?' said Gil. Vary straightened up in the saddle and gathered up his reins.

'As— as Mistress Mason says,' he said. 'We mak siccar.'

As Euan had reported, the gate stood open in the drystone wall of the barmekin. They approached cautiously, but behind the windows of the house nothing stirred. Within the barmekin, two storehouses also lay open to the warm evening, empty and shadowy. In one a ripped sack on the earthen floor had a scatter of grains around it; when Gil slipped in at the door something with a long tail whisked away into a dark corner. The other held only a broken bucket. He peered out round the doorway, and looked about the yard. Euan was right, he was certain; the place was still, apart from the rats, and he had no feeling of being watched, but he would swear to it that some living thing was present, somewhere within the drystone wall.

The rest of the group had gathered in the cover of the empty storehouse.

'The house,' said Vary. 'We need to check the house.'

'We should secure it first,' Gil said. 'It could be a trap. Euan, Henry, wi me.' He looked at Alys. 'Will you wait where we tethered the horses, sweetheart? Take the dog, if you would.'

The house, as Vary had said that afternoon, was timber-framed above a stone ground floor; there was a single jettied upper floor and an attic with windows set into the mouldering thatch. The house door, above two broad steps, stood ajar as the gate had done, nothing stirring beyond it. Shuttered windows on either side suggested a conventional hall within.

With a nagging feeling of life repeating itself – of course, he thought, last night at The Cleuch – Gil made a dash for the door, kicked it wide, sprang aside waiting. Still nothing moved. First Euan and then Henry followed him across the yard to the steps and paused, listening like him for any sound from within. After the length of an *Ave* he stepped into the dark interior, senses at a stretch, the other two following him.

The hall was empty, almost as empty as the store-houses. It contained two broken stools, a table which must have been built in its place, since it would certainly not go out of the door, and a central hearth with a heap of cold ashes. After a wary look about him Gil went to open the shutters, filling the chamber with sudden light. Euan, sword in hand, kicked open first one, then the other of the doors at one end of the chamber.

'There is nothing there,' he reported. 'Not so much as a cut of peat.'

'The fire's been out since last night,' said Henry, straightening up and blowing ash off his hand. 'They've stripped the place. Displenished it as if they was tenants. I'm surprised they've left the rafters.'

'The laddie never said they rode,' Gil recollected. 'They took all the horses, was what he said. I'll wager they used them as pack-beasts.'

'Unless it was the tinkers,' said Euan darkly, 'that has found the door open and emptied the house.'

Gil went back to the door, and waved the rest of the company forward. Vary came across the yard at a run ahead of the other men. 'Is she here?' he demanded, bursting into the house. 'Have they taken her away and all? Where is she?'

'We've yet to check overhead,' Gil said, looking about him for the stair as the other men tramped in.

'There is someone here,' Euan said positively. 'I am not knowing just where, but someone is here.'

'You said that afore,' said someone. 'I canny see anyb'dy. Can you, Tammas?'

218

'Would the dog no scent her out?' Henry suggested. 'I ken he's a sight-hound, but he's a good nose for a' that.'

'Gil,' said Alys in the doorway. He turned, opening his mouth to remonstrate, and she let go of the dog's collar. 'Gil, someone is moving in the attic.'

He stared at her. She stepped into the house, and Socrates began exploring the hall, sniffing carefully in corners, his claws clicking on the flagstones.

'I was out among the horses,' she said quietly in French, 'as you bade me, and when you kicked the door open someone stirred behind one of the attic windows. You wouldn't have seen it from the yard, but from where I was I could just see the movement.'

'No more than that?' he asked, frowning.

'No more. It could be man or woman.' She thought briefly. 'I think quite tall, and taking care not to be seen from below.'

'Here,' said Tottie Tammas, opening another door in a corner of the chamber. 'The dog's found the stair. Will I gang up, maister?'

'Let me,' said Gil. 'Euan, Henry.'

The stair was narrow, uneven, shadowed. He listened, but could hear nothing. As quietly as he could, Socrates at his knee, he climbed the first turn of the spiral, into the light falling from the upper floor, and then two more steps. Pausing just below the sill of the upper room, Henry and Euan at his back, he drew off his hat, balanced it on the point of his whinger, and extended it into the chamber. Nothing stirred. Socrates looked up at him, clearly puzzled.

Well, he thought, *either there's nobody there, or it's someone who knows that trick.* Retrieving the hat he clapped it on his head, and took the remaining two steps and one more.

This chamber was roughly panelled in Norway pine, and was as empty as the hall, indeed emptier since there was no table. A few papers were scattered under the window, some other odds and ends were heaped in a corner, one shoe with the sole gaping lay at the top of the stair. The dog tick-tocked round the chamber, pawing at the shoe, snuffling briefly at the papers.

'Is there another stair?' Henry wondered, while Euan tried the door at their left, and found another, smaller chamber. Gil looked up; overhead the beams sagged worryingly, the broad planks of the ceiling, which formed the floor of the attic chambers above, adrift from their pegs in more than one place. Whoever was up there must be frozen in place, not daring to stir for fear of making the planks creak.

'Go down,' he said to Henry, very clearly, 'and fetch Maister Vary up.'

Overhead, someone drew an audible, sharp breath. There was a pause; then, as if it had been squeezed or disturbed by a sudden movement, a baby wailed. A very young baby.

Henry grinned broadly, and clattered off down the stair. He was back a moment later with a wild-eyed Vary. 'Where is she? Where's my lassie? Is she here, Gil? Is she here?'

'Vary!' called someone overhead. 'Come up, maister, come up!'

'Where?' Vary stared about, as if expecting a ladder to drop in front of him. 'Where are you, lass?'

The boards creaked above them as someone moved across them. Footsteps descended behind the panelling, and a door opened, invisible before it moved, identical with the panels on either side. A woman came through it, ducking under the low lintel, and Vary took a step back as the dog rushed forward, tail waving.

'Who are you?' he demanded. 'Where's— where's— where's Mistress Madur? Where's my wife?'

220

'Vary, I'm here!' called the first voice. The woman stood aside, gesturing ironically, and Vary plunged into the stairway and up out of their sight. She turned to look at Gil, a tall angular woman with pale blue eyes, wisps of reddish hair escaping from her cap. Gil pulled off the hat again and bowed to her.

'Well met, Mistress Lithgo,' he said.

'Well, Maister Cunningham,' said Beatrice Lithgo, curtsying in return. 'You took your time finding us.'

'They kept moving us,' Mistress Lithgo said. 'I made it plain, it was no way to treat a new-made mother, but they'd not listen.'

'We tracked you to Castlehill,' Gil said, 'and then to The Cleuch, but it's taken us till today to calculate that you were here and to come for you.'

'Aye, and sic an escort,' she said, smiling faintly at the men gathered round. They were out in the yard in the warm evening, Alys close against Gil's side, Mistress Lithgo seated on the mounting-block and looking much as ever, unperturbed by her five or six days' imprisonment. 'There was more places than that,' she went on now, 'but I never heard their names.' She counted on her fingers. 'Four different houses, we were in. I was sick o the sight o that horse-litter by the time we fetched up here. And every time, the bairn was taken from Audrey, and we were threatened no to make a sound, or they'd slit his wee wame. Though I will say they carried him safe enough,' she added. 'She had nightmares about it, poor lass.'

'Did you hear any names?' Gil asked. 'Names of people, I mean.'

'Aye,' she said, and closed her mouth firmly. He nodded.

'And when did they clear out of here?' he asked. She gave him an approving look.

221

'First light, I think, or little after. We were asleep, in the small chamber up yonder,' she pointed at the end window, 'and they cam in and seized the blankets from us. I tried to get some sense from them, but all I got was, They'd send folk to fetch us, they'd send her kin to fetch us.' She grimaced. 'There's a well, that's clean enough, so we'd water, but they've left us no food, and I'd a trouble to keep the blanket we'd rowed the wee fellow in, till they found he'd fouled it. It's been a long day.'

'And then we turned up,' said Alys. Mistress Lithgo looked at her, her expression softening.

'Aye. I'd got Audrey up to the loft for safety. She was asleep when you all rode up, and I was feart at first, for I saw nobody I kent. Then I saw you,' she said to Henry, 'and I kent Tammas there, the wee bauchle that he is.' The gigantic Tammas grinned, and his neighbours dug him in the ribs and guffawed. 'And then I kent your voice, maister.'

'And here we all are,' said Alys, 'wi no food, and no fire, nothing for the horses, and one fouled blanket among us all.'

'We'd best ride out,' Gil said thoughtfully. 'It's more appealing than a night on the bare floor in there. There's maybe an hour to sunset, and the beasts have rested and grazed a bit. We could be most of the way home by dark.'

Alys turned to look up at him, but said nothing.

'I'd as soon no spend another night from my own roof,' said Mistress Lithgo. 'I was to be at Laigh Quarter on Sunday past, they'll be wondering what's come o me. And I'm famished wi hunger.'

'Raffie's searching for you all across the county,' Alys said.

'Can the mistress ride?' asked Vary's man Archie. 'She's no one to sit astride, how would we carry her?'

222

Gil turned this over in his mind, considering Mistress Madur's appearance when he had seen her just now.

He had given Vary as long as he could bear to before following the man up the attic stair. By the time he emerged on to the creaking floorboards, whatever raptures the couple had indulged in were over, but he somehow felt there had been none; Vary and his wife were seated decorously side by side on a balk of timber, gazing raptly at their infant, the only sign of deep emotion the grasp Vary had on Mistress Madur's free hand, as tight as a drowning man's. As if, Gil found himself thinking, the man had indeed felt himself drowning, out in the world without her support. How foolish a fancy was that, he thought, and stepped forward to congratulate the new parents on the crumpled red creature on its mother's lap. The baby did bear a startling resemblance to Vary, he realised, and had a remarkable amount of hair.

'He's well?' he said. 'He looks strong.'

'Oh, he's strong!' said Audrey Madur, smiling up at him with that stunned expression he had seen on his sisters' faces at a like time. 'He's like to suck me dry!'

She was not what he had expected. He had formed the impression of a dainty creature, perhaps a little clinging, a little shy. Instead, Audrey Madur was a big-framed girl with bright blue eyes and curling mouse-coloured hair, a high colour and a bountiful figure, though that might be due to the present circumstances; her voice was soft but very cheerful and she smiled a lot, and looked at Vary with affection.

The baby stirred and snuffled, and Vary said anxiously, 'What's wrong? Is he waking? What's he need? You've nothing for him, lass, what can we do?'

'He's well, maister,' she said, turning to smile at him. 'Beattie says he's a fine lad, like to do well. Beattie's been such a support, Vary, you'd never believe. From the time they brought her to me in yon cave where he was born, she's been like a mother to me.'

'In a cave?' he repeated incredulously. 'Oh, my lassie!'

Gil slipped away unnoticed; finding Alys below he sent her up to admire the infant, and prowled about the first floor, lifting the scatter of papers, and looking in a press in the smaller chamber.

When Alys came down again she was standing by the window, leafing through the papers. She came to lean against him, and he put his arm about her and hugged her firmly to his side. She put her head on his chest for a moment, then drew a deep breath.

'What have you there?' she said, in the resolute tone of one changing a difficult subject.

'Interesting,' he said. 'I've no idea how these came to be left behind, they should be in the steward's possession. Pages waiting to be pasted into an account roll, I suppose. But look at this.'

She ran her finger down the page, her lips moving silently, apparently totalling the amounts as she went. It seemed to be a list of incoming entries, rents in coin and a few in kind. In the midst of the page her finger stopped. She glanced at Gil, and he nodded.

'*Item fro mr varrie*,' she read, '*c merk*. One hundred merks? Whatever for?'

'I take this to be the man who called at The Cleuch,' Gil said. She nodded absently, still staring at the page.

'He can't add up,' she said suddenly. 'The total is off by a good sum. Fifty merk short, I should say.'

'Doubly interesting,' said Gil. 'I wonder where the money went to?'

'And twenty on this page,' she added, turning the sheets over, 'and ten – another ten – he is skimming off a great deal. No wonder Somerville has been short of money. And yet he was building.' She paused, staring at nothing. 'Perhaps the coin for the building came from elsewhere, into Somerville's own hands.'

'I need to talk to Vary,' said Gil. 'When I can get sense from him.'

Now he looked at the men about him.

'Henry,' he said. 'You and Archie bring the horses into the yard and make disposition. Two of them must be fit to carry an extra burden surely. The rest of you, I want the house searched.'

'They've stripped it bare,' objected someone.

'There's aye something left. I saw an odd shoe above stairs. Anything that's not nailed down, bring it here to me. Bits of wood, that broken stool, a black plack out a corner. Check the panelling upstairs for presses, look ahint the doors, look in all the corners.'

'You are thinking they are maybe leaving something that will tell us who they are, maister?' said Euan.

'We ken who they are,' said Gil, 'or at least who they were working for. I want anything that lets us have proof o't.'

When the men had drifted off, Mistress Lithgo said, 'They're ower weary.'

'We all are,' said Gil. 'We've been seeking you all across the Middle Ward. So what names did you hear, mistress? What did you jalouse? They came for you on Thursday night, right?'

'They did,' she agreed. 'A man I didny ken, tirling at the door in the twilight, just as I was sat down for a late bite. Couldny wait, said the lass was groaning strong. So I put my things thegither, and lucky I did, seeing where she was, and taken by surprise, no a thing wi her to hap the bairn in. So it went well, in that mother and bairn survived, and I says to the man that fetched me there, *Now you can take me back to Belstane*, and he says, *No, no, we'll just take you wi us.* And since he'd a great knife in his hand at the time,' she said, with that faint tone of irony he remembered from their first encounter, 'I accepted the invitation. So they cut sticks and made a hurdle for Audrey, and when there was light enough to go by we went on up the Mouse. I think that was Castlehill they took us to.' Gil nodded. 'We'd the day there, shut in a storehouse somewhere, and they fed us and brought some clouts for the bairn, moved us on by twilight again.' She grimaced. 'I heard the steward there, what's his name again, Richie Thomson, I've made him up a bottle for his hair once or twice, so I ken his voice. I heard him telling someone we couldny stay there, they'd never keep us hid. So it was on to Throwburn, which I've been at once, I think. We were there just the one night, and elsewhere after that, in a barn full wi sacks; we lay in more comfort that night. Then they moved us to The Cleuch, shut us in the old tower up there. Two days we were there, or was it three? And then yestreen they brought us on here, and left us.'

'You've been well treated?' Alys said.

'Oh, aye. We lay no worse than the men themselves, I'd say, and they fed us, brought us a jordan and gied us privacy to use it. And in this weather we wereny cold.'

'Names,' prompted Gil.

'Aye, well, for all I never saw them, Audrey guessed it was by order o two o her uncles she'd been lifted, for she kent some o their men, and she said the lad that was slain, her groom, was he? kent them and all. I did lay eyes on Jackie Somerville, the sleekit fellow.' She considered. 'There was others. I never met wi her uncles, so I'd no ken their voices, but I heard one or two gie orders, outside wherever we were held, and there was some mention o an Irishman, O'Donnell I think they cried him, folk all seemed feart for him. Even the ones that gied orders.'

'Did you ever hear Maister Vary?' Alys asked casually. Mistress Lithgo looked at her, puzzled.

'Vary? No, how would I hear him? And if we did, Audrey would ken his voice,' she added, 'though I'd not. How would he ha been about? D'you think he ordered this done?'

'It's no clear who ordered it,' said Gil. 'It seems a daft scheme, stealing Vary's wife to persuade him to approve some plans they had for land on the Burgh Muir. I reckon someone else is behind it, someone wi a bigger plan.'

'The Irishman?' she asked. He shrugged.

'Maister?' said Euan at his elbow. 'Maister, I found a press, like you said, and they've forgot to clear it. See, there was all sorts there.'

The other men were arriving, by ones and twos. Nobody else had found anything more significant than the single shoe and broken stool, but Euan had a strange assortment of items, stowed and stacked in a dusty basket of plaited reeds.

'Set it here, man,' said Mistress Lithgo, moving aside on the mounting-block to make room.

'What have you got there?' Gil said, poking at the assemblage. 'That looks like the neighbour to that shoe. A broken mousetrap, a cracked beaker, some broken staveware. These should all ha gone on the midden long ago. What's this?' He pulled out a sacking bundle, the kind of packing in which a merchant would ship a number of small items. To judge by the folds and stitches in the sacking it had held rather more than it presently contained.

'Is it—?' said Alys, craning to see what was inside. He reached into the rough folds and drew out a couple of the flat rectangular objects they concealed.

227

'Tablets,' said Mistress Lithgo.

'Some of the tablets on which they sent word to Vary,' said Gil, setting them out on the mounting-block.

'Excellent!' said Alys. 'St Bartholomew, another Crucifixion, and a very bad Annunciation. The dove looks as if it will peck her eyes out.' She lifted the nearest. 'These are from the same batch as the first messages. This one has not been written on.'

'None of them has,' said Gil, investigating. 'Very useful, Euan.'

'What else is in there?' Alys was poking in the basket of finds. 'Nothing of any import, I think. No, here is a – something off a horse-harness, is it, Gil? An ornament from a bridle or the like?'

'Could be.' He held out a hand, and she dropped the little metal object into his palm. It was of gilded lead, the gilt rubbing badly, and the loop by which it had been attached to something was broken. He turned it over; it seemed to be a badge, depicting a horse's head, perhaps a couple of inches across.

'Whose badge is it?' she asked.

'There's a many uses a horse's heid,' observed Henry, approaching the mounting-block leading several reluctant horses. 'Him at Ravenstruther, for one, though I'd think his looks the other way, and someone up by Cam'nethan has one wi the background cut out, like a pilgrim badge. These beasts is about ready, Maister Gil, and we should get on the road if we're to get back afore the light goes.'

'Are we leaving, then?' said Vary from the house door. He came down the steps. 'I was just coming to say that. I'd like to get Mistress Madur back to Lanark, and the wee one washed and in his cradle.' He looked at Mistress Lithgo and smiled, probably for the first time in days, and went on, 'We've named him, mistress. His name is Lithgo Vary.'

'You didny need to do that,' she said, looking embarrassed.

'We did,' he said. 'What's that, Gil? It looks like a trinket off my brother's horse-harness. My brother o Kersewell,' he elaborated. 'Gregory. What's it doing here?'

Chapter Eleven

'So you've sorted the matter,' said Sandy Boyd.

'No entirely,' said Gil, equally softly. 'The lassie's home safe, but I've yet to find who was at the back of this. I don't believe it was her uncles on their lone, they'd encouragement from somewhere at the very least, and maybe funds and all.'

'Mmm,' said his cousin, on a sceptical note. From beyond him, where the dark shape of William Doig showed against the sky, came a quiet laugh.

They were seated in the shadow of a clump of hawthorns, overlooking the ford at Hyndford Lea. The moon would not rise for another hour, but the night was not dark, and a blaze of stars showed the outlines of Tinto Hill, Culter Fell, a row of other hills as black shapes across the horizon, and glinted on the Clyde where it coiled lazily across the landscape on its way to the Falls of Clyde and the gorge which ran past Lanark. The road from Lanark down to the ford showed faintly, paler in the dimness. The night smelled of dust, of the trees behind them, of a fox which had passed that way a day or so since, of honeysuckle and wild garlic and the yellow flowers of the broom thicket behind them.

'But the women's all got home safe,' said Doig.

'Aye,' said Gil, hoping it was true. Alys had certainly appeared very weary; it seemed likely she would ride for Belstane as he had asked her to.

He had parted from her not far from Tarbrax, when Henry had announced that the best way to Belstane lay through Forth and not by the Lanark road.

'I'm for Lanark,' he had said. She looked sharply at his face, then put her hand out. He took it, and she squeezed his fingers briefly and let go.

'Take care,' she said. 'Put Sandy in front of you.'

'You're a rare huntsman, maister,' said Mistress Lithgo from the crupper of Alys's horse. 'I'm owing you much for the day's work.'

'He is,' Alys agreed over her shoulder.

Mistress Lithgo and her patient exchanged farewells, emotional on Audrey's part, matter-of-fact but with much blinking on Mistress Lithgo's, and promises to meet again soon. Then the Belstane party rode off into the fading light. The dog looked anxiously after them and then up at Gil, till he said, 'Home, Socrates. Go home with Alys.'

'Right, my lass,' said Vary as the wolfhound loped off, and settled his arms about his wife where she sat uncomfortably across his saddlebow. 'Let's get you hame.'

It had been surprisingly easy to locate Sandy Boyd in Lanark; Doig had been drinking in Juggling Nick's, had followed him when he went out the back, with a muttered, 'East port, an hour afore midnight,' and had spoken from the shadows of the east gate when he drifted up there. Sandy had materialised a few minutes later, black-clad, pale face and hair floating ghostly in the light night, completely unsurprised to see him. They had left the sleeping burgh not by the gate, which was well barred at that hour, but by going up a vennel, out across someone's garden where they startled a pair of cats discussing hunting rights, and through a break in the fence at the end of the toft.

'You can come by this way the morn's morn, Billy,' said Sandy as they made for the road to the ford, 'offer to mend their fence.'

'D'ye think they'll turn up?' Doig asked now.

'No idea,' said Sandy lightly. 'If they hope for their coin, they'll show.'

Doig snorted. 'If they believe in it,' he said sceptically.

'What's the aim of the meeting?' Gil asked. 'Are you looking for your quarry to be there?'

'No him,' said Sandy. 'He'll be hiding up somewhere. But I'm hoping I might get a word of where he is, or the like. Depends who he's sent to collect.'

The night wore on. Gil, his back against a hawthorn trunk, was grateful for the rest, the silence, the time to do nothing whatever, even to think. When Sandy hissed he came awake slowly, to find the horizon lightening away to their left where the moon would rise.

'I see them,' said Doig, barely audible. Gil concentrated, rubbing sleep from his eyes, and recognised movement near the river, more like wind in a barley-field than any actual moving figure. A shadow flitted between two trees, and another, and a third.

'Five or six at least,' he said quietly. 'The tinkers?'

'Aye.' His cousin was silent for a space, still watching. Finally he said, speaking hardly above a breath, 'Changes things. We wait till moonrise.'

The stealthy movements down by the ford continued. It seemed to Gil that the group, whether the tinkers or another party, now had the ford surrounded, with people on both banks, hidden under trees, melted into the bushes. He saw the wisdom in arriving as early as they had; someone simply obeying the summons for moonrise would have walked blind into a trap, unless he had brought an armed escort.

How dangerous were the tinkers, he wondered. The boy who had appeared this evening up at Tarbrax had seemed well disposed, on the whole (and how had he known they would be there? Why was he watching the place? Did he know the two women were in the house? Surely not, since he had claimed the place was empty.) These groups of wanderers had a bad reputation, of course, but principally for opportune theft and general dishonesty and stealing children, for fighting and drunkenness. They were not given to organised violence, though they were held to be bonnie fighters.

The moon lifted above the Lothian hills, only a day older than last night at The Cleuch but somehow much thinner. It cast some light on the scene before them, though the greater effect was to deepen the shadows where the stealthy movements had settled. Trying to keep a tally in his head of where one dimly seen figure and another had halted, Gil gathered his feet under him, preparing to rise.

'Right,' said Sandy beside him. 'Let's away down there.'

Emerging from the shadows of their clump of trees, he sauntered down the slope. Gil followed him, Doig with his rolling gait alongside. By the ford, first one, then another figure emerged from obscurity, till there were four people standing where the track ran down the river bank, watching them approach. Their stance was vigilant, rather than threatening; they did not seem to be armed. Without turning his head or seeming to look, Gil reckoned there were perhaps two more still lurking this side of the ford, ready to appear, and another four or five on the opposite bank.

Sandy strolled down to a point perhaps ten feet from the four men, and halted, nodding to the nearest.

'A bonnie evening,' he said casually.

'It is that, maister, indeed it is that,' agreed the man. 'Been a while, Blue Doo.'

'It has that. It's been away too long, indeed.' The accent, like the boy's up by Tarbrax, was lilting, strange.

'Cauf's Heid,' continued Sandy, with a nod to another man. 'Hauf a Sark. Wooden Toe. A bonnie evening.'

There was general agreement on this. After a few moments, the man addressed as Blue Doo remarked, 'And I see you ha freens at your back, maister. A bonnie evening, wee man.'

Doig grunted, apparently impatient with this ritual. There was a waiting pause, and Sandy finally said, 'My cousin.'

'A bonnie evening,' Gil contributed, raising his hat to the four.

'A bean gadgie like yoursel, maister, I can tell that,' said Blue Doo to Sandy.

'Oh, aye, a course he is,' said Sandy.

There was another pause. Doig fidgeted slightly, but Sandy stood unmoving, waiting. Gil did likewise, thinking of the cats they had seen earlier and wondering at what point his cousin would strike out with an ear-piercing shriek, and how the four tinkers would react.

'I'm wondering,' said Blue Doo, giving in, 'what would bring yourself out to take the air at this hour, maister. It's a time for honest folks to be in their beds, so it is.'

'I could say the same to you,' Sandy returned. 'I suppose there's some errand brings you out in the moonlight. An unchancy hour to be abroad, so it is.'

'Well, as to that,' said Blue Doo easily, 'and as it falls out, we've an errand indeed. It's a freen o ours, you see, has asked us to come down here and collect a wee parcel from a fellow, a gadgie like yoursel, maister. Which we're doing as a favour to him, he being a guest o the

MacPhersons, and we had word that it would be a good thing to be doing.'

'Is that right?' said Sandy with great interest. 'Now that's a remarkable thing, for a freen of ours has sent us down here in the hope of getting a word wi a fellow that summoned him here concerning the very same wee parcel.'

'Oh, aye, that's a remarkable thing indeed,' agreed Blue Doo. 'Is that no a remarkable thing, Cauf's Heid?'

One of his companions nodded. Another said, 'Aye, it is that. Now what's to be done about it, d'ye suppose, Blue Doo?'

'I ken what I'd think we might do,' said Blue Doo. 'We might offer these bean gadgies, and the wee man and all, our hospitality for the nicht, to lie in our tents wi us, and then the morn's morn when it's day and we can all see what's afoot, we can take him to meet our freen. Now how's that appear to you, maister?'

Sandy Boyd cocked his head on one side, apparently considering this.

'It's a generous offer,' he said at length. 'You'd see us back on our road after, a course.'

'Och, indeed, we'd do that,' Blue Doo assured him. 'To the very gates o Lanark itsel, and no mistake.'

'I'd think that might be a good thing to be doing,' said Sandy, 'and a good offer to be accepting.'

'I hoped you'd see it that way,' said Blue Doo. 'Indeed, I did.'

He turned, put two fingers to his mouth, and whistled sharply. The watchers in the shadows emerged, one and two at a time, and he spoke to them in a language Gil did not recognise. Some of it seemed to be Ersche, and there were Scots words in there, but much of it was unfamiliar. Like *bean gadgie*, he reflected; *bean* was possibly the good Scots word *bien*, lifted from the

French, but was a *gadgie* a man, a human being, a gentleman?

'Well, now,' said Blue Doo. 'It's just a wee step up the river, so it is, to the sweetest place to be setting our tents we ever did see. Will we be off, then, freens, while the moon's still watching us?'

The next hour or so stayed with Gil as the stuff of dreams. He could not imagine how Doig was coping with the journey. The tinkers' notion of a wee step, it turned out, was four or five miles, mostly by the banks of the Clyde where it looped and curved across the flat ground below Carstairs. The going was rough grass and bushes, the occasional cattle-track, open land which the men around him crossed crouching low on principle, in case anyone should chance to see them.

'For it would astonish you how people are willing to think we must be up to no good, maister, I can be assuring you,' said the fellow guiding him, who seemed to be the one called Wooden Toe. 'Your eyebrows would be rising off the top o your heid, so they would, if I was telling you all I've been accused of, and me as honest as the day's long. Mind your feet, maister, the Carstairs herd laddie brings the beasts to drink here,' he added unnecessarily. Gil's nose had warned him some time since.

Moving rapidly, they reached what Gil reckoned must be the foot of the Carnwath Burn and turned up its narrow valley. The going was even rougher here, and the waterside was overgrown with bushes and brambles, which the company threaded its way through expertly, tugging the three strangers this way and that to avoid furze bushes and overhanging branches. Suddenly very tired, Gil plodded after Wooden Toe, ducking when ordered to, aware of Doig cursing behind him and his cousin discoursing on what seemed to be the doings of the Court ahead of him, and thinking

237

about how far he had ridden or walked in the past two days.

Then, abruptly, they came out into an open area, with a fire burning at its centre, and a number of low tents disposed under the trees at its margins. Beyond the ring of tents, ponies' eyes gleamed in the firelight, hooves stamped; the burn burbled happily ten feet away, a stewpot simmered on a base of stones by the fire, and several women sat in the flickering light watching them.

'Come in at the fire, maisters, and welcome,' said Blue Doo formally.

'A blessing on the hearth,' said Boyd. Gil murmured an Ersche blessing he had heard in Perthshire, and sank down where he was directed. One of the women leaned forward and put a leather beaker into his hands. It was hot, and steamed with a scent which made his nose tickle.

'Drink that, maister,' she said. 'You'll no be liking it, but it will be liking you.'

He sniffed more carefully, detecting thyme and wild garlic and other herbs with an undernote of, was it fennel?

'Drink,' encouraged the woman. 'It's what was ordered for you.'

'Ordered?' he said warily, looking at her across the beaker. 'Who by?'

'Him wi the red hair, a course.' She made a sign with one hand. 'Drink up, maister, and be easy, I'd no poison a guest at my fireside.' Bright eyes watched him intently as he tasted the tisane, then swallowed a mouthful. 'Aye, you were brought here in a good hour. Sleep now, maister, and get the word you came for.'

The voices woke him from a dream. He lay for a while, working out where he was, hearing birdsong beyond the voices, not the loud rejoicing just after the dawn but the chirrups and whistles of the morning feeding session. It must be a couple of hours after Prime. There was a mixture of odours, of cut bracken and heather, ancient canvas, trampled grass. Other, more pungent smells floated past, and then the scent of fresh bannocks. The voices became clearer as if the speakers were closer or something had moved out of the way. He was in a tent in the tinkers' camp, he realised, wrapped in some-one's ancient, greasy plaid. He had slept like a log until the dream, and the scent of the bannocks toasting had set his belly rumbling.

The dream was oddly disturbing, and showed no tendency to evaporate now he was awake, as dreams usually did. He had walked under a shadowed hazel alley, like the one in Vary's garden, with a companion who seemed familiar, seemed to know him well. The man had said, *Not here, but in the orchard. Get your son in the orchard, under the apple trees by the midsummer moon.* Then he had turned to look at Gil. He had red hair which fell over a long gown with wide lapels, of blue plaid shot through with many colours; under the gown he wore a linen sark bound with a fox-skin belt. *Guard yourself,* he said. *Break out of the hazel grove. Beware of thunder.* Gil had answered, *I don't know a hazel grove.* The red-haired man reached out and touched him, with three fingers, just below the breastbone. And then the voices woke him.

They were still conversing, not far away.

'Can you no get rid of him?' said his cousin quite clearly. 'You could just leave these parts, steal away in the night and leave him sleeping. You're well able to do a thing like that, and vanish away into the hills.'

Gil sat up and unwound the plaid, settling his clothes about his person, pulling on the doublet which someone had removed before rolling him up in the plaid, patting the purse at his belt.

'The trouble wi that, your lordship,' said another voice, 'is that we'd no want to be leaving this neighbourhood yet. We're trysted wi the McEwans after St John's Eve, see, over by Tweedsmuir, but for sure that's a day or two away yet. We'd no want to be ower soon to the tryst, the way you'd think we was all young lassies.'

'Tell him to leave.'

'Now what kind of hospitality would that be, maister? And yet he is eating all we can find, though he never hunts, and he has taken Pitmedden Maggie's Annie to his bed though she was not willing, and he demands a fourth part of the coin we are promised for planting all the wee trees, up on the muir above Lanark town.'

'Aye, the trees.' That was Doig. 'Who was to pay you for the planting, then?'

'Och, the same man that was to be paying you,' said the tinker. It sounded like the man called Blue Doo. Reflecting on the oddness of the tinkers' by-names, Gil folded the plaid, emerged stooping from the tent and set off into the trees in search of privacy.

When he came back to the clearing one of the women from last night looked up from the spitting bakestone on the fire, studied him, then gave him what was clearly a blessing in Gaelic, and handed him a bannock from the heap arranged on a dock-leaf at her side. He returned the hearth-blessing he had used last night, at which she smiled, and turned back to her bakestone. She was clad in a worn and patched kirtle, much faded but still showing the original tawny in places; the shift under it was cleaner than one might have expected, and the linen on her head was neat and decent, though it was folded in a different way from that worn by the women he was used to.

Looking around, he discovered two other women seated in the next tent, gossiping happily over their spindles while four or five men of the tribe sprawled about on the grass, some whittling at sticks or staves with their great gully-knives, one spinning like the women a remarkably fine thread from a collection of tufts of wool. There were no children visible. Off to one side, his cousin and William Doig sat with three of the tinkers.

As he joined them Sandy looked up and nodded, but went on with what he was saying: 'What you tell me, man, is you'd like rid of this fellow.'

'Och, no, no,' protested Blue Doo. 'No rid o him, precisely, your lordship, just that we'd be well pleased if he were to be elsewhere, and us no wi him.'

'Where is he the now?' Doig asked.

'Well, when we left,' said one of the other men, 'he would be wi the rest o the MacPhersons, see, where we last saw all of them.'

'And that was?' Doig looked as if he found the tinkers' inability to speak directly to a subject exasperating. Gil, thinking that dealing with Euan Campbell had had its uses after all, chewed his bannock and listened as the man, who might be Wooden Toe by his voice, worked his way round to locating the other camp on the other side of Carnwath town, no so far from the Medwin, in a bonnie wee spot—

'Kersewell?' said Boyd.

'Och, indeed, your wisdom, you're setting me a trap,' said Wooden Toe. 'For indeed it is no more than a wee step away from the very house o Kersewell. If you kent that, surely you were never needing to ask.'

'Will we go there now?' said Doig bluntly.

'Now, wee man, I can see you're in a great hurry,' said Blue Doo. Seen by daylight he was a lanky man with

241

shaggy iron-dark hair and beard, the threads of grey pronounced at his temples; he was clad in a tattered doublet over a well-washed shirt and belted plaid, a great gully-knife at his waist and a felted bonnet on his head, of the natural brown of the wool rather than the woad-blue worn by most house-dwellers. 'But we can get away if you're wishful, the six o us you see here, and leave Bella,' the woman by the fire looked up and he nodded to her, 'and the rest to be breaking the hearth and following us by dark.'

'Is that where the bairns are? Up at Kersewell, I mean,' Gil asked. Blue Doo shot him a penetrating look, and glanced away again. Under his shaggy eyebrows his eyes were a bright blue, but did not meet anyone's directly.

'No need to be bringing the bairns down here,' he said, 'when there was no telling who'd be answering the invitation we left.'

'Will we get away then?' said Doig impatiently.

'Haud your horses, wee man,' said Boyd. 'There's one or two other matters I need to deal wi.'

'Is there, now?' said Blue Doo. Wooden Toe casually began gathering his feet under him to rise. The third man in the group, a small wiry fellow with fairish hair receding under his mottled brown bonnet, was grinning uneasily.

'Och, surely no, maister,' he said ingratiatingly, 'your honour can have nothing to discuss wi poor tinker folk like us. We've no reason to mix wi the likes o yoursel.'

'You're mixing wi me now,' observed Boyd, grinning in his turn, rather like a cockatrice Gil had once seen in a bestiary.

'No, no, your wisdom's mixing wi us,' corrected Blue Doo politely. 'It would be a different thing altogether were we to be mixing wi you.'

'Be that as it may,' said Boyd firmly across something Doig was about to say, 'I've matters to deal wi. For a start, when did you say you were to meet the McEwans?'

'Did I say so?' said Blue Doo evasively. Wooden Toe, still moving casually, ambled away from the group.

'St John's tide, he said,' said Doig. 'No more than a week away.'

Too direct, thought Gil. *These folk are even more devious than the Campbell brothers; they'll not respond to the direct approach.*

'What road d'you take to Tweedsmuir?' he asked idly. 'I was never over that way, I'd not ken how to start.'

'Well, I wouldny start from here, maister, if I was you,' Blue Doo assured him. 'You want to be over by Biggar, for sure, and work your way down the Biggar Water and then away up the Tweed. A bonnie river, the Tweed, and teeming wi salmon and trout, so it is, and hazelnuts all along the banks in a couple o months, there will be.'

'I can imagine,' agreed Gil. 'Is that the way the McEwans take and all?'

'Och, no, they are coming over from Lochmaben way. It's an easy climb up from Annandale, so it is, the auld grandmother would have it so.'

'And the Lees come over the border from England, do they?'

The bright blue eyes flicked sharply to his face and away again; in the corner of his vision Gil was aware of his cousin turning to look at him as well. He waited a moment, but neither Blue Doo nor his remaining companion commented. 'It's a long way into the hills,' he went on, 'just to meet another group o travelling folk. I'd look for there to be a better reason than the McEwans, and the Lees wouldny come any further into Scotland than that, would they?'

243

'No, no, maister,' said Blue Doo softly. 'Surely you must be mistaken, for the Lees are English travellers. They'd no be welcome in the Marches, no this side o the Border. I couldny say they would gather at sic a tryst as you describe.'

'I see,' said Gil. 'I can see that. Maybe they'd send a messenger, I suppose.'

'I suppose they might,' agreed Blue Doo. 'I suppose they might, maister, though it's hard to be sure.'

'And if they did,' said Gil, 'he could bring anything across the Border, anything small, a message or a letter or a package, I expect. Or a cartload of guns or a barrel of gunpowder, maybe.'

There was a silence, in which he felt the tinkers were carefully not looking at one another.

'Aye, aye,' agreed Blue Doo again. 'I dare say sic a one might, maister, I dare say he might. But I couldny tell you aught about sic a thing, for neither guns nor gunpowther has come near me, I'd say, and I've no knowledge o messages or letters, being as I'm no a man that can read or write. Someone wi book-learning, the like o yoursel, maister, could likely tell us more.'

'You think so?' said Gil. 'But I've no knowledge of messages either, since I've never been into Tweeddale, nor met a messenger from the Lees. I wonder where the gunpowder came from.' He gazed at a blackbird which was hunting under the bushes opposite, turning leaves energetically. Feeling his eye on it, the bird scurried off into the shadows, and he added, 'And I wonder who might be able to tell us of sic things.'

'I tell you who might,' said the other tinker who was still sitting with them. Blue Doo glanced at him, frowning, but he continued with an innocent smile, 'Yon fellow we was just speaking o, maister, he might ken all sort o things. Him being a travelled man, you ken, and been to all sort o places, and outside Scotland, and into Ireland, and all.'

'I'm thinking,' said Blue Doo, 'the wee man here, that's seated like a statue in some great lord's garden, might be able to tell you more o messages and packages than us poor gangrel bodies.'

'Aye, that's a true word, Blue Doo,' said the other tinker, while Doig preserved a stillness like the statue he had been compared with. 'For one thing, he can read, Maister Doig can, I ken that.'

'He can indeed, Cauf's Heid,' agreed Blue Doo. 'And he's a travelled man, forbye.'

'Billy?' said Boyd, breaking a long silence.

Doig glared at him, and said in a goaded tone, 'Aye, I suppose. Like maybe the letter I delivered to you a'ready?'

'Billy, the day you're working for one man and only one, I'll dance naked through Edinburgh,' said Boyd. 'Who else have you carried for this trip, and what?'

'I've gave you all that's yours, you can be certain,' said Doig aggressively. 'You've no need to get on at me.'

'Oh, but I think I do, Billy,' said Boyd, his tone silky. 'What did you carry to the Irishman?'

'Nothing.'

'And what will you carry for him? Where is it to go?'

'I'm carrying nothing for the Irishman,' said Doig, the anger still rumbling in his voice. 'You can search me if you will. I've nothing to carry away for the Irishman nor anyone else, unless you're planning to gie me an errand to the back o' the North Wind.'

Yes, we can search you, thought Gil, sitting impassive in the circle, *because the packet you were carrying is in my purse.* When had the small man put it there, he wondered, and why? And just how much did he know about the cartload of guns, about the gunpowder?

245

The letter in the packet had made interesting reading earlier, under the trees, a missive in diplomatic Latin addressed to the Earl of Buchan, invoking his aid in disposing of 'he who styles himself of York' should 'the boy' set foot in Scotland. It mentioned significant amounts of money, and appeared to be from John Ramsay, the former Lord Bothwell, one of the favourites of James Third, dispossessed after that king's death at Sauchieburn and currently resident in England. Gil hoped the seals could be reinstated if necessary; it seemed likely that Sandy would be better at that than he was.

'And you reckon none of the MacPhersons carries sic things back and forth?' Boyd remarked to Blue Doo. 'I'm surprised at that, for it seems to me like an easy way to be earning a coin or two, or a few favours, when you're acquaint wi the Lees and all.'

'Would you say so?' returned Blue Doo, sounding interested. 'Maybe we should be looking about us for messages to take, if that's the case, would you think, Cauf's Heid?'

'Aye, mebbe,' agreed Cauf's Heid. 'We could be asking at himself, likely, up at Kersewell.'

'But you've already run errands for Vary of Kersewell,' said Gil politely, 'have you no? That's how you've got setting down on his land.'

'What, the MacPhersons?' said Cauf's Heid, looking alarmed. 'Och, you're thinking o someone else, maister. Maybe the McEwans. Aye, that'll be it,' he nodded sagely, 'likely the McEwans. Turn their hand to anything, they will.'

'So what did you do for Vary?' asked Sandy Boyd. 'Him at Kersewell, Gregor or Gregory or whatever his name is.'

'Kept a watch on Mistress Somerville at Kettlands, I'd say, for one,' said Gil. Cauf's Heid's alarmed look intensified. 'And on his brother Ambrose in Lanark. Maybe no yourselves, maybe no the elders of the group, but your bairns seem to me to get all ower Lanarkshire, and who notices a tinker laddie?'

'They did more than that,' said Doig sourly. 'Planted out five hunner slips o timber, hid the Irishman—'

'Set fire to The Cleuch,' suggested Boyd.

'Indeed we never!' said Blue Doo, his hand going to the gully-knife at his belt. A silence fell across the clearing. Gil looked up, to find the rest of the group of tinkers watching intently. 'That was the Irish gadgie fired the house, so it was, and none o our doing. You'll no hang that one on our necks!'

'You think no?' said Boyd mildly.

'No, I think no,' said Gil. 'I think the worst they've done there is hide the fellow, as Doig says, and convoy him about.'

A strange expression flitted across Blue Doo's face, surprise and – what? Something else. Could it have been relief?

'We were guiding him to The Cleuch,' he conceded. 'Seeing he has no great knowledge o the tracks and tramping-ways o Scotland. And when he came away from the place in a great hurry in the midnight, we were taking him back to Kersewell, and it was only when we looked back we were seeing the place, the way it was burning. I'm right glad to learn you were all getting away safe,' he added, 'for I'd no wish sic bean gadgies as yoursels to be hurt in a fire, so I wouldny.'

So they knew we were there, thought Gil.

'What did the Irishman want at that house?' he asked.

'Och, we'd have no knowledge o that,' protested Cauf's Heid. 'He'd no share that wi the likes o us!'

'Maybe no,' said Sandy Boyd, 'but you might ha been in a position to overhear some of their talk, being as close as you were. It would be interesting to ken what they found to converse about.'

Gil flinched, as the image of Robert Somerville's ruined face came to mind. Blue Doo's glance flicked to him and away again, and the man nodded, infinitesimally.

'I'm thinking maybe Somerville didny ha much joy o the conversation,' observed Cauf's Heid drily.

'How was that?' asked Boyd, his tone casual.

'Och, surely your worship kens as much as we do,' said Blue Doo. 'Being as you were there and all, afore the fire spread.'

Boyd waited. Gil waited. Doig looked from one to another of the faces about him. Finally Blue Doo fell into the trap and broke the silence.

'He was asking a many questions, so he was,' he admitted. 'The Irishman. So he was. Somerville didny seem right willing to answer them, neither.'

'Questions?' prompted Boyd in the same casual tone.

'Aye, questions. Where was the missing lady, did she bear a boy or a bairn, was it like to live, questions o that sort. No to mention, where was the coin, who had paid him. I think he never had any answer, did he, Cauf's Heid?'

'No that I heard,' admitted Cauf's Heid. 'At least, no in words.'

'Was that all he asked after?' Boyd asked. 'Just the missing lady?'

'I'd ha thought he'd only to ask at you and your family,' said Gil, and a flicker of annoyance crossed his cousin's face. 'The way you've been watching her and those about her.'

'Och, indeed no!' protested Cauf's Heid. 'What we kenned o the lady and her kin we were keeping to

248

oursels, for that's nothing to do wi wanderers out o Ireland, nor it isny.'

'But more to do wi Vary of Kersewell?' suggested Gil. 'Since he's paying you. Do you think he will?'

'He'll pay us,' said Blue Doo confidently. There was a certain threat in the tone.

'And was that all the fellow was speiring at Somerville?' Sandy Boyd asked. 'Or at Henry Madur? Och, no, I suppose that was all you heard,' he added. 'Likely you wouldny want to get near enough to hear right.'

'We heard plenty,' said Blue Doo. 'We heard enough.'

There was another silence. After it had dragged on for a while, Blue Doo unfolded his legs and said, 'Maybe we should be setting out for Kersewell. It's a fine day we're wasting, your honours, so it is.'

'Aye,' said Doig grimly. 'I've had enough o the giff-gaff, time we were on our feet.'

Watching the MacPhersons sorting out who would accompany them and who would stay to strike the camp, with much discussion in that strange mix of Ersche and another tongue, Gil remarked softly, 'Interesting.'

Doig grunted. 'No interesting enough.'

'Billy's right,' said Sandy Boyd. 'No interesting enough.' He switched to French. 'Did you hear what you wanted?'

'More or less,' Gil returned. '*I wol now singen, yif I kan, the armes and also the man.* Accusations are not proof, of course, but a conversation with the eldest brother will be of value. I'm assuming it was him brought in the guns, whoever carried them. It may have been the McEwans rather than this crew. Do you know, Maister Doig?' Doig gave him an impassive stare. Gil grinned suddenly. 'That's if Vary will speak to me. I won't

249

convince as Blacader's quaestor, will I, rising up out of the heather like this.'

'Use your knife on him,' recommended Doig in Scots. 'Most folks will listen to that.'

Chapter Twelve

'And an invitation scribed in Vary's own hand,' said Mistress Somerville, dabbing at her eyes, 'to stay at Lanark wi them to see the bairn baptised and longer. There was ne'er sic a good-son as mine, madam, I tell you, attentive and respectful, just as he ought.'

Alys met Lady Egidia's eye and looked away quickly, hiding a smile. Behind Mistress Somerville her maid, less successful, bent her head hastily to scrutinise the elaborate folds of her mistress's veil.

They were in the solar at Kettlands, having ridden out shortly after noon to call on several people. Alys would have much preferred to stay at home after yesterday's wide excursions, but her mother-in-law had insisted on her presence. She sat quietly on the padded backstool, studying Mistress Somerville's collection of strange objects, wondering why she kept them and how rapidly the new grandchild, for whom they had brought a suitable gift extracted from the attics at Belstane, would destroy most of them.

'And your daughter is well?' said Lady Egidia. 'And the bairn? What have they named him, again?'

'Wee Lithgo,' said Mistress Somerville dubiously. 'It's a right strange name for a laddie, though I can see why they gied him it. I hope he doesny get teased at the school. Aye, my lassie's well, or she was this morn when

Vary sent me word. I'm that grateful to Maister Cunningham, for I understand it was entirely his doing that they were found. And how her uncles could ha done sic a thing to her – but maybe best nothing's said on that head.'

Not entirely Gil's doing, thought Alys, but said nothing. Lady Egidia, seated opposite, the wide skirts of her green riding-gown pooling about her feet, set her empty glass down on the tray with a little click. 'I'm right glad my son has been of service, madam,' she said. 'As for the other matter, that's a sore loss to you, to have your brother and good-brother both dead in the one night.'

'No loss they!' said Mistress Somerville on a vindictive note. 'Our Rab was aye a sleekit creature, and as for Jocelyn Madur o Eastshiel, well! Thought himsel a judge o horses, so he did, tried to tell me what I should be riding, offered to buy it for me. And how much o my price would ha gone into his purse, tell me that?' she demanded rhetorically. 'It's a right shame The Cleuch went up in flames,' she added. 'I'd heard it was a fine house, and I'm sorry for the eldest boy, that's the heir, but Rab's no loss to the world, I can tell you, madam.'

'You've no notion what could ha brought your brother to do sic a thing?' Lady Egidia asked.

'Likely money,' said Mistress Somerville sourly. 'He'd be after money from Vary, or some way to get it, or maybe someone gied him money to do it. He's aye been short o money, since he was a laddie, it slid out his fingers like water.'

'You'd wonder how he managed to build sic a great house,' said Lady Egidia. 'Hall and two wings, so my son tellt me, and everything fine about it, as you say. And some handsome plenishings too, Gil said.'

'Aye, all lost,' said Mistress Somerville, shaking her head. 'He'd a long tale last I seen him, o doing a favour

252

for Commendator Knollys, him that used to be Lord Treasurer, o being far ben wi him. *More use*, says I, *to be well ben wi the man that's Treasurer now*, but he wouldny hear me. So maybe that's where he had the coin fro. No saying now, it's all lost, every stick, save for a great cabinet, a' fu' o wee drawers like a spice kist, that the Depute sent across on a cart yestreen. Right kind o him to do that. He sent word wi it that was the only piece they'd got out undamaged and would I like to take it for safety. I'll maybe no mention to my nevvie it's here,' she added, with a complicit glance, 'till he asks for it.'

'They make those in the Low Countries,' said Alys, without looking at her mother-in-law. 'I've seen one or two. They can be bonnie things. Is this one carved, or painted, or the like?'

'I've not seen it.' Mistress Somerville shook her head again, so that her barbe slid back and forward over her bosom. Today's gown was not the magnificent black brocade construction she had worn to visit Belstane, but a plainer brown garment with huge sleeves turned back with black velvet; the kirtle visible beneath it was well worn. She must have assumed the gown in a hurry, like Provost Lockhart the other day, when the guests were seen riding up the track. 'It's still out in the stables,' she continued now, 'till it loses the stink o the fire. I'll need to set them to wash it wi vinegar and water.'

'What did your brother use it for?' Alys asked. 'Some keep papers in them, but some keep curiosities, the likes o these that you collect, madam. You could make good use o't in this chamber.'

'Och, it's full o all sorts, says Billy,' said their hostess dismissively. 'Stones and strange coins and the like. You're welcome to take a look, if it interests you, lassie. Tell Billy I bade him show you it, as you leave.'

'And we ought to be taking our leave,' said Lady Egidia, gathering her skirts together to rise. 'You'll have to see to your packing, mistress, if you're to stay at Lanark for some days. I've no doubt Mistress Madur will be glad to have you wi her.'

Billy, once he accepted that they were to see the cabinet, was quite happy to show them where it was, and to describe the trouble they had had getting it off the cart and into the storeroom where he had placed it.

'Four o us, it took,' he said, grimacing, 'what wi the legs drapping off as soon's look at it, and the wee draws sliding out, save for the one that jammed when I tried to open it to get a grip o the thing. Here it's, mistress, and here it can stay for all o me.'

'Very handsome,' said Lady Egidia, studying the item. 'That must hold a deal o clutter. From the Low Countries, you said, my dear?'

Alys stepped forward, and froze, realising just in time that she could hardly go through the contents in front of Mistress Somerville's servants.

'It's empty,' said Billy. 'I emptied all the wee draws into yon basket.' He indicated a stout willow basket sitting by the foot of the cabinet. 'There was all sorts in it, stones and wee carvings and boxes, empty purses and old seals, you name it. Load o rubbish, fit for the midden, all o't.'

'I would keep papers in it,' said Alys. She peered into the basket, and felt that Billy was right in his valuation of the contents.

'He didny. That's one thing there wasny, papers.'

'I think we've seen enough,' said Lady Egidia, looking over her shoulder at the yard, where their horses were just being led out. 'Let's away, my dear. We've other calls to make.'

254

'Where now, mem?' asked Steenie as they rode down the track towards the Lanark road. 'Is it Lockharthill now?'

'I'd like to go into Lanark,' said Alys.

Lady Egidia looked curiously at her, but only said, 'Very well. Lanark first, Steenie, and then likely Lockharthill after. You men can wait at Juggling Nick's as usual.'

'Did you see the cabinet, Steenie?' Alys asked.

'What, the now, mem? I'd a look at it. It's an orra thing, right enough. There'd be a fair bit o carpentry in it, wi all they wee boxes to match to size. Skilled work, right enough. My cousin Will's a furniture-maker, chairs and kists and the like, but he's never made aught like that.'

'And up at The Cleuch? Did you see it come out the house?'

'No me, mem. I was down the stables.'

'What is your interest?' asked Lady Egidia in French.

'Gil saw the piece in the man's closet,' Alys returned. 'He kept secrets in it, coins and documents, but now they are missing. I wonder who has them.'

'Ah.' Lady Egidia turned her horse on to the Lanark road, and remarked after a few paces, 'I have not yet met this Madame Olympe.'

'She may not be in Lanark just now,' Alys said.

'I understand that. She seems to be a most interesting person.'

'I would rather say *étonnant*,' said Alys with care.

'*Étonnant*,' her mother-in-law repeated, her eyes dancing.

'Precisely.'

Much to Alys's relief, Agnes opened the door to Madame Olympe's lodging when she rattled at the pin. Her expression was anxious, and lifted only slightly when she saw Alys.

'Oh, it's yoursel, mem,' she said, bobbing a curtsy. 'I fear I canny ask you in, mem, madam,' her glance flicked over Alys's shoulder to Lady Egidia, and then to Steenie waiting at the foot of the steps. 'My mistress is no weel. Something she's ate, I've no doubt, I've emptied the jordan as many times the day—'

'Oh, poor lady,' said Alys, suppressing a giggle at this level of verisimilitude.

Below the forestair the Lightbodys' inquisitive elderly maidservant leaned out of her window and called up to them, 'She's needing a good dose o rhubart, Agnes, and then some o my rice porridge. I'll make her a wee drop and send it up.'

'Aye, thank you kindly, Annet,' responded Agnes. 'That'd be right neighbourly in you. So you see, mem,' she continued to Alys, 'how I'm placed.'

'That's no easy for you. This is my good-mother, Lady Cunningham, Agnes. May we no step in for a moment?' Alys said, trying to give Agnes a significant look. 'Only for a moment, we'd not wish to disturb Madame.'

After a slight pause Agnes stepped aside to let them enter, biting her lip.

'D'ye ken where—' she began, in a low voice, as if taking care not to disturb an invalid in the inner chamber.

'No,' said Alys, equally softly, 'nor Gil either, but I've to get the papers that came from The Cleuch.' Beside her she was aware of Lady Egidia very carefully not reacting. 'The papers that came home after the fire,' she prompted, at Agnes's dubious look. 'Out the cabinet in Somerville's closet.'

'Ah.' Agnes still looked doubtful. Alys, in the absence of any truthful exhortation she could come up with, kept silence, and finally the woman said, 'I'll see if I can put my hand on them, mem. Hae a seat, ladies, why

256

don't ye. And I hope ye'll forgive me if I don't offer you a refreshment, what wi illness in the house.'

'That's well understood,' said Lady Egidia. She seated herself elegantly on the backstool Agnes indicated, and raised her eyebrows in some amusement as the door to the inner chamber closed behind the woman. Alys nodded, pointed at the floorboards, touched her ear. Annet might be listening in the kitchen below them, though it was also possible she was at the window, interrogating Steenie where he waited in the street.

They waited in silence for the length of a *Te Deum* or so, while sounds from the inner chamber suggested that Agnes was searching for the papers in one kist or another, one bag or garment or another. Eventually she emerged, slipping sideways through the door, making certain they could not see past her. She held a small bundle of folded papers; the outermost one had a bright green seal on it.

'I think this must be them, mem,' she said, 'for I canny mind that I've seen the seal afore. Did he— do you ken what's wanted wi them?'

'No entirely,' said Alys, with perfect truth, tucking the wad of paper into her purse, straightening her skirts over it again. 'Just that they're wanted. My thanks, Agnes, and I hope Madame will be about soon.'

Agnes acknowledged this with a wry smile, and curt-sied again as they rose to leave.

'I've a good purging mix,' said Lady Egidia. 'I can send some over if this continues. Tell your mistress,' she added as she made her way down the forestair, 'I'm right sorry to find her in sic state. I'll call again when she's more herself.'

'You'll aye be welcome, madam,' Agnes assured her, almost credibly, and below them Annet withdrew and Steenie straightened up from where he leaned against the wall, and offered Lady Egidia his arm to step down off the stair.

In the private chamber at Juggling Nick's which she and Gil had used before, Alys laid the papers out on the table, Lady Egidia watching her with interest.

'That was cleverly done. I've seen Gil use the same methods. It's like guddling for trout,' she commented. 'And here's the men reporting several o my beasts in the stable waiting. What's that about?'

'We hired fresh horses last night,' Alys explained. 'Those we came home on, that we brought back the now. But it troubles me that Gil's animal is still here. He must have gone to the ford on foot. I wish I knew where he went from there.'

'So do I,' admitted her mother-in-law. 'What do you have there?'

'I'm not certain,' Alys said. 'There are many papers here, but still I think some must be missing.' She looked from one to another of the documents before her. 'As for why he would keep such material, it seems the height of foolishness to me. This one mentions a barrel of gunpowder, sent with the bearer.'

'Gunpowder?' Lady Egidia repeated. 'So the rumours are true? Does it mention guns as well?'

'Not so far. Who is Ramsay?'

'John Ramsay?' Lady Egidia craned to see the papers.

'There are three letters signed only R,' Alys shuffled them round on the table so that the older woman could study them, 'brief ones, but this one in another hand refers to Ramsay.' She grimaced at the crooked writing. 'There is no Christian name. And another refers to B.'

'That could be the same man. Ramsay was Lord Bothwell till he was forfeit after Sauchieburn.'

'It says *R has scrievit B*,' Alys reported.

'So obviously not.' Lady Egidia considered the letters before her. 'It might be Stewart of Buchan, I suppose, who is half-uncle to the King. They aye ran thegither, if I recall right.'

And were not friends to the young King, Alys surmised, if Ramsay had forfeited his lands and title after the uprising in which James Third had *happenit to be slain,* as the next Parliament had put it.

'Buchan was aye plotting one thing or another in corners when I was at Court,' Lady Egidia continued. 'I never understood why the King put up wi him. The late King, that is. The Queen my mistress never put any trust in him, nor in Ramsay, for all he was one o the King's favourites.'

'But what are they planning now,' Alys wondered, not trying to distinguish between kings, 'and what had Somerville to do with it?'

'Here is *Ios M,*' Lady Egidia pointed. 'So Jocelyn Madur is in it as well. But what is it? What are they planning, as you say? I canny make out.'

'Nor can I.' Alys rearranged the papers, setting them in the order of the dates they bore. 'These three from R, who may be Ramsay, refer to one RH, on embassy to C. He is to ask for the person of John of Albany.'

'One of the heralds, perhaps,' said her mother-in-law. 'The English have a Richmond Herald, I believe. Sent to France on Embassy, and asking your king to give them the Duke of Albany, who must be first cousin to James Stewart and would make a useful pretender for England to wield against us. He might get him, too,' she said thoughtfully, 'Charles of France is busy harrying the Pope this year, rather than looking north.'

'That makes sense,' Alys agreed. 'Not that Charles de Valois is my king,' she added. 'I am married to a Scot, after all. But in the third letter, when the Valois has given

259

no answer, Ramsay turns to discussing making sure of the death of someone.'

'Who?' demanded Lady Egidia pertinently.

'It calls him *the boy*. His name is not here.' She turned the letter over. 'I suppose it is the same boy as Michael heard discussed.'

'The Duke of York,' said Lady Egidia. 'Or whoever he is. They seem very sure he will come to Scotland.'

'It seems certain he is invited, at the least, by what Sandy told Gil, and a bride picked out for him as well. Poor girl. I see why Sandy wanted these,' Alys said absently, unfolding the letter with the bright splash of green wax on the outer folds. 'But why Somerville kept them, as I said—'

Lady Egidia was reading Ramsay's third letter, brows knitted over the cramped lines.

'This makes it clear there is a third player,' she said, 'though it never names him. But is that the Irishman Gil spoke of, or another?'

'This one names him,' said Alys. 'It's not the Irishman. It also names a very great sum of money. We must speak to the Depute, I think, ask him for armed support and a warrant. Perhaps he will come with us.'

Lady Egidia looked up from the letter.

'How could I ever have been against your marriage?' she wondered. 'You are an ornament to our house, my dear.'

'I try,' Alys said, feeling her face warming. 'Do you know what is an espinyard?'

'I've seen them in action,' said Robert Hamilton. 'Nasty things they are, for all they're no that big, no more than an ell in length. I can tell you, madam, they're as like to slay the gunners as their target. A kick like a mule, no wonderful accurate, and one o the three I watched

260

blew into schairds and the two men wi't, a dreadfu sicht.'

'Dreadfu!' declared Provost Lockhart, refilling the glasses. 'An instrument o the Deil, clearly!'

'Indeed aye,' said Lady Egidia, crossing herself. 'A sorry end to meet wi. And as you can see here in these letters, maisters, there's now a half-dozen o the things wandering about the countryside wi these tinkers, though they don't belong to them, they're for delivery to someone unnamed. They might no even ken what they're carrying.'

'Believe that, madam—' began Hamilton, grinning wryly.

'Believe the moon's made o green cheese, aye,' she agreed, and sat back, watching him study the letter. Alys kept silence and nibbled a little cake, allowing the older woman the discussion; she had yet to meet the man, other than Gil, who could withstand Lady Egidia at full tilt. And not even Gil, she reflected, most of the time.

It was sheer good fortune that they had found Hamilton in the burgh, discussing the capture and release of Audrey Madur with the Provost. The two ladies had been made welcome, and offered a refreshment; the ale was good, the little cakes were light and crisp. But Alys was aware of a growing anxiety about Gil, probably baseless but hard to ignore, a gathering feeling that he was going into danger.

Where was he? she wondered. It seemed likely that he had compeared at the ford as demanded in the ransom note, and equally likely that Sandy Boyd was with him, and probably also Doig. Since Boyd was not back in Lanark, they had presumably all gone elsewhere with the messenger who came for the ransom money. But had they gone willingly, or otherwise? Who was the messenger? Where had they gone, and had they gone afoot, as she had speculated, or had someone provided ponies? That would affect how far they might have gone since moonrise, particularly if Doig was still with them.

All this reasoning is a waste of time, she admitted to herself. *You know perfectly well where he has gone, and that is —*

'Kersewell?' said Robert Hamilton. 'Why Kersewell, madam? Gregory Vary's a dismal fellow, but the law kens nothing o the man. What gars ye think we should ask at his yett about these guns?'

'The place, and the man himsel, are named clear enough in this paper here,' Lady Egidia said, pointing with a long forefinger. 'It all reads to me as if Somerville's been in correspondence wi more than one person furth o Lanarkshire, furth o Scotland indeed, to more than one purpose, none o them good. But since the man's deid, we'll say no more o that,' she said inaccurately, 'save for this matter o the Spanish goods. You see, this section here.' She pointed again, and read aloud, interpreting the very individual spelling with ease. '*Your Spanish goods are sent, and will reach K by Midsummer.*'

'There's mony another place in Scotland begins wi a K,' observed the Provost reasonably, and Hamilton nodded agreement. 'Kirkcaldy, Kirkcudbright, Kirkpatrick. Or a C. Cauldhope, Cambuslang, Cadzow. No need to assume it's Kersewell that's meant here.'

'No need to assume it isny,' Lady Egidia countered. 'I hope you areny going to be misobliging, Robert. This is important, and I think we're short o time.'

Hamilton's fair-skinned, handsome countenance reddened.

'I'd be pleased to oblige you, madam, gin matters were otherwise! But this sounds to me like a hunt-the-peesweep, wi no evidence to go by but some ill-scribed letters from the Deil kens where. You've not let me hear yet where you got them.'

'We are not free to tell you that,' Alys offered. Hamilton's head jerked round, as if he had forgotten she was there, and he frowned at her. She smiled sweetly in return. 'If you reckon my good-mother's kin, sir – my husband's kin – you'll see why.'

The frown intensified. She maintained the smile, and after a moment he turned away, looking dissatisfied. The Provost, however, gave him a significant nod and hitched up his gown again.

'If that's the case, madam,' he said, 'I'll can let ye have a few o the constables, which at least looks better as an escort, however good your own men might be.'

'I suppose,' said Hamilton. 'I can send Richie to round up a few and all.'

'I kent you'd see your way to helping us,' said Lady Egidia in satisfied tones. 'You're a good laddie, Robert. And my thanks, Provost. A few o your constables will be a good help.'

Maybe, thought Alys, reviewing the constables she had seen so far. *But maybe not.*

There was a rasping at the door. Lockhart broke off his reply to Lady Egidia and called, 'Aye, Dandy, what is it?'

'If you please, sir,' said his clerk, putting his head round the door, 'here's a fellow from up the coalheugh, seeking Lady Cunningham, says it's an urgent matter.'

'Seeking me?' Alarm flared in Lady Egidia's face, and she looked from Lockhart to his man. 'May I—?'

'Bid him come ben, Dandy,' the Provost said, nodding. The clerk stepped aside for a man in the mud-caked garments the miners wore, breathing heavily, his face and hands grimy with coal-dust, his padded bonnet in his hand. He cast a swift glance about the group, and went down on one knee to Lady Egidia, who rose, staring intently down at him, one hand at her mouth, her face unreadable. The other three people in the chamber also stood perforce.

'If you please, mem,' he said, 'it's the mistress. Lady Tib. It's her time. The maister sent me to find you.'

'Already,' she said, on a little gasp. 'How – when did it start? Do you ken—?'

'All I ken's what Maister Michael bade me say, mem,' said the miner in apologetic tones. 'Which is that she was groaning hard when I left, and eager for you to come to her. That was maybe an hour since. Beattie's wi her,' he added reassuringly, 'doesny seem ower concerned.'

'You must go, madam,' Alys said. 'Tib will need you. I can go to Kersewell—'

'That you'll no,' said Hamilton. 'I'll no be responsible for you your lone, madam. Two ladies is bad enough,' he glanced at Lady Egidia and went scarlet again at his clumsiness, 'I mean, two ladies is a trouble to keep safe if we meet wi any problems at Kersewell, one lady by her lone is more than I'll be answerable for. You'd take up the attention o two o my men, when they're maybe needed elsewhere.'

Alys was considering her reply to this, and noting how the situation had gone from being a peesweep-chase to needing all Hamilton's men, when her mother-in-law caught her eye and said firmly, 'Well, we'd best get away then. Thank you both for hearing us, gentle-men, and I can take it you'll send a company to Kersewell as soon as it's gathered?'

'Aye, well,' said Hamilton, clearly taken aback, as if he had been expecting an argument. 'Aye, you need to get on the road, madam, and I hope matters go well for Lady Tib. Her first, is it no?'

'It is,' agreed Lady Egidia, gathering her skirts together. 'And we thought she'd a month yet. Pray for her, if you will, sir. Forgive me, man,' she added to the miner, who had risen and was standing aside for her, 'I dinna ken your name. Get to Juggling Nick's and bid Henry see to the horses, if you would. We can ride out as soon as maybe. Here.' She reached for the purse which she wore at her belt like a man, and handed him some coins. 'Get yoursel some food and a stoup o the good brew, and follow us when you're rested.'

He clapped his padded bonnet back on his head in order to remove it again to her, gabbled something grateful, and left the chamber precipitately. The two ladies, bidding farewell as rapidly as was polite, followed him. Down in the street where Steenie waited for them Lady Egidia took Alys's arm.

'Thank you, my dear,' she said. 'We'd no time for an argument. If you take Steenie and Euan and Henry, I'll be for the Pow Burn wi the other lad. One man's enough. There's none will get between me and my lassie at a time like this.'

'I was about to suggest the same,' Alys said, making for the Nicholas Tavern at a half-run to keep up with her mother-in-law's long strides, wondering what would happen to the man who got between Lady Egidia and her target at any time. 'You'll give my love to Tib, tell her I'm praying for a successful outcome.'

'Be sure I will.' Lady Egidia halted at the mouth of the pend which led through to the tavern's busy yard, and tugged Alys into a fierce embrace. 'My dear child. Keep Gil safe for me.'

'I will,' Alys promised, as Henry led the first of the Belstane horses through the pend, the animal's head tossing indignantly at the speed with which it had been saddled up.

'It's Lady Tib, I hear. She miscounted, then?' said Henry, placing the beast for his mistress to mount up. 'She'll be a while, mem, what wi it being her first.'

265

'Aye, and you ken what happens when you rely on that,' retorted his mistress, arranging her wide skirts about her. 'Jaikie, you're wi me. Henry, you and Steenie and Euan do Mistress Mason's bidding. You ken the way to Kersewell, I think? And avoiding Lockharthill,' she added, gathering up the reins. 'God speed ye.'

'And you, mistress,' said Henry, and Steenie echoed it. Euan, leading the remaining beasts out into the street, looked after the Lady of Belstane and then at Alys.

'They'll be helping Maister Michael get through it,' he said wistfully. 'Plenty ale and cheese, there will be.'

'We need to find Maister Gil,' Alys said, patting her horse's nose.

'Avoiding Lockharthill,' said Henry intelligently. 'The Depute forbade ye to go wi him then, mem?'

'How far is it?' she asked, wondering how the servants always seemed to know what they were about almost before they knew themselves.

'No that far, even if we go roundabout. Ten mile, maybe?'

'Then we must get on the road,' she said.

The road was much the same as they had taken up to Tarbrax, winding eastward through Carstairs and Carnwath. Steenie seemed to know the tracks and byways of Carstairs parish well, and kept them hidden from the house of Lockharthill and its policies by slipping among small lumpy hills from one sand-digging to another.

'They are quarrying sand?' Alys said in surprise. 'What is it used for?'

'Folk's gairdens,' said Henry. 'It makes rare paths, so I believe, though the mistress doesny like it so much. Or it's wanted for tilting grounds or the like, or maybe the ground for a riding school, a covered one. Like a great barn, you ken, for schooling the beasts.'

'It makes a right good bed for growing carrots,' said Steenie.

'They's a gravel quarry yonder and all,' Henry added, 'that the Belstane paths came fro. Haud on a wee, Steenie, there's horses on the other road.'

'I have seen them already,' said Euan from the rear. 'It is a fat merchant, just, and all his men. I'll wager they are carrying coin, for they are all well armed. Not the Lanark constables, any road, I would be knowing that Mattha Speirs from a mile off, seeing he is riding like a great sack o neeps.'

'So what's afoot up at Kersewell, mem?' Steenie asked. 'What's Maister Gil got hissel into now?'

'We'll find that out when we get there,' Alys answered. 'Does either of you ken the house? How does it lie?'

'I've rid there once or twice,' Henry said. 'It's an auld tower-house, no so unlike Belstane, but he's set out a pleas-ance inside the barmekin, so all the stables and offices and that's outside it, an orra way o doing things to my mind.'

'Indeed, yes,' Alys agreed. 'So how does one approach the place?'

Between them, Henry and Steenie described for her a tower set in a valley, by a burn which ran eastward down to the Medwin Water. There was thick woodland to the west, with a track through it; the main approach was from the south, off the Peebles road.

'We should take the track through the woodland,' Alys said, wondering where Peebles was.

'If those tinkers are there,' observed Euan. 'they will be hiding in the trees.'

'Why should they be there?' Steenie demanded.

'They've been a' the places we've been the last few days,' Henry said. 'He's right.'

'I think they are friendly,' said Alys. Henry made a dubious noise, but did not comment.

They pressed on, despite the heat of the afternoon, through Carnwath, passing St Mary's church again, and on to the Edinburgh road. The landscape had changed; they had left the small lumpy hillocks behind and rode among higher, round-shouldered hills, with the blue bulk of the Pentlands up ahead of them. A couple of miles beyond St Mary's they came upon a track which led off eastward, climbing gently into a dense woodland which clothed the saddle between two hills.

'It's down the other side o that,' said Steenie. 'Less than a mile, it is.'

'I hope the track is going through those trees,' said Euan. 'They are growing thick together.'

'I can be showing you the way through, maisters, bonnie lady,' said a voice from the roadside. Alys's horse shied sideways, tossing its head in surprise, and she checked it as another of the tinker laddies, or possibly the same one, rose up out of the ditch and stood grinning at them, his face and his long belted shirt grubby with earth, bracken fronds in his shaggy dark hair. No, it was certainly the same one, the one who had told her Isa's advice was a true word. She put that firmly aside, and studied the youngster.

'What do you want?' demanded Henry.

'Why, to offer you help,' said the boy, opening his eyes wide in innocent surprise. 'What else would I be doing, maisters, bonnie lady, but helping sic travellers as yoursels?'

'I keep expecting you to turn into a fox,' said Alys. The boy grinned at that, and touched his brow. In five years or so, she recognised, he would break hearts.

'If you was the King's daughter of Ireland, bonnie lady,' he said, 'then I surely would. And that's my by-name you've given me, and I thank you for it.'

'And how would you be helping us?' Euan asked.

'I can be showing you the road through the wood, the way I was telling you already.'

'Och, we'll find that for oursels,' said Steenie.

'And I can be showing you where the fine merchants will be looking at the cannon.'

'That would be a help indeed,' said Alys, smiling at him. 'Do you ken where my man is and all?'

'Oh, aye,' said the boy. 'You'll be wanting to free him, I don't doubt.'

Chapter Thirteen

'It could be worse, I suppose,' said Gil, looking round their prison.

Doig snorted in scepticism, but Sandy Boyd stretched and said, 'Aye, we could be in the cellars wi the rats, or down the bottle-hole. This is almost civilised, compared wi that.'

'We shouldny ha trusted those tinkers,' said Doig, rubbing the graze on his jaw.

Gil rose stiffly and went to the window. The shutters stood wide, but the chamber was right under the roof and the air did not stir. This tower was higher than Belstane, and that rose four floors above its undercroft; a long way below him he could see Gregory Vary strolling in the pleasance which occupied the whole extent of the barmekin, in friendly conversation with the black-bearded man.

Beyond the walls, there was a huddle of the outbuildings which were more usually inside them, the stables, the bakehouse, stores and barns and byres. Vary must be confident in the peaceable nature of his neighbours, Gil thought, studying these. It would hardly take much of a raid to carry off an entire year's stores, and the horses to bear it away as well. This was not Armstrong country, but it was not so far removed from it.

271

Further off, a burn ran eastward, down towards the wide valley of the Medwin, where the hay lay out drying in the long strips in the fields. In the other direction the land closed in, and a track rose towards a low pass clothed in thick woodland. Away from the track he could make out movement under the trees, low tents or shelters like those in the camp below Carnwath, one or two dogs roaming about.

'I think they were as taken aback as we were,' he said, replying to Doig. 'Wooden Toe was ready to argue, till Blue Doo stopped him.'

'Aye, and why did he stop him?' Doig glowered at Gil. 'You're in gey weel wi the tinkers, I must say, for one that's never met them afore.'

'No so far in as you,' Gil countered. He turned from the window, surveying again the dusty chamber where they were imprisoned. It contained remarkably little: a broken settle, two worm-eaten stools, a roll of moulder-ing tapestry. The walls were limewashed and draped in cobwebs, and there was no hearth, so no chimney; over-head the rafters, purlins, sarking, supported whatever covered the roof. Probably slate, he considered, looking at the angle of the boards. There was no sound of any other movement up here, only the squeal and thump of the jackdaws on the roof, distant birdsong and lowing of cattle, and someone singing at his work beyond the barmekin wall.

They had reached the bounds of Kersewell's policies about midday, to be accosted by a pair of scowling men in leather jacks and helmets, one with a businesslike quarterstaff, one with a whinger, who had insisted grimly on escorting them to meet Maister Vary. Half the tinkers had melted into the landscape at the sight, but Blue Doo and Wooden Toe had accompanied them, protesting that all they wished was a word wi the

272

black-haired Irish fellow, so it was, and no need to be disturbing himself.

Gregory Vary had received them in the hall of the tower, a wide chamber occupying the whole of the first floor, hung with damp and decaying tapestries, its ceiling painted on planks and beams with irritatingly uneven lozenges. Vary himself was remarkably like his brother, thin and narrowly made, but his face was lined and bitter, and there was an odd triumphant look in his eyes. He was seated behind a table which was draped in a handsome carpet and held a Gospel-book and a stack of papers, as if this was about to become a trial or a hearing at law. Gil did not glance at his cousin, but was aware of him tensing warily by his side. Behind them the two armed men stood alert and waiting, and the tinkers looked uneasily about them. The Irishman was not to be seen.

'You call yoursel Maister Cunningham, I hear,' Vary said. 'And who are these?'

'I am Gil Cunningham,' Gil agreed, 'the Archbishop's quaestor.'

Boyd held his peace. Doig growled something unintelligible.

'What, going about the country wi a band o tinkers?' scoffed Vary, much as Gil had predicted. 'You'll forgive me if I canny believe you, man. So what are you after? What brings you on to my lands?'

'There's a few things I'd like to discuss wi you, and maybe wi a guest under your roof,' Gil said politely. 'We could start wi the abduction o your good-sister Mistress Madur, to the endangerment o her life and her bairn's. Then there's the arson at The Cleuch, wi the death o—'

'That's havers and lees!' said Vary forcefully. 'I had naught to do wi any o that, and you canny show that I did. Whereas here's you and your retinue,' his lip curled at the word, 'traipsing across my lands spying out the saints ken what, in broad daylight, planning and plotting a' sort o nefarious deeds!'

'No, no, maister,' said Blue Doo, and swallowed nervously. 'Deed they wereny, for we brought them here quite openly and were about to put them afore you, so we were, just as we agreed on—'

Just as who agreed on? Gil wondered.

'We'll ha nothing from you vagand rannagants,' said Vary contemptuously. Behind him the tapestries stirred, and a tall man with a black beard stepped into the hall. The tinkers cringed at sight of him, but he ignored them, studying Gil with an interested and slightly disturbing smile.

'And who might these be, Gregory?' he asked, his voice buttery with the accents of Ireland. 'For I'm sure they're not the company we looked for, seeing they have but the one follower between them.'

'I'm the Archbishop's quaestor, as I said,' Gil repeated, studying the newcomer. He was a big man, taller and broader than Gil, clad in workmanlike leather doublet and upperstocks, his legs bare below the knee but for a thick pelt of black hair, his feet encased in soft brogans such as the men of the Isles wore. The black beard rippled down his chest, a strange style for a fighting man, Gil thought, and this was certainly a fighting man. 'And what's your interest?' he challenged in return.

'None o your mind,' said Vary, at the same time as the Irishman smiled more broadly and said, 'Ah, I've an interest in all kind of things, so I have. Where our wandering friends get to,' he nodded at the tinkers, who were trying to become invisible without moving, 'who it is that's buying and selling the black powder, where royal dukes are to be found. All kind of things. So what is it interests you, Maister Cunningham?'

'None of these,' said Gil firmly, somehow chilled by the use of his name, though he reminded himself that the fellow must have heard Vary address him. 'As I've already told Maister Gregory Vary, I'm pursuing the abduction of his good-sister Mistress Audrey Madur, and the arson at The Cleuch. If any of these things you mention are connected wi those, then I'd like to ken more, but otherwise they're none of my concern.'

'And you, the silent man at the side there,' said the Irishman, scorn in his tone. 'Have you naught to say for yourself? I've heard all about you, Maister Boyd, that I have, but to tell you truth, I'd not have expected to see you wi a train as short as this at your back.'

Doig growled, deep in his chest like Socrates. Boyd remained silent, though one eyebrow twitched, and after a few moments Blue Doo stirred uneasily. 'The likes o the MacPhersons would be having nothing to do wi royal dukes at all, and that's a true word, your honour, so it is. So it is,' he repeated, his words slowing as if he was a toy whose string was running out.

So it was you shifted the black powder in truth, thought Gil. *I wonder did it get here?*

Another of those smiles stirred the black beard, and the Irishman said happily, 'Indeed, and I would say royal dukes would be having little to do with the likes of you, except it's strange what you find among the heather when the need presses. Maister Vary, what will we be doing with these gentry? For I hardly think the guests we look for will be wanting to keep company with them, do you?'

Vary nodded at this, and signalled to the man with the quarterstaff. The door opened behind Gil, and he glanced over his shoulder to see several more sturdy men enter the hall.

'I'll talk to you later, Cunningham, or whatever your name is,' Vary pronounced sourly. 'Take them away, lads. Put them above.' He gestured towards the painted ceiling.

'I'd rather talk now, if you would,' Gil said, since Boyd remained silent. Little hope of persuading the man, he thought. *Whatever I said or sang, it would be better received by a billy goat, or by a rotting tree trunk.* 'I've a deal o questions for you, like I said, and it's a long walk back to Belstane, where I'll be looked for the night.'

'Oh, we'll put you on the road later,' the Irishman assured them casually. *Dead or alive?* Gil wondered, and could not predict the answer from the tone of voice.

'Take them away, lads,' Vary said again, and two of his men laid hands on Gil.

It was Doig who swung the first punch, level with his own big head, but Vary's men took it as a signal to use force on all three of them and waded in joyously. Gil ducked to avoid a blow aimed at his throat, and his attacker tripped over Doig's writhing victim; Gil parried another blow, managed to catch a joint-stool which was hurtling towards his cousin's back, and heard one of the tinkers protesting.

'There's no need o this, maisters, sure there's no, and if himself's the Archbishop's man like he says, this is bad luck, and I want none o't. The red-haired fellow never—'

'Begone, then!' said Vary impatiently.

Gil found his feet hooked from under him and he went down, with a solid weight on top of him, the breath driven from his body. Before he could try to scramble up to recover, something struck his head and the whole melée whirled away into shadows; he was only distantly aware of being dragged up many flights of stairs and flung on to a bare floor in a cloud of choking dust, of hearing a key turn in a heavy lock.

Now he touched his head gingerly where the lump was, surveying his fellow-prisoners. Doig displayed a number of bruises, the graze on his jaw, and the beginning of a splendid black eye; Gil himself was aware of more scrapes and contusions on his back and arms than were visible. Boyd, on the other hand, appeared undamaged, which Gil felt was somehow typical.

'So why are we here?' he asked. 'Locked in like this, I mean. And why at the top o the house, rather than the cellars?'

'In cause they tinkers are a crowd o cheatin, jankin sniggerts,' said Doig roundly. 'And that Vary and a'.'

'No the tinkers, Billy,' said Sandy Boyd. 'As Gil said, they were ready to argue when we were taken up. No, it's Vary we need to look at, and his guest.' *Who has signed his own death-warrant*, Gil thought, *with that crack about the length of Sandy's train. He can't be allowed to live long with the knowledge that implies.* 'Though I wouldny trust the tinkers full reach,' Boyd added musingly. 'Wi my life, maybe, but no my purse.'

'So what's Vary at?' Gil asked casually. His cousin glanced briefly at him, then at the folds of tapestry in the corner of the chamber. Overhead a scuffling and thumping on the slates suggested jackdaw politics was being enacted. 'So far I reckon he prompted the abduction o his good-sister, probably suggested the trees on the Burgh Muir, brought in this Irishman that goes about torturing and killing and committing arson. He'd likely get away wi those, though I doubt if his brother will ever forgive him when he finds out the whole, so why's he so coy about answering questions the day?'

'I wouldny ken,' growled Doig.

'It does seem he's expecting company,' remarked Boyd, still eyeing the threads fraying from the tapestry. 'The Abbot o Melrose coming for his dinner, or the like.'

'The hall didny look set for a feast,' Gil countered, and Boyd grinned and nodded. 'Though I must say,' Gil went on, turning back to the window, 'if he's expecting company, he's got it now. Come and see this.'

Below them, on the track which led up from the Medwin, a cloud of dust had appeared, with what seemed like a large party of riders at its centre. They seemed to be peaceful, to judge by their leisurely approach, and to be expected, to judge by the way the barmekin gates had swung open and Vary was making his way to welcome them. As the dust settled, Gil made out a group of persuasively armed guards, who wore black cloaks with a white device on the left shoulder. In their midst rode a well-padded, well-gowned man, with another fighting man at his side, presumably the leader of the guard. The first of the guests dismounted, removed his broad hat and fanned himself with it, accepted Vary's bowing welcome. Gil craned to see better. Even at this distance, he could recognise the dusty face and sweaty, balding pate which were revealed. Suddenly the device on the guards' cloaks became clear: the fishtailed Cross of St John.

'Sweet St Giles,' he said. 'William Knollys.'

'Who?' said Doig from behind him. 'Are you certain? What's he after?'

'It's him,' agreed Sandy Boyd. Gil looked along his shoulder at his cousin, and found him staring intently at the scene by the gate. 'It's Will Knollys right enough. Whatever can Gregor Vary have to attract him? It takes a mighty big bit o cheese to tempt Will out o his hole these days.'

'It's the espinyards, surely,' said Gil. 'How many is the Crown wanting?'

Sandy turned his head to meet Gil's gaze, the pale eyes sparkling with amusement.

'The lot, a course,' he said. 'But at our price, no at Will Knollys's price.'

'I thought Knollys was out o favour wi the Crown,' said Doig, who had not stirred from the settle. 'Dismissed two-three year ago from the Treasury, wasn't he no?'

Gil preserved his countenance. He had been instrumental in Knollys's fall from favour, after he had recovered, quite unintentionally, a quantity of the late king's coin and jewels which the Treasurer had rather hoped to keep for himself. James Fourth, the present king, had been appropriately grateful to Gil, but Knollys had left office all incontinent, and currently had to content himself with his income as Preceptor of the Knights Hospitaller at Torphichen. Gil suddenly recalled Mistress Somerville's waiting-woman mentioning Commendator Noll. So Somerville was acquainted with Knollys, it seemed.

'He was.' Boyd was watching the display at the gate again. Servants had emerged from the house with refreshments, the horses were being led away, some of the armed escort had left with the horses. Some of it had not. 'This is how he wants to get back in favour, I'd say. This king hasny the same interest in gunpowder his grandsire had, but he wouldny say no to a set o matched espinyards. So what we want is to get them at a price suits us, no a price that suits some middle man or other.'

'I can see that,' Gil agreed. 'You should get my mother in to bargain wi Vary. Did you ever see her chaffering for horses?'

'Even Vary doesny deserve that,' said his kinsman. 'Who d'you suppose that is wi Will Knollys? I canny tell from this angle.'

Below them, the guests were being escorted to the house with some ceremony, Vary offering an arm to the former Treasurer of Scotland, the Irishman conversing with Knollys's companion behind them. Gil frowned down at the scene: the companion was lean and dark, his helmet removed to show neatly clipped hair and beard. Where had he seen him before?

'Maybe we should get out o here, then,' said Doig from the settle, 'let you get a right look at him. Yon tapestry's away too rotten to make us a rope, let alone there's no enough o it. How stout would you say the door is?'

He slid down off the settle and marched across to the door, kicking it hard with no great effect, and began poking at the lock and hinges.

Gil looked about the chamber again, paying more attention this time. Below the window, the limewash on the wall clearly covered raw stone, but the other three walls seemed to be plastered. Drawing his dagger, he stepped to the nearest and knocked on it with the pommel, then struck it harder. The wall shook visibly under the blow, and a lump of plaster fell out, revealing a framework of woven hazel behind it.

The hazel grove, he thought, *I must break out of the hazel grove.*

'You're a handy fellow to have by in a crisis,' Sandy Boyd commented, joining him. 'I suppose the whole chamber is wattle and daub?'

'The inside walls, at least,' Gil said. 'None o Vary's folk stayed up here, did they?'

'Naw.' Doig kicked the door again. 'I heard them all away down the stair. You think we could get through this?' He drew a sturdy dagger, and began digging at the limewashed surface by the jamb of the door.

'I'm thinking more o how far up the partitions go.' Gil tilted his head back, looking up at the rafters.

'Oh, aye, your good-father's a mason,' said Boyd.

'Pierre doesny deal in wattle and daub.' Gil began to drag the settle nearer the wall. 'You were never in the attics in the Darngaber house, were you?'

280

'No, I was only there the once.' Boyd took an end of the settle. 'Will we tip it up on end, or is this high enough?'

'High enough for me.' Gil placed his end of the piece and stepped up on to the seat. 'You'll maybe want to tip it up for Billy, unless he can fly.'

'You mind your tongue,' said Doig, turning away from the door to watch as Gil reached up, took a firm grasp, and swung himself up on to one of the crossbeams.

'As I thought,' he said. 'They haveny taken the wattle right to the roof – there's a gap at the side here.' He leaned over to seize hold of the wattle panel and shook it. It creaked slightly, but stood firm. 'That's why we're up here, a course,' he added, leaning further to peer into the next chamber. 'The cellars must be full o guns. He'd want to store those secure, wi a band o tinkers on the policies, and they'd be a bit heavy to drag up as many stairs.'

The next chamber was just as dusty as the one they were in, and contained more disused furniture. More to the purpose, its door stood ajar. Gil got his head and shoulders through the little gap, kicked off from the beam he had been sitting on, and rolled forward to land crouching in the other chamber. Moving quickly to the door, he listened carefully. There was movement in the distance, footsteps and voices, a rattling of crockery. Beyond the window of this chamber, the man was still singing. The tune was unfamiliar.

He slipped through the door, into a further chamber. The one in which they had been imprisoned clearly opened off this as well.

'Well? What fortune?' demanded his cousin beyond the thin walls.

'Excellent fortune,' he answered, turning the key in the lock. 'No need for Maister Doig to fly after all.'

Doig growled at him, rolling past him with his awkward gait.

'Well done,' said Boyd, clapping Gil on the shoulder as he emerged. He paused to brush a dusty hank of cobweb from Gil's arm and shook it fastidiously from his fingers, adding, 'And have you a map o the disposition o the enemy and all?'

'I've no surveying gear on me,' said Gil. 'You'll have to make your own.'

They picked their way quietly out of the maze of small chambers which had been partitioned out of the topmost floor of the tower, just as in the attic of the house Gil had known in childhood. The floorboards creaked under their feet, no matter how carefully they stepped, but it seemed, if there was anybody on the floor immediately below, that nobody was listening, and they reached the top of a stone newel stair without being heard.

'Up or down?' said Boyd.

'Up, of course,' said Gil, setting off downward, whinger in hand. 'Likely the jackdaws will bear you off the roof, if you cozen them a bit.'

'I've no bread,' said Boyd, following him.

'Wheesht, the pair o you,' said Doig, bringing up the rear.

No tower was ever built with a stair which ran from top to bottom: how would one defend such a place? This stair ended at the floor below, and the door at its foot stood ajar; Gil paused, ears stretched, before slipping into the chamber sideways, back against the wall. This level was clearly used, the chamber roughly furnished with a low bed, several kists, and three stools. Servants' quarters, perhaps, Gil surmised, making his way cautiously along the wall.

Crossing two more similar chambers, they found the next stair, and paused at the doorway to listen. The rattling of crockery had ceased, and the voices were fainter, as if further away.

'It's awfy quiet,' said Doig in a hoarse whisper. 'I'm no liking it.'

Boyd moved past him, to set foot on the topmost stair, but Gil put out a hand to stop him.

'Wait,' he breathed. They listened, frozen in place, and Gil heard again what had alerted him: the soft pad and shuffle of feet, bare feet, on the stairs. He fell back a step or two, waving the other two back with him, watching the shadowy aperture of the stairs. In a few moments the light changed as someone ascended. The padding feet stopped.

'Maisters?' said a voice. A boy's voice. 'Are ye there? Blue Doo sent me.'

Gil looked from his cousin to Doig. Before he could answer, Doig said, 'And how'd we ken that?'

'Och, maisters, would I play ye fause?'

'Ye have done a'ready,' Doig pointed out.

'That wasny me, maisters. Nor it was Blue Doo neither. It's none o our doing if Maister Vary's forsworn, so it isny. Maisters, I'm sent to fetch ye out o here, to where the bonnie lady's waiting for ye. Are ye coming, or no?'

'Bonnie lady?' said Gil, with a sinking feeling. Beside him, Boyd was grinning broadly. 'What bonnie lady?'

'The one your lordship's mairriet on, a course,' said the voice scornfully. 'What other would it be would come to find you? Is yir lordships to company us, or will we be going back and telling her ye're minded to stay the night?'

'We're coming,' said Doig, and stumped off down the stairs. Gil glanced at his cousin, pulled a face, and followed him.

One floor down, they emerged from the stair to be surrounded by a troop of tinker children, who tugged at their hands and clothing and hurried them to find the next descent. While the song outside changed to another, equally unfamiliar, they glimpsed more elaborate, neglected chambers, some with high beds and painted kists set on their flagstone floors, one a dusty solar with moth-eaten embroidery on a stand near the window-seat, but there was no time to take in details, and attempts to question their escort were hushed. When they reached the stair Gil recognised why: there was much more stirring below them, voices and movement, sounds and scents of food being served, a great waft of roasted mutton smells. Doig's stomach rumbled loudly. The boy who had spoken to them, who seemed to be the leader of the group, halted them here.

'Donnie,' he pointed at one of his henchmen, 'away and mak siccar o the door, and see a'body's in place. Yir lordships'll ha to be quiet,' he instructed the three men, 'for we'll be passing the big hall, where they're a' eating and drinking o the best, and we'd no want to be noticed.'

'And the armed men?' Boyd asked lightly. 'Where are they?'

'Och, they're all out-by, the most o them, making siccar we canny be getting into the house.' A two-note call sounded in the stairwell. 'Right, yir lordships. One at a time, in case they would be seeing us, and we'll ha you first, maister.'

'My turn, indeed.' Boyd stepped forward, and Gil realised his cousin had neither sword nor whinger but only his dagger on him. 'Wish me luck, Gil.'

Gil watched him go, listening to his quiet steps on the stairs. There was a quick exchange with the boy on guard, and more soft steps which faded into silence, and then, at the edge of hearing, a scuffle, a choking sound, a thump and scrape, and another silence, broken by

284

more serving sounds from the hall. What was Sandy up to, he wondered.

When the soft call was repeated, he followed his cousin down the stairs as quietly as he could manage. The stairs led down past a sturdy door, behind which clinking of knives and glassware could be heard and the smell of roast mutton drifted out again. The grubby boy waiting beside it, Donnie, waved him on urgently, and he hastened downward, hearing the door open above him.

'Here, you!' said a voice. 'Get down to the kitchen, fetch another jug o the good ale, and be quick about it. And you'll no be tasting it on the way back, neither!'

'Aye, maister!' said Donnie's voice, and after a moment his bare feet pattered on the stairs and he appeared beside Gil, clutching a jug and grinning broadly. Above them the door closed, and Donnie called up to his leader again, a different signal, and led Gil on downward. The stair curled down past the kitchen, where the door stood ajar on the bustle and scurry, but nobody looked round as they slipped by, and a few steps below it ended abruptly in a low, wide cellar, dimly lit from barred openings high up under the vaults.

Gil stopped as his feet met the flagstones, and peered around in the shadows, sniffing the air of the place. There was a lot to see as well as scent, and little light to see by. The usual stacked barrels and sacks were ranged along the walls, with pools of shadow beneath them, and dark objects lurking in the spaces. There seemed to be a lot of people about, not all of them child-sized. Directly in front of him was a row of packing-cases, long and narrow, with twisted straw sticking out of the gaps in the wood. Several figures were bending over these. As he stepped forward, one of them leaned hard on a crowbar, and there was a sound of splitting wood.

'Ah! Got you, you *diabhal*,' said a familiar voice. *Euan Campbell*, he thought, *and if Euan is here, so must Alys be.* Searching for her, he recognised his mother's groom Steenie.

'Let's get a look at it,' said his cousin in the crowd. People shifted, and he saw Alys, neat in her riding-dress and the hat like a man's, bending over the opened case, and Boyd's head of light hair beside hers.

Something impelled him forward, very rapidly, but when he reached them all he said was, 'If you wanted one of these for your birthday, you'd only to say.'

She did not look round, but her hand came up and tucked itself unerringly, tightly, into his.

'We've nowhere to keep it,' she said in Scots. 'It wouldny rest on the sideboard.'

He looked down at his cousin; he could smell blood, but Sandy seemed to be undamaged, though he was shivering.

'Maister Gil,' said Euan. 'What will we be doing wi these handguns? Are they to be left here, or what?'

'Can we get a better look at them?' Boyd asked. 'Anyone got a light?'

'I think we shouldny have a light in here,' said Alys. 'There's a sack o what I take to be black powder on yon barrel. I hope it's the right grade for these.'

'You know powder, cousin?' Boyd said in surprise.

'My father dealt once wi a quarryman who used it,' she replied.

'We can be taking them outside,' said another of the figures in the shadows, and Gil recognised Wooden Toe. 'We can be fetching them out to the other side o the wall, if your honours think it fitting, if once we can get them all out o these kists. They are not being that heavy outside the kists, see.'

'That's a true word,' said Boyd, straightening up. He had the gun in his arms, a long pipe of cast metal, strengthened with hoops of iron here and there along its length, with a wooden stock at one end which extended its length by another half an ell or so. 'One man can carry it, no bother.' He raised one hand to his nose and sniffed, grimacing. 'Though he'll be greased like new leather when he's done.'

'Wullie,' said Wooden Toe, 'you'll see to clearing the way, then?'

'My name's no Wullie,' said the leader of the troop of children, stepping in from the stair. 'I'm The Fox now, see. That's my by-name. This bonnie lady, that has a' the wisdom o Scotland and France both, was naming me hersel.' The pride in his voice would have inflated several footballs, Gil thought.

'Fox,' said Wooden Toe patiently, accepting this. 'You'll be seeing the way's clear, then, till we get these cannons out of here.'

Euan Campbell was already applying the crowbar to the next packing case. The newly named Fox turned back to direct his henchmen, just as Doig stumped in off the stair.

'This isny the way out,' he said irritably, looking about him.

'No, it's where the guns are,' said Boyd. 'Gin you'll wait a wee, you can carry one out for me. I need a right look at them afore I bargain wi Vary for them.'

Alys looked up at him and nodded, but did not speak. Gil pulled her against him, and watched as the remaining guns were freed from their packing and shared out round the group. By the time the Fox returned, a procession had formed up waiting for him, Boyd at its head with the first gun cradled in his arms and the leather sack of gunpowder dangling from one wrist by its sturdy ties, Gil with a small barrel on his shoulder which seemed, by its markings, to hold more powder.

'We'll gang out through the kitchen,' the boy said, his voice full of suppressed excitement. 'I've tellt them we're to take the guns outside. Just walk out through and they'll no stop ye.'

'One can see,' said Alys softly in French, 'how these people are said to be related to the fairy folk. They know well how to make themselves unregarded, and so invisible.'

'And how to cover others with the same invisibility,' Gil agreed. Wooden Toe, just in front of them, turned and nodded, grinning widely.

'And this laddie will be the maist skilled in his generation,' he assured them in Scots.

Wondering where Knollys's armed men might be, and whether he was committing a felony, and if so which one, Gil followed the rest of the procession up the stair, into the kitchen, where the kitchen hands looked up to stare at the guns and sand crunched under their feet, up another flight, and across the screens passage at the end of the hall. Through its openings, out of the tail of his eye, he could see the back of Vary's head, a full view of Knollys, a side view of Knollys's companion who was still tantalisingly familiar. The three were seated round a small table, their meal now at the nuts and sweetmeats stage, with the cloth removed and glasses of claret wine set out. Some of Knollys's men stood about; they peered suspiciously at the movement in the screens passage, but did not act. The Irishman was not present.

From the screens passage, predictably, they descended by another stair to a richly appointed chamber, designed to impress and better kept than those above, where a heavy door stood open to the daylight. Tapestries stirred in a breeze; two great chairs and several upholstered

288

backstools stood about; a sideboard boasted an array of pewter which gleamed faintly. The actual silver, Gil assumed, would be kept on another sideboard further into the tower. He stepped out on to the platform at the head of the wooden forestair, and found the weather much changed from what it had been when they arrived at Kersewell.

'We'll no need to hang about,' declared Wooden Toe, 'if we're to test these cannons. I'm thinking it will rain within the hour, by the look o the sky.'

'I'd say you would be right,' agreed Gil, looking about him.

It was not just the sky, now half-full of mountainous clouds, which foreboded rain. A wind had risen, hectic and unpredictable, turning leaves upward, tossing blooms about in the neat flowerbeds of the pleasance. It tugged at Alys's hat, and she put up a hand to the brim.

'Come on!' urged the Fox from the stairfoot. 'You'll no be waiting about here, there's men wi big swords just the other side the wall. We need to be ganging that way!' He pointed along one of the sanded paths, where half the guns were already processing hastily towards a door in the wall, the swarm of children running beside and ahead of the bearers.

The door was narrow, with slots in the stonework for two heavy bars. Gil noted this only in passing, finding himself thrust out and along the hillside, away from the barmekin wall towards the encroaching wood, Alys hustled after him. Several of the tinkers' dogs came loping silently towards them, heads down, but a word from Wooden Toe and a whistle from the margins of the trees sent them circling back uphill. The party rounded the flank of the hill and found themselves in the valley of the burn which Gil had seen earlier from the top of the tower.

'There you are,' said Sandy Boyd, looking up as Gil set down his barrel and gave Alys a hand down the slope. 'What d'you ken about guns, Gil?'

'No a lot,' Gil said frankly. 'I value my hearing.'

'If these are the ones Brosie Vary mentioned,' said Alys, 'he said they're something like an arquebus, but Maister Hamilton the Depute described something bigger, that needed two men to work it. I suppose one must hold it and the other apply the match.'

'Cousin,' said Boyd, smiling at her in delight, 'I tell you, if I'd seen you first, Gil would never ha stood a chance.'

'Oh no, maister,' she said, with demure ambiguity. 'You'd never ha got into my gowns.'

Boyd uttered a crack of laughter, and then turned, punching Gil hard in the shoulder.

'Come on then. I'll not risk men to hold them. We need to prop them somehow so they willny fly about when we fire them.'

'Why have we no been observed?' Gil said uneasily, looking about. 'I'd have expected Knollys's men to come down on us, let alone Vary's own.'

'I was telling Knollys's folk,' said Euan cheerfully, 'that we would be testing the guns out here, and to be staying away from this side the castle meantime. Likely they'll be spying round the corners at us, but it will keep them out of our way for a bit.'

'And it was me was suggesting it to him,' observed Wooden Toe, 'thinking it would come better from a smartly dressed fellow like him, see.'

'It was not,' said Euan indignantly. 'I was thinking of it my own self!'

'I was just borrowing this fleuchter, see,' said the Fox, ignoring them. He brandished the peat-spade, narrowly missing Doig's head with the metal-shod wooden blade, 'that was lying about down by the wall. Your lordship could be using it to cut holes in the ground, and put the cannons into them, maybe?' he ended diffidently.

'Aye, that's a good thought,' said Boyd with enthusiasm. 'Can you find us another one? Just we'll need to make haste.' He glanced at the sky, which was darkening steadily as the clouds advanced.

'Do we have slow-match?' Gil asked.

'There is some here,' said Alys, looking up from the sack of gunpowder. 'In a purse inside the sack, to keep the powder off it. Cousin, was the sack split when you lifted it?'

Boyd looked up from the hole he was making in the slope beside the burn, and shrugged.

'Never thought to look,' he said innocently. 'Why, is it damaged now?'

'There is a hole in this seam. I'd say we've lost the half o the powder,' she said, running the black grains through her fingers. 'It's the good corned stuff, at least, but we've no way to know how strong it might be.'

There was a distant rumble, and Gil looked up in time to see another flicker of lightning in the approaching clouds. The thunder which followed it was long delayed.

'I'm not happy about the weather,' he said. 'We'll all get very wet, if nothing else. It's picked a bad time to break.'

'Someone else is no happy, maister,' observed Steenie from further down the bank, as two of Vary's men emerged shouting from the narrow gate they had used. 'I'd say we've been seen fro the house.'

'I'd say you're right,' agreed Gil, watching the two approach. They were shouting such remarks as 'Stop thief!' and 'Stand away!' but as they neared the group by the burn they slowed, recognising the numbers they had to deal with. Finally they stopped, just within easy earshot.

'My maister bids ye stand away from the guns,' called one of them.

Behind them, Vary and his guests had emerged from the same gate, staring indignantly along the slope.

'The cannons is to be tested,' said Wooden Toe hardily. 'Your maister wouldny sell cannons untested, surely?'

'Hah!' said Boyd at this, handing the fleuchter to Euan Campbell. 'Cut another hole like this, will you, ten paces that way.'

'Steenie, will you attend me,' said Alys, setting down the sack of powder. 'Let me talk to them, Gil.'

She set off towards the house, Steenie following hastily, a hand on his whinger. Nodding to the two manservants, she went on past them, and curtsied politely to the three men by the wall. Gil watched a moment longer, but the conversation seemed to remain civil, and he turned back to assist his cousin in bracing the espinyard in the hole he had cut for it, wedging the stock in with the turves.

'What do they throw?' he asked. 'Are there balls or bullets or the like? I believe they have to fit exactly.'

'I can see they might,' said Boyd, stamping on the turf he had just placed. 'We'll ha to ask your bonnie wee wife, who seems to ken everything. I suppose she has no sisters? No, the best ones never do.'

Another rumble of thunder reached them, and Gil paused to study the sky. The clouds were closer and heavier, and an unpleasant colour, but there did not seem to be rain beneath them yet.

'I found another fleuchter, your lordship,' announced the Fox, returning along the waterside with a second peat-spade. 'They've no care for their tools here, nor they have, the way they're leaving them all about. And I

292

can tell you where all the other folks has went to,' he added proudly. 'They're all down by the Medwin at the hay, to get it in afore the rain comes.'

'Good luck to them,' said Boyd, moving on to where Euan was digging with more enthusiasm than accuracy. 'No, no, man, no like that! Here, gie me the thing till I show you.'

By the time Alys returned, led ceremoniously on the arm of William Knollys, Lord of St Johns, himself, with Steenie watchful at the back of the group, five of the guns were bedded in the bank of the burn and the sixth was awaiting its turn, and the sky had darkened almost right across. The wind was tugging the grass in all directions, rustling the bushes along the bank and turning up their leaves, but no rain had fallen yet, nor was there any sign of approaching rainfall, only the relentless rumble and the distant flicker of lightning.

'I ken not, my lord,' said Alys with great aplomb as they approached, 'gin you're acquaint wi my husband, Maister Gil Cunningham, Archbishop Blacader's quaestor.' Gil turned as she spoke, and bowed suitably deep, aware of earth on his hands and on his hose. 'And our kinsman, Maister Alexander Boyd.'

Boyd looked up, rose and bowed with equal formality.

'Grandson to Boyd o Knockentiber,' he elaborated.

Knollys, large, plump and blue-jowled, dressed for travel in crimson leather and blue linen, fat hands gloved and studded with rings, nodded in a casual way at Gil, but stared inimically from pale round eyes at Sandy Boyd. After a moment he grunted, and turned to Vary.

'So this is your guns,' he said. 'They're no very big. I suppose you're right,' he said to the world at large, 'they're as well being tested afore we conclude the bargain, till we see what they can do.'

'They're big enough to cause a might o damage,' protested Vary. 'If they're to be carried, they canny be too big, else they'd throw the gunners flat every time they got fired. Gin O'Donnell was here he'd tell you all about them. I canny think where he's got to, I'd expeckit him to be here. Here, you!' he said abruptly to Gil. 'Cunningham, or whoever you are. Have you seen O'Donnell? Thon Irish fellow wi a black beard, you met him earlier.'

'I've not had that pleasure since we parted in the hall,' responded Gil, with extreme politeness, carefully not looking at his cousin. Knollys's companion, still irritatingly familiar, caught his eye and grimaced in curiously, and suddenly Gil knew the man. 'De Brinay!' he exclaimed. 'Well met!'

'Well met indeed, Maister Cunningham,' agreed Raoul de Brinay, knight of the Order of St John, whom Gil had last encountered on a hillside above Linlithgow. 'I would not have looked to find you in this affair,' he added in French.

'*Ni moi non plus,*' returned Gil.

'Cousin,' said Boyd urgently, 'do we have a charge for these guns?'

Alys murmured her excuses to Knollys and stepped down to join them by the burnside, which by now looked as if it had been ploughed. De Brinay, with a tiny jerk of his head at Gil, drifted away along the bank. When Gil joined him he asked in friendly tones, 'May one enquire for your companion, the learned builder?'

'He's well,' Gil assured him, 'and is now my father-in-law. My wife is yonder, engaged in measuring gunpowder.' He glanced over his shoulder, in time to see Alys apparently loading one of the guns. Where did she learn these skills, he wondered.

'Ah!' De Brinay's eyes widened. 'My felicitations. And can you tell me,' he murmured, still in swift idiomatic French, 'what authority our host has to dispose of this equipment?'

'This is not clear to me,' Gil replied, 'but I believe little or none.'

'I suspected as much. What can you tell me of the matter?'

Briefly, Gil recounted the tale as he knew it, of the band between Gregory Vary, Somerville and Madur, the presence of the Irishman, the involvement of the tinkers. De Brinay listened carefully.

'This is a very different version from our host's,' he said when it ended.

'You don't surprise me.' Gil stopped, studying the sky again. 'Is the Order of Knights Hospitaller interested in the merchandise, or is this an enterprise of my lord's alone?'

'I could not say,' said de Brinay, without expression. 'Our host mentioned the Irishman also. Do you know where he might be?'

'I could not say,' Gil replied, equally without expression. He knew his cousin was capable of carrying out an execution, without benefit of accusation or trial; now he tried not to think about what he had overheard on the stair earlier or the dark smell of blood he had encountered at the entrance to the cellar. And where, it now occurred to him, was Billy Doig? He had not seen the little man since they had reached this spot. Well, he reflected briefly, Doig was well able to look after himself. No doubt he had good reason for vanishing.

Thunder grumbled again, rather nearer.

'Perhaps we should encourage the gunners to make haste,' said De Brinay, studying the sky in his turn. 'I mislike this light.'

When they returned to the crowd milling about by the guns, Alys was just straightening up from the last one, and Knollys was saying angrily, 'I canny see that it's safe or wise to let a—' He bit off the word he was about to use, and substituted, 'lady see to the charging o the things. How does she ken what she's about?'

'I charged the half o them, my lord,' observed Boyd sweetly. 'I've *laid my wares, a buckler broad,* and I'd like to see you all withdraw now, maisters, ayont the bank, maybe twenty paces nearer the walls. In case o mishap,' he explained, as Knollys stared at him with those round eyes, as pale as his own. 'You'd not want to be struck by flying metal, would you now? Or by earth and mud,' he added. This was clearly more persuasive, and when Vary added his urging the Preceptor turned reluctantly to move away.

Vary watched him go, then swung back to seize Gil's arm. 'That young woman,' he began.

'My wife,' said Gil pleasantly, freeing his arm.

'Aye, is she? Says my brother Ambrose has a son.'

'That's correct, maister.'

'Damn him to perdition,' said Vary, with a casual fervour which chilled. 'And what d'ye think you're about, any road, you and your wife,' the tone was unpleasantly sceptical, 'and him yonder, thieving my guns out my cellar and burying them like this? I'll be talking to the Depute about this, I can tell you, the minute I've sealed the bargain wi my lord.'

'You may have your chance sooner than that,' observed Gil, looking along the slope. 'I think this is Robert Hamilton now, wi half o Lanarkshire under arms. Were I you, maister, I'd away up and keep him back. It wouldny look good if he were to be slain by a misfiring gun below your walls.'

Vary, muttering curses, set off hastily after Knollys, and Gil bent to give Alys a hand up the bank. She took

296

it, smiling up at him, and suddenly said, 'Gil, I have just recollected, word came from the coalheugh about noon. Tib is in labour. Your mother is gone to her.'

'That should shorten her time,' said Gil. 'Will you come well back from this, sweetheart? I don't trust these constructions.'

'Nor do I,' she admitted. There was a sudden brilliant flicker of lightning, and she flinched as a much louder crack of thunder followed almost instantly. 'That was too close. I wish everyone would come away, we need to get on before the rain starts.'

By the time the strip of digging along the burnside was cleared of tinkers, tinkers' children, St John's men and the servants who had come with Alys, the storm was upon them. There was still no rain, but the wind was wilder, and stronger, and lightning flashed and danced in the heavy clouds.

'Confound this!' said Sandy Boyd in Gil's ear. 'It will blow the slow match out!'

'You'll contrive,' said Gil, cutting thumbs' lengths of the twisted bark cord. 'You aye do. Any idea how fast this burns?'

'None at all.'

'It's a pity we don't have the Irishman here.'

'Isn't it,' agreed his cousin. 'Here, if we light all the fuses at the once we can set them faster and get away afore the first goes up.' He was striking flint on steel as he spoke, coaxing a little heap of tinder to a flame on top of a flat stone. 'Come on, come on! Ah, that's caught. See us the fuses, Gil.'

As Gil set the third fuse, fitting the unlit end firmly into the touchhole, watching to make certain that the other end was still burning, that it would not blow out, there was another, closer roar of thunder, almost on top of them, which crashed and rumbled on for ever, or so it seemed. He stepped away, looked round for his cousin, found him beckoning wildly and followed him up the bank.

'They'd never forgive me if I let you come to harm,' Boyd shouted over the thunder, 'and I don't know whether I'd fear my aunt or your bonnie wee wife the more. As for—'

A number of things seemed to happen at once. There was a loud crackling sound, and a fierce bright light suddenly illuminated the slope in front of them, the crowd of watching people, the barmekin wall and the tower beyond it. A huge hand lifted Gil up in the air and flung him flat. Astonished, he managed to cover his head with his arms, as a volley of small stuff beat down on him, pebbles and clods of grass and sharp bright things, all falling silently around him thick as hailstones. And then, most alarmingly, the ground trembled and quivered under him like a custard pudding set on a table, and he was enveloped in more dust as bigger excussa battered down on his back and arms.

Then something struck him on the head.

Chapter Fourteen

'But why did all the cannons explode?' asked Tib, round-eyed, cradling her swaddled daughter. 'Had you put too much powder in them or something, Alys?'

'I had not,' said Alys firmly. 'It was the lightning. It struck the espinyards, because lightning is drawn to metal things, and they all exploded, and the gunpowder that was beside them as well. It was a very great explosion,' she said, reaching for Gil's hand. 'I thought— I thought Gil had been buried alive.'

'He's harder to dispose of than that,' said Lady Egidia.

Two days had passed, in which a great deal had happened, and the party from Belstane had judged the time suitable to call and congratulate Tib on her safe delivery, Michael on his fatherhood. Tib had received them in full state, sitting up in the box bed with the brocade curtain elegantly drawn back, the bedclothes surmounted by the same embroidered counterpane and pillow-bere which Gil recalled both Kate and Margaret having used on like occasions. Tib herself was enveloped in a garment of velvet trimmed with braid and bunches of ribbon and the infant Gelis, a dainty bundle on a matching bearing-cloth, had been much admired, had had several gold or silver coins slipped into her miniature grasp, and was now re-wrapped and asleep, making little snuffling sounds, in the crook of her mother's arm.

'It must ha been, if it brought down the tower,' said Tib, rocking the baby slightly. 'Joanna, thank you! Set the tray down and take a seat, my brother can pour out the wine.'

'And the cordial,' said Joanna Brownlie, sweet-faced and soft-spoken, wife of Michael's grieve and Tib's chief support in the community. 'It's made wi apples, you mind. Well, mostly apples. It was right good this year.' She set the tray by the bedside and curtsied to the visitors. 'Is that right, Maister Cunningham, that the tower was brought down and all? Guns are terrible things, so they are, and so's gunpowder. Jamesie wants to use it in the mine, he says it would do for opening up a new seam, but I canny bear the thought.'

'Nor can I, lass,' said Michael, moving reluctantly from his post by the bed-foot, where he was gazing admiringly at his wife and child. 'And so I've told Jamesie.'

'But is that right about the tower?' Tib asked. As a child, Gil reflected, watching Michael pour the cordial, she had been annoyingly persistent about her questions, and it had not worn off as she got older. 'I think it thundered and lightened here and all, but I wasny paying that much mind to the weather.' She smiled dotingly at her infant.

'The tower of Kersewell is fallen,' he agreed repressively. 'It wasny the espinyards exploding that did it, all they did was cover Sandy and me in flying turfs and divert the burn.'

'Then what—?' she began.

'It was the lightning.' Alys shivered, and looked up at Gil over her glass of cordial. He touched her other hand reassuringly and accepted his own glass from Michael.

*　　*　　*

300

He had roused, flat on his back with all his limbs throbbing with bruises, in one of the outhouses by the barmekin wall. At his side, Alys, with tear-tracks in the dirt on her face, had seemed unable to let go of him.

'I thought you were—' she said. 'I thought—'

He struggled up onto one elbow, but she pushed him back down again, and began patting at his chest and shoulders, feeling for broken bones.

'I'm not damaged,' he protested. 'Sandy—?'

'Unharmed,' she said, and smiled rather wryly. *'Naturellement.'*

She seemed to be speaking very faintly. About them the world was almost silent, though he was aware of movement, of people coming and going. He could feel footsteps in the ground under him, though they made no sound. This reminded him of the moments before he had lost consciousness, when the ground had quivered under him, and he began to get up on his elbow again.

'What happened?' he demanded. 'The guns— was it only the guns?'

Alys shook her head.

'It was the lightning,' she said, still in that diminished voice, and he realised that his ears were stopped. By earth? By the great noise? 'The lightning set off the guns, all at once,' she went on, 'all six of them, and I think the barrel of gunpowder as well, so there was a very great explosion. But then,' she swallowed, 'but then another great fork of lightning struck the tower-house, and I think perhaps there was more gunpowder in the cellars, for it— for it— I never heard such a loud noise. We owe a candle to St Barbara, many candles. She must have been watching all we did, and protected us. Gil, the house is fallen, the whole house, fallen into a great mound of stones. They are searching now for, for any that were in there.'

'The lightning?' he repeated. 'You're sure of that?' She nodded earnestly.

'Many saw it strike, including the Chevalier de Brinay. The trail of gunpowder did not catch. I had made certain to break it where I could, with my foot, but it never burned anyway. And now it's raining hard.'

'*To me is vengeance, I will repay, says the Lord,*' he quoted in the Latin. She nodded again, still holding tightly to his hand, and he returned the clasp, thinking that to a mason's daughter the fall of a stone tower must be particularly terrible, thinking of St Barbara, who watched over towers, protected against lightning, protected gunners and those who used gunpowder. 'I must get up.'

'You're still bleeding.' She used her free hand to raise the cloth on his temple to check beneath it. 'I think that will scar. Lie still. Maister Hamilton has taken charge, and arrested Maister Vary. The tinkers have vanished into the trees. All is well.'

'I doubt Vary thinks so,' he observed, and a shaky giggle escaped her. 'I should report to Hamilton.'

'He will come for your report when he needs it,' she soothed him. He lay still for a little, looking up at the beams of the roof, which were hung with assorted gardeners' tools. This was probably where the fleuchter had come from, he thought.

'What's happening?' he asked. 'Where is everybody? Is anyone hurt? Did Doig turn up?'

Michael was asking the same thing now.

'It must ha been a dreadful thing to see, an entire tower falling. Did anyone get out? Do they ken how many are slain?'

'If you'll believe it,' said Gil, 'one man only. They were all down by the river getting the hay in afore the storm

302

struck, the cooks and the kitchen-boys and all, and there was only the one corp found under the rubble. Even Doig turned up like a false coin, said he'd been talking to the tinkers, probably about who owed how much to whom.'

'That's a miracle,' said Tib, crossing herself. 'Thanks be to all the saints it was no worse. Who was it that died?'

'They think it was this Irishman we've been tracking across Lanarkshire. Though what wi the explosion, and the building falling on him, he wasny that easy to name.' Gil's mouth tightened as he thought of what had been carried out of the ruins; the clothing was recognisable, but the flesh inside was so tattered that it was barely discerned to be a man; the fellow had been identified by the clothing and the great black beard, caked with dust and blood. Distinguishing such a thing as a knife-wound was not possible.

'The Irishman?' Michael repeated. 'So he was in it wi Vary after all?'

'It seems like it,' agreed Gil. Michael sat down with his own glass, and they drank the baby's health.

'So what is the tale, then?' Tib asked. 'What was it Michael helped with, riding all across Lanarkshire in the hot weather?'

'He helped us find Audrey Madur,' said Alys. 'You'll have heard about her bairn?'

'Aye, Beattie told me all about him, in between the pains. Lithgo Vary! Poor wee soul, he'll get teased to ribbons at the school. But what was it happened? Tell me it all, Gil, I want to understand.'

'I should like to understand better too,' said Lady Egidia. 'We learned little enough this morning.'

Gil managed not to catch Alys's eye.

They had begun the day by riding into Lanark, where his mother had awarded herself the pleasure of calling on Madame Olympe Archibecque, as she had previously threatened. Despite the bruises which made the ride a penance, Gil was glad to have witnessed the event, from the moment the maidservant Agnes stared at them on the doorstep.

'Good day, Agnes,' he had said. 'Is madame at home? I've brought my mother to call on her. Again,' he added, on a nudge from Alys.

Below them, the maidservant in the Lightbodys' kitchen leaned out, craning to see who was at the door.

'Aye, she's in, and she's up and about,' she called, 'for I can hear her up there. The two o them's been back and forrit all day, ye'd think they was packing!'

'Come away in,' said Agnes, her smile rather fixed. 'Hae a seat, madam, why don't ye? My lady'll be wi ye in a wee bit.'

She stood back to allow them to enter, and placed the padded backstool for Lady Egidia, who sat down and looked expectantly at the door to the inner chamber. Agnes moved awkwardly about, offering wellwater and fruit vinegar to drink, asking politely about their ride in from Carluke. There was some movement in the other chamber. Gil took it his cousin was not assuming Madame Olympe's garments by himself, which was probably impossible, but was more likely stowing something he did not wish to leave lying about.

In quite a short time the inner door opened, and Madame stood revealed. Today she wore the sky-blue and tawny brocade garment in which Gil and Alys had first seen her in the marketplace; its wide sleeves and spreading train seemed to fill the doorway. Her headdress was equally imposing, a towering pile of wired and folded linen, and her face was elaborately painted. Lady Egidia rose slowly to her feet, her face almost expressionless; Gil could just detect a faint twitching of her mouth.

'Ah, madame!' protested the vision in the doorway in French. 'Your promised visit! How you honour me, how I am unworthy of this distinction! But Agnes, where are the cakes? Where are the sweetmeats? *Fruit of Paradise kind, upon a napkin white in colour*?'

'I was waiting for yoursel, madam,' said Agnes in Scots, not quite rolling her eyes. 'I'll away out for them the now, will I?'

'Not for our delectation, I beg you,' protested Lady Egidia in equally fluent French. 'We make a brief call only.'

Madame protested in turn; Agnes was despatched. They were all seated, the two redoubtable ladies eyeing one another, the one blandly, the other warily, Gil and Alys trying to conceal their amusement.

'And had you an easy ride from your home?' Madame enquired.

'Trivial,' pronounced Lady Egidia. 'But you, madame, you were not yourself when last we called, and could not be at home to us. I trust matters are much improved now?'

'Thank you, yes, I am quite restored to myself.'

'*Ça se voit, heureusement.* I have a receipt for a good purge for such cases. I must let your woman, Agnes is it? — have a note of it.'

'Ah, no, I am certain that will not be necessary, I find myself quite recovered. And your own health, madame?'

'I keep well, I thank you. I believe we have a mutual acquaintance, in Mistress Somerville of Kettlands.'

'Mistress Somerville!' Madame threw up her large white hands. 'A lady of the most informative. You will have heard that her daughter is restored to her family? And a fine son with her?'

305

'I hope to call on the girl later,' Lady Egidia admitted. 'Might you accompany us?'

'Alas, no, madame, I am spoken for. I must call on Maister Hamilton the Depute, for I believe he may have found something which I had mislaid. I must retrieve it before I leave Lanark,' pronounced Madame Olympe, with a pointed glance at Alys, who gave her an enigmatic smile.

'What a pity. I hope you regain your property, madame. Perhaps the Depute will have made good use of it meantime. But tell me, what is the French custom when there is a birth in the neighbourhood?'

Alarm flickered in Madame's painted face.

'Why, it—' she began. 'It varies, in different parts of—'

'In Paris,' observed Alys, 'it was very much as here. All the gossips would call on the new mother, with small gifts of money or clothes, and admire the baby.'

'Why yes!' agreed Madame, with scarcely audible relief, as Agnes returned with a little basket of sweet cakes from the baker's stall along the High Street. 'Like that!'

They consumed the cakes, and a second round of fruit vinegar (Gil rather thought it was blackcurrant), along with some more barbed conversation. Finally, Lady Egidia rose to take her leave.

'I am much gratified to have met you, madame,' she announced. 'One had described you to me as *étonnant*, but I should much rather say you are impressive.'

'*Impressionant*,' repeated Madame Olympe. Alys's glance slid sideways to Gil.

'*Oui, impressionant. Et aussi plus fort et puissant.*' Lady Egidia put out her hands to take Madame's, smiling into the painted eyes. 'This meeting has much amused me. I shall remember it.'

'And I, madame.' Madame Olympe curtsied low, gave the elder lady a rapid and practised double kiss, swooped on Alys and did likewise, and advanced on Gil.

He reached out to take her hands, contriving to hold her off, and said cordially, 'I've no doubt we'll meet again, madame. Until then, good fortune.'

Agnes, at her mistress's gesture, held the door open. Gil stepped out, waiting to offer Lady Egidia his arm. She paused on the doorstep, nodded to Agnes and said in quiet Scots, 'Tell your mother I was asking for her.'

'Aye, mem, I'll do that,' said Agnes, equally quietly, and bobbed a curtsy.

'And then we called on Audrey,' said Alys now. 'They're both doing well, and she and Maister Ambrose Vary are very happy together, though much shaken by Maister Gregory Vary's actions.' Her hand tightened in Gil's, and he rubbed his thumb across her knuckles. 'I should think the bairn must be twice the size of Gelis here.'

'Ouch,' said Tib without thinking, and shifted uneasily against her pillows.

'How much did they tell you?' Michael asked.

'Little enough,' said Gil. 'It's clear Brosie was nowhere near his brother's schemes. About all he knew was what the Depute had let him know, and the Depute doesny have the whole of it, though he seems to have contrived somehow to get hold of a lot of papers relative to the matter.'

'Strange, that,' murmured Lady Egidia. 'Come, Gil, begin at the beginning and let us have the whole tale. Michael should know what he has assisted in.'

'I think Gregory Vary was in several plots,' said Gil, thinking of his last sight of the man. Alys had told him

307

that Robert Hamilton had been inclined to indignation at first, thinking he had been decoyed up to this end of Lanarkshire on a ruse, but once he grasped the whole of the matter, with the help of the papers which he retained firmly despite Sandy Boyd's best efforts, he had taken and bound Vary, to hold him for the Assize at Edinburgh. 'In the first place, it was Vary prompted the plan to abduct Mistress Madur, to his own ends, though I suspect her uncles joined him happily enough.'

'But why?' demanded Tib. 'They never asked a ransom, did they? Was it for money, or to make Maister Ambrose do as he wished, or what?'

'That, I think,' Gil agreed. 'Forbye, Gregory had the notion about growing timber on the Burgh Muir, which I rather think the burgh itsel will take over entire, to the benefit of the burgh coffers, if not to the folk who graze their beasts out there.' He paused to reflect. 'Somerville and Madur were in that plan as well. Indeed that and the abduction were two halves of the one scheme.'

'Maister Ambrose would never have agreed to it,' said Alys. Gil nodded agreement.

'Then there was this half-brewed intention to kill the Duke o York, or whoever he is, when he comes to Scotland. Somerville and Madur have been in correspondence wi John Ramsay, the former Lord Bothwell, now resident in England, concerning more than one daft plan to owerset this king and put someone the Tudor likes in his place. I think that may be where the most of Somerville's money came from, and the powder was part of the payment as well.'

'Is that where the tinkers came into it?' Michael asked doubtfully.

'Aye, well, it's my belief the tinkers carried letters and goods and gunpowder too, no matter what they said.'

308

Alys made a sound of agreement. 'Their friends the Lees come across the Border from England, and Ramsay makes good use of them.'

'Ramsay,' repeated Tib.

'One of the old king's — er —' began Michael, stopped, and looked at Lady Egidia in embarrassment.

'Not so very er,' she said in amusement. 'The King liked him, and he was friends wi Buchan, but he was never more than passing bonnie, even as a young man. He'd not have won that much favour.'

'Och, Michael,' said Tib. 'We all ken the old king was that way inclined, you've no need to be so mim about it.' She looked down at the baby. 'This wee one will be wanting fed soon, Gil. Let us have the rest o the tale, will you? So far that's,' she counted hastily on her fingers, 'is it three separate plots the man was in. Is there more? What did the Irishman have to do wi it all?'

'The guns,' said Michael.

'Aye, the guns,' said Gil. 'I suspect the Irishman was in the country along with the guns, bringing them in from Spain through Ireland, though he then got entangled in the other matters. It was certainly him slew Robert Somerville, and probably Jocelyn Madur and all, likely because it was all coming apart and he could see the rewards slipping away from him. By what Vary was saying, Gregory Vary I mean, O'Donnell was demanding payment for the guns immediately, which may have been part of his quarrel with Somerville and Madur, since I can imagine they'd be reluctant to give him anything.'

'So there was a cartload o gunpowder right enough,' said Michael, 'and a cartload o guns as well.'

'There was,' Gil agreed. 'And if they hadn't carried off Audrey Madur and set us looking for her, the conspiracy might have succeeded.'

'You think?' said Alys.

'Oh, no, dear,' said his mother. 'You and your cousin would have dealt with it.'

They rode home to Belstane in the cooler evening. The day of thunderstorms, all across Lanarkshire, had wrought less damage in these parts of the county, but had made way for a less oppressive weather, with light fluffy clouds in a deep blue sky and the occasional breeze to freshen the air.

'And your cousin,' remarked Lady Egidia in French, when Michael had turned back to the sprawling mess of the coalheugh, with promises to send word of how Tib and Gelis went on. 'I take it the Treasury put him here to go into the matter.'

'Something like that,' agreed Gil.

'Is he satisfied with the outcome?'

'I think so.' Gil considered the last glimpse he had had of Sandy Boyd, rather than Madame Olympe. He had been discussing possession of several bundles of papers with Robert Hamilton, arguing his case patiently and without noticeable success, but there had been about him an indefinable air of triumph, rather like Socrates after a successful hunt. At least the Irishman had not survived to spread his information around.

'He needs a wife,' said Lady Egidia reflectively.

'You think?' said Gil, startled.

'Oh, yes,' said Alys. 'But it would need to be no ordinary lady. I can think of nobody suitable.'

'Nor I,' agreed her mother-in-law. 'I must pass my acquaintance under review. And their daughters.'

'How would you promote the match?' Gil challenged. 'Sandy's like smoke: he's in your face and then he's not there.'

310

'There are ways,' said Lady Egidia. 'It may take a little time.'

Later, in their chamber, her eyes dancing, Alys said, 'Should you write to your cousin to warn him of his marriage?'

'How? He's never there, as I told my mother,' said Gil abstractedly. He was gazing at the window; its twisted horn panes showed light and shade and indistinct yellowed clouds, but he hardly saw them. His dream in the tinkers' camp had come back to him, had been with him all day, the red-haired man lurking at the back of his mind in his many-coloured checked gown. Was it the same red-haired man of whom the tinkers spoke? They seemed to hold him in respect.

'It's a bonnie evening,' he observed.

'It is.' Alys was beginning to unpin the cap she wore under her hat. He put out a hand to stop her, though he loved to see her honey-coloured hair fall loose.

'We could go out and walk in the orchard,' he said. Her gaze snapped to his, and her breath seemed to stop. Had she dreamed too, he wondered. 'It's a new moon, so it will be quite dark, quite private. We could take a blanket,' he added airily, and smiled at her.

She went scarlet, then white, and drew a long quivering breath. Then she turned and gathered up the topmost blanket from their bed, folding it carefully.

'It's a bonnie evening,' she said, as he had done. She stepped to his side and put her free hand in his.